Bath Pond

Bath Pond

A Heart-Warming Story of an Early Florida Family

Lowell Teal

Oakhill Press
Winchester, VA

10 9 8 7 6 5 4 3 2 1

Book design and production by Bookwrights Design
Jacket design by Michael Komarck
Printed in the United States of America

Library of Congress Cataloging-in-Publication Data

Teal, Lowell, 1933-
Bath Pond : a heart-warming story of an early Florida family / Lowell Teal.
p. cm.
ISBN 1-886939-63-2 (alk. paper) -- ISBN 1-886939-70-5 (pbk. : alk. paper)
1. Rural families—Fiction. 2. Florida—Fiction. I. Title.
PS3620.E426B37 2004
813'.6—dc22 2004053148

Oakhill Press
1647 Cedar Grove Road
Winchester, VA 22603
800-32-books

Dedication

For Robyne and Martha
"Your entrance into our world made our family complete."

and

Ali and Rob
"Keep your 'lamps burning' as brightly as they are today."

Foreword

Florida's first settlers were rugged. Adventurous souls, men and women willing to claw a meager living from marginal land largely uninhabited, save the Seminoles. Florida was a territory unlike any other in the Union. Extraordinary beauty of the Atlantic and Gulf shorelines, vast virgin timber lands, pristine lakes and bubbling streams drew restless pioneers searching for a better life. Florida weather was almost more than newcomers could imagine. Abundant wild game, fish, and cattle sustained the early settlers.

Timber harvesting paved the way for farmland and grazing pastures, to be followed by railroads and visions of development.

Agriculture was the linchpin to Florida's economy, notwithstanding physical hardships, disease, crop failure, hurricanes and lack of transportation to outside markets. Overcoming those obstacles provided imaginative insights of success and lucrative professions. Villages, cities, and boundless urban complexes would eventually emerge.

Through it all, agriculture was the bedrock of success, influence, and the financial resource that took Florida to worldwide prominence. Today tourism drives Florida's economy, but agriculture continues its steady, solid support through a myriad of jobs and support industries, maintaining thousands of acres in farming enterprises.

Largely unrecognized are the many benefits of agricultural lands providing wildlife habitat, water conservation, and a major source of food and fiber for the state, the nation, and the world.

Without question, those who paid a price with sweat, toil, and determination would look with envy to what has been transformed on the foundation they established.

Charles H. Bronson
Commissioner of Agriculture
State of Florida

Preface

Those traveling to Florida today have little knowledge of the incredible anguish and hardship early pioneers encountered. Their effort evolved into the magnificent world of fantasy and fun it is today. People are still people, however, not "cut from the same cloth."

The creation and development of Florida's agricultural industry was far more than a vast unprecedented feat of tilling the land and marketing to those waiting to buy. It was a "guts and glory" enterprise. They were tough, resilient individuals willing to risk everything for success or failure. Many lost it all, but always found a way to come back. Few quit!

With advances in agricultural machinery and adequate transportation methods, it became lucratively apparent that Florida agriculturalists were actually farming the weather, not the soil. Using their unique ability to grow vegetables in winter opened the floodgates for citrus and other commodities to be marketed across the nation and later the world.

Bath Pond is the story of one family's ability to rely on each other and every natural and man-made asset to exist, given the difficult circumstances from which their story is told.

Lowell Teal

Acknowledgements

The "bath pond" itself is not fiction. It actually exists and has been the source of enjoyment for many. Growing up, I was among many other farm laborers who stopped by after work for a quick "dip!" I offer my sincere appreciation to Betty Duppenthaler, whose family owned the property, for allowing me to use its name within the pages of this book. After the devastating freezes of the 1980's, the Florida citrus industry changed drastically. It moved south. Today the "bath pond" is located within an upscale subdivision and the residents have no idea of its existence or history, nor will they ever.

It would be unforgivable not to mention Lucy Harward without whose assistance this book would never have been completed. Bob Hoenshel, Earl Wells and Ruth Miller were all, from time to time, advisors sometimes unaware of what was happening. To these people my heartfelt gratitude.

The love of my life, my wife Jackie, willingly gave untold hours listening to frustrations and reading drafts of the unfinished manuscript. She always offered just the right amount of praise or criticism I needed to keep me going. For her assistance, kindness and continuing love, I feel the most blessed man on the face of the earth.

Author's Note

Garrett Gregson Jr. grew into manhood before the Great Depression without his mother. His father, with the assistance of Essay, his black housekeeper, raised him. Essay's grandson Beau also lived with them. Though reared in this type of home, Garrett never felt any sense of personal insecurity.

Hidden deep inside Garrett was an inborn trait of which few others were aware. He liked challenge. Later in life, he fashioned from these challenges opportunities that required tremendous financial burdens. He then transformed these burdens into a comfortable life, and more importantly, adventure!

"God promised to feed the birds, but He didn't promise to put it into their nests."

John Langford

PART ONE

The Beginning Years

1

It was late afternoon in early spring. The orange glow of the sun was fading fast in the west. Night sounds were already beginning in rural Florida including the occasional grunt of the bull gator, the chirping of crickets, and the croaking of frogs.

The long white house with green shutters was nestled perfectly under giant oak trees. Planted years ago, they complemented this opulent home. The landscaping boasted the perfect plants in the right places, with trees professionally trimmed. The lawn was beautifully manicured and meticulously kept, all of which completed the framing of a home that most people can only fantasize about owning.

While most everyone dreams of living in and possessing a home like this, the truth is that, financially and personally, this physical setting is misleading, and few are willing to pay the price. The activities behind its walls privately speak of extraordinary toil, frustration, and sorrow, in addition to the happiness and hilarity. Unless the home is the gift of inheritance, this type of wealth is usually the product of risk, the agony of loss, and the uncertainty of always operating on the fringes of the unknown.

Garrett's private wish was to decrease his daily activities in order to spend more time with his wife, Mary Fran. They had discussed doing so many things together, and yet as they grew older, the family's business required greater demands of his time.

Today was a good example. Problems at the office consumed every minute, yet he was expected home early. Not being able to walk away from the office was the source of another agitation. The problems followed him home. The phone rang constantly from the moment he stepped inside to ready himself for an evening out with Mary Fran. "Sorry to bother you again, Mr. Gregson, but there is someone asking for you on the phone," said the maid. "I tried to get him to call your office tomorrow, but he would have none of that."

"Who is it?" yelled Garrett from the shower.

"I can't say his name, but he says he is in New York," was the reply.

"I'll take it in here, thanks," replied Garrett.

"Garrett, we received two loads of your grapefruit late this afternoon. We estimate, tentatively, both contain more than 5 percent decay. Do you want us to work it out for your account or order a federal inspection?" asked the voice, easily recognizable to Garrett as Vincent Agronelli of Agronelli Produce.

"Get an inspection and let me know the results when completed. Thanks for the call." Returning to the shower he was on a slow sizzle. He had felt all along that the grapefruit had been packed and on the floor too long because of the salesmen's inability to sell it. *It should have been dumped into the cannery bin,* he thought.

"Hurry, Garrett," said Mary Fran. "We only have a few minutes to make it to the hospice banquet."

"Why don't I just meet you there?" asked Garrett.

"No, I'll wait. The phone will keep ringing, and you will miss dessert," said Mary Fran.

"Lay out my clothes. I'm almost finished."

Rushing out of the bedroom, he could hear the phone continue to ring. Mary Fran told the maid not to inform Garrett of any further calls, instructing her to go to the study and make a list of those he needed to return the next day. She always had a special talent to not only handle Garrett, but the moment as well.

While driving to the dinner, Garrett was grumbling about always being in a rush. He finally asked, "Why in the world would anyone have a dinner on Monday night? Monday night is always bad."

"I don't know, Garrett. That is just the way it is."

Arriving at the resort hotel, he was fortunate to locate a parking place almost in front of the entrance door and said,

"This kind of good fortune will never happen again. Why can't we be this lucky when we go see the Gators play?"

"Hurry, Garrett, let's try not to be late."

Turning down the long corridor toward the Grand Ballroom, Garrett recognized Governor Alan Wright deep in conversation with four highway patrolmen at the entrance.

"What's Alan doing here?" inquired Garrett of Mary Fran.

"I don't know," she said. "You do remember hospice took care of Mildred before she died? Maybe that's the reason."

Approaching the door, Alan turned and greeted Garrett and Mary Fran. "Well it's about time you two showed up. I have been waiting so we could go in together."

"It's great to see you, Alan. I certainly didn't expect to," replied Garrett as they shook hands.

The troopers opened both doors. Inside was a room filled with lavishly decorated banquet tables and people, all of whom immediately stood. Peering through the open doors, Garrett could see a number of their friends. After a long moment, Alan took Mary Fran's arm, and the troopers began escorting the two of them into the room.

Walking in, Garrett became aware that the evening must have something to do with Mary Fran because she was so heavily involved in the community. Looking at Mary Fran, she appeared astounded at the terrific ovation and everyone standing.

Approaching the stage, the troopers ushered Garrett and Mary Fran to their table. Each of their family members had already been seated there. When they were seated, Alan approached the lectern.

When the shouts, whistles, and clapping subsided and the guests were again seated, Alan paused to collect his thoughts. He said, "Garrett, Mary Fran, this is an evening which has been planned for a long, long time. Initially, it was intended to honor you for service to our community through the years. However, the more planning we did the more irons we recognized you had in the fire. You had fires going we had no way of knowing about without a great deal of digging and snooping." The audience again erupted with laughter and applause.

Alan continued, "This evening was initially conceived as a tribute to the two of you for your generosity to hospice by financially providing for patients and their families. Yet, so much more of your good works has come to the forefront, we will not be able to stop with one honor. We will, and must, go back in time more than fifty years, at the very least, to that special occasion in your lives: that Sunday afternoon of your wedding."

Garrett sat in utter amazement listening to Alan. His memories of that Sunday afternoon were still very real and vivid. So much had happened since that day, good times and profound sorrow. Yet the thought of that day within their lives has always been the source of a beginning for them and private happiness for him.

Revisiting this thought, Garrett's mind began to wander, and he became oblivious to Alan's continuing accolades and recalled only that Sunday afternoon filled with bright sunshine.

2

The little one-room country church sat atop a sandy knoll nestled comfortably within a group of scrub oaks. Cattle grazed in all directions from its fenced yard. Some of the more inquisitive animals on this Sunday appeared to be listening to the singing of the hymn "Just As I Am" as the services ended.

The church was old and in serious need of paint and repairs. The interior had never been painted. Its benches and pulpit could best be described as early primitive. A small bell was mounted to a fat pine post near the entry gate, and eleven steps led to a small open porch with rickety handrails. The setting is clearly Depression South.

The entire countryside was alive with the music of the hymn as Beau James opened the front gate of the churchyard for a nervous Garrett Gregson. Garrett sat on the front bench of his father's farm wagon.

The day was Sunday, April 15, 1933: Garrett's and Mary Frances Johnston's wedding day.

Seated beside Garrett was his father, Garrett Senior. His friend Alan Wright and cousin Brett Moore were stationed with Beau in the rear of the old one-horse wagon.

Worshipers watched as Garrett brought the wagon to a stop adjacent to the back door of the church as Rev. Boggs had previously instructed. After a few taut moments with no conversation, Garrett said, "Well, I guess this is it," as he stepped to the ground.

"Are you nervous?" Alan asked. "I know I would be."

"Relax, son. You'll be alright," Garrett's father said in a strong, slow, deep voice with a smirk on his face.

"Sure, you'll be alright. That is, if you can get past this wedding ceremony, and the dinner, and then the honeymoon. The honeymoon is when this 'alright' business will begin," offered Brett as only an uncomfortably shy young man can in the presence of his cousin's father, and, of course, his uncle.

Rev. Boggs opened the back door of the church, looking down the rutted sandy road waving to the Coble wagon bringing Mary Fran to the church. "Here come the Cobles, Garrett. Are you ready?" asked the preacher.

"As ready as I can be, I guess," replied Garrett haltingly. "How do I look?"

"You look fine to me, maybe just a little peaked and sickly around the gills," said the preacher while hugging Garrett strongly with a heavy slap to his back. "You and Mary Fran will be very happy. You are a lucky young man."

"He looks like a man who will be henpecked soon. I hope he's got his huntin' and fishin' behind him for a while, cause the good time has ended," laughed Alan.

"It'll be worse than that, Preacher. He'll be hooked and won't have any way to get loose for a breather," Brett said.

"Now, don't you let these boys spook you, son. You will be the happiest man in the settlement. Mary Fran is a fine young lady, and the two of you will be happy together. We have been having fun off you at your expense," the preacher said with a smile, gently touching Garrett's arm.

"The preacher is right," said Mr. Gregson gruffly. "Don't let these boys make you break and run." Garrett's dad was a big man, thoroughly hardened by long days in the sun. He was a distinguished-looking gentleman and thoroughly respected in the settlement. He was thought to be honorable and his word good. After all, these two attributes were the most important to a person's positive character.

All the while, Mr. Gregson had been watching Gator trailing their wagon about a quarter-mile back. Gator was a mixed-breed bob-tailed brindle bitch, a fine cow dog and his personal companion.

Breaking and running had never occurred to Garrett. At the moment he was more concerned about his wedding clothes. He had wanted a new suit but couldn't afford it. Had the Depression not been raging there might have been some possibility of a new outfit. Instead he wore a faded blue suit, now a little tight fitting, a new white shirt, and a red tie with brown shoes. He was self-conscious because his coat was a darker blue than his pants, yet he was well aware that everyone in the church couldn't afford a new suit either.

Running around the corner of the building, Beau said nervously, "Garrett, Miss Mary Fran and the Cobles are unloading. I think they are ready."

"They are, Garrett," said the preacher. "The congregation is singing the last verse of the closing hymn. I'm going back in now, and when they finish the verse the pianist will then play the last few notes of the wedding song. You and your dad will come into the church house through the back door. Come to me at the middle of the altar and face the congregation. When you are in place the pianist will begin the wedding song, and Mary Fran, escorted by Mr. Coble, will enter from the front door."

Everyone in the settlement was aware Mary Fran was an orphan. She didn't remember her parents and had no known family. Her only memories were of foster homes until the Cobles took her in about five years ago.

The Cobles had no children of their own. Working for the state of Florida, they cared for orphans, abused children, and illegitimate babies until permanent homes could be located. On Mary Fran's wedding day they had fourteen kids, ranging from a few days old to Mary Fran, who was nineteen, the same age as Garrett.

Immediately upon stopping the wagon, Mrs. Coble quickly took a last look at the dress she made for Mary Fran. It was a very plain but attractive white dress noticeably homemade. Of course, Mary Fran was understandably proud of the only new dress she had ever had. She was also wearing white shoes, the only new shoes she had ever had, provided by an anonymous benefactor.

Her clothing had always been something other people had worn first and then given to foster homes and orphanages. Today, Mary Fran's clothing, all of it, was new for the first time in her life. She felt very proud of it, as well as for the circumstances that had brought her to this hour on this day within her life.

Realizing the sacrifice the Cobles and the other kids had to make in order for her to have these new clothes was the only unhappiness Mary Fran knew surrounding the circumstances of her wedding. She was acutely aware that she would soon have someone and some place she could call her own. She would no longer have to worry about when or where she would be moving the next time.

Life had provided few good times or pleasant memories for Mary Fran. Her earliest recollections were of being placed within one foster home after the other. Of course, that is, except for the time at the Cobles. They were genuinely interested in her, and it showed. Life with the Cobles made a difference for her.

The Cobles' problems were no different from everyone else's: no money and very little food.

Most foster homes were the source of a bed, such as it was, and meals that except on special occasions were meager at best. But most of all, foster homes lacked the love and trust for which Mary Fran yearned. She wanted to feel needed and have a sense of belonging instead of the uncertainty of always awaiting the next move. She wanted to be consumed with passion for another, and Garrett more than filled her expectations in a prospective husband.

Mary Fran was now confident of a better life, a loving husband, and a home of her own for the very first time in her life. The last few days had been very emotional, as she was realizing her newfound happiness. This was the high point of her life!

After being sure that Mary Fran's dress was as it should be, Mrs. Coble kissed her and took the rest of the kids inside the front door of the church, making her way to the front pew reserved for her entire family. Alan and Brett had been asked to join her and help with the kids, which they did.

The Reverend Silas Boggs was stately in appearance as he stood in the chancel area in front of his pulpit and behind the altar. Ramrod straight, he was the typical minister of the day. Long shocks of unmanageable white hair sorely in need of a trim covered his entire head and ears, all the way to his collar. His black suit was shiny from countless pressings with a flat iron. He was wearing a white shirt with fringed cuffs and a black string tie. With a slight smile he gave the pianist the nod to begin the wedding song.

The pianist, noticeably nervous, adjusted her position for the final time at an old upright piano desperately in need of tuning. She could play every hymn in the hymnal, but when other occasions presented themselves, she was at a severe loss. Today was no exception. Her nervousness was apparent, and the entire congregation ached for her at this moment.

Just before the time came for Garrett to enter the church, Mr. Gregson turned to Beau and said, "Beau, did you see Gator trailing us? Don't let her cause any problem during this ceremony. She will if she can, you know."

"Yes, sir, Mr. Gregson. I'll do my best to watch her," Beau replied.

The Coble family now seated, the pianist began the last few bars of the wedding song, at which time Garrett and his father entered through the rear door. It was an endless journey for Garrett as he made his way through those seated in the amen corner to the altar, which was constructed simply from rough-sawed lumber. The choir was seated directly across from the amen corner. Each choir member was closely scrutinizing Garrett, and he could feel every eye. When the journey to the altar was over, all of ten steps, the pianist took a long pause and a deep breath, and then began the wedding song in a very slow, deliberate tempo, so soft that those hard of hearing might not know she was playing.

One of the older church sisters seated in the back seized the moment to straighten Mary Fran's dress for the last time as she and Mr. Coble entered the door. The trip down the aisle was slow, and Mary Fran was beaming with happiness.

The moment Garrett saw Mary Fran, he knew, without a doubt, that he was doing the right thing. She was everything he had ever hoped to have in a wife, and at this moment she was more beautiful than he had ever remembered seeing her. In fact, she was the most beautiful woman he had ever seen.

Her eyes were glued to Garrett, and his to hers, as she slowly walked toward the altar. She saw in him the security she had always sought and never known. She recognized in him an honorable character who made her proud. This was the right marriage for her. She could feel his love as positive and his loyalty as a profound element within their marriage.

Ending the trip to the altar, both Garrett and Mary Fran turned to face Rev. Boggs, who began, "Dearly beloved, we are gathered here in the sight of God and before these witnesses to join together this man and this woman into the holy estate of matrimony."

Garrett wondered if all couples faced with enduring a wedding ceremony reacted as he did at that moment. While he wanted more than anything else to marry Mary Fran, he was working hard at standing still. His instinct was to break and run—not that the ceremony itself was so bad, but in front of all these people, knowing full well every one of them was carefully scrutinizing every detail at this very moment. They were noticing what he and Mary Fran were wearing, and wondering how they would get along in the midst of these hard times.

The ceremony ended in about five minutes, with Rev. Boggs concluding, "And now by the power vested in me by the state of Florida, and as a minister of the gospel, I now pronounce Garrett and Mary Fran to be husband and wife. What, therefore, God has joined together, let no man put asunder.

"You may kiss your bride, Garrett."

Looking into Mary Fran's eyes and taking her into his arms, Garrett had all his fears dispelled. Kissing her, he forgot about all the others present and drifted but for a moment into a world away.

Taking Garrett and Mary Fran's arms, the minister turned them until they were facing the congregation, saying, "Folks, Mr. and Mrs. Garrett Gregson Jr. Speaking for them, they would like each of you to join them for a covered dish dinner on the grounds, held at the Coble home at the conclusion of this service.

"Shall we bow for a moment together? Our Father, we thank you for Garrett and Mary Fran and earnestly ask you to watch over their lives with favor. Guide them with the direction that comes only from you and safely see them through all their tomorrows in your service. Amen."

The moment the preacher finished the prayer, Gator slipped around to the opposite side of the church from Beau. She quietly eased under the building to do a routine K-9 investigation while Beau was watching and listening to the ceremony inside. What she found was a fully mature female bobcat with a couple of kittens, and Gator couldn't back down from a fight.

The two went head to head. The noise of the fight brought all the dogs left with the horses at full gallop, all of which were anxious to enter the fray.

To stop the fight under the church, Beau grabbed a cow whip from someone's saddle and lashed into the fighting animals. The dogs, including Gator, retreated in one direction, and the bobcat with her kittens in another.

The fight did relieve the tension for Garrett and Mary Fran. It also drew laughter from those inside the church who were ready for lunch.

The minister gave a nod to the pianist who again struggled through part of the wedding song as the new couple quickly made their way out the front door of the church. Following close behind were all the members of the congregation.

The couple stopped on the top landing of the little porch. Everyone coming out wanted to hug and wish them well. These were country folks who enjoyed simple pleasures and who were sincerely interested in the couple's successful future together.

The last two out were Alan and Brett, both of whom shook hands with Garrett, then hugged him, and finally planted their very biggest kiss on Mary Fran, which of course had the temporary effect of embarrassing her beyond words. It was no great surprise to Garrett that the pair kissed her squarely on the lips, embracing her passionately.

Garrett and Mary Fran made their way to the Gregson wagon. Beau, who was black, was waiting with Gator. He wanted to say something to them, to wish them well, but somehow words failed and he could say nothing. Sensing this, Garrett pushed Mary Fran over to him and said, "Beau, this is Mrs. Gregson. What do you think of that?"

"I think it is mighty fine. I'm proud for both of you," said Beau. Both Garrett and Mary Fran hugged him.

Mr. Gregson walked up to them, put his arms around them and they him, and said, "I didn't get to have a word with you at the front door just now, but I did want you to know you have done the proper thing, in my view, and I know you will be very happy together. My only regret is that your parents, Mary Fran, and Garrett's mother couldn't be here to share in the joy of this day." Tears started to run down his cheek as he spoke, since he now realized that he, in fact, was alone, except for Essay and Beau.

"Beau, turn this wagon around and let's get on to the festivities since everyone else is lining up behind us," said Mr. Gregson, who now had Gator tied to the wagon seat.

Garrett and Mary Fran took the front seat with Beau driving. Mr. Gregson, Alan, and Brett sat on the tailgate with their feet hanging off. The Gregson party led the other members of the congregation as they traveled to the Coble home and dinner on the grounds.

3

The Coble home was located about thirty minutes from the church traveling by horse and wagon. It was built shotgun-style with multiple add-ons, a pitiful example of a home in need of paint and a new roof. Sitting high off the ground, there was plenty of room underneath for every kind of animal not larger than a hog normally found on a farm. Guineas filled the lawn and fields during the day and roosted at night in the jack oaks and scrub pines located around the clean swept yard. The soil was sand soaked and of very poor quality. Unfortunately, it was all the family could afford. They had twenty usable acres suitable for a garden and to pasture a couple of milk cows. They grew pork and poultry for meat and eggs. Occasionally they were able to kill a bull calf for additional meat.

The Cobles were good and decent people. Everyone in the settlement thought well of them. Because of the good work they did with kids, neighbors shared extra eggs and vegetables and old clothes for the kids. Strange, but no one ever thought to send new clothes to the kids. Because everyone was aware of the Coble effort with kids in need, their outreach actually became a community effort.

When the Gregson wagon arrived, Mr. Gregson said, "Beau, find your grandmother and be sure you mind her."

"Yes, sir, Mr. Gregson. She told me to come to the kitchen door as soon as we got here," answered Beau. With these words he tied the horse and followed her instructions.

Beau was part black, part Indian, part white, and an integral part of the Gregson family. His grandmother, Essay James, was hired years ago shortly after Garrett's birth. Garrett's mother developed pneumonia, and Essay was hired to keep house and look after him. She stayed employed ever since.

When Mrs. Gregson died, Essay moved into the bedroom behind the kitchen. She not only raised Garrett, but also did the household and garden chores.

Essay's daughter, Florence, left home prior to Essay's Gregson employment. She returned later with the news she was pregnant. The prospective father was a white man of unknown identity. She had no husband, no home, and no place to go. Mr. Gregson allowed her to live in a room in the barn.

Florence disappeared shortly after the birth of Beau. Essay was the only mother Beau ever knew, and the Gregson family was his family. Living with a white family was always the source of uneasiness, yet the Gregson family accepted him and his circumstances. His real fear came from members of other white families knowing his situation, which, of course, he couldn't change.

It had always been difficult for Beau to comprehend the fact that because he was regarded locally as black, he could not go certain places, and there were certain public privileges of which he could not avail himself. This was particularly difficult since he was considered an equal in the Gregson household. While the community considered him unequal, he was fully aware that the Gregson family regarded him with no inequality.

Beau's complexion was very light olive, not black. His hair was straight, not curly. His lips were thin, not thick. His appearance was that of a white person. In fact, without knowledge of his past, one would have considered him white, even at first glance. At fourteen he was tall and muscular, a handsome young man, well disciplined, and one who practiced only the best Southern manners.

Essay had been preparing for Garrett's wedding dinner for days. She cooked pies, cakes, and an assortment of vegetables. She prepared for the crowd a gigantic pot of Brunswick stew from rabbits and squirrels.

She had arrived at the Coble home early in the day using the other Gregson wagon to continue preparations for the mid-afternoon meal. After the Cobles left for the wedding, Essay took over the kitchen and attended a small baby.

Arriving at the kitchen door, Beau found Essay overflowing with jobs for him. "You take this to the table, do that, go see about so-and-so," as well as an endless list of other duties.

For Mary Fran, the day was unbelievable. Her entire life was spent going from home to home. Within each of the homes her days were filled with very little schooling but an abundance of chores. She felt total hopelessness and the need to be a part of a real family.

To know that the entire congregation of the church was coming to share her wedding dinner was an honor more than she could comprehend. Other than Garrett, this was the nicest thing that had ever happened for her.

As they stopped the wagon at the edge of the yard, some of the younger folks were already welcoming Garrett and Mary Fran, in particular, those who were dodging helping with mealtime preparations.

It was a happy time—a time when she could become better acquainted with more of Garrett's friends.

Garrett had one particular chore: to pay the preacher for performing the wedding ceremony. He had spoken to his dad about this and learned that this was the accepted thing to do. He desperately wanted to satisfy Rev. Boggs, but he didn't have much with which to satisfy him. Garrett had fifteen dollars and twelve cents to his name, and his problem was how much to offer the preacher.

Garrett located Rev. Boggs on the west side of the house where Beau was setting up the tables to hold the food. Field boxes from a local citrus and vegetable packinghouse were borrowed for folks to sit on, and he was placing them around the side yard.

"Preacher, could I speak to you for a minute?" inquired Garrett.

"Certainly, Garrett. Let's sit here under this sapling. There is a little breeze and shade," answered the preacher.

In his usual slow and deliberate manner, Garrett began to work his way into the subject of a love offering for the preacher. Garrett's dad did offer to take care of this, but feeling it his responsibility Garrett told his dad he wanted to do it.

"Preacher, I want you to know that Mary Fran and I appreciate the friend you have been to us during these past weeks as we gradually worked our way to this special day. You know we have had some misgivings about it all, but with your assistance and the help of others who love us, I know we've made the right decision and I'm proud of that. Now comes the really difficult time for me. I want to honor you, in some way, with a gratuity for marrying us. The problem is we have very little to offer, and if I had a great deal, I still wouldn't know what to give," stumbled Garrett.

"Son, don't feel like you have to pay me anything. I am your minister, and all these things are part of my job. While it is part of my job as minister, you know the church pays me for such duties. I have the added good fortune of having you and the rest of the membership for friends. With friends like you folks, what more could one ask?" the preacher replied in a very reassuring voice with a sincere smile.

This answer wasn't exactly what Garrett had hoped for. He wanted the preacher to say what the job was worth, but he didn't. Now it was up to Garrett to arrive at some just payment within his range. "Preacher, if I offered you one dollar, would you be offended by this small amount?" asked Garrett.

"Garrett, I wouldn't be offended if you gave me a penny. I know that you want to do something because you feel it is the right thing to do, even though I've tried to discourage your thinking this way. You have the right spirit, and whatever you do is fine. If you do nothing, that is fine as well," the preacher concluded.

"Well, I want to do something, and I can comfortably afford to do this amount," Garrett replied, handing Rev. Boggs one dollar.

"I do appreciate this and will always know the gift came from your heart," Rev. Boggs said. In his wisdom, the preacher could feel Garrett swell with pride as the dollar was accepted and put inside the preacher's change purse.

Garrett was mature beyond his nineteen years. Few men this young would have been so intent upon being certain the preacher was taken care of and satisfied. But then, this was Garrett's nature.

The preacher said to Garrett, "I want you to pause and take a look at what is normal within this household. Look at the old house. It is no better than your dad's barn. The farm itself isn't worthy of being called a farm. Its soil is so poor the total acreage won't provide vegetables for the family. Look at the barnyard. There are chickens and guineas everywhere. Then take a look at those cages. Do you know what is in them, Garrett?"

"Yes, sir, I do," replied Garrett. "They've almost cleaned the gophers out of this end of the county. Mr. Coble knows how and where to catch fish, too."

"Tell me, who else do you know who traps rabbits to eat? Who else do you know constantly on the alert for other wildlife like possums and coons to trap and cage them above ground level? There must be twenty possums over there and a couple of coons. Then look toward the end of the barnyard. Those are wild hogs Coble trapped, and the family will eat them, such as they are."

The preacher continued, "It is not dishonorable to be without financial resources. It is very honorable to conduct oneself as the Cobles do within the community and to benefit all these disadvantaged kids. In order to follow their dream, both are up way before daylight cooking breakfast, making school lunches, milking cows, and tending to their animals, and I'm certain neither get to bed at a reasonable hour either. The worst part is that their schedule is never ending. Seven days each week, year round."

Garrett said, "It's a sad situation, but I've always admired the Cobles for sticking to these kids like they do. I'm happy that Mary Fran and I will be able to have our own home, and by day's end that is exactly what will happen."

After the preacher's remarks, Garrett paused and studied the entire group from the settlement there to have lunch and celebrate their wedding. Most of the kids had no shoes. If they did they were saving them for winter and school. The women wore dresses that were clearly handmade. One woman was wearing a pair of men's brogan shoes, another had on men's khaki work clothes. All the ladies cut their own hair, or each other's, and washed it when they could get to it. The teenage girls were clean, but dressed in hand-me-down clothing. The one thing noticeable was that everyone was clean, very clean, including the clothing.

The men were, for the most part, clean-shaven. Their wives cut their hair. Few had collars that fit, and most had a single tie that was worn whenever the occasion called for one. All the men wore clean work clothes. The preacher, Garrett, and Mr. Gregson wore the only three suits in the crowd. The truth is that if it had been any other occasion, Garrett and Mr. Gregson would not have had a suit on either.

Perusing the crowd, Garrett wondered if everyone put the cash money in a central location and counted it, could they muster one hundred dollars? He doubted it.

Times were very difficult, and there seemed to be no winners. It was tough just to scratch out a living, as evidenced by people spending hours and hours in the sunshine, their skins parched almost to a mahogany pitch. Their hands were cracked and cut.

Garrett even had questions as to whether he could support Mary Fran or not. But one thing he was confident of: She would be better off with him than living like she had all her life.

Mr. Coble stepped upon an orange box and called the folks over to him. Then he said, "Mrs. Coble and I are glad in our hearts that each of you came to our home at such a happy time. It is our hope and prayer that Mary Fran and Garrett will have many happy years together and that our settlement can watch as they grow older among us. I am told the table is set and dinner is ready. I will ask the preacher if he will bless the table," concluded Mr. Coble.

After the preacher blessed the table the folks unloaded the food as fast as only Methodists can. Everyone brought their favorite dishes, and based on the way the meal had begun, only empty bowls would go home.

When everyone finished, most of the older men found a spot to themselves for a smoke or chew. The ladies busied themselves cleaning up the table and dishes while the younger folks gathered around Garrett and Mary Fran.

Later in the afternoon, when the house and yard were clean, the ladies joined the young folks' conversation, bringing a few gifts for the newlyweds. The gifts were practical things like homemade dishtowels, pillowcases, and quilts, and various types of dishes, pots, and pans. Some brought canned vegetables and meats. One person brought fresh homemade cottage cheese. Rev. Boggs, long recognized as an expert in making cane syrup, brought a gallon as his wedding gift. There was a dollar bill tucked into the jar lid.

Garrett and Mary Fran left for their house after the gifts were opened and everyone was adequately thanked for their part in making the day one the couple would treasure in memory. Garrett hitched up one of the Gregson horses to the small wagon and loaded their gifts, including Mary Fran's meager belongings. Essay had prepared enough for their supper in a pan she had brought along for this purpose. And now they were off!

The trip to their new home took them away from the mostly unproductive sand hills to the gently rolling lands of citrus, truck farming, and cattle operations. The land was heavy and black, with large bodies of clear sand-bottomed lakes filling the countryside. While the roads were rutted and sandy, they passed through acre after acre of citrus groves, all of which were flushed with new spring growth. This being April, the remnants of orange blossoms were disappearing and honey bees were still singing as they desperately tried not to miss even the slightest amount of nectar. The afternoon was filled with the smell of the blossoms and the music of the bees, both in tune with the feelings of the two young people madly in love on their way to their first night together. There were also some good laughs that eased the apprehensions of the moment, the uncertainties, the uneasiness of the next hour, the next day. It was tough for one horse pulling a wagon through the sand hills. The weaker the horse became, the more gas he allowed to escape aimed in their direction. This added some levity. They thought about leading the horse through the deep sand. The odors also took the edge off the couple's passion, but it was quickly regained when they reached their destination.

The trip to their new home took more than two hours. It was almost dark when they arrived. In fact, the crickets had begun their noise and the nighthawks had taken flight. The young couple had rented from John Langford a two-room house with a shed-roofed kitchen and a small open front porch. Mr. Langford and his wife lived not too far from their little house.

The house had never been painted, or ceiled, and holes were rusting through the tin roof. Even so, it was home to the newlyweds, and the holes in the roof made not a particle of difference. The house was located in an area boasting giant water oaks, black land, and lots of lakes.

A lane entered the property between the Langford fences. The horse was slightly spooked by the shadows lengthening under the oaks as the house came into view.

Stepping up to the front door of the little house, all Garrett could think of were Brett's words before the wedding: "If you can get past this wedding ceremony and the dinner, and then get on with the business of the honeymoon . . . this alright business will begin!"

The alright business had begun.

4

The first full day of their lives together began with the sun peeping over the trees into the windows of the little house. A heavy fog hung low under the oak trees.

The morning stillness was broken by the sounds of a cow whip and cattle moving with a yelp that could only be Garrett's dad. The other indication of who was coming up was Gator's vicious bark. Gator was a "gather and drive" dog, not a "catch" dog. Even though she was taught not to catch, her demeanor had certainly fooled every cow with which she would ever come in contact. She conducted herself as if around cattle she were the meanest dog in captivity.

Jumping from bed, Garrett could not imagine what his dad was doing herding cattle there on horseback. It was barely sunup.

Just when the cattle passed the bedroom window, Mr. Gregson cracked his whip yelling, "Garrett, Mary Fran, come out and see what I've brought you." The cattle congregated under oak saplings in the backyard and were satisfied with a few moments to relax and graze. The cattle, held by Gator, were bunched behind the little house. When Gator saw Garrett, it took all her discipline to remain connected to her appointed job. In fact, on a couple of occasions she came to Garrett for a visit. She looked at Mary Fran questionably.

The young couple could not believe this. The first day of their lives together . . . awakened at daylight with a cow whip and a herd of cattle.

Garrett was up and out quickly. It took Mary Fran just a little longer.

"I wanted to surprise you, son. This is your wedding present from me. Here is one heifer for each month of the year, all of which are with calf. You will have twenty-six cows in the near future, because there is also a bull for breeding purposes and a steer for the table in the bunch," said Mr. Gregson, with an unmistakable sparkle in his eye. The old man was proud of his son, and it showed. He hoped this gift would give them a financial lift at the very beginning of their marriage. He considered Mary Fran a wonderful young lady.

"But, Dad," questioned Garrett, "what in the world will I do with them? You know I don't have any place to keep them."

"Don't worry, son. I've made arrangements with John Langford for you to put them in this pasture. You visit him and arrange some method of repayment for the use of the pasture," he said. "He is looking forward to your coming."

"I don't know, Dad, I had not thought of anything like this," replied Garrett. Mary Fran stepped out the back door with a look of total disbelief with her hand over her mouth.

"Look, honey, Dad has given us our wedding present from him. Twelve springing heifers, a bull, and a steer for the table," explained Garrett. "What do you think of this?"

While Garrett was talking, Mr. Gregson got off his horse, carefully coiling his whip and hooking it onto his saddle horn. Turning to face them, Mary Fran walked up to him, giving him her biggest hug and kiss. Visibly shaken, she said, "Mr. Gregson, up until yesterday I never had a dress or shoes that were truly my own. These were my first new clothes. During the past twenty-four hours I now have Garrett, a home I can claim as ours, a beginning family of which you are a part, twelve cows, a bull, and a steer. I can't believe this is happening to me," she reacted.

As she spoke these words, Garrett moved beside her, taking her hand as she took Mr. Gregson's, and the three of them moved closer to the cattle for a better look.

After a few minutes of silence, Mary Fran said to Mr. Gregson, "You know, yesterday and today means I'm accepted into this family, but there is something that bothers me," concluded Mary Fran.

"What's that?" asked Mr. Gregson.

"You already know I've never known my parents. Since I am a part of this family now, would you mind if I called you 'Dad'? You see, I've gained a husband, a home, twelve cows, a bull, and a steer, and now a dad, which means more to me than anyone could ever hope for," said Mary Fran.

"You just don't know how good that would make me feel for you to call me 'Dad,'" the old man said through tear-filled eyes. "I really don't feel I've lost a son, but rounded out my family with you. This is a happy time for us all, even though I am reduced to living with Beau and Essay.

"Garrett, open the gap and let's put these cows in the pasture," instructed Mr. Gregson.

"When you finish with the cattle, come into the house and I'll have a pot of coffee going," Mary Fran said.

With the gap open, Gator started the cattle moving in the direction of the opening. All of them went into the pasture. Immediately upon their being safely inside the pasture, Gator came to Garrett as if he were a long-lost relative. She was still puzzled that Garrett wasn't at home last night and then finding him in a strange place.

When Mr. Gregson and Garrett entered the kitchen, Mary Fran said, "You two sit down at the table. The coffee will be ready directly."

Following her directions they sat down. Mr. Gregson noticed the pan Essay had fixed them for last night's supper sitting in the middle of the table, untouched. With Mary Fran's back to them, Mr. Gregson peeked inside to confirm his suspicion that they didn't eat the food. Placing the cover back, he looked over at Garrett, who had a sheepish look on his face, very close to total embarrassment. He was embarrassed because he remembered the conversation his dad had had with Essay about being sure there was a pan to go with them from the Cobles. Mr. Gregson didn't embarrass them further, but did get a personal chuckle from it all.

While they were having coffee, Garrett said to Mary Fran, "Let's make a pact now. Unless we really get into financial trouble, let's never sell a female cow until she is past bearing future calves. We will sell only the male calves. If we can keep them in pasture, we will always multiply. What do you think?"

"Sounds good to me," she said.

"That's the best news I've heard in a long time. A man with a cow and calf operation is hard to break financially," Mr. Gregson said.

"Dad, do you know with all the good fortune that has come my way in the past couple of days, I feel next to a millionaire," Mary Fran said.

"You just keep right on feeling this way, and one day you will be one," Dad said.

While talking, Mr. Gregson was unbuttoning his shirt pocket, in which he was carrying a small tin box. As he pulled it out into plain view, Garrett immediately knew what it was and had the most pleasant expression on his face. When Mr. Gregson saw Garrett's face, his began to assume the same appearance. Observing them, Mary Fran had a feeling the box had special meaning just for them.

The box was noticeably old and worn smooth. Not that it had had a great deal of use, it simply was an old tin box with a foldover top.

With an expressive voice, Mr. Gregson said, "Mary Fran, Garrett did not know I was going to do this, but I hope it meets his approval. This small box was his mother's container that held what little jewelry she had. There aren't a lot of items in the box, but what there is I know of no one I want to have them other than you. The total contents aren't worth much in money, but in heart value they are priceless to me. I hope you will accept the jewelry and when the occasion arises wear it proudly."

Handing her the box, she took it with a shaking hand. Her emotions were lodged within her throat. She actually couldn't speak.

Opening the box, she found various little pins, a couple or three necklaces, and a ring or two. There was nothing of real value except to the family. Even so, it was the first piece of jewelry she had ever had, and the tears began to flow.

The tears were running freely as Garrett stood up and moved around the table to try and console her, "Hon, don't cry. Daddy wanted you to have the jewelry so that you could have something that was dear to this family. Other than a picture or two, this is all we have left of my mother. It is right that you have the jewelry and wear it proudly when the occasion comes."

"Oh Garrett, I will, I will. I just didn't think there would come a time in my life when I'd be so proud and yet so completely without words. This is just wonderful. I will always cherish the thought and the jewelry," cried Mary Fran.

As they finished their coffee, a wagon pulled into the front yard. It was a neighbor, Silas Smith, with four pigs for the newlyweds.

"Morning, Silas," Garrett said. "Come on in for a cup of coffee."

"Thanks, Garrett, but I can't," replied Silas. "The missus and I just wanted you and Mary Fran to have these four shoats for your pigpen. By hog killing time you should have some fine meat."

"You mean you are giving us these pigs?" asked Garrett.

"Sure we are. This is about all we can give as a wedding gift, but we are proud to do this. I fixed up the old hog pen out back the other day. Why don't you help me get them into it?" asked Silas.

The pigs were red and weighed about forty pounds each. They were not only tough to get hold of, but a real chore to get into the pen.

"Garrett, I couldn't bring these pigs without some feed for them. I brought you these ten sacks of shorts, which will help you get them started," said Silas.

"I can't believe this, Silas. You are not only giving us pigs but also the feed for them. This is just about the nicest thing that has ever happened to us, and we really do appreciate it."

"Well, we wanted to do something and this was the best we could. Besides the meat will come in handy in the fall.

"Hope you have good luck with them," Silas said, climbing back onto his wagon. "The missus told me to come right back. I think she has some chores stacked up for me today. You young folks come visiting one day."

"Thanks, Silas, we will, and you bring Mrs. Smith back over for a visit with us," Garrett countered.

"If you don't mind, Silas, I believe I will ride along with you. I was just leaving anyway," said Mr. Gregson. With that he whistled for Gator to follow. A little perplexed, Gator didn't know whether to go to Garrett or follow Mr. Gregson's instructions. Reluctantly, she looked at Garrett, who motioned for her to follow Mr. Gregson. The dog obediently followed.

"Thanks, Dad. Thanks, Mr. Smith. You both have been more than generous this morning. What a way to begin the first day of our marriage," said Mary Fran.

Watching them leave, Garrett said to Mary Fran, "Isn't this a wonderful way to start our first day, even before breakfast? Speaking of breakfast, what about some?"

"Give me a few minutes, and I'll see what I can do," she replied.

Essay never allowed Garrett or Beau in the kitchen when she was cooking, so Garrett walked from the back fence to the hog pen, admiring his newly acquired livestock. He absolutely couldn't believe what had happened to them. They were in business!

As they finished breakfast, another wagon came up the lane. It was Loretta Higgins, a neighbor of the Gregsons. She stopped in the front yard and stepped down from her buggy.

"Morning, Mrs. Higgins, how nice of you to visit," Garrett said.

"Can't stay, Garrett, just had a present for you two. I thought you might like to have these layers and a few fryers," Mrs. Higgins replied. "I had your chicken pen tightened up a few days ago and felt like you could use these Domaniker chickens with a rooster."

"Well, how nice," responded Mary Fran. "Garrett and I will never catch up repaying all the kindness that has come our way today."

"Help me get them into the pen, Garrett," instructed Mrs. Higgins. "I also brought you some of my extra scratch feed and laying mash."

Now the newly married couple had cattle, hogs, and chickens—all before lunch on the first day of their lives together. In addition, they still had their original fifteen dollars and twelve cents. With these kinds of friends, how could one lose?

Sitting on the edge of their front porch with feet hanging off, they were trying to comprehend the good fortune that had come their way this morning. It was unbelievable that so many good folks did so many wonderful things for them.

While discussing their bonanza, the sounds of people talking coming down the lane were getting louder by the second. They were laughing along with the sounds of horses' hooves.

"Hi, Mary Fran and Garrett," screamed Mr. Coble as the group came into view. Mr. Coble and a group of friends from the little church had come together with those who had been there already, and now the whole group came to complete another job. Up to this point, everything had been planned and executed perfectly.

"We've come to get your vegetable garden started, Garrett," said one of the men in the group.

"That's nice, but my ground isn't broken."

"Don't worry," Mr. Coble said. "It will be in just a few minutes.

No sooner had Mr. Coble said this than all the women and men were unloaded from three wagons. Two teams were unhitched from the wagons and hitched to plows the wagons were carrying. Just as soon as they were hitched to the plows, they immediately went to work turning the garden spot.

"I've never heard of anyone doing this for another except for those who were sick," said Garrett to the entire group.

Mr. Coble said, "According to Brett and Alan, we figured you would be sick after last night and the action you've already had this morning. You can bet this will be one of the last favors of this kind you will ever receive from this group until you get too old to do them for yourselves. Just relax and relish your good fortune."

The ground was quickly plowed and then leveled. The women removed their shoes and started to plant seeds of various kinds. They dropped seeds into the drill, carefully covering each with their bare feet.

This operation would have taken Garrett and Mary Fran a couple of days to accomplish. This group finished the entire job within a couple of hours and was gone.

Garrett said to the folks as they were loading equipment onto one of the wagons, "People, this is just about the nicest thing that has ever happened to me, except for Mary Fran, that is. It is doubtful I will live long enough to repay this favor, but you can believe we will certainly work trying to repay each of you."

"Forget it, Garrett," said one of the men. "If we had wanted thanks or pay for the job, we would have told you how much before we did it. We just wanted to help the two of you out, and this was about the only way we could. We've had a good time as if we had been at a party. In fact, this was a party, and we feel good about it. See you later, newlyweds. Come to visit when you are out of hibernation!"

There were many farewells as the group left. It was a happy group of loving folk to do such a nice thing for a young couple. But then, in the grips of the Depression these kinds of things were about all anyone could do for another. The young couple stood and watched them leave, thinking how nice to have friends like these.

When supper was finished and the kitchen clean, Garrett said, "You know, some way must be devised for us to take baths every day. We have only a shallow well with a hand pump, no tub, and only a washrag and a bar of lye soap some of the church folks gave us. We've got a problem!"

"Maybe we do have a problem, but only a small one. Think of all the good things that have happened to us today. What more could a couple ask on the first day of their married life? What has happened feels more like a fairy tale to me. I really think we can work out a simple thing like taking a bath," Mary Fran said.

"Well, what do you suggest we do? Go out to the pump after dark?" asked Garrett.

"Why don't we take the soap and go back to the little sand-bottomed pond in the pasture where our cows are and take a bath in the lake?" she asked.

The little pond was about one hundred feet across and very deep, indicating a spring-fed body of water, and was perfectly round, perhaps a sinkhole. It was a beautiful little lake with water as clear as drinking water. Fish could be seen around the edges.

Knowing there was no one around for probably three miles, Garrett screamed, "The last one in is a rotten egg," stripping his clothes off and diving into the water.

"Well, I must be a rotten egg because I'm not going in this water without some sort of suitable clothing," said Mary Fran.

"That's what you think," Garrett said. With this, he had already grabbed her and was wading into the water, and before she could stop him, he was taking her underwater.

When they surfaced, she decided there was no need to allow modesty to spoil a good time, and off came her clothes. Besides, how can one take a bath with clothes on?

From having been reared close to nature in the manner he was, and having Brett, Alan, and Beau as constant companions, Garrett was an excellent swimmer. Being tall and lanky, with sufficient muscle, his performance in the water was extraordinary. No person in the settlement could match his swimming skills. Friends in the past had recommended his entering swimming competition, but, of course, he never did.

Garrett said, "Coming here every night would be a good thing to do. We can keep it to ourselves and come for our baths. This is a super-clean little lake, and I think we should name it Bath Pond."

"That is the best idea you've had lately, Garrett Gregson, I agree. But, if I ever get word of you boasting about our taking a bath 'jay bird,' it will be the last time it will happen. You got that?" Mary Fran announced firmly.

"Agreed," Garrett answered. "It's our secret." Then the business of the honeymoon started all over again. When the bath and frolicking were over, the couple lay at water's edge until the mosquitoes drove them home.

5

Garrett knew he would have to visit Mr. Langford and make arrangements regarding his house and pasture rent. It was tough for him to ponder, given his total savings of fifteen dollars and twelve cents.

Knowing the task must be attended to, Garrett left home early using the horse and wagon on loan from his father. He had no way to ask Mr. Langford if it was alright for him to come, which bothered him. The only option was to visit his home, and if a visit wasn't possible, to make an appointment to return at a more convenient time.

The trip took almost an hour. Garrett's house was at one of the far corners of the Langford property. At least this was his guess because it was such a long trip.

Mr. Langford's property was an unimproved cattle ranch. Cattlemen during this time in the history of Florida's cattle industry were cutting timber, removing the stumps if possible and planting the ground to new and improved grasses. Mr. Langford had done none of this.

In early life, Mr. Langford was a corporate executive and a highly educated man. Mrs. Langford was also extremely well educated. Their financial success early on was impressive.

Because his son was interested in sawmilling, he purchased this very large tract of land. He was neither a cattleman nor a citrus grower. His hope was to develop the sawmill, taking his son into the family business, since lumber appeared one of the more lucrative ventures in the early part of the century.

Fate was to spoil his plan. His son, John Jr., was excited about going into the lumber business with his father, but it wasn't to be. John Jr. was killed in France during World War I.

The death of Mr. Langford's son diminished all his enthusiasm for the lumber business. Mrs. Langford was so upset because of her son's death that she stayed in bed most of the time for an extended period afterwards. Both she and Mr. Langford withdrew from every normal activity. Even though both were highly educated, she continued to be adamant about not having any community connection or responsibilities. Neither had been to church in so long that some of the younger folks in the settlement had never seen them. Both Langfords were recluses.

Their original plans were that while John Jr. was in France, Mr. Langford would begin setting up the mill using timber located on their property. His calculations indicated it would take about fifteen years to cut. While this operation was under way, with John Jr. in charge, the elder Langford would spend his time looking for new timber acquisitions.

With these plans in mind and excited about being in business with their only child, the very best in every kind of equipment was purchased for the business. The mill was expertly engineered, and operational tests were beginning when word of their son's death came. With this, the operation was closed down and remained idle. Rust and inactivity over the years had taken a terrible toll on the physical condition of the equipment.

Garrett was uneasy about how to approach Mr. Langford. When Garrett made the deal for the little house, he felt Mr. Langford was difficult to talk to, in the sense that he did not add anything along the way to the conversation. After settling the agreement for the little house, Garrett left as soon as possible. Maybe the uneasiness was all Garrett's?

The Langford home was a large one-story wooden structure. In years past it had been a showplace. It was painted white, and its lawn had a number of formal evergreen gardens. It was one of those lovely older homes with a porch around three sides. The front porch was screened. The outbuildings were located well away from the main house, leaving it in a beautiful setting to itself.

The perimeter of the lawn had planted oaks with a number of native cabbage palms interspersed throughout. Some areas held clusters of cabbage palms. These giant oaks were filled with Spanish moss, and cabbage palms were framed with the remnants of a white board fence.

Entering the lawn area, Garrett saw Mr. Langford sitting on the side porch in a rocking chair rolling a cigarette. Garrett was happy not to have to roust him out of the house as on the previous visit. He proceeded to the barn area to tie his horse. This way, if the horse decided to fertilize the lawn, it would be on the opposite side of the fence and out of sight.

Passing the porch, Garrett waved to Mr. Langford and received the return of what looked like a feeble exchange but no change of facial expression. Making his way back to the steps of the porch, Garrett said, "Hidy, Mr. Langford. How you getting along today?"

"Okay for an old man. Why don't you come on up here and tell me about your wife and how you are liking married life?" Mr. Langford said, much to Garrett's surprise.

"Well, I like it," taking a seat in the adjoining rocking chair. "I think it is the best thing that has ever happened to me. The neighbors and friends at church have been so nice to us." He described how the settlement folks had given them cattle, pigs, and chickens, and plowed and planted his garden. He still couldn't believe it, and Mr. Langford understood why he couldn't.

"Garrett, you know we take care of our own in this settlement. You and Mary Fran are now our own, and I know everyone who was a part of whatever was done for the two of you did it because they wanted to and they feel proud of their effort. They did it because it would be helpful to the two of you," concluded Mr. Langford.

"The truth is, if I hadn't been trying to act mature and be grown up about it in front of Mary Fran, I believe I would have cried when all those folks finally did leave after bringing all the livestock and planting our garden," Garrett said.

Garrett continued, "You surely do have a nice place. I have always liked the house, its location and setting. I think if I could ever build a home anywhere, I would want it to be here. It is high enough so that you will never have water worries and low enough that the soil is good. Not sandy like the sand hills."

"Well, you know, Garrett, I do have some sand hills on the western side of the property, and I had planned some day that my son and I would plant them to citrus," explained Mr. Langford. "But, as you know, that day will never come for me now. John's death ended all my interests and dreams. Mrs. Langford and I are doing little more than sitting here waiting to die. This is a very sad way to end one's life."

"I know it must be, Mr. Langford, and you know everyone in the settlement have the two of you close in their thoughts and prayers. I guess there isn't any measurable way to help anyone who has lost as much as you folks have," said Garrett.

"You said it, there is just nothing to live for anymore. When your interests die, you may as well, too," Mr. Langford said.

Garrett continued, "Sometime when we know each other better, maybe you will take the time to tell me about John Jr.? What he was like? The things he liked to do? What you and he did together? How you passed the time and all this? I'd sure like to know more about him. He must have been a fine person," Garrett said.

"He was, Garrett. We might be a bit biased, but he was all we had. Don't make the mistake of just having one child. When you do and something happens to this child, you lose all your reason to live, particularly if that child is grown. This is the tragic thing. If we had another, we could transfer all our affections to the survivor and always remember the good things about the deceased. We could then climb new hills and meet new challenges. When you lose your only child, your world dies and that's it!" concluded Mr. Langford. "Yes, when the time comes, I would like to tell you about John Jr. I think you and he would have been great friends, even though he would have been much older than you."

After a long, long pause, Garrett pulled his thoughts together and said, "Mr. Langford, you know my dad gave Mary Fran and me some cows as a wedding present. Dad told me he spoke to you prior to bringing them over, and you agreed to let me keep them at my place with the understanding I would make arrangements with you to somehow work out the rent."

"That's right, your dad did come by, and I told him it would be okay. I've thought about what the rent should be, but I really have no firm ideas as to what I want to do about it."

Garrett let the subject lie for a while in silence, hoping it would draw out Mr. Langford's intentions. He decided to let Langford continue with the conversation rather than respond to his remark.

"The truth is, Mrs. Langford and I need a little assistance from time to time more than we need rent money. I also know money at this time is hard to come by. Would you agree to do some of our chores and errands in exchange for the rent on the house and pasture?" asked Mr. Langford.

"Yes, sir," Garrett enthusiastically responded. "That would be fine with me, because money is really scarce. What did you have in mind?"

"Maybe on Friday or Saturday, either you or Mary Fran could grocery shop for us and get the other things we might need from town like medicine and such. Maybe planting us a small garden so we can enjoy fresh vegetables from time to time would also be nice. More than this, I want you to either walk or ride my fence lines and let me know their condition," Mr. Langford said.

"I can do these things. In fact, it would really be a help to satisfy my debt with you this way instead of with money," replied Garrett.

"Then it is a deal," said Mr. Langford, offering his hand. They shook, securing the deal.

"Come on into the house and meet Mrs. Langford." Entering the parlor they found her sitting in a straight chair gazing out the window. She was a frail little woman with an unhealthy look and a face that was almost blank. Even as she spoke to them, she exhibited little expression.

"Oh, yes," she said in a weak voice. "I remember your telling me about the young couple. I'm pleased to meet you, Garrett. Is Mary Fran with you, and are you settled in yet?" she inquired.

"No'm, she isn't. She didn't come this trip, but I will bring her soon so that you can become acquainted with her," he replied. "Yes'm, we are settled. We don't have much furniture yet, so it didn't take long." Then Garrett told them about all the nice things the folks in the settlement had already done for them in terms of livestock and the garden.

"We live amongst good people, Garrett," Mr. Langford said. With this, he turned toward his wife.

"Okay. You remember to bring Mary Fran to see me, Garrett, and good luck to you," said Mrs. Langford as she turned back to the window.

"Yes'm, and so nice to have met you," said Garrett as they were leaving the room. He was also thinking about the way she abruptly ended the conversation, yet all she did was turn toward the window again.

Garrett couldn't help but notice the inside of the big house. It was furnished with what looked to him to be only the best furniture and rugs on all the floors. He thought it was the finest home he'd ever been in. One thing was strange. All the drapes were pulled except the window in front of which Mrs. Langford was sitting. The house was extremely dark, particularly so because it was also located under the oaks, providing even more shade.

"Garrett, let's see if the pick-up will crank. It is in the garage," said Mr. Langford as they left the house.

"I didn't know you had a truck, Mr. Langford," Garrett said with an obvious excitement in his voice.

"I've had it a number of years, but it hasn't been driven much lately."

Opening the garage, Garrett saw a dusty pick-up truck sitting there that looked relatively new to him. It was perfect inside the cab, and even the cargo bed wasn't scratched, indicating very little use.

"Can you drive, Garrett?" Langford asked.

"Yes, sir, but not very well," Garrett replied.

"You've got to learn sometime, and it might as well be now. Get in."

Garrett stepped in on the driver's side and sat there in amazement trying to see through the dirty windshield. He had driven enough to know how to begin, and he hoped to be able to get the feel of the truck with little problem, and quick.

"Back her out, Garrett."

Turning the ignition switch to the on position, he pressed the foot starter. As they both expected, the battery was gone.

"You'll have to crank it with the crank. This is the reason I haven't driven it lately. The crank is behind the seat in the bracket made for it."

Following the instructions, Garrett pulled the crank only once and the truck's motor started to run. It ran with ease, like one having very little use, and he thought it must be almost new.

Garrett backed out of the garage with Mr. Langford on the opposite side of the cab. "Which way?" he asked.

"Go down the center road, and let's just take a short look south."

The center road divided the Langford property and was a private road. From lack of use it was not in very good shape. It had washouts that badly needed repairs. The countryside was palmetto flats interspersed with very large pines. These pines initially attracted Mr. Langford to the property for his sawmilling operation. They were fully mature.

There were also a number of beautiful sand-bottomed lakes on the property. All the lakes were much larger than Bath

Pond yet not quite as special to Garrett, nor as clean. He was sure Bath Pond must be spring fed.

They spent about two hours slowly driving down the center and various other side roads. It was obvious the fences were in a horrible state of repair and much more needed doing on all the outbuildings and even the main house. Everything was falling down around the Langfords'.

Arriving back at the main house and parking the truck, Mr. Langford said, "Garrett, I'm just a little tired. Thank you for coming, and I'll see you again soon."

"Yes, sir, Mr. Langford. I'll be back tomorrow to break up your garden spot and also get started walking your fence line. The fences look as though they need some help. Are there any other chores you need done before I get back tomorrow?" inquired Garrett.

"I think not. I'll see you tomorrow," replied Mr. Langford with a noticeably tired voice. "Thanks, Garrett, for coming over. Your youth has already made me feel lots better." This sort of a statement left Garrett puzzled as he hitched up his wagon.

Arriving home, Mary Fran was standing inside the little front room looking out the window. She came onto the porch as he pulled the wagon into the yard.

"I've been kind of worried about you, Garrett. You were gone all morning. I sure hope you got things worked out with Mr. Langford," inquired Mary Fran.

"Sure did, everything is fine. They are really nice people. It's a shame they were dealt such a tough blow by the loss of their only child. They are sitting over there waiting to die, it looks like to me. Mr. Langford treated me fine, but when we went into that dark house to meet her, I felt like I was in another world," Garrett said.

"They don't have much to live for, do they? Why don't we see if we can make life just a bit more enjoyable for them?" she replied.

"Like how?"

"I'm sure we can find a way. I really don't know now, but maybe we can take them something like a cooked fish, a mess of fish, or kill some fresh meat. Or, maybe something as simple as a visit when the opportunity comes up," she said.

"Then we will just look for a way. They sure were nice about letting me work out our rent. They know we don't have money, and they will go as far as they can to accommodate us. I believe they are good and honorable people who won't take advantage of us—the kind of folks we want to be associated with," Garrett said.

Finishing his chores, Garrett was thinking about how lucky he was. He and Mary Fran had been married only a few days, and so many good things had happened to them already.

They were given livestock and the place to keep them, and their garden and now the Langfords had agreed to let them work out their rent by doing odd jobs. *No one was more fortunate*, he thought.

When the work was finished and the pair went to Bath Pond, Garrett said, "I plan to get started at the Langfords tomorrow. He wants a small garden and also thinks I should ride his fences soon. I believe I'll give a little more and clean up their lawn first. It sure is a mess. When the lawn is finished, I'll begin the garden and then get on the fence. Why don't you come with me tomorrow so that you can meet the Langfords? We can take our lunch and plan on being home by mid-afternoon. What do you think?"

"I think it's a good idea. You've talked about them so much, I sure would like to meet them," she said.

6

Garrett and Mary Fran arrived at the Langford home before 7 a.m. Unhitching the horse from the wagon, they saw Mr. Langford coming out of the kitchen door aiming for his chair on the side porch with tobacco and cigarette paper in hand.

Sitting down while finishing rolling his cigarette, he waved to the young couple saying, "Morning, folks. You sure are out early."

"Yes, sir, we wanted to get a good start on the chores this morning, and I wanted you and Mrs. Langford to meet my wife."

The two stepped upon the porch. "Mr. Langford, this is my wife, Mary Fran. Mary Fran, Mr. Langford," he managed to get out while pointing in both directions.

"How do, Mary Fran? Garrett has told us about you and how good the neighbors were the other day. I think that is wonderful when people remember that they can be of service to others in such a kind way," he said. "It is good to meet you. Mrs. Langford and I want to get to know both of you much better."

"Well, I'm happy to meet you, Mr. Langford. I know we will be good friends," she said.

While Mary Fran was talking, the old man was getting up from his rocker. He took her hand very politely and made his way to the kitchen door, "Mama, come out here. There is someone I want you to meet."

Mary Fran could see a very small, frail woman with son-white hair in a bun on top of her head. *She looks so very old,* Mary Fran thought.

"Mama, you met Garrett yesterday, and now this is his wife, Mary Fran," said Mr. Langford.

"Oh, Mary Fran, I'm so glad to meet you. It has been such a long time since I've had the opportunity to talk to another woman, let alone one so young. Why don't you come on into the kitchen, and we'll have a cup of coffee?" replied Mrs. Langford.

The two of them disappeared into the kitchen.

"Mr. Langford, I brought my horse this morning so that before I started on your garden spot I could take my wagon and clean up your yards. I thought I'd get all this moss and dead limbs out of the lawn and maybe trim up some of the bushes," Garrett said.

"You don't have to do this, Garrett. The lawn wasn't a part of our agreement, you know."

"Yes, sir, I know, but I want to do this. Besides, it will make the place look so much better. It'll be tough on you to do these things, and I just wanted to do them for you."

"It's not tough, but impossible. This is very nice of you, Garrett, and I'll try to find a way to make it up to you."

Garrett really had in mind that when he started the yard work, Mary Fran would come out and begin to help him. After the first load of moss and limbs, he thought surely she would soon be there. But no Mary Fran.

About three hours passed, and he was still working alone. Mr. Langford was sitting on the porch watching his every move while smoking one cigarette after the other. Occasionally he would doze off for a few moments, and when his head fell forward the brim of his hat completely covered his head from view.

Garrett counted seven full loads of moss, limbs, and other debris when he finished cleaning just the front lawn. Not having any shears, he went into Mr. Langford's toolshed and was amazed at the number and kinds of tools there. Every kind of farm tool one could imagine was there, all of which were without use. Clouds of dust and spiderwebs were everywhere. Dirt dobber nests were in every crack, and rat droppings covered the floor.

He was astounded at such a collection of tools, none of which had seen any, or much, use. He selected a pair of shears with which to trim some of the larger plants.

Someone in the past had done a fantastic job landscaping the main house and lawn. The house itself was framed with just the right plants, and the lawn had interspersed within it a number of formal evergreen gardens that sorely needed attention. St. Augustine grass had been allowed to grow up into the hedges, and in some places it was the same height as the hedge.

After another hour of trimming, Mary Fran still had not come from the house and Garrett was getting hungry. Just as he was quitting for lunch, she came to him and said, "Garrett, Mrs. Langford wants us to have dinner with her and Mr. Langford. I told her we brought ours, and she said they never get to break bread with anyone anymore and she wanted us to eat with them. I couldn't say no, Garrett. Will you do it?"

"If you told her we would, we will. Where were you this morning? I thought you were going to help me with the lawn?"

"I did intend to, but Mrs. Langford got to talking, and the next thing I knew we were in the kitchen fixing dinner. Besides, she said the lawn was man's work and a woman should stay in the house where she belongs anyway," she said with a snicker.

"I can see now that me and that woman are headed for trouble if she keeps pumping your head full of that kind of trash."

There was a pump at the side of the house that Garrett used to wash his face, hands, and arms before going into the kitchen. Mr. Langford was waiting on him as he came onto the porch. "I'm sure glad you two are having dinner with us. It is so seldom we have anyone for a meal that it is a real treat when it does happen," Mr. Langford said.

The four were seated, and Garrett thought how much more lively the house sounded with someone in it. The room seemed more delightful with the windows and curtains open. The atmosphere was lighter. This was probably because Mrs. Langford was sitting in a dark room looking out of the window when he last saw her. On this day she was full of energy with a smile. She and Mary Fran were having a good time together. The thought of sharing a meal with others gave both the Langfords a lift.

"John, will you return thanks?" Mrs. Langford asked.

After the table was graced and the food consumed, in no time, it seemed to Garrett, it was two o'clock. They had finished eating and had so much in common that they lost all track of time during their conversation. The older couple seemed to enjoy every minute, which was understandable for two people who had been alone together with little contact with the outside world for such a long period of time.

"If I don't get back in the yard, I won't finish the things I want to do today," Garrett said.

"Well, I want both of you to come often so that we can have some time together again. This has been the most fun of anything I can think of in a long time," Mrs. Langford said.

Garrett was finished by 4:30 p.m. He and Mary Fran decided to go home through the Langford property instead of along the clay road.

Traveling through the palmetto flats and pine woods Mary Fran remarked, "Can you imagine anyone ever having enough money to buy this much land? Here it is, I have had one new pair of shoes and one dress in my entire lifetime that I can call my own, and this couple has all this land and such a beautiful home to boot. How many acres do you suppose they own?"

"I can't tell you that except to say my dad has said in the past he has heard they have more than fifteen thousand acres."

Later that afternoon at Bath Pond, Mary Fran asked, "Do you think we will ever have any such place as the Langfords'?"

"Sure. We'll probably buy them out!" Garrett replied, squirting water into her face through his clasped hands.

7

After a few weeks Garrett and Mary Fran's pigs were almost large enough to kill, their garden was doing well, the cattle had found a home with them, and their chickens were producing eggs. The two of them couldn't have adjusted to life together any better. Each complemented the other. Evidently Mary Fran wasn't following Mrs. Langford's advice because she had not only been working in the garden, harvesting and canning, but working on the development of their lawn as well.

"Garrett, we have more squash than we will ever eat. They won't be good canned, and they are going to waste. In fact, I'm just a little tired of eating them. Why don't we pick those ready for harvest early in the morning and take them to the Cobles? With all their kids, the squash will disappear in a hurry. What do you think?" she inquired.

"Good idea. The squash are getting ahead of us, and it will give us a chance to visit the Cobles. We haven't seen them since our wedding."

Garrett was in their garden picking squash as the sun was coming up the next morning. When he finished there was more than a bushel for the Cobles. They also included other vegetables and eggs within their package.

The trip was enjoyable because they had not been anywhere but to the Langfords' since their marriage. While they had plenty to keep them occupied, it was good to get out and go somewhere.

Arriving at the Cobles', Mary Fran immediately noticed the place wasn't as well kept as it normally was—things like the milk cows standing in the lot lowing for food, their udders strutted by not having been milked that morning, a few of the smaller kids playing in the sandy yard without any supervision, all of which was totally unlike the Cobles.

Entering the house by the kitchen door, Mary Fran saw that one child had no diaper at all and the other's was soiled. Kitchen pots and pans were left unwashed and piled everywhere, totally unlike anything she had ever known in the household.

Stepping into the front room, Mary Fran asked one of the older kids where Mrs. Coble was, and the child pointed toward the bedroom.

Mr. Coble was sitting by the side of the bed holding her hand. She was wrapped in quilts and appeared to be having a chill.

"What's wrong, Mr. Coble?" asked Mary Fran.

The old man looked up and said, "Mary Fran, she started with a cold a few days ago, and it has turned into something much worse, I'm afraid. I really don't know what's wrong, but I do know she isn't getting any better."

"What have you done for her?"

"All I could do was offer her aspirin and food and coffee, and she is now to the point of refusing it all," the old man replied.

Garrett walked into the bedroom and immediately recognized the gravity of the situation. It couldn't be good.

He asked about the cows and the other livestock. "Garrett, I completely forgot to tend to the stock this morning."

"Don't worry about it, Mr. Coble. I'll go take care of them."

When Garrett reached the barn, he realized it had probably been longer than one day that the stock hadn't been tended to. He pitched in milking the cows first, followed by taking care of the rest of the stock.

Bringing the milk into the kitchen, he found Mary Fran in there trying to clean up the mess and feed the children. "What do you think?" he asked.

"I don't know what to think. I do know she is very sick, and I wish I knew how to go about helping her."

They both worked the rest of the day taking care of the necessities. When mid-afternoon came, the older children, home from school, told them that Mr. Coble had not left her side since she went down. They said they had been doing the housework and chores, which explained a great deal.

Mary Fran cooked their supper and did the necessary things around the house. Garrett tended the stock later in the afternoon.

As Garrett was outside watering the horse, Mary Fran came out and said, "Garrett, I hate to leave Mr. Coble here with all these kids and Mrs. Coble as sick as she is. I think she needs the doctor, and she needs him soon."

"You mean you want to stay here and look after the Cobles and their kids?" Garrett asked.

"I don't have much of a choice as I see it. They were good to me, and they need help now if they ever needed it. What do you think I should do?"

"I don't guess you have much of a choice. Why don't I go by town and ask the doctor if he will look in on her soon?"

"I think that is a good idea, if Mr. Coble will agree," she said.

When they entered the kitchen from outside, Mr. Coble was sitting at the kitchen table, appearing very tired. He was completely worn out from looking after the kids and trying to take care of his wife. Because of these problems he had not shaved for a few days, which also didn't help the way he looked. A good bath and shave was what he really needed.

"Mr. Coble, Garrett and I have decided I should stay with you for a few days—at least until Mrs. Coble gets back on her feet, so that I can help take care of these kids and look after her," Mary Fran announced.

"Oh, honey, I couldn't let you do that. You and Garrett have been married such a short time, and you need to be together. I can manage," he said.

"Nothing doing, Mr. Coble. Mary Fran wants to stay. I want her to stay for a short time, and I want to go by town and ask the doctor to come out to see Mrs. Coble," Garrett replied.

"Garrett, I don't have a penny of money I can pay the doctor with. I know she needs help, but I am not in position to pay the doctor," he replied.

"We're not going to worry about how the doctor will be paid. We'll take care of him somehow," said Garrett.

Arriving at the doctor's office, Garrett didn't quite know how to approach him. He wanted him to go but didn't have any money with him, and he didn't want the doctor asking Mr. Coble for money for the house call.

When Garrett entered the office, the doctor was in a back room and immediately came out. "Hi, Doc, I'm Garrett Gregson Jr. My wife is out at the Cobles trying to take care of the kids and Mrs. Coble. She is terrible sick and in desperate need of a doctor. Will you look in on her?"

"What sort of illness does she have, Garrett?" the doctor inquired.

"They say it started as a cold and has gone into something like the flu."

"Do you think I need to go tonight?"

"I sure do, Doc. If she weren't in such bad shape you might wait until tomorrow. She does have a high fever and is pretty much unresponsive," Garrett said.

"Okay. I'll go now."

"One thing, Doc. Please don't ask Mr. Coble for money. I will come back into town in a few days and stop by to take care of your bill myself. Mr. Coble doesn't have any money, and it would only embarrass him. I don't have any with me, but I will be in soon and take care of it," Garrett said.

"That's fine with me, Garrett," the doctor said. "I'll do my best with Mrs. Coble, and we won't worry about the money."

Leaving the doctor's office, Garrett realized Mary Fran would not be home anytime soon. Mrs. Coble was too sick to get well quick. Even if she did make good progress, it would take a long time for her to get well enough to handle all those kids. She probably had worked so long and so hard that she had no resistance to any type of ailment. She was worked down, he reasoned. It was a cinch that Mr. Coble could not look after her and do the things necessary to take care of the kids too.

Garrett was not only going to have to look after their home and chores alone, but he was also going to have to go to the Cobles often to look in on Mary Fran. Someone had to feed their livestock and milk their cows probably for some time to come. Mary Fran couldn't do all this alone and take care of the kids and the Cobles. It was also in his hands to assist.

He thought of the doctor and wondered what he found at the Cobles. Could he do her any good?

Garrett was up before the sun the next morning taking care of the chores and packing Mary Fran a few of her necessary items. He was at the Cobles by mid-morning.

Arriving, Garrett went directly to the kitchen, finding Mary Fran wrestling with a mound of kids' clothing, sorting them and trying to get started washing. Some of the kids were gathering firewood for the wash pot out back of the old house.

"Hi, honey. Did the doctor get here last night?" he said, embracing her.

"Yes, and the diagnosis is bad. He says he thinks the flu has gone into pneumonia. If it is, there isn't much he can do because her condition is so low at the moment. He's coming back today but didn't offer much encouragement," she replied.

"Where is Mr. Coble?"

"He's in the bedroom with her. He won't leave her, and she won't talk to him. I don't believe she knows he is there," she said.

Garrett walked to the bedroom door and saw the old man sitting in a straight chair beside the bed. He must have been there all night because he was still unshaven and looked extremely worn and tired.

"Howdy, Mr. Coble. How are things today?"

"I don't know, Garrett, she sure is sick," he replied. "The doctor did come last night and gave her some medicine, and I guess it hasn't had time to take effect yet. Maybe she will begin to respond soon. He will be back late this afternoon."

"Why don't you take a breather? I'll sit with her," Garrett said.

"No, I can't do that. She might need me and I won't be here. Thanks anyway," Coble said.

"In that case, I'll give Mary Fran a hand."

Garrett found Mary Fran at the wash pot. "I think she is in really bad shape, maybe even worse than yesterday when I saw her. She has a long way to go to be well again, I think."

Garrett stayed around all day, helping Mary Fran get caught up with the chores and trying to satisfy some of the kids. It was really a mystery to him how this older couple could ever take care of this many children. He had been on the job only a few hours, and the kids were about to drive him out of his mind. *Where did the Cobles get the patience to continue day in and day out taking care of these kids*, he wondered.

The doctor arrived mid-afternoon, going directly to the bedroom. By this time Mary Fran had made some inroads inside the house and it looked decently picked up.

The doctor sat down on a straight chair and observed Mrs. Coble for a few minutes without saying anything. Then he said, "Mary Fran, have you been able to get any food inside her since I was here yesterday?"

"No, sir. She won't eat and has taken very little liquid by mouth. She refuses," replied Mary Fran.

"What kind of liquids did you try?"

"Everything I could think of, like fresh orange juice, cooled coffee, warm milk, soup, but nothing seems to work. She just won't take food."

The doctor gave her a complete examination and was with her maybe thirty minutes before coming back outside where

Garrett was waiting. He said, "Garrett, Mrs. Coble is a mighty sick woman. I don't know if she will make it. I know she won't if some way isn't found to get some nourishment inside her. All I can do is hope the medicine I've given her will help to reduce her temperature, and if this can happen maybe she will regain enough responsiveness to realize she must take liquids and some kind of food."

"Is there anything we can do that isn't being done?" asked Garrett.

"I don't think so. You're doing all that can be done at the moment," said the doctor as he drove away. "See you day after tomorrow."

Garrett decided to leave at mid-afternoon, realizing he had to take care of his stock at home. He had done everything he could to help Mary Fran catch up, and daylight was fast running out for him.

He approached her as she was trying to rinse the heavy soap residue from the edges of the wash pot after it had cooled, "I think I ought to go. I need to be home to look after our stock. What do you need for tomorrow?"

"I need some good luck with Mrs. Coble. I've never really seen anyone this sick. She is in such bad shape it will probably be a long time before she can take care of herself, let alone these kids. I've only been here two days, and I don't really know how she does it. You get home before dark," Mary Fran responded.

Driving home, Garrett thought how long it had been since he had seen his dad. Since their wedding his dad had been to their house several times, but he had not been home nor visited with Essay and Beau. He decided to visit and let the milk cow wait on him tonight.

Driving into his dad's yard he smelled the aroma from the supper Essay was preparing. He couldn't tell what all the good smells were, but part of the aroma indicated biscuits in the oven. His mind raced backward to some of the great food she had provided him over the years. She was one of the best cooks he had ever known. Mary Fran was learning well, but Essay was an accomplished chef.

"Hello, son," Mr. Gregson said as Garrett was tying his horse. "Mary Fran already run you off?"

"Hey, Dad. She's over at the Cobles. Mrs. Coble is sick."

"What's wrong?"

"Don't exactly know. Mr. Coble said she caught what he thought was a cold from one of the kids a few weeks ago, and before she could get over it some sort of flu bug jumped on her. I asked the doc to go by and take a look, and he said it was probably pneumonia."

"Then I guess Mary Fran is over helping look after Mrs. Coble and the kids?"

"Yes, sir, she has been there for two days now. We took them some vegetables day before yesterday and found them in this fix, and Mary Fran decided she ought to stay."

"Since you are here, why don't you stay for supper? We'd be glad for you to stay. Essay and Beau will be glad you are here. I sent him to the store, and he should be back soon."

"I thought you might not invite me. I planned to stay anyway, with or without an invitation," Garrett said with a laugh and a hug for his father.

Garrett entered the house from the front door, going directly to the kitchen where Essay was cooking. Did it ever smell good.

Entering the kitchen, Essay's back was to him and he said, "I knew when I smelled supper you had to be cooking a pan of biscuits. You always did have the best smells in your kitchen of anyone I've ever known," Garrett said to Essay.

Essay turned around and saw Garrett. Her face turned into a big smile as she hugged him and said, "What are you doing here, and where is Mary Fran?"

"She's at the Cobles. Miz Coble is sick and she's helping out. Have you got enough going in that stove to feed me tonight?"

"If we don't, we'll make Beau go without supper," she laughed. "It is sho good to see you."

Mr. Gregson walked into the kitchen and said, "I think he came planning to stay for supper, Essay. Maybe we should make him wait until we've eaten and give him the scraps."

About this time Beau came in the back door and immediately went for Garrett with a bear hug, saying, "I thought you had forgotten all about us now that you are married."

Smiling to Beau, he said, "Not really. I've been busy."

"Y'all get washed up. Supper will be ready in five minutes," she declared.

Going out onto the back porch, Mr. Gregson said, "Son, it is good to have you home for a meal. It has been right lonesome without you around here for the past few weeks. I'm glad you stopped by. Can you spend the night?"

"Dad, I don't think I should. My milk cow has to be tended to when I get home tonight."

"Well, I guess you are right."

Essay's supper couldn't have been prepared any better. Garrett always thought she was one of the best cooks he had ever known. Of course, she had been cooking for him all his life, and her food was all he had ever known. She served fresh black-eyed peas with rice, a squash casserole, stewed apples, a sweet onion, corn left over from dinner, and a pan of hot biscuits. Her meat was fried pork shoulder, and they had hot coffee. Garrett ate his fill.

On his way home Garrett felt sorry for Mary Fran, knowing she was up to her elbows in dishwater and chores, and he had just eaten a good meal with his dad. He actually felt guilty. He also wondered how she tolerated all those kids. The Cobles were his first exposure to this many kids, and it was nerve-wracking for him to be around so many at one time.

The ride home gave Garrett the opportunity to think again about his dad's successes. He wasn't a rich man, but he was one who always had a little something in his pocket, whether it was money or livestock or a farming venture. He always said, "If others can do well and make lots of money, the Gregsons can do pretty well and get by."

His dad was an honorable man and had done well. He thought of how his mother had died at such an early age and wondered how his dad managed to raise him. Garrett's mother must have been about Mary Fran's age now. How could his dad stand up under such grief?

His mind wandered to his dad taking care of him as a baby. *How did he do it and work at the same time*? Then Essay came to look after him, and life around the house improved for everyone. When Beau came, his dad never flinched but did what was required to look after them all. He did it and was proud of them all.

Garrett could hear his milk cow bawling a mile from the house. He was glad he didn't have neighbors who could guess what was happening.

8

For some reason Garrett woke up early, maybe because Mary Fran wasn't there. For whatever the reason, he had an uncomfortable feeling within. Since Mrs. Coble was ill and Mary Fran wasn't there with him, maybe this was it?

He was up before 5 a.m. Sitting at the kitchen table drinking coffee, he decided to go to the Langfords and tell them what was happening. He might be scarce for a few days until the Coble household returned to normal.

Mr. Langford was in his usual place, rolling a Prince Albert cigarette. He was fully dressed, including the big felt hat pulled down to his glasses.

"Morning, Garrett. I've been wondering what happened to you for the past day or two."

"We've had a little problem. We took some vegetables and eggs over to the Cobles. Mrs. Coble is pretty sick, and Mary Fran is over there helping Mr. Coble out with the house, Mrs. Coble, and the kids. She really has her hands full."

"What's her trouble?"

"I don't really know for sure, except she started with a cold that went into flu and now the doctor thinks she might have pneumonia."

"That's bad. Is she making any progress that you can recognize?"

"I can't measure any. She has been totally unresponsive since I saw her the first time. Whatever her progress, I know she has a long way to go before she's much better."

"Garrett, I couldn't help hearing what you said about Mrs. Coble," Mrs. Langford said as she came out onto the side porch. "Has the sickness run through all the children?"

"Mr. Coble thinks that is how she got sick in the first place," Garrett replied.

"I'm so sorry Mary Fran has to face such a thing this early in her life. Maybe Mrs. Coble will begin to show some improvement real soon and she can come home," Mrs. Langford said as she went back into the house.

"I'm ready for that! She's only been gone a few days, and it seems like forever to me," Garrett said.

A very serious expression came to Mr. Langford's face as she went back into the house. "Garrett, I've done lots of thinking since our last visit. You know I was all set up for my son when he returned from the war. When he didn't come home, I thought it was the end of the line for me, and I lost interest in almost everything, including developing this place."

"I know it must have been a terrible shock for you and Mrs. Langford."

"Until you experience something like this, you can never really understand the shock of losing a son and being robbed of all of your dreams," he said.

Mr. Langford continued, "I was thinking of all the preparation I did for my son's return, and it is now wasted unless someone can take it and run with it. Mrs. Langford and I have discussed this, and we like Mary Fran and you. We've known your dad for years. He is honorable and trustworthy. We think this has rubbed off on you.

"Our wish is that you will think about putting the fences back into condition, begin clearing the sand hills for grove, and doing it by cutting the timber from the land, and sawing and selling it to finance the entire operation. We've discussed this at length and hope you will consider our proposal."

"I don't know what to say, Mr. Langford," Garrett said.

"There is no need to say anything. You and Mary Fran need to think about the proposition and probably talk it over with your dad before you make any sort of decision," Langford said.

"I sure will need to do lots of thinking," Garrett replied.

"I don't want you to think it is a way to take advantage of you, or for you to become wealthy overnight. If you think these things I had rather you didn't take any part in the deal at all. I simply wanted someone to continue with the plans for this place and see them through. I don't know of a person I'd rather have do it than you. That is, unless you have other things you're interested in?" the old man questioned.

"No, sir, not that. In fact, I've wondered lots lately what I'd do to make a living. I certainly don't have enough stock to live off of. My garden won't do it, and I don't have any money to begin any sort of business."

"Remember, you haven't been offered an easy task. My dad told me when I finished college that 'God promised to feed the birds, but He didn't promise to put it in their nests.' God, you see, doesn't do it all, but He does give us a brain and muscle that will see us through most any situation," said Langford.

He continued, "I'd expect not to put any cash money into the deal from this point forward. You would simply cut the timber, saw it, sell it, and use the returns to develop this place. Of course, I would expect you to take enough cash to live on. This way you won't be flat broke all the time. For Mrs. Langford and me, we won't need any cash out of it. Our hope is the total amount, less what you take, will be put back into the place. You have my word not to second-guess any of your actions as it relates to developing the place. Your only job is to keep me posted on what you are doing and use me for any advice you might need as it relates to the development of the land. The sawmill is already set up and has sawed only enough timber to check the operation out to be sure it works properly. At least, it did when the engineers checked it out. You must resurrect it and begin if you want to follow through with the deal," Langford concluded.

"I need to think about this proposition and talk it over with Mary Fran. After all, she will be affected too."

"I understand."

"And Garrett, I know you are anxious to go see Mary Fran and how Mrs. Coble is today. You need to be able to cover ground faster than you have been. Turn your horse out into the barnyard, feed him, and take the pick-up. It not only needs to be driven, but it will help you out too. I'll take care of your horse. You won't need to worry about him."

"Mr. Langford, this is about the nicest thing anyone has ever offered me, but I would be on pins and needles every minute thinking something would happen to the truck. I don't know if I should or not?" questioned Garrett.

"Look at it this way. We might be partners someday. If we are, the pick-up will be driven by you, not me. If we don't become partners, you'd be doing the neighborly thing to drive an old man's truck to keep the battery up, particularly if he asked you, which I am."

"Yes, sir, I want to do the right thing, but the offer is such a shock."

Mrs. Langford, standing at the screen door, said, "You know where the keys are kept in the barn, and you know where the fuel tank is. Now, you fill it up and don't worry about it, because if you are too particular with it, something will certainly happen to it. Oh yes, keep us posted on Mrs. Coble."

While fueling the pick-up, Garrett couldn't get over such a generous gesture—an offer he never really expected, yet realistically was a time saver for him instead of traveling horseback.

Driving over to the Cobles, Garrett felt richer than any other person in the settlement. How could such a nice thing happen to him? After all, he wasn't close to Mr. Langford at all. At best he was a casual acquaintance, yet the man seemingly wanted to take him under his wing and help him get a foothold. This just might be his big break!

Garrett's intentions were to discuss it at some length with Mary Fran when he arrived at the Cobles, then visit his dad to get his ideas.

Entering the Cobles' back door, Garrett sensed things weren't as good as they were when he left yesterday. There were very few kids in the yard, and it was awfully quiet inside the house.

Kids were lying all over the living room floor, all visibly sick. He walked into the bedroom seeing Mr. Coble in his usual straight chair with about a week's growth of beard. Mary Fran was standing at the foot of the bed. When she saw him, she walked to his side and took his hand. He could see Mrs. Coble was totally out of it, and her breathing was now very labored. She was a grayish pale, and he was certain they had put nothing into her stomach.

Pausing at her bedside for a moment, the two then went into the kitchen. "Garrett, this place is falling apart. Last night I looked in on the kids and found all these in the living room and bedrooms with fevers. I sent the rest of them to school this morning, hoping I could find a home for them to sleep tonight to keep them from coming back here and catching whatever this is. The other side is that if we farm them out, we will be subjecting healthy families to the problem."

"Who in the world would take the kids in if they don't come back here after school?" Garrett asked.

"I don't know, but I do know if they come back here all of them will come down with whatever bug is here," she said. "Why don't you go to the doctor and ask him what we should do?"

"I think that is the only sensible thing to do. I will go now and be back as soon as I can."

After explaining the situation, the doctor said, "Garrett, I don't know what to do with the well kids to keep them away from the house. I can take all the sick kids to the county hospital and get them some relief there. The state will take care of this bill since they are wards of the state anyway. In fact, I believe the thing to do would be to take the kids and Mrs. Coble to the hospital."

"I think that is a good idea, Doc. How do we go about it?"

"I'll send a deputy sheriff to the hospital to tell them to expect us late this afternoon. We'll have to make several trips in my roadster until we get them all there."

"Doc, Mr. Langford loaned me his pick-up, and we could use it too," Garrett offered.

"Good, let's go."

When Garrett explained to Mary Fran what the doctor was doing, she knew it was the right thing to do. To boot, she knew she had had about all she could take with the three nights she had been there. Up all night and working all day trying to keep the kids together was about more than she could take.

Mr. Coble knew the doctor was right also. While he couldn't afford the doctor, he had to do all he could for his wife, even if it meant going to the county hospital at the expense of taxpayers. The kids had to be taken care of, and this was the only way it could be done.

The doctor said to Mr. Coble, "Mr. Coble, a deputy has gone to the county hospital to alert them of our arrival with Mrs. Coble and the sick kids. I also went by the welfare office, and they are going to pick up the well kids from school and farm them out into other homes until this epidemic is over. You are not the only folks with the flu. Many others in the settlement have it also, and it is a bad strain."

The doctor and Garrett carried Mrs. Coble to the doctor's car. Mr. Coble sat in the middle holding her. Two kids climbed into the rumble seat and the rest went with Garrett and Mary Fran in the pick-up.

The trip took about an hour and a half. Upon arrival, kids were laying all over the bed of the truck, their conditions noticeably worsened from earlier in the day. Mrs. Coble was deteriorating.

The nurses were expecting them and had a ward ready for the kids. Mrs. Coble was placed into a private room. The nurses knew Mr. Coble wouldn't leave her and had a cot for him placed beside her bed.

The doctor came to Garrett and Mary Fran and said, "I want the two of you to leave now. Go back to the Coble house and boil all the bedclothes in lye soap, scrub the floors, and scald all the kitchen utensils and dishes."

9

It was already late afternoon. Because of the time, Garrett and Mary Fran decided the germs and house cleaning could wait until tomorrow morning. They had been separated for a few days, so they decided to go home and begin the clean-up tomorrow.

After the animals were cared for, they decided a visit to Bath Pond was in order. It was good to be together again, since in their minds they were still honeymooning.

They were at the Coble home early the next morning. Garrett immediately began to cut firewood for the wash pot and didn't stop the entire day. They washed and boiled everything, including scrubbing the floors with boiling water.

They left at first dark, bone tired.

Mary Fran went to sleep as the pick-up made its way through the palmetto flats, truck farms, and citrus groves.

Arriving home Garrett said, "You were tired and took a nap coming home."

"I know. Let's take a quick swim, and while you tend to the animals I'll fix supper."

Mary Fran put up little resistance to Garrett's urging her to go to bed early. She was extremely tired.

Sometime before morning she was up looking for aspirin. Hoping not to wake Garrett she did not light a lamp.

"What are you doing?" he asked.

"Looking for aspirin," she said. "I don't feel good."

"Do you think you have the flu?"

"I hope not. Go back to sleep. I'm alright for now."

At sunrise, both knew she was sick. Garrett felt he had to have help and immediately went to the doctor's house to alert him to Mary Fran's illness. He was given medicine and the promise to visit later in the afternoon.

Garrett decided he needed help looking after Mary Fran. He'd never cared for anyone who was sick. The only person he could think of was Essay, and off to his dad's house he went.

"Dad, Mary Fran is coming down with the same flu bug that has everyone at the Coble house sick. I need help. Can Essay come home with me to take care of her?" he asked.

"I don't know of any reason why she can't. Beau and I can get along alright for a few days."

Arriving home, Garrett knew immediately Mary Fran was worse. Her fever was higher than when he had left her earlier in the morning. Essay pumped cool water and immediately begin bathing her, hoping this would provide the relief she needed. She was also given the medicine the doctor had sent.

"Mr. Garrett, would you go to the garden and see if you can scratch a few new taters? If you can, I'll make Miss Mary Fran some tater soup. Maybe that would taste good to her," Essay asked.

All morning Mary Fran continued to worsen. Just before the soup was ready she became nauseated and vomited several times. She was very sick and listless, and her color was pale. She was slow to respond to any kind of conversation. She was so sick she just wanted to be left alone.

The doctor came at sundown. Garrett was out with the animals and happened to hear the car as it pulled into the front of the house.

"How's Mary Fran?" the doctor inquired of Garrett.

"I really believe she has been getting worse all day, Doc. I'm anxious for you to take a look at her."

"I've got some bad news, Garrett. Mrs. Coble died shortly before noon," the doctor said. Her condition continued to worsen and everything they did for her did her no good. He also explained that the rest of the kids would continue to live at the Children's Home until foster homes could be located. Those kids in the hospital would remain there until they were able to go to the Children's Home.

"And, by the way, I took Mr. Coble home on the way out here," the doctor said. "He's very shaken and naturally so. I think you should look in on him tonight. I've told the preacher, and he headed out to get some of the ladies in the settlement to carry some food in tonight for him."

"Yes, sir, I'll do that, but right now will you look at Mary Fran?" Garrett asked. Being told of Mrs. Coble's death only caused Garrett greater concern for Mary Fran's condition.

After spending a good thirty minutes with her, the doctor came out of the little shed bedroom and said to Garrett and Essay, "Mary Fran has the same ailment all the rest at the Coble house have. She is very sick, and you must remember to give her the medicine just as I have instructed. Also Essay, you keep a little broth from a chicken or some stewed vegetables or fruit handy at all times. Don't miss any opportunity to get some into her. Try to find out from her what she might like to eat. She probably won't tell you, so it will be up to you to convince her to eat something," the doctor concluded.

"Garrett, I'll be back tomorrow morning," the doctor said as he gathered his things to leave.

Following the doctor out to his car, Garrett said, "Doc, with all the calls you've made to the Cobles plus coming out to see about Mary Fran, I am probably at the point of having no more money myself. Do you know how much I owe you now?"

Very gently the doctor said, "Garrett, we've more important things to worry about now besides money. No, I don't know what you owe me and I'm not worried about it. Let's get Mary Fran on her feet, and we will worry about money later. I know you will pay me when you can. The important thing now is not to worry about it. We have more important things to be concerned with."

When Garrett returned to the house, Essay said, "Mr. Garrett, I heard the doctor tell you to go to see about Mr. Coble. Do you think you could get hold of some stew beef and bring it back with you? I guess I can kill a fryer, can't I?"

"Sure, kill the fryer and I'll bring the stew beef home with me."

"If you can get some beef, I'll put it in a canning jar in boiling water until it cooks the broth off the meat. This broth will have lots of power in it for Miss Mary Fran. You go now and don't worry about Miss Mary Fran. I'll take good care of her."

The trip to the Coble house was endless. Not only did Garrett not know how to confront someone who had just lost another through death, he was actually nervous and scared about the entire situation. He kept telling himself that if others could do it, so could he. While he didn't know what to say to Mr. Coble, he thought that maybe at that moment the words would somehow be miraculously provided. This had to be one of God's mysterious ways he'd always heard about.

It was late afternoon when he arrived. There was a lamp burning very low in the kitchen and a lady was just leaving by the back door of the old house. *At least the house is clean,* Garrett thought.

Garrett entered the kitchen door to find Mr. Coble sitting at the table with his head in his hands. Mr. Coble did not look up as he entered. Garrett walked over to the table and sat in a chair directly across from Mr. Coble. Putting his hand on the old man's arm, he said, "Mr. Coble, the doctor just left my house looking after Mary Fran and told me about Mrs. Coble's passing. This is the first time I've had to console a person who has lost a loved one, but at least I think I know something of how you must feel. I'm so sorry. She was a good woman."

Very slowly Mr. Coble raised his head from his hands, looked at Garrett, and said, "Mary Fran is sick too, isn't she?"

"I'm afraid so."

"She got it looking after us, and I feel like we are to blame."

"You are not to blame, Mr. Coble. You are the only true family she has ever known. She had to do what she did. She is young and strong, and I believe she will be alright," Garrett said. "Essay is looking after her every need even now."

"Garrett, Mrs. Coble and I were married forty-three years. We never had much but each other, but we did have this. When we learned we couldn't have children, we began taking in children without homes. Of course, this was satisfying. We not only got attached to many of them over the years, but we enjoyed having a small part in the lives of those who couldn't help themselves when they needed it. This was our family."

Garrett could see the old man's eyes were bloodshot with dark circles under them. His face was more lined than usual, and his beard was worse looking than ever. He appeared as if he hadn't slept for several nights and was visibly very tired.

Talking seemed to help, and the old man continued. "When we had time to talk, which was not very often, most of what we talked about was what we could do for a child or the children together. Very few times did she have ready-made clothes or any of the finery after which most women lust. She was content to make do with what we had, which was close to nothing most of the time. And now she's dead and I don't have the money to provide her a decent burial. I guess the county will have to help me. It is sad to get to the end like this with no money and very little except memories. But we do have assets like you and Mary Fran and all the other kids we've been fortunate enough to help over the years. This means something. In fact, it is the real meaning within our lives.

"I've been worrying ever since her death what will happen to the children. There is no way I can look after them, and yet I know they are expecting me to come for them when they find out she's dead."

"You know the community has a debt to you and Mrs. Coble. What would our settlement have been like if it hadn't been for the two of you? What would all the kids have done if it wasn't for your love and care? There is no way to determine what you have meant to this community."

"The truth is, Garrett, no one received more blessings from what we did for the kids than the two of us. We truly found our calling early in life and managed a way to do it in the only fashion we could afford," Coble said.

A group of ladies from the church came with food and to visit. They were prepared to stay or do whatever he required.

"Garrett, since you have Mr. Langford's truck, will you go by the undertaker's and tell him I need to see him? I need to know what his charges will be, and how can I pay them on time?" he asked.

"Sure, I'll slip out now and let you visit with the ladies."

"Oh, by the way, Garrett, thank you and Mary Fran for coming by to clean up the house and sterilizing things while I was away. It has never been cleaner."

"We were glad to do it," Garrett said as he was leaving the house. "You are looking after the animals now, aren't you, Mr. Coble?"

"Yes, don't you worry about them."

The process of maturing was tough for Garrett. Too much grief with such tremendous consequences was happening too soon to one so young.

Garrett really needed some consoling himself. Mary Fran's present condition was of grave concern to him, yet Mr. Coble had barely brushed past this subject during their conversation.

The undertaker told Garrett the price of Mrs. Coble's burial would be $145 total, including two cemetery lots at the little church cemetery in the settlement.

"I'm sure you know Mr. Coble doesn't have any money. I have a plan. My wife was raised, in part, by the Cobles, and I believe I can get those who are now grown but raised by them to chip in and pay the bill if you will be kind enough to give me some time?" Garrett asked.

"Let's look at it this way, Garrett. I've known your dad for a number of years. I buried your mother. I have known you all your life. I know Mr. Coble doesn't have any money. Unfortunately, the county won't help because it can't. Maybe the welfare agency of the county who helped the Cobles look after the kids will be in position to do something. If so, this is the best thing that could happen. If I can be assured the return of my out-of-pocket costs, I can rest lots easier," the mortician said.

Garrett said, "If I personally guarantee your fee, would you not bother Mr. Coble?"

"Sure," he replied.

"Further, Mr. Coble asked me to ask you to come visit him. Will you ride out to his house early evening and tell him to rest easy about the bill without disclosing the person taking the responsibility? Tell him when everything is concluded, it will be soon enough to worry about paying."

The undertaker said, "I think that is the least I could do. I'll be glad to go out."

After picking up some stew beef, Garrett decided to visit his dad and tell him what had happened.

"You did right, son, with what you told the undertaker. We'll take care of it somehow. After all, the Cobles are most of the family Mary Fran has ever known. I guess you could say we owe it because of Mary Fran," Mr. Gregson said.

"You don't think I should ask others who the Cobles have helped in the past?"

"Not unless some of them ask. If they do, let them help. If not, we'll figure a way to satisfy the bill."

Arriving home, as the sun was setting behind the giant oaks in the front yard, Garrett could see the lamplight in the bedroom, a sure sign Essay was taking care of Mary Fran. As he entered the front door, she was coming from the bedroom.

"How is she, Essay?" he asked.

"She ain't doing no good atall, Mr. Garrett. She don't want to talk to me. She puking all over everything. She won't eat nothing. She won't drink nothing. Her fever won't come down.

I thought it was going down early this afternoon, but now as the sun going down it coming back, which is natural," she said.

"Here is the beef. You need anything else to take care of her now?" Garrett asked.

"Nawsa, dis it."

Garrett went into the bedroom, "Hi, hon, how you feel?"

"Not too good," taking his hand and drifting off.

Garrett sat there for a moment as she snoozed. When she was asleep he went into the kitchen.

"Has doc been out yet?"

"Nawsa, not yet."

Garrett could see chicken soup cooking with about half the fryer killed earlier. The other half was in a pot of chicken and rice she was cooking for their supper. It sure smelled good because he had eaten very little during the day. She was also cooking a pan of biscuits and fresh peas from the garden.

The doctor arrived as Garrett was finishing feeding the animals. After looking in on Mary Fran, he came out to the front porch where Garrett was waiting on the front steps and motioned him to follow out to the woodpile where each sat down on the same log.

"She is a sick woman. I don't believe she is any worse than yesterday, but I think what we must do now is take care of her as best we can and let the flu run its course. Believe me, we are doing all we know to do," the doctor concluded.

"The fever worries me, Doc. Is washing her down all we can do?"

"Yes, that and keep some aspirin in her. I think she is beginning to make a comeback from being so sick, but it will take about another week for her to get to feeling decent again. By the way, did you see Coble today?"

"Sure did. He's worrying over the bills that will be coming his way with no money to pay them with. Some of the church ladies brought him food and are still with him, I think."

"How do you think he'd like going to live at the County Children's Home and working there? In a sense he might feel he was at least doing the best he could to look after the kids that were in their home," explained the doctor.

"It might be a good idea, Doc. At least it would give him some reason to get up in the morning. I don't believe he will want to stay in their home without Mrs. Coble."

"There is an opening, and that is a possibility. I think I'll go by there and talk to him when the time is right," the doctor said.

Mrs. Coble's funeral was held late the next afternoon. It was a bright, clear, hot day. The sun was fading but still in position to shine brightly on the front of the little church. Its tin roof was just a little rusty and absorbed the heat well.

Everyone in the settlement attended. Even a number of those kids the Cobles raised in their home over the years came, who now lived in other towns. It was a full house for the little church.

Rev. Silas Boggs did his best with the eulogy and delivered a powerful personal salvation sermon. The burial concluding the services for Mrs. Coble was very late in the afternoon.

Mr. Gregson decided to visit Mary Fran before going home. Garrett had picked him up in the Langford truck and agreed to take him home. On the way, he said to Garrett, "Not anyone offered to help with funeral expenses, did they, son?"

"Not really. At least not money anyway. Several did come to me and said they would like to but because of the hard times they just didn't have a spare dime."

"Well, at least that shows their intentions were good. The truth is that good intentions won't pay bills. You know, Coble doesn't have money and we've very little. I think the thing to do is join forces with the doctor and see if we can't encourage the county to pick up part of the tab, and we will take care of the rest. Since the Cobles worked for the county, they should be given some benefits since they did it for almost nothing."

"That's good. Let's get on that in the morning and work it out."

"Fine with me," Garrett's dad said.

Mary Fran was propped up in bed with a straight chair lying down, back up, with a pillow on top. She looked very weak and sick, Mr. Gregson thought.

"How are you, Mary Fran?" he asked.

"Oh, hello, Dad. I think I'm some better, but I know I'm a long way from being well."

"You are looking a whole lot better to me," Garrett said, though privately he thought not much.

"Was there a good crowd at Mrs. Coble's funeral?" she asked.

"Yes, just about everyone in the settlement and a number of the foster children from years ago were there also. The church was full," Mr. Gregson said.

"I'm glad. My only regret is that I couldn't go. I do feel bad about this," she said.

"Everyone did ask about you," Garrett said.

Walking out of the bedroom, Garrett saw headlights coming up the lane.

"Dad, here comes the doctor. We can talk to him about going to the county and getting some help with the funeral," Garrett said.

The doctor entered the front room and said, "I was out in this direction and thought I'd look in on Mary Fran," making his way into the bedroom.

A few minutes later he came out. "Thank goodness, she's much better tonight. Keep her on the medicine until you use it all up. Be sure to continue to watch her temperature, and as it comes up give her aspirin and sponge baths as necessary."

That was the best news Garrett had heard in days. He and his dad also took the opportunity to work out a plan with the doctor's assistance whereby they hoped to encourage the county to assist with the funeral expenses. Garrett was tense about working it out because he had personally guaranteed the bill to the undertaker. Yet he did feel better about it since his dad was on his side, and he'd never let Garrett down.

When Garrett was taking Mr. Gregson home after supper, he carried a plate to Beau from Essay. "Son, don't worry about the bill. We will get by it somehow. The main thing now is not to let Mary Fran's progress slow. If she doesn't have a setback, I believe she will be okay soon."

10

Waking the next morning, Garrett was still tired from all the worry, anxiety, and work he'd been exposed to for the last few days. He didn't want to get up, yet knew he had to and began thinking about all the things that had happened the past few days and the opportunities offered for the future, which he had to talk to Mary Fran about.

Entering the kitchen, he found Essay was already working on breakfast. "We is having something different this morning. I is tired of grits and eggs. What "bout hotcakes?" she asked.

"Fine with me. I don't know when I've had hotcakes, and I know Mary Fran would like some too," he said.

"I is already give her a bath, and she be much better this mawnin'," Essay gleamed.

Garrett said, "I guess you are taking all the credit for getting her well?"

"Yes, sir, I is," she replied with a big laugh.

Entering the bedroom, Garrett said, "Mornin', sug, how do you feel?"

"Better than I have since I got sick."

"Essay's fixing hotcakes this morning. How's that sound?"

"Good. Maybe I can eat one."

After breakfast, Mary Fran asked Garrett to help her sit on the porch in the sun for a while. Thinking this might help, he moved a chair to the porch and helped her get to it.

After they were settled and Essay was out feeding the chickens and doing a few things in the garden, Garrett said, "Mary Fran, we have something we need to talk about. Do you feel like talking now for a few minutes?"

"Sure, what is it?"

"With all the things happening as they have, I haven't had the time or opportunity to talk to you about a conversation

I had with Mr. and Mrs. Langford a few days ago. You see, they made us a proposition. He wants me to begin thinning his timber and resurrect the sawmill he built for his son. By selling the timber, we can live and begin to develop the place from the proceeds. When money comes in, we clear land to set citrus and plant pastures for the cattle. Mr. Langford says he won't need any of the money for himself, and we can take wages from the returns and put the rest in improvements to the place. What do you think?"

Surprised she said, "I can't believe it! You mean the Langfords are going to trust you to continue with the same business they started for their son?"

"That's right. I talked it over with Dad, and he says it sounds good to him. He believes the Langfords are good people and won't take advantage of us. Because of Dad's judgment, I want to take advantage of the offer—that is, if you do. I believe it will be a chance for us to get ahead," Garrett concluded.

Both agreed they should take advantage of Mr. Langford's offer. Mary Fran began feeling weak, and Garrett helped her back to bed.

Being sure that everything was proceeding well at home, and seeing Mary Fran safely back to bed, Garrett decided to visit Mr. Langford and discuss the offer in detail.

"I am going over to Mr. Langford's to talk further. Expect me by lunch," Garrett said as he left.

11

The trip didn't last long because Garrett was lost in thought regarding those things he wanted to discuss with Mr. Langford. He was happy about the prospect and scared of failure at the same time. The adventure of it all was the best thing that had happened since his marriage to Mary Fran. Now that she was feeling better, their lives were looking up again.

Entering the side yard fence, Garrett saw Mr. Langford in his usual rocking chair rolling a Prince Albert cigarette. He parked the truck at the gas tank and walked back to the side porch where Mr. Langford was sitting.

Walking up the steps while glancing in Mr. Langford's direction, Garrett felt something was wrong. The old man's eyes were red and filled with tears. He couldn't look at Garrett.

"Hi, Mr. Langford, how is it this morning?"

After a few moments with no response, Garrett asked, "Is there something wrong, Mr. Langford?"

The old man broke into tears and turned away as if crying took away from his manhood. His weeping became uncontrollable.

Garrett was standing there not knowing what to do. Should he hug the old man, say something to him? If so, what? He was totally without any knowledge of what his next action should be.

He moved closer and said, "Try to get hold of yourself, Mr. Langford, and tell me what's wrong."

Still completely unable to control his emotions, Mr. Langford motioned to Garrett to follow him into the house. The house was almost dark. No lamps were on, and the giant oaks had completely shaded out the sunlight.

Following Mr. Langford, Garrett wondered where Mrs. Langford was. A sense of fright began to come over him.

Approaching the bedroom, his worst fears were realized. She was lying on the bed in her nightgown. She wasn't moving or breathing.

Garrett looked at Mr. Langford and asked, "Is she?"

The old man nodded affirmatively, sat down on the bedroom rocker, and completely lost control of his emotions. Garrett continued to look at the lady. She must have died in her sleep. Her face had a pleasant expression, and her hair wasn't in disarray. When the realization really hit Garrett, he turned toward the old man and, seeing his profound grief, squatted beside him, putting his arm around him and letting him cry it out. Garrett did not one time try to say anything to him or get him out of the room to ease the situation. His thought was that if he could get it out of his system maybe it would help.

When he did regain control, Garrett asked, "When did this happen?"

"I don't know. When I woke up this morning, she was already gone. Must have been during the early part of the night because her body was cold when I got up."

Allowing the shock to subside, Garrett wondered what he should do. The two of them decided the undertaker should come and take her body. Garrett went to town to get him.

After arriving in town Garrett heard the undertaker say, "You've turned out to be one of my best customers lately, haven't you?" Recognizing that his remark was not humorous to Garrett, the undertaker put his arm around him and let him know he wasn't attempting to make a joke out of Mrs. Langford's death.

"Sure looks that way, doesn't it?"

"Garrett, there is more to this than me just going out and picking up the body. First the doctor must go out and pronounce her dead, and then the sheriff must release the body before I can pick it up. The sheriff must get involved to satisfy himself that no foul play has taken place. Why don't you go back and stay with Mr. Langford, and I will notify the doctor and the sheriff, and we will all meet out at the Langford place as soon as possible?"

Garrett's dad's place was not far from the road to Mr. Langford's home, and he decided to get his dad to go with him. If his dad would come, it would make things a lot easier for him.

Lucky for him, Mr. Gregson had just finished his bath and was standing on the back porch shaving. Upon hearing the news, it didn't take him long to get into the truck.

They went directly to the bedroom and found Mr. Langford sitting on the side of the bed with his wife's body. With little difficulty, one could tell he was deeply emotional over his loss and personally devastated.

Mr. Gregson walked over to him and put his hand on his shoulder and said simply, "I'm sorry, John. Having gone though this kind of loss, I think I know something about how you feel. It is an awful time to have to face, and regardless of how you prepare for it, you're never ready for it to come."

The three sat in the bedroom, with very little conversation, until the sheriff arrived. He asked Mr. Langford if he knew when she died, and the answer was no. He then asked if she was sick when she went to bed, and he answered, "Not more than usual." She had several ailments. She had diabetes, high blood pressure, and a goiter, all in addition to a very severe case of crippling arthritis.

Finishing his questions, the sheriff sat quietly and waited for the doctor and undertaker. After a thorough examination to be sure she did not die of foul play, the doctor determined she must have died early in last evening of heart failure given her past medical history. The sheriff released her body to the undertaker, and in a few minutes there was only Garrett, his dad, and Mr. Langford standing on the side porch watching as the hearse pulled away.

"John, are there any kinfolks Garrett and I can contact for you?" Mr. Gregson asked.

"No, thank you. Both our families are gone, and we are all that is left. There is no one to notify except the preacher," he replied.

"Garrett, why don't you just go get the preacher, and I'll stay with John until you get back?"

12

When the funeral was concluded, many of those attending came by the Langford home for the customary visit. There was food everywhere that folks had brought, and Mr. Langford was overwhelmed by their generosity. To help out, Garrett brought Essay over early in the morning to manage the kitchen and clean the house. She was in full charge, dressed in her freshly washed and starched Sunday clothes.

Essay came to Garrett and said, "Mr. Garrett, Miss Mary Fran is home alone and is feeling good. She is most over the flu bug but just weak. Why don't you go get her and bring her here for supper? It will do her good, and it might help Mr. Langford."

Thinking this was a good idea, he asked Mr. Langford what he thought. His reply was, "I was just thinking the same thing, son. Why don't you do that?"

Mr. Gregson said, "If you don't mind, maybe you'll drop me off at my place on your way?" Essay fixed Beau and Mr. Gregson large plates of food to go with them.

After supper, and with all the visitors gone but Garrett and Mary Fran, and while Essay was washing dishes in the kitchen, Mr. Langford said, "I have a proposition to bring to you. It is not something that is a must, but something I would very much like to see happen. Garrett, why don't you and Mary Fran move in with me? This house has five bedrooms and rambles all over the place. Essay, there is a smaller house out back that is fully furnished and can be yours. If you folks would do that, it would not only make it much easier on me but on you because of the cramped quarters you are now living in. Garrett, if we get together on the deal we discussed that's fine. If we don't, that is okay, too. It has nothing to do with you folks moving in. If it works out fine and if not, we can make other arrangements later. But for now, I think it is a good idea, beginning tonight."

"Lawd, what would Mr. Gregson say, Mr. Garrett?" Essay asked as she was later told.

Garrett turned to her and said, "This is probably just a temporary arrangement for you. Why not let me handle Dad?" To which she replied, "Yes, sir."

After a thorough discussion, they decided to try it. Garrett and Essay went home for their bedclothes and essentials.

Arriving back at the Langford home, Garrett went to the bedroom assigned to them and found Mary Fran sitting on an easy chair in the room. She appeared as if she didn't know what to do next.

"What's wrong, hon?"

"Garrett, do you realize I've never seen a bedroom decorated like this one with furniture like this except in magazines? It is too pretty to mess up by sleeping in this bed."

"What are we going to do, sleep on the floor?"

"The other thing I was thinking of is that I've never spent the night in a house with indoor plumbing! Would you believe I've never had a bath except with a washrag and basin, a washtub, or with you at Bath Pond? What a change all this has been."

"Come now, you need some rest. You've been up a long time today. Besides, I want to feel how this bed will sleep."

13

Garrett was up early the next morning, feeling apprehensive about moving in with Mr. Langford. He longed for their independence, and now they had done the very thing he wanted to avoid. He went out onto the side porch and found Mr. Langford rolling a cigarette.

"Morning, Mr. Langford."

"Morning, son. You're up mighty early."

"It is a nice morning, so quiet and peaceful here. Cool too," Garrett said.

"The morning is my time of day," Mr. Langford said. "It has always been. I like to get up early."

"I like the morning too, but sundown is my favorite time of day. Dad always thought we should be up and at 'em by about five o'clock, and I guess I always thought this was too early. However, now I can't sleep much past five, if I do at all."

"I hope you rested well, son?"

"Sure did. Thanks."

"I miss my wife, Garrett. This is an awful period of life to be required to face. We both grieved over our son's death, but now to part with my wife after more than fifty years is much too much to face alone. Up till now I've always had her, and now I don't."

"I know it must be tough, Mr. Langford," as Garrett groped for words.

Essay came around the back of the house. "Mawning, everbody. I'll have coffee in just a few minutes and breakfast a little later. I is having trouble getting use to this kitchen."

"That's fine, Essay. If you need help let me know," Mr. Langford replied.

"Mr. Langford, I don't know if we made the right choice by moving in with you last night. We, of course, want to be helpful, and it was a nice gesture on your part. But honestly, I have second thoughts about it all," Garrett said.

"I was hoping you wouldn't have, because I have no ulterior motive in asking you and Mary Fran to move in. I certainly can get along okay without anyone. My thought remains today, as I explained last night, if we are going to develop this place—correction—if you are going to develop this place, it would be lots more convenient for you and Mary Fran to live here. If you are uncomfortable with this arrangement, it might even be better if I moved over to your house and let the two of you have this place for yourselves. Would that make you feel better?"

"No, sir. It isn't the fact that you are in the house with us. It's not that at all. I just feel funny about it all, I guess because it happened so fast. I really want the proposition you've offered to develop this place to work out to everyone's best interest. Further, I don't believe you are trying, in any way, to take advantage of us. I believe you are genuine in your offer and genuine in wanting the place developed, and I don't have one thought that I can't do the job. I can! Maybe the thing we need is a few days just to get used to one another and the whole idea?"

"Why don't we just leave it like that? After a few days, if there are some adjustments that need making in our living arrangements, we will just do it. In the meantime, we ought to think about how we will proceed with the things we need to be doing on the place. Since we need the sawmill first, why don't you go to the sawmill when you are up to it and see what it will need to get started?"

"Sounds good to me."

"Before I forget it, Garrett, I know Coble is in bad shape, and you told me it has been arranged for him to work at the County Children's Home. Why don't you see if you can buy his place from him? That forty acres would square up that section, and we would then own it all," stated Mr. Langford.

"I'll be glad to do that, but I don't have any money to buy him out," Garrett replied.

"No need for you to have any money. I have it, and we will just throw the forty in with the rest of the land and develop it as we go," Langford said.

"Good, this might solve another problem. By doing this—that is, if Mr. Coble will sell—it will provide him enough money to take care of Mrs. Coble's funeral expenses and then some for his pocket," Garrett concluded.

Mary Fran came onto the side porch and told them breakfast was ready. She looked much better this morning and appeared to Garrett as if she was right at home, much to his surprise.

After breakfast, Garrett walked out to the sawmill to check out the equipment. There were dog fennels six feet tall all around the machinery. The weeds and carriage were filled with rats. The tin roof was falling down around the engine, and everything was in shambles. Trees had grown up toward the sunlight through the rusty roof. Some had grown through the holes in the roof. Rust had taken its toll on the outside of most of the equipment, but the one thing that he had noticed was that all the equipment was weatherproofed on the inside about as much as was physically possible.

The worst thing he faced that morning were the wasps' nests under the rusty roof. Some nests were as large as a shovel blade. Hundreds of wasps were circling, becoming more furious by the minute. He retreated to the tool shed and located a broken hoe handle. He wrapped the handle with a big bundle of old rags he found and dowsed the end with motor oil. On top of the oil he poured just enough gasoline to start the fire.

In addition to the wasps there were very large rat snakes lying all over the roof structure of the old building. They were under the carriage and every other place that would afford them a quick meal. Garrett was taught never to kill a rat snake or a black snake. The size of these snakes, though, caused him to wonder if this was good advice. Yet, when he invaded their territory, they immediately left but were seen around the barnyard often.

A safe distance away from the barn he threw a match onto the rags, lighting his torch. It blazed up and effectively caught fire. He then marched back into the shed and did away with all the wasps. Luckily, he was only bitten a couple of times, not catching the barn on fire.

The wasp job finished, he took a large bush hook and began the difficult job of knocking down the dog fennels and trees that were growing around the sawmill apparatus. He pulled all the debris out into the center of the barnyard and began a pile of grass, limbs, and other items that needed burning. When he had the pile of sufficient size that he could keep it going, he torched it. Then the idea was to work fast enough to keep it going. It was a hot, difficult job to finish, but he intended to hang on until it was complete.

Burning the brush only added to an extremely hot and miserable day out in the broad open sunshine. The weather was brutally hot. Working with and by the burning pile was a job only for a very tough young man. Yet as tough as Garrett was, there were a few times when he wondered if it would all be worth it in the end. Mid-morning the sun was bearing down with not a breath of air stirring except the noise and hot air coming from the brush pile he was burning.

The more he cut away from the engine, the more evidence surfaced that it was of extremely high quality. Given the manner in which it had been weatherproofed, he had strong feelings that it would probably start. Finishing what he felt would be a good start on resurrecting the sawmill, he decided to change the engine's oil. Looking into the radiator, he saw that it needed only a little water, and he filled it. Garrett was careful not to spill any water on the outside of the radiator so leaks would be easily apparent. To his great surprise, there were none in the radiator.

He greased every grease fitting he could locate. He checked all the engine belts. He drained the diesel fuel for fear water had somehow seeped into it and refilled the engine. Then he drained the petcock valve to be sure all the water was out.

Inserting the crank into the engine he pulled it over a few times, and to his amazement it wasn't frozen up because of sitting so long. He decided to determine if it would run. After he pulled the engine over a few times, it fired. A few more pulls and it sputtered to life for a few seconds. The wasps' nests were discovered between the motor and the hood over the motor. Thousands of wasps came thundering out thoroughly confused and went out toward the barnyard as opposed to attacking Garrett. When the wasps quit coming, he pulled it again and it started to run again. After about twenty minutes of this exhausting effort trying to crank the engine, it gave a loud cough and sputtered to life. When the fan began to turn up, it was blowing hay and rats' nests everywhere. When the cover over the exhaust pipe opened up from the engine pressure, it blew nests to the ceiling of the old shed. Heating up the remaining hay and nests on the engine caught them on fire and rapidly burned the residue. The engine began to smoke and smelled like yard rakings being burned. Even though the smoke and smoldering fire concerned Garrett, he knew what was happening and decided to wait it out, certain that the engine would not be harmed. He was right.

The engine was not operating well, but it was running. He decided to give it more power after it warmed up. When he did, it seemed to settle down into what he calculated to be a perfect rhythm for the large engine, so large that Garrett had to reach above his head to remove the radiator cap.

Garrett thought as he stood there observing and listening to the engine run that a great adventure was beginning right now, and his heart began to pound from the excitement.

Now that the engine would run, he was certain the blade on the sawmill needed sharpening. The blades had been removed from the spindle and were inside the tool room immediately adjacent to the carriage. Inside were all types of files necessary to sharpen the blades. While sharpening the blades and observing the rest of the sawmill equipment, he began to realize what an extensive unit Mr. Langford had assembled. From where he sat sharpening the blade, he could see dog fennels and all types of weeds and vines had completely covered the operating portion of the mill. He could see the bull chain that ran from the log pile to the log deck from which the logs rolled down to the log turner. From the log turner the carriage that carried the logs through the saw blades was visible. There was a chain that deposited sawdust in a pile about one hundred feet from the carriage. A slab chain removed the slabs from the area, and an edger and trimmer saw were suitably situated at the end of the chain. Another chain deposited the trimmed particles into an area where an employee could sort through them and remove any good lumber and throw the rest into the slab fire. It was a fine set-up, and although Garrett had never seen a sawmill operate, he was excited about the possibilities that were before him.

As he finished the first blade, Mr. Langford walked up. Garrett didn't realized how stooped the old man appeared until he saw him walking with a cane and wearing a much larger hat.

"Didn't I hear the engine running just now?" he asked.

"Yes, sir, you sure did. I cleaned the weeds from around it, serviced it, and pulled it a couple of times. It was not frozen up, so I decided to see if I could crank it. It cranked without much trouble," he answered.

"What you might think about doing is cranking the engine and running it a bit daily whether you saw or not. This will usually keep it in good operating condition. The Langford rule of thumb when operating any kind of engine is always be sure it has plenty of oil, and the fuel will take care of itself," he said with a smile.

"I've had high hopes for this place, Garrett, that seemed hopeless until you came along. Now I'm depending upon you to make my dreams come true."

"Working here all morning, I've begun to develop a few dreams of my own. I didn't realize the size and style of the unit you have put together here. I believe with some work on all these wooden buildings, I can have this place ready to go soon," Garrett said.

"Garrett, I have an old Fordson tractor we used to snake logs to the log wagon to bring them to the mill. It is in one of these barns here. I also have two oxen we were planning on using to snake cypress logs out of the swamps. They have been turned out with the cattle. Maybe you will want to bring them to the barn and keep them up, feeding them dry feed and use them also? They were well trained and followed instructions well."

"Sounds good to me. I'll see if I can locate them."

When Mr. Langford left, Garrett found a scythe and begun to cut the weeds from around the sawmill. He piled them to the side and started to burn them with the debris from the mill unit. The next morning he hitched a team to a cycle bar mower and not only mowed around the sawmill itself but carried the rig to the house and mowed around the house also. This was the first time this had happened in some time. It seemed the cleaning would never end.

While he was cleaning around the outbuildings, he decided to fix up enough pens so that he could retrieve his livestock and bring them over to Mr. Langford's. His chickens, pigs, and cattle had to be tended daily, and the trip back and forth was taking too much of his time needlessly. The eggs would come in handy given that Mr. Langford had no chickens, nor did he have any swine.

The only thing that really kept him going was Mary Fran's recovery. She was stronger each day and usually sat on the side porch visiting with Mr. Langford. It was good to see her feeling good, and she spent every available moment talking to Garrett, offering him all the encouragement she possibly could. She was also forging a strong relationship with Mr. Langford while she recuperated.

14

When the sawmill was cleaned and serviced and ready to go, Garrett decided it was time to bring in the oxen and begin feeding them inside the barn. He saddled a cow pony and went hunting them early in the morning. He was aware Mr. Langford had a big place, but it wasn't until he started to ride it that he realized just how expansive it really was. He rode for over two hours before he saw the first cow. Of course, the oxen were not with this group of cattle, all of which ran with explosive speed in the opposite direction. On the first day out, he barely made it home in time for supper.

While they were having supper, Garrett was telling Mr. Langford where he looked for the oxen. "Try more into the flat woods to the west. They always like to graze in that area. You can probably located them there," Mr. Langford said.

Early the next morning, Garrett found them among a group of cattle in one of the better grazing areas. Surprisingly the oxen were gentle and posed little trouble in bringing them in—after he convinced them with a cow whip. When they realized he knew how to use it, they were more than eager to come along.

It was evident from the two-day hunt for the oxen that the cattle all needed worming. They also needed spraying for flies, and every pasture needed salt.

Observing the vastness of the land itself and the dreams the two held, it became painfully evident there was a big job ahead. Garrett didn't quite know how he was going to get the work done alone. In fact, he didn't know how to start. He would begin by taking it one day at the time.

Garrett mentioned to Mr. Langford at supper that evening the need for salt and worm medicine. Langford's reply was, "Well, you know where the truck is, you know where the fuel tank for it is, and you know the way to town. Why don't you go and get whatever you need and charge it to me? This is the way to handle that."

"Thanks, I'll do that tomorrow."

"Garrett, while you are in town tomorrow, why don't you go by the depot and make preliminary arrangements for us to begin getting flat cars to haul our sawed lumber to the finishing mill? Here is the name and address of the mill and its manager. Stop at Western Union and wire the manager, telling him we expect to begin shipping rough-sawn timber soon and for him to expect it. Ask him to confirm our request to ship. Be sure to tell him we will only be sending him what we cannot sell as rough-sawn lumber here at the mill. He should understand now he will not get our full production," he concluded.

The next day was a long one for Garrett. He was off early and arrived home just in time for supper, having completed every chore assigned him.

15

Early the next morning Garrett took a one-man crosscut saw from the barn and walked out to a large stand of pines not far from the sawmill. He wanted to be close enough to start with so that he could take the tractor, or oxen, and drag the logs to the bull chain instead of having to load them onto the log trailer and haul them to the mill. He was interested in starting slow and working his way gradually into the mill while learning how to work it alone. This was something he had never done, but he had watched others as they sawed lumber.

The day was no different from the preceding one—hot as blazes! Murderously hot. Garrett wondered whether or not he was man enough to continue in the sawmilling business. Not only was it tough work, the temperature only seemed to cause serious apprehensions. It might be too much, but his determination was such that he was not going to let it whip him before beginning.

"Getting ready to get started I see, son?" Mr. Langford asked.

"Yes, sir, only I don't know how or where to begin," Garrett replied.

"I figured we ought to chat before you get too serious, so I decided to make a trip out to see you. Why don't we agree now that all the sand hills, where we plant citrus, will be cut clean? On the land destined to be improved pasture, we will only cut those logs large enough to sawmill. This way we will just have to get the stumps out of the grove land, and if we thin the pines in the pasture we can come back later and cut again. This way there won't be any waste. If we decide we want to truck farm, we will carefully pick the best land and clean-cut it."

"Where we are standing now would be best as pasture. Is that right?"

"Right," Langford replied.

Now that the two of them had come to an understanding, there was nothing to do but begin. The first tree seemed to take an eternity for him to fell. When it went down, it went the wrong way—further proof that he had lots to learn about sawmilling. Plus, he needed to develop some new muscles for this sort of work. Presently his muscles felt puny.

At this point he thought of Mr. Langford's admonition: "God promised to feed the birds, but He didn't promise to put it into their nests." He wondered if he would ever find his nest.

When day's end finally arrived, he was almost too tired to get home. It was a horrible feeling since he wasn't used to this type of work. The side porch looked really good to him. Better still, the thought of going to Bath Pond would be the perfect ending to a grueling day. Mary Fran went with him, but did not go into the water since she still wasn't quite well. She also felt her newfound comfort with the indoor plumbing was too much to give up at the moment.

Just before noon the next day, Garrett's dad came riding up on his wagon. "Son, you've got a man-sized job, haven't you?"

"Yes, sir, I sure have. In fact, I don't know if I'm man enough to do this job."

"Sure you are. All it takes is guts to see it through. It's always okay to quit for a day, just don't give up."

"I know you're right, but it sure seems like success is a long way away when you are down on your knees trying to saw one of these big trees down."

"I'm sure it does, but remember you've got the chance of a lifetime here. If you make the best of it, you can go places, and if you louse it up, it's over."

"Yes, sir, I know that. I don't intend to louse it up. I plan on making it. Why don't we go to the house? It's about dinnertime, and you stay and eat with us. How about it?"

"Sounds good to me. Get on the wagon. You don't look like you could make it walking," his dad replied with a chuckle.

The next day Garrett was out early again. By mid-morning he was utterly surprised at how well he was getting the hang of the crosscut saw. Pausing for a drink of water, he saw his dad coming in the wagon again. Beau was with him.

"How is it going today, son?"

"Better I think. I believe I'm learning how. Hey, Beau," Garrett said.

Beau was off the wagon before it stopped and walked over to Garrett, "You look like you just ain't big enough for this job, boy."

Garrett said, "Who are you calling 'boy'?"

"Garrett, I've sure missed you," Beau said with a hug.

Before Beau could say another word, Garrett's dad said, "Garrett, I've brought Beau to you. He and I have talked about it and decided you need him far more than I do. This is under one condition. The condition is when I have cattle to work or fences to build or any job I can't handle alone, the two of you will come help me. So, under those circumstances, I've brought Beau to stay, and I want to leave Essay also until Mary Fran is on her feet again," Garrett's dad said.

Garrett grew weak in his knees. It was true he could use them, but feeding them was what worried him. Besides, he didn't know how Mr. Langford would take to it. And that's what he told his father.

"Don't worry about John. I talked to him yesterday after lunch, and he thought it was a good idea." Garrett's dad was ahead of him again.

About this time Mr. Langford came up in the truck. "Well, I see you've brought Beau over already. What do you think about it, Garrett?"

"I think it is a wonderful idea. I sure could use help if a way can be found to feed everyone."

"You don't eat much, do you, Beau?" Langford laughingly asked.

"No, sir," Beau replied.

Langford looked at Garrett's dad. "Then I think it is a good deal. Garrett needs the help, and I'm sure we won't starve to death."

"If you think so, Mr. Langford, then it must be a good idea," Garrett replied.

"Beau, there is plenty of room with your grandmother, and she knows you are coming," Mr. Langford said.

"Yes, sir," Beau replied.

Garrett's dad and Mr. Langford went back to the house in the pick-up with instructions to Garrett to bring the wagon in at dinnertime.

"Garrett, I'm sure glad to be here. I'm glad because I hope you need me and also because I want to be with you. Your dad always treated me just like a member of the family, but he is slowing down and there really isn't enough to keep him busy, let alone the both of us. I want to help you, and I want to do the best job possible with you," Beau said.

"I know you do, Beau. You've lived with us so long, you are one of the family and the closest thing to a brother I'll ever have. You know I can't pay you anything now, but one of these days I'll be able to, and I'll always remember you helped me when I needed it most. I won't let you down. You know that, don't you, Beau?"

"Yes, I do know that, and I'll never let you down. You can count on that."

16

Garrett and Beau quickly learned that working around a sawmill was not easy. It was the hardest work either had ever done. Not only was it brutally hot around the machinery, but in the field as well while wrestling with the logs. The work was tough, and it took a full-grown man with plenty of staying power to stick.

The two of them cut timber for a week and decided it was time to begin sawing. Both were careful to be sure the carriage and motor and every possible part was well greased. The engine was fully serviced.

Now it was time to begin sawing, and neither knew anything about how to begin. Just before they cranked the engine, Garrett went to the side porch and said to Mr. Langford, "We are almost ready to begin sawing. The thing that is puzzling us is how do we measure the thickness of each board we saw?"

"Why don't I come down to the mill and help you get started? There is nothing to it that five minutes worth of help won't solve."

Sure enough, after a short lesson and completely destroying two logs, Garrett and Beau were sawing lumber. Garrett operated the saw and carriage, and Beau caught the slabs and threw them onto the slab fire. The worst thing they had to contend with were concerns about starting an uncontrolled fire around the mill. They thought they could find a use for the sawdust, but felt the best thing to do with the slabs and trimmed ends was to burn them, making their lives unbearably hot.

They had cut timber for a week, but it only took two days to saw the logs they had felled. It was now time to go back into the woods.

Beau said, "Tell me again what Mr. Langford said about the birds?" Garrett recited the prose again, for about the fiftieth time.

A few weeks passed, and the lumber began to pile up. Garrett wired the lumber mill, asking them for permission to ship a flatcar of rough-cut lumber. The return wire stated the price and asked him to ship immediately.

To his great surprise, the folks in the settlement had heard of Garrett's sawmill venture and visited, wanting to buy lumber. It was a good feeling having neighbors wanting to do business with him, particularly with those able to pay for it. During the next few days he was barely able to get the flatcar loaded for lumber lookers.

Now the two were felling trees until about three in the afternoon and doing their best to get them sawed before it became too dark to see. Their newfound success was working them almost beyond their ability and staying power. When their strength was low, the thought of the "bird story," as they labeled it, always lightened the moment.

With practice, their ability to operate the mill improved. They could now saw professionally with most mills, and if their strength would hold, they could certainly fell the trees necessary.

The area they had been cutting was beginning to shape up. The trees were thinned, and the pastures were beginning to open up. Everything was well, even to the point of both making some wages. Also, their operating capital was beginning to accumulate. Because of this, Garrett began to think of clearing some land to plant grove and pasture.

17

It was late in the afternoon when a dilapidated old car coughed and gagged to a stop in the side yard next to the porch where Mr. Langford sat smoking. There was steam coming from everywhere under its hood. From the manner in which it was spewing, it appeared as if it might blow up.

Inside sat a young man and his wife. The car had a West Virginia license plate.

Mary Fran heard the commotion and walked out onto the porch as the young man stepped out of the car. Mr. Langford was sitting beside where she was standing.

"Hidy, my name is Bill Mathews. My wife, Cindy, and I are headed to South Florida hoping we can find some work. We've heard there are jobs in the fields, but our worn-out old car has come about as far as it will. Somehow we got off the main highway and don't know how to get back to it," Bill said.

"What's wrong with your car?" Mr. Langford inquired.

"To tell you the truth, the car was worn out when I got hold of it. I think the biggest thing wrong is it needs a valve and ring job since I can't keep oil in it. It also needs a clutch, and second gear is gone. It's probably ready for the junk yard," Bill concluded.

"Sounds to me like there ain't much left," Langford said.

Garrett saw the strangers from his vantage point at the barn and walked over to where they were. Mary Fran said, "Garrett, this couple is lost. Their car is about finished, and they are headed from West Virginia to South Florida to get work in the fields."

"Sounds like you've got trouble to me," Garrett said.

"We sure have," Bill replied.

"Why don't you ask your wife to get out and stretch her legs? Maybe you would like a drink of water?"

"That sure would be nice." Bill went to the car and said something to his wife. He brought her over to the porch and introduced her to everyone.

"This is my wife, Cindy. We've been married just a little over six months now and not been able to find any sort of work at home."

"We're happy to meet the both of you," Garrett said. "This is my wife, Mary Fran. This is Mr. Langford, and my name is Garrett Gregson. Why don't you come onto the porch and sit for a spell?"

"I sure wish we could relax, Garrett, but I've got to see if I can get this old car running and get back toward the main highway headed south. It is getting dark and we need to be moving," Bill said.

"Cindy, why don't you visit with Mary Fran for a few minutes, and I'll see if I can help Bill with the car?" Garrett replied.

The pair went into the kitchen where Essay was preparing supper. Both sat down at the kitchen table, and Essay poured them a cup of coffee.

"How long have you two been on the road?" Mary Fran asked.

"Today makes four. Lots of the roads between here and home are not paved and hard to travel on. We also got lost several times, like now for instance," she said.

"Have you been sleeping in the car?" Mary Fran inquired.

Very embarrassed, Cindy said, "We had no other choice. We stopped where we could and cooked us a little something to eat, and the car is the only shelter we have. The other thing is that the roads are full of folks trying to find a better life. People everywhere trying to hitch a ride, asking for food, asking for money. The truth is we barely had enough to get us this far, and now I don't know what we will do."

Trying to change the subject, Mary Fran said, "Tell me about your family."

"Really not much to tell. There were five kids. My dad is dead. My mom couldn't raise us, and we had to move in with her folks. My grandparents have been taking care of all of us for a few years. I'm the oldest, and it was probably a relief when Bill and I slipped off and got married. The truth is, if it were not for his parents, we would have already starved to death. There is no work or money in our part of West Virginia," she concluded.

"It's tough, isn't it?" Mary Fran asked.

After working on the old car for more than an hour, it was apparent that the both of them not only didn't know what was wrong but if they could have determined the cause, they probably couldn't fix it. One thing that worried Garrett was the water running out the side of the motor, which indicated to him that something dreadful was wrong.

"You may as well give up on the car for the day, Bill. It is certain we don't know how to get it going."

"I hate to mention it, Garrett, but we've spent everything we have trying to get to South Florida. I do have a full tank of gas I figured would get us there, but no more money. How would you feel if I asked you if we could sleep in the car here tonight and maybe we could figure out something tomorrow?"

"There is no problem with us making arrangements for the night," Garrett said.

Mr. Langford walked up and said, "Bill, I saw Cindy inside with Mary Fran. She sure seems a might tired to me. Is she well?"

"Yes, sir, as far as I know she is. Most of both our problems are that we are tired. We've been fighting this old car for almost a week now without any place to call home except it, and both of us are close to the end."

"Bill, you and Cindy wash up and have supper with us and plan on spending the night. Somehow when you are rested, problems don't look as big as they do when you are tired."

Bill replied, "I sure don't know how to thank you for this. It means a lot to us, and maybe we can find a way to repay the favor."

Garrett took Bill inside and made arrangements with Essay for them to stay for supper. After returning to the side porch, Mr. Langford said to him, "Son, why don't you let them sleep tonight, and bright and early in the morning, after a full breakfast, ask them to stay? Work out some arrangement with Bill to help you and Beau, and let them move into your old house. You need the help, and they need a house and some way to make a living. Above all they need to regain their self-esteem. Besides, I like them, don't you?"

"You are reading my mind, Mr. Langford. This is just what I had in mind," Garrett said.

During supper, Bill and Cindy painted a dismal picture of how the folks in West Virginia and bordering states were making a living. Most were not. All the big cities had long bread lines, and folks were standing in them listlessly. There was no work and no hope in many cases, and the Great Depression was still running rampant everywhere they'd been.

Garrett was at the mill at five o'clock the next morning greasing up the carriage. He thought he would get a head start on the day. He also wanted to get some of his necessary work done so that he could find time to talk to Bill before work time. When he was heading back to the house for breakfast, and after he had awakened Beau, Bill was coming down the path toward the mill from the house.

"Morning, Bill. How is it this morning?" Garrett asked.

"I can't tell you how much that night's sleep meant to us," Bill said. "I feel like a new man this morning thanks to your good heart."

"I'm glad you and Cindy stayed. Let me ask you something."

"Okay."

"Is it necessary that you go to South Florida? Could you be satisfied here if we could get together on some basis?"

"South Florida has no magic for us except we heard there was work there. What we need is a way to eat and exist," Bill said.

"I'll make you a deal. We have a small tenant house Mary Fran and I used to live in that the two of you can live. We're just getting started here, and if you will work with us you can have a milk cow, a garden spot with seed and fertilizer, laying hens and a rooster, a hog, and we will kill a steer once in a while. We will squeeze out a few bucks as they come into the sawmill. When things get better, we will make things better for you."

Bill was noticeably shaken. He was far from home, in a strange land taken in by hospitable strangers. No money, no transportation, and now this. Bill became so overcome with emotion he was unable to speak for a few seconds. Because he couldn't express himself verbally, he simply offered his hand and they shook on it.

Realizing Bill's predicament, Garrett said, "Good. After breakfast we will take the tractor and pull your car over to the house, and you can get settled today and be ready for work tomorrow. It can be a good arrangement for both of us. But remember, no money until we take it in."

"Okay," Bill replied. "Whatever and whenever you decide will be fine with me as long as we can just exist and not worry about it."

Beau and Garrett did not leave the Mathews until all their belongings were unloaded. On the way back to the sawmill, Garrett was trying to figure how to best use Bill. He had to get the most mileage from him, whatever his job turned out to be. Bill looked as though he was able to handle the tough work he and Beau had become accustomed to. His greatest problem was how he was going to take care of all the personal needs of the people he had taken on.

Entering the house for dinner, Garrett said to Mary Fran, "Bill and Cindy are just as happy in the little house as we were when we first moved in there. I really like them, and I believe their stay with us is going to be good."

"They are nice people, and I'm looking forward to having Cindy around so that I can have someone to visit with. I think we have lots in common," Mary Fran said.

The next morning Bill was standing at the side porch before daylight waiting on Garrett and Beau to begin the day's work. Having a job is an exciting experience—that is, since almost no one in his hometown could say the same this morning. He felt fortunate and blessed.

When Mr. Langford came onto the porch rolling a cigarette, he saw Bill and said, "Good morning, Bill. You're up a might early, I'd say."

"Yes, sir, Mr. Langford. I'm ready to get started. This is as close to Christmas as it can get for me."

"Garrett will be out shortly. Why don't you go to the mill and begin greasing the machinery and fueling the rigs?" Langford suggested.

"Yes, sir, I sure will do that. Just let him know where I am."

When Garrett came out Mr. Langford said, "I think we have us a good man in Bill. He was standing outside the porch when I came out and is now greasing and servicing the machinery at the mill."

With the addition of Bill's help, Garrett and Beau sawed more than twice as much lumber as they normally did. "We've hit the jackpot with Bill," Garrett said to Mary Fran. "We did not have to stop the mill once today to clear away slabs and trim. We cut lots more than we usually do."

For the next couple of weeks the three could only cut enough timber in the field in a week to last them two days of sawing. It was amazing how well the mill operated and how efficient it was when the organization was right.

Garrett could readily understand his need for a crew in the field cutting the timber and delivering it to the mill. If he could find a way to keep the mill operating all the time, his volume could greatly increase, and with it the income.

18

Often at Bath Pond, Garrett and Mary Fran discussed when they were married all they had was each other. Then the conversation inevitably turned to some of the events that led them to where they had progressed to now. They not only had each other, but a nice home, a business, and all the hope anyone could ever ask for. They were particularly lucky because most people were experiencing severe financial difficulties.

How sad it was to them to see all the people passing through town in search of work. The kids who were directly affected by this level of poverty were particularly tough to watch. Garrett and Mary Fran tried to help all they could with their limited resources.

With all of this, the two of them did have foresight enough to know that if it were not for Mr. Langford, they could be in the same shape as the migrating laborers. The couple recognized their good fortune.

Even more depressing than the families with kids were the older folks who were uprooted and faced the necessity of having to leave their lifetime homes and who were now looking for some way just to subsist.

This day at Bath Pond was no different. Their hearts went out to all those folks who couldn't, or didn't, share their good fortune. Because of Mary Fran's life in foster homes and living the life she had, they could empathize with those without. She was always the one to notice the unfortunate folks first. Yet their good fortune did not arrive without an extreme amount of very hard work, which both were capable of doing and willing to do.

Bill and Cindy had been there two months when Garrett decided everyone needed a break from their difficult daily routine. Thinking of what he might do, the decision was made to take everyone to the coast for a day and night and fish, sunbathe, and just relax for a bit.

Garrett could never plan an outing without inviting Brett Moore and Alan Wright. This was no exception, and both accepted.

To get the most out of a weekend, they decided to leave well before daybreak on Saturday, fish all day and night, then come home Sunday when they were tired. Garrett borrowed a rowboat and a shrimp net, and everyone took their own fishing gear, mostly cane poles.

Because they were black, Essay and Beau were just a little apprehensive about going. Beau, however, had many times passed as being white since his ancestry was also partly white. After some coaxing, they agreed to come.

19

Four a.m. was the appointed time to leave. Essay had a pot of coffee for the trip and a few biscuits for the road. She also carried meal, grits, lard, and coffee, along with her three-legged frying pan and plenty of firewood.

They were fishing by 9 a.m. at Eau Gallie. There were plenty of fish caught early, and Essay began to fry them for lunch. The afternoon was spent fishing and lounging around in the sun, relaxing and napping.

Shortly after dark, the men began watching other fishermen catching shrimp. They watched where the men went and how they threw their net. Because their boat wasn't large enough to accommodate everyone, they took turns.

After netting shrimp most of the night, their catch was slim. Everyone but Beau had had a chance, and now it was his turn. Beau hit the jackpot. His net was so full of shrimp on several casts that he could hardly bring it in. He caught more shrimp during his time than everyone else did put together.

During the night, those not casting for shrimp were fishing from an old dock. If they weren't fishing, they were sleeping. At first light Essay had a pot of coffee, grits, and shrimp for everyone. It was the first time any of the group had ever had shrimp for breakfast. After the night's fishing, shrimp and grits tasted mighty good. When they ate their fill, home sounded like a good idea. They wanted to fry fish and boil shrimp at home, knowing Mr. Langford and Garrett's dad would enjoy them as well.

The trip home was endless because everyone was tired and sleepy. They arrived after what seemed like an eternity, and the men immediately went about the task of cleaning fish and shrimp. The girls helped Essay cook the meal. In no time they had a feast fit for a king.

The outing was good for everyone because it afforded a break from the daily routine. Everyone was tired and ready for bed shortly after dark.

20

Before daylight Mary Fran was up feeling nauseated. When Garrett woke up, she was in the kitchen taking a dose of soda water, trying to control her stomach.

"Something didn't set well with me last night. I woke up about an hour ago feeling awfully nauseated," she said.

"Is it any better?"

"Yes, some better, but it has a long way to go before it is back to normal," she replied.

Garrett left home worried about Mary Fran. His day began at the sawmill.

Arriving there he found Bill already greasing the equipment. After exchanging a few words of greeting, Bill said Cindy was sick.

"They both must have had too much to eat or gotten hold of the wrong thing since both are down," Garrett said.

Shortly before lunch, Cindy visited Mary Fran, and both sat on the side porch with Mr. Langford. Both now felt okay.

"You girls alright now?" Bill asked, walking up to the porch.

"I think so," Cindy replied. "I'm just a little weak from it all, but my stomach is at least under control."

"If the two of you hadn't been so hoggish, you probably wouldn't have gotten sick. You should have seen the pile of groceries these two ate last weekend when we went fishing, Mr. Langford," Bill said.

"I'll bet it wasn't near the pile the rest of you ate," Langford replied.

"You're right about that, Mr. Langford," Mary Fran said.

Both Cindy and Mary Fran got along good for the next few days. The stomach problems reoccurred every so often.

Deciding there might be something more than a bad food problem, Garrett insisted both the girls visit the doctor to determine what was wrong. In fact, he was so strong about it that he decided to take them.

The doctor examined both the girls. Knowing Garrett was in the waiting room, he called him in.

"Garrett, I'm glad you brought these girls in when you did, because if you had waited longer, it might have been too late for me to be of any service."

Garrett's face turned gray and asked, "Doc, is it that serious?"

"To the best of my knowledge it doesn't seem to be anything terminal at this point." He paused for a long period of time. "That is, I guess you could say that. It is, however, serious and will require constant monitoring. Now I need to ask you a question, Garrett. Can I depend upon you to remember to bring them back at regular intervals so I can continue to check on them until they get over their problems? Can I?"

"You sure can, Doc. Is it going to be a long, drawn-out illness?"

"Relatively speaking, no. It will be just about seven and one-half months before they are cured."

"That long? What in the world is wrong with them?"

"They are both pregnant."

With this news, Cindy and Mary Fran broke down crying, and Garrett didn't know quite what to think or do. First of all, he didn't realize they were crying tears of joy. He thought they were sad about having a baby, yet he knew both wanted children. With nothing more being said, he walked over and put his arms around both as the only means he knew to console them.

Arriving back at the house, Garrett began to blow the horn when he entered the gate. Thinking an emergency was at hand, everyone came running.

"You can take this pick-up and go home. I just left Cindy there, and she needs you now," Garrett said to Bill.

Without replying Bill jumped into the truck and headed home.

"Is the problem serious, Garrett?" Langford asked.

"Oh, there is no problem. Mary Fran and I thought Cindy would personally like to tell Bill she's pregnant. Mary Fran wanted to tell all of you that she is pregnant too. There will be little folks around here soon!"

"That's great! In fact, that is the best news I've heard in a long time," Langford said.

Hearing the news, Essay was beside herself. Beau, though embarrassed, lit up. Seldom had any of these folks been presented with such news, and everyone was just a little uneasy with it all.

The word that Cindy and Mary Fran were pregnant gave some fuel to their workload. Production at the mill was the best it had been for some time. Even so, they weren't able to keep up with the lumber orders and sorely needed more lumber. Everyone talked about ways they could cut more timber and saw more lumber. Nothing they tried improved their volume.

21

Lumber orders began to pile up. Garrett just couldn't fill them quickly enough to satisfy his potential customers, not because he wasn't doing a good job, but because the other sawmills in the area were forced to close because they couldn't make their loan payments on the equipment. Economically, times were very tough for anyone in business.

Because his mill was paid for and everyone else had hard luck, that turned out to be Garrett's very good fortune. He was in the right place at the right time with the right product.

Late in the afternoon, Garrett, Beau, and Bill were quitting for the day and decided to go to Bath Pond for a swim. They had been talking about how good it would feel and had been looking forward to it most of the afternoon.

As they left the mill yard, they saw coming up the main road a totally dilapidated old truck. It was a one-and-one-half-ton truck that they couldn't believe was running and moving. It was a moving junkyard. Its truck bed was a boxlike structure built out of rough lumber, and it leaned to one side. The carpentry to build the box was primitive at best. Its motor was sputtering and sounded as if it wouldn't make it to the barn. It looked like a red truck, but the coloring was actually clay dust and rust. The truck was between the Langford place and a terrible rainstorm that was building to the north.

The truck made it to the edge of the house yard, spitting and spewing, when with a loud wheezing sound and a backfire it came to a stop. There was water running in a sizeable stream from the radiator. It was smoking, and it smelled as if it was about to catch on fire.

The driver and another man in the cab began to brush their hair back under railroad caps. Both stepped out.

Approaching Garrett, the driver said, "How do, mister? My name is John Haney and this here is Jim Lawrence and this is Jim Morgan over there getting out of the back of the truck. Right nice place you've got here. We admired it a long time from the road before coming on in," Haney said. Garrett noticed the rags they were wearing. Their appearance was totally unkempt. Not only were each of them sorely in need of a bath, but the wet mattresses in the back of the truck were producing an odor too. Garrett shook their hands callused from years of hard work.

"Why, thank you," Garrett replied. "Where you folks going?"

"We don't rightly know, I guess. We left south Alabama about two months ago looking for just any kind of work. We lost our farms, and all we've got left are our families and this old truck. We decided we could starve to death while moving searching for work as easy as we could holding up in this old truck in Alabama with nothing to do. Truth is we've found very little to do in the two months we've been on the road. We've had to live in and under this old truck, and we are about to the point of reaching the end," Haney replied.

While Haney was talking to Garrett, people were unloading from the back of the truck. Someone placed a short ladder as steps to exit the truck. It turned out there were three men along with their wives and children. The men were unshaven and dirty. They were living evidence of very hard work and a hard life in the past. None were well groomed. The men's hair was shaggy, and they hadn't shaved in a very long time. But more, they were openly self-conscious about their appearance, particularly the women.

They were plain country folks down on their luck. In fact, they had had no luck at all finding enough to keep food on the table.

The women were dressed in long dresses, and their hands also offered evidence of a difficult existence. They had clearly worked in fields and done all sorts of work just to survive. All the women had aprons down to their dress hems.

Mary Fran was a close witness to these folks' appearance. Her background was one that allowed her to immediately empathize with them. She knew exactly how they felt, and while she didn't become emotional in front of them, she did do her best to put them at ease with her conversation and actions.

The kids were in various stages of undress. They were also dirty and needed a haircut in the worst way. Just to chop it off would have been an improvement.

"You mean you have been on the road for two months and slept in this old truck the entire time?" Bill inquired.

"Yes, sir," Haney replied. "We had no choice with nothing to do in Alabama. Most of us didn't sleep in it, we slept under it."

While Bill and the group talked, Mr. Langford motioned Garrett away from the group. "God sent this group, son. Why don't you hire them?"

"How can I hire them, Mr. Langford? We barely can keep ourselves in groceries. What can I pay them with?" he asked.

"Looks to me like they might be the answer to running the wheels off the sawmill. These folks know how to work, and they desperately need to eat. You can look at them and tell that. On top of that, I believe they have known nothing lately but abject poverty. They are survivors trying to dig up something to do for an honest living. Because they are survivors, I believe they know how to bite corn close to the cob," Langford concluded.

"I agree, but that still doesn't tell me how we can hire them and us live up to our end of the bargain with you."

"Hiring them might help you. Make a deal with them."

"What kind of a deal? Tell me and I'll try."

Langford continued, "These folks are desperate and in need of only the basics. They need food and they need shelter. They probably aren't as interested in money as in something to eat and a dry place for shelter. We want to do the honorable thing. We don't want to take advantage of their bad luck."

"Yes, sir, keep going. I'm beginning to see what you mean."

"Why don't you make some sort of a deal with them that doesn't require much money—in fact, none for a while? That is, until we can begin to make the sawmill a little more profitable. Give them a milk cow or two, but on second thought and looking at the size of the group, you'd better cut out about five for them. The Coble house is doing us no good, and the place needs someone there to look after it. There are probably enough beds there to take care of them. Remember, we bought this place furnished."

Continuing, Langford said, "I believe it will look like a castle to these folks after living in that truck for two months. What you want to do is give them just enough to keep the monkey off their backs. Don't welcome them with open arms, but give just enough to provide them a chance so that they will have to want to work to gain your respect. Your assistance and loyalty to them now will reap tremendous benefits for you somewhere down the road if they accept the deal and stay with you. Throw in the garden spot, a few pigs, and all that stuff, but don't throw in money we don't have yet. I believe you need their labor way worse than they need you at this point, though they don't know this. They could be a substantial part of the success you will make out of the sawmill and the entire place. The bottom line is we've got the assets to make everyone a living; however, we don't have enough hands to make it happen. If you can make this deal work, we'll be on the mend. Remember the 'birds'!"

"You're right. They might be just the people who can keep the old Coble house from falling down," Garrett said. "I'll do my best with them."

Beau and Bill were talking to the group. They had been told Garrett was the boss, and what he said was gospel.

Everyone was church-mouse quiet as Garrett approached the gathering, "Where you folks plan to end up?" he inquired.

"Anywhere we can survive. All we are looking for is some way to live. Our problem is we have about come to the end of our road. We left with one hundred pounds of our black-eyed pea and butter bean seeds and almost that amount of coarse grits. All of it is about gone. We had two fifty-five-gallon drums of gasoline for the truck, and we put the last in this morning, and we are now just a few miles from the end," Jim Lawrence said.

Haney spoke up. "Worse still, our women and children are tired of traveling and living out of this old truck. We brung our pots and pans, some furniture and bedclothes and that's all. We were forced to leave the rest behind because we couldn't haul it. We've asked a few friends to keep some of our goods, and if we ever get settled we can get them."

Mary Fran and Mr. Langford were visiting with the kids and ladies while Garrett and the menfolk talked. Mary Fran was reliving her past in her mind, though her life was not so traumatic as being on the road with no place to go. Her problems were different, but she had others looking out for her as best they could. From her vantage point, someone who has experienced no place to go, no place to belong, nothing to do, and no place to make a living leaves a feeling of no self-worth or self-esteem.

"You folks ever worked at a sawmill?" Garrett asked.

"Yes, sir," Haney said. "We've all worked at a sawmill. The question here is if you would let us work on your mill. Our problem is getting the chance to show you we can do you a good job."

Based on Haney's remarks, Garrett immediately recalled his previous conversation with Mr. Langford about not welcoming them with open arms but rather give them just enough to let them get their foot in the door. He felt like Mr. Langford had more wisdom in his head than Garrett would ever be able to absorb.

"I could use just a little help for a short time, I guess. But I have problems the same as you have problems. My problem is very little money. We have plenty to do, we have enough groceries, we have shelter, and that's about it until we get on our feet."

"To backwoods people who get nervous every time we see a paved road, if we had what you do, we'd feel like the king of England," one of the men said.

"I'll tell you what we can try for a few days, but only for a few days to be sure we can make it work," Garrett began. They were all ears. "We have a rambling old frame house that used to be an orphanage. It is located on the western boundary of our place. It is furnished, such as it is, and I think it will hold all of you for the time being. The house can provide you with shelter. We have need of help at the sawmill beginning in the morning. The bottom line is I have no money to pay you. If use of the house is worth something to you, if a milk cow or two is worth something, including their feed, if a garden spot is worth something, and the promise of money when we have it is worth something, then I think we might can make a short-term deal. If we can't make it work, we can still part friends," Garrett concluded.

When Garrett finished, the three men looked with a nod of acceptance to each other, and all three approached and offered their hand to Garrett. When they were finished shaking on the deal the women came forward, thrilled sufficiently that each hugged Garrett, something he wasn't expecting.

While all the hugging was going on, standing to the side and watching Garrett's utter amazement at what was happening was Mr. Langford, who had a smug grin looking as if he had just swallowed a cup full of store-bought liquor. Mr. Langford's private opinion was that Garrett had just hit the mother lode!

"Do you think you have enough gas in your truck to drive about five miles from here and then back in the morning?" Garrett asked.

"Yes, sir. We just put our last five gallons in before driving onto your property. By the way, I thought you said the house was on your place here," Haney answered.

"It is, and it's about five miles from here. You folks follow me."

Beau went with Garrett to get the Alabama folks settled. On the way over Beau said, "I think you just made the best deal you've made in a long time. In fact, it was the best deal since Mary Fran agreed to marry you. These folks are hungry, and I believe they can really help us with that sawmill."

"That's just what I'm banking on. If we can run that sawmill, we can generate money to pay them and ourselves," Garrett said.

Arriving at the Coble place they unloaded quickly and were all over the grounds and house, deliriously happy. Tears ran down the faces of the road-weary women as they examined the house, and particularly the kitchen. The kitchen was well equipped because of the mouths it had to feed when utilized as an orphanage. Five gallons of kerosene for the stove and lamps sat under the back stoop.

The ladies were congregated around Garrett when he said, "Send a list of the things you will need with the men in the morning. Some of us will be going into town tomorrow, and we'll see about getting it to you."

"We thought we would be helping at the mill," one of the women said.

Not realizing they had this idea, but after thinking about it a quick minute, the idea seemed like a very good one. Garrett replied, "Why not get settled tomorrow, and we can talk about what you can do at the mill?"

Going back to the truck, Haney approached Garrett and said, "We do appreciate your letting us stay in this house. It not only looks like a mansion to us, we will take care of it just like it belonged to us. You should also know my mother is in the back of the truck on a pallet. She's old and sick, and one of the womenfolk will have to stay with her until she is back on her feet. I hope that is not a problem."

"Not at all. Does she need anything you don't have?" Garrett asked.

"No, sir. We've got her medicine the doctor gave us before we left, but she just ain't getting no better. She's right sick," Haney replied.

"Does she need a doctor?" Garrett asked.

"Let's give her a day or two to rest here, and then take another look at a doctor," Haney said.

Garrett left them at about 8 p.m. as they were settling down and cooking supper. He could hear the women laughing and talking in the kitchen, something they had not enjoyed for a long time.

While they were not blood relatives, the Alabama folks had grown up together. Their families settled the area of southern Alabama well in advance of the Civil War. Of course, each of the families had their favorite stories told by their grandparents regarding their participation in the war.

Without exception all the families aboard the truck on that afternoon came from an ancestry of financial substance. Their resources were not squandered over the years, but depleted as a result of the Depression.

During the Civil War stories emerged of farmers in the area increasing the number of hogs they normally raised for the purpose of helping the southern troops eat regularly. In order to do this, smokehouses had to be greatly enlarged. Smoking the meat was a monumental chore to most of the farmers.

The area in southern Georgia south of Quitman and north of Tallahassee was known as "The Smokehouse of the South." The cured pork was transported to the troops as it became available The southern Alabama farmers contributed their smoked hams to this group to feed the troops. They all worked together.

Also during this period Confederate troops had enlisted the aid of Florida ranchers to round up scrub cattle and drive them north, crossing the Suwannee River somewhere around Lake City, headed to a rail siding for shipment north.

Occasionally, the South Alabama farmers had extra beef that they drove to the rail siding for shipment. For dirt farmers, this was a tremendous undertaking yet filled with adventure, and the stories were tremendously exaggerated as the years passed.

During the last days of the war, seven Northern soldiers were found hiding on John Haney's grandparents' Alabama farm. They were on foot actually trying to steal corn that had been left on the stalk drying for later use as livestock feed.

John's granddaddy saw them and captured them with a single-shot shotgun, which was all he had. The capture had the makings of fashioning a real wartime hero in stories of later years. The soldiers were happy to be captured in an area that at least had food.

Grandfather Haney noticed that his captives were kids not old enough to shave. They were separated from their unit weeks prior with no weapons except pocketknives.

Haney marched the boys into the front yard of his home, where he summoned the entire family to witness his trophies. He also had them file by the front steps and give up their pocketknives.

Grandmother Haney saw each of them scratching their heads and bodies. She also saw them munching on their horses' corn for next year.

She instructed her husband to take them to the creek, make them strip their clothing off, shear their hair to get rid of the lice, and make each take a bath totally with strong lye soap. When the shearing and bathing was over, she had a meal prepared for them on a table under a chinaberry tree in the backyard. The food was simple country cooking, and the boys ate as if it were prepared for the finest banquet planned for royalty.

The boys were totally harmless. In fact, Grandpa Haney left his shotgun leaning beside the front door of his house in view of all the captives.

Later the same day word came that General Lee had surrendered to Grant at Appomattox. While the news was devastating to those who had sacrificed so much to feed the troops, at least the killing had stopped.

The young soldiers were allowed to sleep in the barn for a few days to rest up for their long trip home—only under the condition that none smoked in there for fear of fire. The walk home would be extremely dangerous for them so soon after the war's end. While they were there, they did what they could to help around the farm and became friends who later in life tried to remain in contact with the family.

Grandfather Haney's descendants, among the others on the truck who had come to Garrett, were good people, once affluent but having lost everything to the Depression and the banks. They were people who had to begin again in order to survive. All they really needed was a chance.

Garrett needed them as much as they needed him. It was a good match and paramount to the success of the entire operation.

They were good people, earthy farm folks, a small traveling community of like-minded people from Alabama. Of the original group, Garrett was never aware of an argument or ill feelings between them. Each had the authority to discipline the others' kids, with a belt if necessary. The atmosphere had the effect of every kid always showing the proper respect for all adults. Of course, as the kids grew older, some found trouble but never anything major.

One of the elements within their lives that held their union together was religion. From the very first Sunday that they worked for Garrett, the newcomers were in the settlement church listening intently to Rev. Boggs.

Attending regularly also included their tithe, regardless of how little the amount. They kept up their responsibility within the church and within the community as Christians. They were welcomed in the area because of their good works.

Because of their current financial circumstances, they looked rough from the very beginning, with tattered but clean clothing. Their bodies had taken a beating, but once they were settled they were always clean.

Over the years their appearance improved as success presented itself, yet their hearts never hardened because of their family's financial losses during the Depression.

22

Driving home that night, Garrett knew he had recognized a good group of people; however, his stomach was in knots knowing he needed to pay them but not knowing how. The money had to be in what they could return by hard work.

Much to his amazement, the Alabama folks were standing quietly outside the side porch at 5 a.m. when he walked outside. He was startled to see them standing there, ready to begin work. Garrett asked, "Have you had anything to eat?"

"Yes, sir. We've had breakfast and brought our lunch. We left one woman at home to look after Granny and the kids and straighten up the place today. She will also have supper ready when we get home."

"While I have breakfast," Garrett said, "why don't you folks meet Bill at the mill? It's just past the big barn area. Get the slab pile burning, and maybe then help him get everything ready to run. We will be ready to crank up just prior to 7 a.m."

Mr. Langford slipped up behind Garrett on the side porch and was standing grinning as the Alabama folks walked away. As Garrett turned to face him, Mr. Langford said, "I told you these folks were what we were looking for. Now in all your generosity don't make it too easy for them. Don't do them any favors. Yes, they are very poor. They are broke, and hungry, and we feel sorry for them. The truth is you yourself need a day's work from each of them to be responsible for a day's pay. You owe them this much."

Arriving at the sawmill Garrett recognized the mill was all ready to go, the slab pile was burning and Bill and Beau were just coming in themselves totally amazed at the morning's progress. Garrett walked over and stepped up on the carriage, while Bill and Beau took Jim Lawrence with them to snake in logs lying cut in the field. Jim Morgan and Haney took up positions around the mill.

Garrett knew how to operate the carriage, but he had never really witnessed someone operate one who truly knew what he was doing. Garrett was always very careful with the engine and the manner in which he operated the carriage, not being too forceful with the way he sawed lumber.

Morgan looked at Haney and said, "When Garrett stops to get a drink of water, you step up on the carriage and I'll give this diesel some gas. Let's show him how to operate a sawmill."

"You've got it," Haney said. "Garrett is lugging the engine anyway. He's not using enough power."

After about an hour, Garrett paused for just a second to step over to the water barrel for a drink. Because there were now women at the slab pile, he stepped around behind the barn to relieve himself.

When he was safely away from the carriage, Haney stepped up on it and Morgan pulled the accelerator back to double the amount of power Garrett was using. When he did, a cloud of diesel smoke rolled up from the big engine through the raggedy shed over it, and away Haney was gliding on the carriage.

Garrett thought something had happened to the engine. He'd heard of a diesel's governor slipping and the engine running away, eventually tearing to pieces. He thought this was what was happening until he heard a log going into the saw with Haney on the carriage. Clearly Haney knew what he was doing. Morgan walked over to Garrett and said, "Mr. Garrett, we think you were lugging the engine, which isn't good for it. The way Haney is operating the carriage is the way we were taught in Alabama. Is it okay if we continue with it this way?"

"It sure is. Haney knows what he's doing, doesn't he?"

"He should. He's ridden one of those carriages a lot of miles in his life," Morgan replied.

Bill and Beau looked up from their jobs in the field. Bill said, "The engine must be running away."

Jim Lawrence said, "Naw, that ain't what's happening. Sounds to me like Haney or Morgan has got hold of the carriage."

The three walked to where they could see what was happening, and there stood Garrett stunned at what Haney was doing with the carriage. He couldn't believe it. Garrett's work was piddling compared to what Haney could do with the mill.

Mr. Langford peeped around the corner of the barn when he heard the loud roar of the engine. Observing what was happening, he grinned and turned back toward the porch.

Garrett walked out to where the three were snaking logs to the mill. "Can you believe what Haney is doing with that carriage?"

Jim Lawrence spoke up and said, "I can tell you that Haney and Morgan can operate that mill in their sleep. They know how to do it."

With that, Garrett began snaking logs to the mill with the three of them. *This was the beginning of a real sawmill operation,* Garrett thought.

Breaking for noon, Bill, Beau, and Garrett started to move toward the house. Rounding the last bend toward the barn and mill area, they saw Morgan wiping his mouth while still chewing the last bite of his lunch, Haney stepping down off the carriage, and Morgan stepping onto it. One of the ladies was coming back to the slab pile after having lunch. The mill would no longer shut down for lunch unless they were out of logs or the engine required servicing. They fired up the engine in the morning, and it was shut down when quitting time came.

By 2 p.m. every felled log on the place had been sawed into rough lumber. The mill crew began to straighten lumber piles and burn trimmings and slabs. Everyone, that is, but Jim Morgan. He came out to the felling crew on Haney's instructions and began helping them. When the lumber was stacked, the entire mill crew joined the field hands and began sawing trees. By dusk, there were more logs at the sawmill than had been at one time since the operation started. Plus, the staging area and the field were filled with logs that were already felled and trimmed, ready for the mill. It was a whale of a day for the sawmill.

Mary Fran, Cindy, and Mr. Langford went to town and filled the order for the needs of the new folks and delivered them to the Coble house. The order was simple—just for the staples and bare necessities, nothing fancy or not needed. Langford had heard them say the women dipped a little snuff and the men chewed Brown Mule chewing tobacco. Though they didn't ask for it, he threw in a case of each.

Garrett was running over with good feelings as the first day with the Alabama people came to an end. He listened to Mr. Langford tell him, "Son, now you've got another problem. You've now got to learn how to be the boss and plan ahead for your laborers. Your job is to always be ahead of them with planned work. Never let their momentum slow, because if you do, it will be difficult to regain. Pushing for more is the name of the game now, while not being overbearing with it. You've got to keep production ever climbing, but more, sales have to keep pace. This is now a new and deeper responsibility for you.

"Now that you have been forced into a leadership role, there is something else you should know," continued Mr. Langford. "When you have a decision to make, and you don't have the foggiest notion of what your response should be, never make a hasty judgment. Do what the corporate executives do. Answer later. This is where I come into play. If after thinking about what your response should be, you are still confused as to what to do, come to me. Usually, as you explain the problem you are wrestling with out loud to another person, the appropriate answer will surface. If it doesn't, we can talk about it. You stay out front, I stay in the background."

With this proclamation from Mr. Langford, Garrett's enthusiasm for their accomplishments for the day paled in comparison to the knot in his stomach, wondering how he would ever measure up. He felt so insignificant in his meager knowledge, yet willing to give it all he had. He was operating on blind faith alone and totally living an adventure.

The next morning, before Garrett, Beau, or Bill could get to the mill, they heard the engine fire off and the carriage begin to roll. Beau was sitting at the table having breakfast and said, "Garrett, we already need about ten more people just to stay with those folks from Alabama. They are going to kill us!"

From the second day working with the Alabama folks, Garrett did his best to fulfill the role of boss. He planned the day's activity, watched everyone work, and did his best to keep sales ahead or equal to production. Being young, this was a tough job, but one that he was to learn well. He was to become highly respected for his ability in this area. The success of the venture rested with him alone, and everyone working there realized this. He did, however, have a secret helper in the advice that came from Mr. Langford. Their daily conference was priceless for Garrett.

Since Beau and Bill were better suited to the field and cutting timber, he placed them there. He kept Jim Lawrence with Haney operating the carriage. Jim Morgan snaked the logs to the bull chain and relieved Haney on the carriage from time to time. The women removed the slabs and stacked lumber after it was trimmed.

Garrett was almost totally consumed with sales. It soon became common knowledge that the supply of lumber was picking up, and folks began to come to the mill at any time. Sometimes meeting the public was a much tougher assignment than running the sawmill.

By mid-December, the sawmill was running well. The logs from the field were well coordinated, and everyone had settled into their jobs. Garrett felt good witnessing his very first business become a small success.

With Christmas only a few days away, Garrett invited Brett and Alan to go deer hunting with everyone. It was the first holiday any of the folks had had in a long time. They made it a practice of not working on Sunday in order to be able to have a day of rest. Additionally, everyone but Mr. Langford, Beau, and Essay were always present at church on Sunday morning.

The truth was that they worked so hard it took Sunday to get back on their feet for Monday. Garrett was always taught to take Sunday off, go to church and spend the time with family, and stay close to home. Fortunately, all the folks associated with him felt the same about it. They fit right into the little church and settlement family.

The hunting trip was in Pasco County, bordering the Gulf of Mexico. The Alabama group wanted to fish in addition to hunting. Because of their condition, Mary Fran and Cindy decided they should stay and prepare for Christmas at home.

The fishing and hunting party arrived home the morning of December 24. They had five deer carcasses, a fifty-five-gallon drum filled with all sorts of fish, and three wild hogs. They immediately dug a barbecue pit, placing an old hog-wire gate with an iron frame over the hole in the ground to cook the hogs. The women began cleaning enough fish to fry for lunch and preserved the rest by smoking them, using wood coals, or salting them inside a wooden barrel.

Essay had never seen anyone do this, and it fascinated her that such an art was possible. She had learned that in order to eat a salted fish, simply soak the salt from them and fry them like any other fish. Of course, over the course of her life, she had eaten her weight in smoked fish, and then some.

During the day of Christmas Eve, Garrett went to Preacher Boggs and invited him for supper. Essay spent her day in the kitchen preparing all the extras that went with the barbecue, like Brunswick stew, grits, slaw, and fried cornbread.

Somewhere around 6 p.m., with everyone gathering in the kitchen of the main house, the minister returned thanks and the feasting began. With all the Alabama folks and the immediate group, the pork and venison went fast.

It was a great time to live, Garrett thought. Everyone was having so much to eat and having a good time together and yet on so little. It was good to see the Alabama group and Bill and Cindy having a good time after such a tough year. The group finally wound down after the kitchen and yards were cleaned around midnight. Everyone agreed to be on the job the day after Christmas.

For all the local people a strange thing happened when everyone was about to disperse and return home. From out of nowhere Jim Lawrence, who had a magnificent voice, began to sing Christmas carols. The Alabama folks were accustomed to this type of singing and joined right in. Jim sang one carol and with little pause began another. Midway through the first carol, everyone was singing.

The group sang for a short while, and before they broke up for the night, the quietest of the three Alabama men, Jim Morgan, said, "Garrett, Haney usually does the talking for us but for fear he will forget—now that he has a whole case of chewing tobacco you gave him for Christmas—I wanted to be sure this gets said. Up to this point, in all our lives, no one has ever done us a greater service than you by taking us in when we needed it most. When we rattled up in our worn-out old truck, every belonging we had was soaking wet, we were at the end of our road. You took us in, gave us food and shelter and work. We felt like second-class citizens, yet we don't anymore. We thank you for believing in us, for all the nice things you have done for us since that late afternoon. Of course, the rest of the men thank you for our case of chewing tobacco and our womenfolk thank you for their case of snuff. You even knew the brands we like. I just wanted you to know how much we appreciate all the kind things you have done for us."

With this, the group, except Beau, Mary Fran, Bill, and Cindy, who were standing on the side porch, gathered close around Garrett and Mr. Langford. Haney said to Garrett, "Would you say a prayer to close the evening, Garrett? It has been such a fine day, and we have so much to be thankful for. I think this is appropriate, and you should be the one to do it."

With this request, Garrett was completely speechless for a moment. There was a long pause while he was in total panic. No one had ever asked such a thing of him; however, this wasn't something he couldn't do. He made an acceptable first attempt with the group, and everyone started home in good spirits. Before they crawled in the old truck, the men shook both Garrett's and Mr. Langford's hands with a "Merry Christmas." The women, already partaking of their Christmas present of snuff, walked up to them methodically, unloaded their cud of snuff, and kissed them squarely on the lips. This was the most they could do to show their appreciation. Then they were off.

Wiping their lips after the truck was out of sight, Mr. Langford asked Garrett, "Could you tell which of the women had Three Thistle and which had Bruton snuff?"

"No, sir, I couldn't. But I learned something tonight. That is the last time I will ever be a part of giving anyone snuff again."

When the two of them turned around to go inside, everyone on the porch was gagging in laughter. When they were approaching the steps, Bill said, "Mary Fran and Cindy said the snuff looked so good to the Alabama women, they are thinking of trying it." Wiping and sputtering, Mr. Langford said to Garrett, "The two of them are too nice to even consider such a horrible habit."

Alan and Bret went home tired after spending a few days with their best friend Garrett. Of course, Beau was also of equal value to their friendship. The four enjoyed a relationship that actually was closer than if they had been blood brothers. They each respected the other, yet no question nor inquiry was off limits, with a truthful answer expected. They intimately knew each other, and they could predict how the other would respond to almost any given circumstance. Their times had been spent hunting and fishing and in heart-to-heart talks as they had proceeded through all the growing pains that young men face.

When they started to leave for the night, they gathered around in the kitchen for a Christmas drink and toast. The toast came from Alan, who said, "Here's to the best friendship a person could ever hope to be a part of. Let us resolve to never take each other for granted and to always respect each others' wishes."

Mr. Langford said, "That drink was successful in washing away all hints of that snuff. Thanks."

And with the drink and toast they all went home for Christmas.

23

New Years' Day was just like any other workday for Garrett's employees. When he arrived at the mill around 6:30 a.m. on January 1, he found the mill running full bore. Bill and Beau arrived, and they felt a little sheepish about standing around with the mill operating the way it was.

Just as they dispersed, the mill slowed to a stop. John Haney, Jim Lawrence, and Jim Morgan walked over to Garrett, with their womenfolks following. "Garrett, I know you know this, but we want to say it again. This has been the best Christmas of our lives because we now have some hope. When the preacher was returning thanks at the Christmas dinner, I knew all of us from Alabama were deep down rejoicing that we found you and that you had a place where we could belong. Not having anywhere to go or anything to do is dreadful. Everybody needs to belong. Not only do we feel we do belong here, but we feel we are doing something that is helpful, something that is necessary, and this makes us feel good. You know we don't have nothing but our time and muscle, and now you have given us hope, and we won't let you down," Haney concluded.

Both Lawrence and Morgan quickly agreed.

Garrett said, "Well, fellows, you know I need you, and you know my limitations, and that is cash money. We've lots to do here, and when we begin clearing land we will all have more than we can say grace over if we can only find the money to do it with."

Jim Morgan said, "Garrett, when the times come that you need more help, we can cover you up with friends and relatives from Alabama. They continue to contact us asking about work in Florida. There are also plenty of folks who don't have enough initiative to get out of there and look for work that are starving to death. We can get the help."

"I hope we need the help," Garrett said.

"Garrett, we've been meaning to ask you," Jim Lawrence said. "Over in the next section where we are now cutting timber, there is about a ten-acre block of good black dirt what would make fine farmland. Do you think we could find the time to clear it and plant it as a garden for ourselves? Our women will be more than glad to help with it, and we believe it will grow more than all of us can eat."

"If we can find the time, I think it would be a good idea. If we could can up enough vegetables to last until the next garden comes in, that would be a big help. Plus we can keep enough fryers and hens for meat and eggs. From time to time we can kill a beef and a hog," Garrett agreed.

Haney said, "You know we are just about to cut over the black dirt now. Maybe when we finish, we could cut it clean and clear it in the afternoons after we quit sawing until dark. It probably wouldn't take too long to knock it out. These oxen would be good stump pullers."

Everyone was agreeing to this idea when Bill and Beau came to work. "We've decided we will clear the black land where we are now cutting timber and make us a big enough garden that all can use from it, kind of a cooperative effort," Garrett filled them in.

Bill said, "Sounds good to me because where I live the dirt is so poor I can't grow anything hardly."

All during the day the group talked about how they were going to get their garden spot operating. When the workday was over, they did start clearing land. The men grubbed stumps and palmettos while the Alabama women started fires, burning them as they went. While sawing dead pines, they were careful to cut them into posts for the purpose of fencing the garden. They were all happy because this area would be a source of food for them, and the land itself was far better than any of the folks had dreamed it would be.

Arriving home around 8 p.m. for supper, Garrett felt good about how all the help was pitching in and working without the necessity of always wanting money or more money. These folks were used to hard times, and they were looking for security. Garrett had all the items that made them feel right at home. They all had a sense of belonging and plenty of land from which everyone could exist well.

Good things always happen when they are least expected. As worn out as Garrett was arriving home after such a grueling day, William Garrett Gregson III was born later in the evening. Billy, as he would be known, was a healthy little boy. His delivery was easy. Mary Fran and Garrett spent their first night with him in their home with little sleep, yet, one of the happiest nights of their lives.

After Billy's birth, Mr. Langford said to Garrett and Mary Fran, "Well, it seems now everything we've done up to this point was worthwhile. Now we have a reason to work even harder to leave something for the future. I'm very glad Billy is here and that everything is okay."

"It is a good feeling to have him, and a better feeling to know he is healthy," Garrett replied.

Within days of Billy's birth, James Robert Mathews was born to Bill and Cindy. He was also a healthy boy, and the Mathews were at a loss to know how to take care of a baby. Mary Fran always came to their rescue because her background was filled with babies in the foster homes, and she was perfectly at ease handling him. In fact a baby could sense her ease and responded in the same manner to her.

Mr. Langford said, "Well, it looks like the population of our little area is growing now. Maybe we should just keep up the population explosion."

"We could, but I hope we don't," Garrett replied.

24

At 4 a.m. Beau's dogs were barking at something in the side yard. They woke everyone up. Garrett looked through the curtains toward the yard, and he thought he could see Haney. Mary Fran asked, "What in the world are the dogs after?"

"I don't know, but it looks like Haney to me, standing about twenty feet away from the side steps. I'm going out to see who it is." Garrett slipped on a pair of pants and picked up his pistol.

Opening the door, Haney said, "Garrett, it's just me, Haney. I'm sorry to cause such a ruckus, but we've had trouble."

"What's the problem?"

"Last night when we got home my mother seemed okay. After supper we were visiting and her face just went blank, and before we could get to her one side of her face dropped. It was her left side. She couldn't talk, and we carried her to bed. She never got to where she could talk to us, and she finally died around midnight."

"Oh, I'm so sorry, Haney," Garrett replied. "We thought she was making good progress since you've been able to leave her alone during the day."

"We thought so too, but I guess it was just her time. We think it must've been a stroke."

"What can I do for you?" Garrett asked.

"Well, Garrett, we need an undertaker to bury her. You know we ain't got no money. The women folk have bathed her and put on her best clothes, and she's laid out. Our problem is we don't know the undertaker and need help with him."

"Let me get dressed, and we will go into town and get him."

On the way, Haney asked, "Garrett, do you think we could get the casket, and do you think we could also get the cemetery lot on credit?"

"I feel like we can work it out. Don't worry about it. Just let me handle it."

"We also talked about not embalming her to save expense and burying her body today sometime. You think this is possible?"

"I can't answer that. We'll have to talk to the undertaker."

The cemetery lot and the undertaker were no problem for Garrett since they had already buried several people. It was sort of like everyone knew the ritual, and "Here we go again burying folks with no money."

The undertaker did say, "Garrett, you already know we'll have to take the sheriff and doctor out so that they can release the body to me, and then we can bury the lady. Why don't we just take the casket as we go? Come on in and pick one out."

Haney said to the undertaker, "Just bring the cheapest one you've got, and we'll be waiting at the Coble place for you."

The undertaker asked Haney about a concrete vault and he said, "We simply cannot afford to buy a vault. Do we have to have a vault?"

The undertaker said, "It's not compulsory, but most people these days are using them because of the high water table at the cemetery."

"We'll have to pass on it, I guess," Haney said.

No one worked that day except Beau and Bill. They only worked until noon.

Garrett and Haney went by the preacher's house on the way, and he agreed to come out in a couple of hours. He also said the cemetery lot could be on credit, and Haney agreed to have the grave dug when the gravesite was pointed out to him.

Mid-afternoon, all the formalities of the death were attended to. The preacher and everyone who worked for Garrett, plus others in the community having heard of the old lady's death, stood around the casket at the cemetery. The preacher offered an appropriate eulogy and sermon, and everyone sang a couple of hymns. The service took about thirty minutes, and the grave was closed.

Everyone went back to the Coble place and talked about Haney's mother. Mary Fran and Garrett were particularly interested in knowing all their backgrounds. This was the logical chance to find out. To their great surprise, at one time most of the Alabama folks were solidly upper-middle-class farmers. When the Depression was starting, they couldn't see what was coming financially and lost just about everything except what the old truck could hold that brought them to Florida. Yet with all the difficult times, they had lost neither interest in making a comeback nor their willingness to work. Privately, Garrett wondered what he would ever do without them. It was as if God had sent them to him.

Being back at the Coble place was nostalgic for Mary Fran. She couldn't help but notice how well it was being kept. The yards looked so different. Flowers were growing, and all the animal cages were mostly gone. There was a little garden, but it wasn't much because the soil was so poor. The entire farm had been turned into a pasture, and it was filled with milk cows and a few calves to eat.

25

The Alabama folks were feeling at home working with Garrett, Bill, and Beau. The mill was running smoothly and far better than Garrett had ever imagined it could. It was doing well because of his good fortune of listening to Mr. Langford and finding a way to work with his newfound employees.

Garrett asked Beau, "Have you seen the cows that belong to me lately?"

"No," he answered. "I've not seen those cows in several weeks."

After lunch Garrett saddled a horse and rode toward the southeastern corner of the property. It was a long ride, but he needed to be away from everyone for a bit to collect his thoughts regarding perceived problems with marketing and managing the operation. These duties were placing heavy burdens on such a young man with absolutely no business training or experience. He did have Mr. Langford's expertise, though, from which he drew daily.

It was a beautiful afternoon, and his horse was walking at a fast gait. Garrett liked this trait in a cow pony, which also acted like he was enjoying the ride.

After about two hours, Garrett arrived at a corner of the property he had never seen. It was a heavy hardwood hammock, according to Mr. Langford called The Great Hammock, and one of the most beautiful places he'd ever seen. He thought, *What a nice place to build a home.*

Carefully making his way through the heavily wooded area filled with giant oaks, magnolias, and bay trees, he caught a faint smell of something cooking—a smell he had never experienced, yet Garrett was sure that it was food. Continuing further into the hammock he passed orange seedling trees more than thirty feet tall that Mr. Langford had told him about. He said Indians had planted them years prior. The oranges were so high that Garrett couldn't reach one. The trees were growing to the light of the sun in the darkened hammock.

Amazed at locating the orange trees, he heard what he thought was a fish strike. He had been told of the lake and had already seen it from a distance. Then he heard what he thought was someone mumbling a few words.

Garrett eased his pony further into the hammock. The pony immediately sensed something out of the ordinary. A wisp of smoke from a campfire was coming up through an oak. Continuing toward the smoke, Garrett received the surprise of his life.

Walking the horse into the clearing, he saw a campsite containing a very small one-horse wagon and a fire burning with a pot hanging over it. Thinking he might be in an unsafe area, he decided not to get off his horse until someone surfaced.

When Garrett had about sized up the camp, a horse whinnied at his pony. The other horse was tied over about twenty yards beyond the wagon and campsite.

About this time an elderly man walked into camp from the lake, carrying a bass that weighed about three pounds. The fish was already cleaned, and the old man simply dropped it into the pot.

Of course, the man had seen Garrett sitting on his horse. He looked up at Garrett and said, "Fixing myself a fish stew for supper. Would you get down and share it with me?"

Garrett, deciding the elderly fellow wasn't harmful, dismounted. He walked over to the old man and immediately determined he was clean of body while ragged in dress. He desperately needed a shave and haircut. His hair was snow-white and down to his shoulders.

Garrett offered his hand and said, "My name is Garrett Gregson. This is Langford property you are camped on."

The old man shook hands very politely with Garrett and answered, "My name is Sawgrass Simpson. I've been camped here for a few days, and I really hope you don't mind. I only take what I need to exist off the land, no more. When I leave, it will be as if Indians were here, because there will be no sign of anyone ever having camped here."

Garrett asked, "Do you just roam around like this all the time?"

"Yes, sir, I do. But I have purpose in what I do."

"Would you mind telling me what that purpose is here?"

"Well, sir, I was a wicked young man who found God. Those who know me call me a 'sawgrass preacher.' I am itinerant. I have little education, but I study the Good Book daily. My purpose is to spread the gospel to those who are down and depressed. I live in the woods. I never try to interfere with other people's Sunday worship if they attend, but I really do try to hold a midweek prayer service on Wednesday night for anyone who will allow me."

"Do you take up a collection to live on?" Garrett asked.

"No, sir, I've never done that. I live simply and live off the land, never taking more than my horse and I need. While I'm on another's land, I do try to be of service by removing the rattlesnakes and other destructive pests and plants."

"What do you do with the snakes?"

"I've found them to be delicious to eat, and I've usually got one or two around."

"How do you catch them?" Garrett asked.

"If you will step over here, I'll show you." The old man walked over to the edge of the camp clearing. He picked up a burlap bag, untied the top, and dumped out a rattler that looked to Garrett to be more than six feet long. The snake had been caught earlier in the day. It was visibly upset, immediately going into a coil and singing his rattles.

By instinct, Garrett backed up out of striking distance. Grimacing his face, he said to the man, "You mean you catch these snakes and keep them in burlap bags? Then what do you do with them?"

"I skin and eat them and then tan the hide. They are delicious roasted over a campfire. Have you had the opportunity to eat one?"

"No, and that isn't where it ends. I'm not going to eat one."

"Mr. Garrett, I surely do hope you are not upset with me being camped here, because I haven't defaced anything. I do have a small trotline for fish and turtles. I occasionally trap a coon, possum, or squirrel to eat. My horse grazes in the area, and I conduct prayer services for anyone who will allow me to."

"I'm not upset with you, but I will be if you don't put that snake up!"

The elderly fellow walked over to the snake, who was really singing now. He started to chant something and waved his left hand crazily around in the air, coming closer and closer to the snake. After about a minute of this, he gently reached down with his right hand and caught the snake behind its head. The snake went wild. The old man held on and gently placed it back into the bag with the snake striking at the side of the bag in rapid motion. The striking caused the bag to roll.

Garrett watched the old man go through this motion, thinking all the while that no one would believe this story. Everyone would think he was lying, and maybe the best way out of this was not to tell it.

"Mr. Garrett, would you please sit on this log with me, and let's get acquainted?"

Garrett sat down and further observed the campsite.

"The last thing I want is for you to be unhappy with me being here. If you want me to leave, I'll be gone very shortly. My real purpose is as I've told you, and if you have employees someplace, I would like to come and hold prayer services on Wednesday evening at whatever time you tell me to come."

Garrett said, "Everyone who works for me attends church regularly in the settlement. We normally don't go to midweek services because of the distance, and the service is actually held too early for us. I really don't guess I have any problem with you camping here if you keep it clean. By the way, how many snakes do you normally catch?"

"It really depends on the location. In flat woods there are more snakes than in sand hills, and I confine my activities usually to flat woods, catching from one to five a day depending on the location. I skin them all, usually eating the younger ones. Occasionally, I find someone who wants to buy the skins, and it provides me a little change for medicine and the like."

"That's your sole income?"

"Yes, plus coon hides. I never kill a deer because I don't have a gun. Just small wildlife I can trap and fish I can catch."

Garrett was undecided what to tell the old man. He looked like something out of a storybook, yet tattered but clean. Then he decided to give him a chance.

"Tell you what, Sawgrass. You show up at our barn area Wednesday afternoon when we quit work—without any snakes—and I'll try to have you a few people to speak to. I can't promise this every week, but I'll at least give you a chance. Now, if you come and my folks decide they don't like your style or whatever, I'll have to ask you to leave and not come back. Is that a deal, and yes, without the snakes?"

"Yes, sir, it is. I won't let you down if you give me this chance. You won't be sorry. Thank you, sir."

Garrett climbed onto his horse, saying, "Today is Monday. We'll see you day after tomorrow at quitting time."

"Thank you, sir." Garrett turned and rode away totally amazed at what he had found and witnessed: a crazy man who made sense.

Garrett was back at the barn when it dawned on him that he didn't locate his cattle. The men were gathered there because of it being quitting time. Stepping down off his horse, he said to them, "You are not going to believe what I've seen this afternoon, and I probably should not tell you."

He told them the whole story and of his invitation to Sawgrass Simpson to visit at quitting time on Wednesday afternoon. Everyone went home discussing the bizarre tale Garrett had told, laughing and talking about it.

All through the day Tuesday, Garrett was sure he had made a mistake, yet something inside kept telling him to relax. *Take it easy. Everything will be okay.*

The excitement increased on Wednesday throughout the day because everyone couldn't wait to see what Garrett had described. About ten minutes before quitting time, even Mr. Langford grabbed his hat and headed for the barn. All the Alabama folks and everyone's wives were there. There was no one associated with Garrett who wasn't there, including his dad, who had kidded him mercilessly since hearing his tale of the preacher in the woods. Garrett's dad also got a full supper out of the deal at Garrett's table.

Everyone was looking in the direction of The Great Hammock, waiting on the sawgrass preacher. He appeared in the distance, and Garrett walked out to greet him.

Arriving back with the group, who by now were totally quiet and observing the strange little man, Garrett said, "Put out your smokes and let's go over to the hay barn where we will be comfortable." Much to Garrett's amazement, Sawgrass had his snow-white hair pulled back in a ponytail and his beard was neatly trimmed and combed. He was wearing a long-sleeved white shirt with a black string tie and a pair of black pants with a crease. His shoes were hightop dress shoes and looked recently polished.

Garrett took Sawgrass to the front of the group and introduced him. Everyone was seated, awaiting his first words.

When Garrett was seated, Sawgrass said to the group, "Would you join me in an opening prayer?" and he offered an extremely eloquent prayer, much to everyone's amazement.

After the prayer, he said, "I know after Mr. Garrett told you who was coming here this evening you could not imagine such a person. The way some of you have been observing me, I can determine you still do not believe your eyes. The answers you seek you already have because I'm sure you already know the truth about me, and I don't want to waste time now, but I will be happy to hang around for as long as you wish to talk."

With this, he said, "Why don't we begin with a brief song session and then I'll lead a short devotion?" With what sounded like a very well-trained voice, he began singing the old hymn "Amazing Grace." Then "Shall We Gather at The River." Then he asked if anyone had a favorite, and someone said, "Can we sing 'The Old Rugged Cross'?"

When this hymn was concluded, Sawgrass opened his Bible and read a short passage from it. Then he delivered what Garrett, Mary Fran, and Mr. Langford later discussed as being a highly learned sermon but that lasted only about fifteen minutes.

Finishing his sermon, he offered another prayer and then said, "I would like to leave you with a gift. This is the only gift I can leave because it is all I have to give. I would like to sing you a song as our benediction." He collected himself and sang "Beautiful Isle of Somewhere." He had a rich baritone voice and was really more than just a poor, uneducated wanderer. He was highly professional.

When he said good-night, someone in the group asked, "Will you come again next Wednesday if Garrett says it is okay?"

Sawgrass looked over at Garrett, who nodded his head affirmatively. After seeing Garrett's agreement he said, "It would be my pleasure to return. I'll look forward to it until then."

After the meeting was over, the Alabama group crowded around him and talked for more than an hour. Garrett broke into the conversation by asking Sawgrass if he would like to eat supper with them, and he very politely declined. Everyone stood and watched him as he left by the cow trail he had arrived on.

"That is the dangdest thing I've ever witnessed," Haney said as he and the Alabama group departed.

During supper, Mr. Gregson said, "John, I don't believe that fellow is uneducated at all, do you?"

"No," he replied. "I would bet money someone, someplace has given him plenty of schooling. His singing voice is very well trained, and this wasn't his first time in front of a group."

The next Wednesday even Rev. Silas Boggs came to hear Sawgrass. Others in the community heard about what had happened and came without invitation, which of course was okay with the regulars. The singing that night was unbelievably strong and wonderful. Mr. Langford couldn't stop talking about Sawgrass and the group singing.

Garrett wondered if he had made an incorrect decision by inviting Sawgrass, yet so many people looked forward to hearing him that he decided this could be his community service. The crowd grew, and those who came brought food for dinner together. Wednesday evening became the social event of the week, with everyone smelling horrible from having worked and perspired all day and then sitting close together.

Silas Boggs asked Sawgrass if he would like to attend and participate in the settlement's church service. Sawgrass replied, "I would like to attend but I would prefer not to participate, because this is your church and I'm not qualified to do what you do."

Thereafter, Sawgrass attended the church in the settlement, sitting very quietly and reverently and participating as a parishioner. When he wasn't with the group on Wednesday or Sunday, he was in the woods alone.

Garrett went out to visit Sawgrass on one occasion and asked him if he could buy him some clothing, to which Sawgrass replied, "I have no real need of anything, but I do appreciate the offer."

Garrett then asked, "If I were just to bring you some items that I feel would make your life easier, would you accept them?"

"I would rather you used your funds to take care of your family, Mr. Garrett."

"Can't I give you anything for what you've done for our community and particularly our employees?"

"The only thing I would really like to have is a pair of Levi's like your men wear. If they are expensive, I don't want that."

"What size do you wear?" Garrett asked.

"I have about a thirty-inch waist and thirty-inch leg measurement," he replied.

"What size coat?"

"Just the pants are all I need."

Garrett said, "Well, Sawgrass. Levi's have a jacket that goes with the pants."

The old man replied, "Well, I wear a 40 regular suit, if that helps."

When Garrett returned he had the Levi's pants and jacket with a matching denim shirt and a pair of snake-bite boots. He also slipped into the little wagon, in a white box wrapped in brown paper, a black suit with a new white shirt and a pair of black shoes suitable for a preacher, with a note inside that said, "Wear this suit to the Glory of God. From Garrett Gregson's employees."

The next Sunday, Sawgrass showed up in church with his new suit on, looking very pleased. He was very humble to all of Garrett's employees, who evidently knew nothing about the gift. Garrett and Mary Fran had done this and figured this was the only way he would accept it.

Sawgrass camped in The Great Hammock for about six months. The crowds continued to grow on Wednesday evening.

To everyone's astonishment Sawgrass failed to show up one Wednesday. Garrett and Beau saddled their horses and rode out to the hammock. It was just as Sawgrass predicted: No one was able to tell anyone had ever camped there. It was swept totally clean, just like the Indians would have left it.

Silas Boggs tried to keep the Wednesday night group going but failed miserably. He lacked Sawgrass's charisma. The singing fizzled, the crowd dwindled, and the meetings drew to a struggling close.

26

By mid-summer everything was going good. The sawmill was working at least eight hours each day, six days a week, sometimes from "can" to "can't." The field crew had learned how to fell enough trees to keep the mill operating constantly. The public had found a constant and steady supply of lumber, and business was good. In fact, Garrett now had a little cash surplus that was kept as a closely guarded secret. The garden had been cleared and the crop was growing, and it looked like a bountiful harvest—so bountiful, in fact, that buying the canning jars for the vegetables turned out to be a major expenditure.

Garrett provided the land, fertilizer, seed, and equipment. Everyone else, including Mary Fran, Mr. Langford, and Essay, provided their time to plant, care for, and harvest the vegetables.

Late one hot summer afternoon, when not a breath of air was stirring, Essay visited the garden to pick some squash for supper. She was there alone because everyone else was working the mill. The garden looked good. The peas were blooming. The corn had tassels, and the tomatoes were almost ready. The squash had been ready for some time. The garden was so beautiful that Essay spent time just looking at what they had accomplished. She was very proud of this gardening project.

The squash plants were between knee high and waist high because they were on the wet side of the garden and were bedded. This gave them the appearance of being much larger than they actually were.

Essay was almost finished picking as much as she would need for supper. Standing straight she didn't realize the hem of her dress was caught on a palmetto root, and as she walked away the root was embedded sufficiently that it pulled her down. She fell across the row she was walking beside into the next row, and her face went down in the middle of a large plant.

Unfortunately, in the shade between the two plants was a coiled rattlesnake cooling from the summer sun. Essay startled the snake, and when she fell the snake struck her squarely in the face. The fangs went deep into her left jaw just below her left eye.

She knew immediately what had happened when the snake began singing his rattles. There was no denying it; the snake had bitten her in a very bad location, and she was well aware of this. She was desperately afraid of rattlesnakes, and realizing she had been bitten only frightened her more.

By reflex, she grabbed the snake just behind its head, pulling the fangs from her face while with the same extended motion she struck the snake across the root that had tripped her. She then took the snake to a large pine tree at the edge of the garden and struck it hard several times against the tree.

She headed home in a trot. Knowing she needed help, she didn't walk, which was the worst thing she could do. The farther she ran, the more excited she became, and by the time she reached the mill, she was not only out of breath but the snake's venom was fast taking effect. Her face was swelling on the left side, and she was beginning to get sick to her stomach. Garrett had stopped work for a moment when he saw her condition, and he came running to her as she started to vomit.

"Essay, my God, what has happened? Why are you running like this?" he inquired.

"Rattler done bit me on the jaw. I was picking squash and fell into a plant where the snake was hiding from the sun, and it bit me."

"Try to be calm, Essay, and we'll get you to the house and get the doctor. Everything will be alright," Garrett reassured her.

Beau saw what was happening as Garrett was trying to calm her down, but he couldn't leave his post at the mill until it was completely shut down. With this, he was at Essay's side inquiring what was wrong.

Garrett yelled at Bill, "Take the pick-up and go for the doctor as quickly as possible. Essay has been bitten by a rattler, and she needs help fast."

Bill was off in a run to the truck.

Garrett asked the others to help him carry Essay to the main house. Balking, Essay said, "I feels like I can walk, Garrett."

"You don't need to be exerting yourself in any way until we get the poison out," he said.

The men had Essay inside the house in short order, and she was placed on a bed in one of the guest rooms. Mary Fran brought a pan of water and was placing wet rags on the area. She also placed some fat meat directly on the bitten area. She had heard an old wives' tale that this would draw out the poison.

Looking at Essay, Garrett thought he could see the side of her face swelling by the moment and turning a bluish black. Garrett began to be worried and frightened for her life at the sight of the affected area.

Beau was at her bedside. He wouldn't leave and was holding her hand.

Time was dragging. After about an hour, the pick-up came up the driveway at a high rate of speed. Just as quickly the kitchen door slammed and the doctor rushed in.

The doctor asked that everyone leave the room while he went to work on Essay. He was in the room alone for about ten minutes before coming to the kitchen.

"Mary Fran, do you have some clean rags I could use for a bandage?" he asked.

"Be right there with them, Doc," she replied. He went back into the room.

Sometime after midnight the doctor came out and said Essay wanted to see Garrett and Beau.

Entering the room, they were not prepared for the hideous swelling of her face, or the apparent agony she was experiencing.

"How is it, Essay?" Garrett inquired.

"Not too good. I'm terrible sick on my stomach and my nerves are just running away with me. You don't need a rattler to bite you," she said.

"Don't worry. You're going to be alright," Beau said.

"That's what I wanted to talk to the two of you about. The doctor says I might not pull through this. I'm an old woman and I have lived a good life, a long life. I know my Maker, and I'm ready to go. The reason I wanted to see you two together is to get some promises. Garrett, will you promise me you will finish raising Beau and take care of him for me if I don't make it?"

"You know I will, Essay, but stop this nonsense about your not making it," he said.

"Now, Beau, Garrett and his family is all you got. They have looked after both of us, and we owe them at least our dues. Promise me you won't do anything off the bat without at least discussing it with Garrett," she asked.

"Mama, you know Garrett is the only family I got, and I'm not going to go off half-cocked. Now is not the time for you to worry about me. You worry about getting well."

The doctor entered the room, saying, "You fellows should let her be quiet and not talk. She needs absolutely no exertion."

Garrett left the room and left Beau with her. Speaking to Mary Fran he said, "I think I should go get Dad. He'll want to know about this and will want to be here."

He walked to the pick-up and left. When he arrived back an hour later, it was all over. Essay was dead. Her body was covered up on the bed, and a distraught Beau was at her side. Garrett walked over to him and placed his hand on his shoulder. He could feel Beau losing control of his composure. He stood up and embraced Garrett, and both sobbed uncontrollably.

After a bit, Beau said, "She was all I had."

"You've forgotten about us, I guess, Beau. We're family and you know it," Garrett said.

"I know it." But with a bitter look he said, "You are just saying that now at this time because you really know I'm not the blood of your family. I'm a nigger, and you are white folks. I can never belong."

Mr. Gregson exploded, "That's not true. You've never been treated like a nigger, now, have you?"

"Naw, sir, I guess I ain't. I'm sorry I said it," Beau sobbed.

Essay's funeral was a couple of days later. Hers was a graveside service in the colored cemetery. Silas Boggs was her minister, and all the Alabama folks and the rest of Garrett's operation were present. There were a few blacks, but mostly whites came because Essay was so closely associated with the Gregson family for so many years. She actually lived with them, only socializing with the black community very little.

Essay's death affected Garrett as much as it did Beau because Essay was the person who raised him. She was his surrogate mother, and a mother is a tough person to bury.

27

When everyone was back at the main house after the service, Garrett took Beau aside and said, "Look, Beau, you know you've always belonged here. You know that we have grown up together, and you know you're still just a kid doing a man's work. Don't be hasty to make any decisions. Continue like you always have here. Together we can make it. If you try anything foolish, both of us will have a much tougher time. We are beginning to make some progress. We have enough to do that we might never get caught up. I need you. What about it?" Garrett asked.

"Garrett, you know I don't know anything but staying here. I don't plan to leave because you are all I have. Where would I go? What would I do? I need to be here doing what I know best. I need to be with you. You know I love you the same as if we were blood brothers. I would never leave unless you wanted me to."

"You know I don't want you to," Garrett continued. "Let's leave it this way. You are home here, and I love you. You will someday begin to receive some of the rewards of your labor. We aren't always going to be this poor. We are going to make something of ourselves, and when we do, you will get your share. Do you trust me on this?"

"You know I do," Beau said. "You also know I would stay with you through thick or thin. I've never really believed you have ever treated me like other blacks are treated. We work together. We have fun together hunting and fishing, swimming and eating. When others look at me like I was second-class, I always see in your face something genuine."

28

During the ensuing two years, Garrett felt the small group associated with him had progressed sufficiently that he wanted to begin to branch out into a larger operation. From his executive abilities, Mr. Langford knew that Garrett had to begin delegating authority in order to achieve the necessary pace for growth. It had been tough because cash was so short, but now the lumber sales had developed a small surplus of cash. In fact, he probably had more cash than the rest of the settlement had all together.

Garrett decided Beau and Bill should head up the cattle operation. They should be responsible for land improvements, as well as fencing and building the herd.

Beau had begun training cow dogs as a hobby because he loved dogs so. He liked mixed-breed dogs. They were not much to look at but tough as nails and mean as they come for handling cattle. Regardless of how many dogs he had to replace, for one reason or another, he never had more than four and their names were always Buford, Booger, Gator, and Precious.

Beau and Bill sometimes would assist others in their operations, but Garrett relied totally on them for managing the entire cattle operation. He knew this operation one day would become a large part of the entire company.

One day Beau and Bill were fencing across a white sandy hill filled with jack oaks. Making their way through the oaks, Bill stumbled upon a yellow jacket nest in the ground. The closer they came to the nest, the more the ground sounded as if it would rise and fly. There was one large entrance hole and a hole of equal size that evidently was the exit, or maybe both were used for entrance and exit.

"How are we going to get around this, Bill?"

"Beats me, Beau. Let's go ask Mr. Langford what we should do about it. I've never seen such a thing."

Pausing at the sawmill to get a cool drink of water, they told Haney and the rest of the group what they had found, whereupon Haney said they would like to have them.

"You've got to be nuts," Bill said. "Those yellow jackets will carry you off, there are so many of them."

"Follow me and I'll show you how to catch them." With this comment Haney was off to the sand hill.

Without as much as a flinch, Haney walked up to the closest hole and turned a five-gallon bucket upside down over it and placed a root on top to hold it down. He then stuck a tomato stake up inside a very large burlap bag. While placing the bag over the other hole he grabbed the tomato stake and began to stick it down into the hole rapidly, which really did create havoc. Every one of the yellow jackets came viciously to life and into the bag. When all were inside the bag, Haney took a short piece of baling wire and closed the sack.

Later that evening the Alabama folks baited their trotline with the yellow jackets and everyone, including Garrett's household, had fish the next morning.

John Haney was as tough as they came. He always believed in a full day's work. For this reason Garrett placed him in charge of the sawmill. Haney knew how to operate a sawmill to its absolute maximum capacity, and he liked doing it. He was a natural.

Of the three Alabama men, Jim Morgan was the farmer. Garrett decided to put him in charge of the citrus nursery. A nursery requires constant attention. Morgan started with seeds to grow seedlings to bud. Three years later they were ready to set out in a grove.

Garrett's goal was to plant one hundred acres of citrus per year on land the clearing crews made available. Morgan's job was to plant the grove and to take care of it from the trees he grew in the nursery.

In addition, Morgan was the proper person to begin the winter vegetable operation. Plenty of suitable land was available, and building a vegetable packinghouse wouldn't be too big of a deal. In fact, Garrett issued instructions to clear land, plant watermelons on the new land, and either plant citrus or vegetables the second year, depending on the soil type.

Jim Lawrence was a people person and a good manager. Garrett decided to place him in charge of land-clearing operations. Land clearing required a large number of employees, and Jim was at his best motivating others. Grubbing and pulling stumps and palmettos was a tough job. Piling and burning all of this was almost more than one could be expected to accomplish, yet Lawrence was a master of encouragement.

Garrett felt bad that the Alabama women wanted to help in the day-to-day operations, knowing there was little to no cash to pay them. When the idea of the vegetable packing shed came into focus, Garrett felt he had found the perfect spot for them. He was thrilled because it would get the women out of the timber woods and swamps, away from the sawmill, and out of the cow pens. They wouldn't have to work the cattle anymore.

Because this ambitious program required much more labor than he presently had, Garrett made arrangements with Jim Haney to make a quick trip to Alabama and see if any people there would like to come and work with them. Haney claimed he already knew the answer to that question.

Haney was back very soon with the promise of more than enough laborers. Garrett arranged for every empty house in the settlement to house the labor. Only laborers with families were allowed to come, to circumvent frequent visits back to Alabama to visit family.

With the arrival of the first laborers from Alabama, Garrett split them between various divisions and work began. Because the folks were new to the area, the sawmill lost part of its production output for a few days. However, they quickly learned under the stern direction of Haney, and production was back at full steam in short order.

29

The area looked like the whole world was on fire because of the land-clearing crews. Jim Lawrence knew exactly how to pace the men, and the clearing progressed even faster than everyone had dreamed it could.

Jim Morgan's nursery was coming along fine. The initial seeds were planted for the seedlings, and they were about ready to line out into the nursery when the new shipment of laborers arrived from Alabama. He was already making plans for his vegetable operation.

Garrett's job was no longer that of laborer. He spent all of his time keeping up with the entire operation and counseling with the various straw bosses. Garrett knew the necessity of counseling his men because of the success he experienced up until now consulting with Mr. Langford. Mr. Langford's input, as always, was to remain in the background and encourage Garrett to go forth. Mr. Langford thought that Garrett should take calculated risks. If it hadn't been for Mr. Langford, Garrett would never have tackled the operation on the scale he had, because he wouldn't have had the guts. But with Mr. Langford's encouragement, experience, and age, he was able to guide Garrett in a successful manner.

In the beginning Garrett only supplied the muscle power. Now that he was beginning to catch on to management, he had begun to focus on how money could be made with the vast land assets with which he had to work. The scope of the operation was mind-boggling and difficult for Garrett because of his inexperience. With the passing of each day, however, management did become a job he could handle, and he had begun to enjoy it. Each day he tried to visit his men and to help work out their problems.

Now came the time when he had to think about selling lumber, collecting money for the sales, and arranging payroll for the labor. The new workers weren't as amenable to working for tomorrow. They needed money when the work was performed.

The vegetable garden had to be expanded because of the additional workers. Now twenty acres would be needed. The cooperative garden had been a good idea because everyone then didn't have to take time off to care for a private plot. The work was accomplished by the family while the men worked during the day. Additionally, the seed and fertilizer for one place seemed less expensive to Garrett than for a whole bunch of little gardens.

30

One day around noon, a frail young man on crutches appeared at the side porch. He was dressed in a black suit with a black string tie and a little black hat. He had tapped on the steps with his crutch until Mary Fran heard him. When she came to the door, he very politely asked, "Ma'am, is Mr. Gregson here? My name is Henry Bates, and the banker sent me here to talk to Mr. Gregson about keeping his books."

"Well, he isn't here right now, but I expect him for lunch any minute. Why don't you sit in one of the rockers here on the porch and wait for him?" Mary Fran asked.

About this time Mr. Langford came out onto the porch rolling a cigarette. He spoke to Henry, "You say the banker sent you?" he inquired.

"Yes, sir, I just finished accounting school and went into the bank looking for a job. The banker said he didn't need anyone but said you folks were the only ones in the county doing any business. He also said he knew firsthand that Garrett Gregson needed help in his office the way he kept his books."

While Mr. Langford was having a real horse laugh as a result of the remarks from the banker, Garrett walked up and asked what was going on. Mr. Langford took great delight in retelling the story with his personal flourishes. It didn't strike Garrett as being all that funny.

"I see you have a handicap, Henry. Do you think you can do the job?" Garrett asked.

"Oh yes, sir, as long as I have a chair that's all I need," he replied.

"Where do you live, Henry?"

"Well, sir, I came from North Florida around Tallahassee, and I don't have any place to live here. I also don't have any transportation. All I have is the need of a job. I have the need to work hard. I just finished my schooling, and I am anxious to try it out," Henry said.

"Tell you what: I have been thinking of either building a small office building or taking in part of the barn for an office. When we build, we can build you a room onto the office. Until then, you can stay in the vacant porch room in the main house," Garrett said.

"Oh, thank you, sir. This is just what I had hoped would happen," Henry said.

Mary Fran came onto the porch and asked everyone to come inside for dinner. "Have you seen Beau?"

"Yes, he's coming. I saw him washing up at the barn," Garrett said.

Garrett continued, "Mary Fran, have you met our new bookkeeper, Henry Bates? The banker thinks we need a bookkeeper because of the way I keep books, and he sent us Henry."

"Yes, I've met Henry, and I'd say he has a whale of a job cleaning up your sloppy record keeping. I want Henry to have lunch with us."

At about the same time Mary Fran said this, Beau came steaming around the side of the porch. "Sorry I'm late. Someone left the gate open, and the weaned calves were getting back into the pasture."

"Beau, this is our new bookkeeper, Henry Bates. Henry, this is Beau James." After a few pleasantries were passed Garrett said, "Come on, let's eat."

31

It was a great time for Garrett and Mary Fran, who by this time had achieved an easier life. They didn't have much money to account for all their labors, but more than enough hope for the future. Everything they had undertaken with Mr. Langford's physical resources was successful, right down to the people involved. Everyone who had been hired seemed as if they were destined to be there. There was a place for everyone, and everyone was happy. Of course, had it not been for the hard times none of these folks would have ever been a part of the operation, and Garrett and Beau would still be felling timber with one cross-cut saw.

Sally Haney was a woman of large frame and the hardest-working woman Garrett had ever witnessed. A few days after Essay's death, Garrett asked her if she would take over the household duties until Mary Fran was on her feet again, to which she graciously agreed. There was no limit to what this woman could accomplish in a day.

Stumbling upon Garrett was like finding Santa Claus for Bill and Cindy, and the Alabama group as well. They each found him when they couldn't go any further. None had any food to speak of or resources to travel further. Together they were able to work out some cash from the Langford resources, and each received on an equitable basis. No one ever questioned the manner in which Garrett paid them. Everyone trusted his judgment and decision to be honestly compensated. Garrett never violated this trust.

Sally took over the house and ran it as if it were hers. She did all the cooking. In fact, she arrived early enough to cook Garrett's breakfast before he was out and about his business for the day. She did all the housework, including the washing and ironing. In her spare time, she tended the formal gardens

Mrs. Langford had planted years before. The garden regained its former splendor. Working with flowers and shrubs was something Sally thoroughly enjoyed. Mr. Langford was quick to heap praises on her for reestablishing the gardens that his wife had loved. This praise was the source of a great deal of fuel and energy for her.

When Mary Fran was able to take over again, Sally convinced them her place was in their house, which is where she wanted to stay. They agreed, and from that day she worked in their home.

32

Progress had been good as summer moved into fall. The land-clearing crews had cleared almost one hundred acres to plant in the spring, and they were feverishly working on pastureland, trying to get Bill and Beau off their backs.

The operation of the sawmill, land-clearing, and cattle operations, and now the beginning of the fresh vegetable operation—not to mention sales of lumber—had Garrett always on the run. Mr. Langford spent lots of his time with Garrett because the two had grown close as friends. Mr. Langford's formal education and the ease of their friendship would prove invaluable to Garrett in later years when even greater risks were involved.

Beau and Bill had a crew cutting fence posts, and they were stringing barbed wire as fast as possible. They were expanding at a much faster rate than the rest of the operation could keep up with. The logical thing for them to do was to fence the designated pasturelands and to cross-fence when it was timbered and cleared. After clearing they improved the land with planted grasses.

Garrett had surveyed the entire property with Mr. Langford. They decided which land to plant in citrus and which to pasture. The citrus always followed a first cash crop of watermelons. They were also very careful to plot the land for the vegetable operation. They calculated about forty-five hundred acres suitable to citrus, twenty-five hundred acres to vegetables, and the balance—up to fifteen thousand acres—in pasture.

John Haney was going wild with the sawmill. The hungry laborers recruited in Alabama were just the right folks for the timber operation. Each day the timber woods were becoming farther and farther from the mill itself, and transportation of the logs became a greater problem. The oxen and one tractor were too slow for optimum operation of the mill. They were constantly in a strain for more saw timber.

The wood yard was spread out with stacks in every direction, every stack kept separate and in logical order.

Customers coming to purchase lumber first visited Henry Bates at the office. He took their order and received their payment for the rough-sawn timber. The paid order form moved from Henry to Haney as approval to have the customers' vehicles loaded. There was one wagon or truck after the other every day, all day.

Everyone knew the money the sawmill was taking in was financing the entire operation. Not only did Haney feel a sense of worth knowing this, but it seemed to compel him to work harder and do the best job possible. Because of his dedication, Haney had one crew come in at daylight and work until one o'clock without a break. The second crew came on at one o'clock and worked until dark without a break. The crew that wasn't sawing was then part of the transportation and loading team.

Henry Bates was another hub of the entire operation. Without his expertise in accounting and organizational abilities, their success would have been much less. He worked from early morning until late night, adequately servicing the lumber customers' accounts. An office had been constructed to his specifications with living quarters for him. Because of his handicap, Mary Fran insisted he eat at their table. Of course, he was glad to do this.

Henry was very particular about his work. He had to have just the right forms, and when it came time to design company stationery, it took him some time to satisfy himself. The Gregson Company was born with his stationery and Mr. Langford's insistence on the company name. The stationery and the public operation of the company could not be more impressive under Henry's leadership. His image to the public was nothing short of extraordinary.

The trees in the citrus nursery weren't old enough to plant in the coming fall after the spring crop of watermelons. Garrett made arrangements with another nursery to swap trees and plant on time. Jim Morgan had the nursery under control. It looked good and was expanding as quickly as they could locate labor to work it.

Jim was also working hard toward a winter vegetable operation. In addition to the first crop of watermelons, he had almost one hundred acres of farmland ready for next fall and winter's operation. He planted cabbage, bell peppers, lettuce, and other truck crops for the winter market. The vegetable house was under construction, and he could hardly wait until his department was in full operation and bringing in cash. His vegetable operation was the second cash contributor to The Gregson Company's developing success.

Jim Lawrence's land-clearing operation had the appearance of an invading army. His crews were advancing with unusual speed. His hand laborers appeared as if their job was the easiest on the place. From first light until sundown, they were in the field wrestling stumps and palmettos.

Crews were cultivating the citrus land, readying it for planting, and crews also cultivated the pastureland for planting. People were working in almost any direction one looked.

Observing all of this was a great comfort to Mr. Langford. Through Garrett, Mr. Langford was achieving what he had always wished he and his son could have accomplished prior to his son's death. Garrett, in fact, was becoming more and more like a son to him.

Garrett was particularly proud of Henry Bates—not only proud of his coping with his handicap even though it did take a great deal of energy just to be present daily and take care of normal business affairs, but for another reason as well. Henry was as honest as any man Garrett had ever known. He was quick to account for all the funds, postage, and even pencils used in the normal operation. All the little things he purchased for the operation were properly tabulated. He insisted on going over with Garrett all the deposits and all the monthly reports. Working with Henry was not only an education for Garrett, but he felt good about leaving all the money activities in Henry's hands. The accounts balanced daily, weekly, and monthly, and at the end of the year every penny was where it was supposed to be. Henry was not only the laborer's paymaster, but Garrett and Mary Fran's as well. Mary Fran never asked Garrett for money. She went to Henry, and he provided those funds she needed.

33

The Gregson Company was becoming just a bit more comfortable. When the opportunity presented itself, Garrett and Mary Fran could stop and take note of how far they had come in so few years. They remembered always that their good fortune was quite by circumstance in being in the right place at the right time; of course, too, Mr. Langford's assets and counsel were invaluable to their success.

They were very proud of the sawmill. After all, it generated the initial cash to begin the rest of the operation. They also had a citrus and beef operation they looked to with pride, and the upcoming vegetable operation was something all of them eagerly anticipated.

More than this, they were proud of their little family. Billy wanted to play with Garrett at every opportunity. Mary Fran was well and had the assistance she needed in the house and, therefore, free time to do some of the things she wanted to do.

Best of all, Mr. Langford was enjoying the newfound success that he had hoped for since the day he purchased the property.

Late one afternoon, Mr. Langford said, "Garrett, I want to use the pick-up in the morning. Do you have any use for it that won't allow my use?"

"No, sir. Help yourself. Is there anything I can do for you?" Garrett inquired.

"No, I've just a little business to attend to," he replied.

After breakfast the next morning and after he had rolled a Prince Albert, Mr. Langford set out in the direction of town. About noon he returned and went directly to Garrett's office and closed the door.

"Garrett," he said, "can I ask you a favor?"

"You know you can, Mr. Langford, anything at all."

"You will remember we used my available cash to begin

developing this place, and I need just a bit of money. What is the possibility you can lend me one thousand dollars?"

"No question about it. It is really your money, and you can have all we have if you want it," Garrett answered.

"No, just one thousand dollars," he said.

Garrett was curious about Mr. Langford's request, but did not ask him what his needs were. After all, it really wasn't any of his business why he wanted the money. Garrett did tell Mary Fran about the unusual incident, and of course she had no idea what he needed the money for either. It was a puzzle for everyone, because when Mr. Langford incurred a debt, the bill was sent to Henry, who promptly paid it. All his needs were provided for.

After lunch the next day, Mr. Langford took the pick-up and was gone for about another two hours. When he came back, he parked the pick-up and resumed his usual place on the side porch with a Prince Albert cigarette.

Nothing more was said about the money, but Garrett did instruct Henry to be sure from that day forward that Mr. Langford always had spending money in his pocket. Henry still asked him about his money needs every week, and he seldom required anything at all.

34

Garrett's pace had been so swift since working with Mr. Langford that the time he spent hunting and fishing had just about disappeared. Other than the few times he had taken all the employees, he had not been at all. Prior to his marriage, he, Brett, and Alan were inseparable when hunting and fishing expeditions were taken—and they were taken often.

Now that the operation was running smoothly, the threesome thought it a good time to get away for a few days and fish for snook on the west coast of Florida. This was always a sport that interested each of them, and they were looking forward to the time together. Garrett felt bad about leaving Beau, given that he had always been a part of their sporting events. But now Beau had responsibilities that would not allow him to leave any time he wanted to, and certainly Garrett couldn't just pick up and go if he had more important things in progress. Beau realized that, because of his duties, he certainly could not go, as badly as he wanted to.

When Garrett told Mr. Langford he had planned for a few days away, he replied, "Garrett, it is always good to get away for a few days. When you are so close to your work, you sometimes lose perspective of what you are attempting to accomplish. You lose the big picture, and when you lose this, you sometimes lose the way. One wants to lose a battle, not a war. My advice is to go fishing and not feel guilty about it. Don't feel like this place can't operate without you. If, in fact, it cannot operate without you for a few days, you don't have it set up appropriately. You don't have the right people in the right places. You need to know this. If it can operate without you, it will be here long after all of us are gone. This can be a test. After all, I will be around, and I believe I can handle any emergency or decision that might come up. So, have a good time, enjoy the time away, and come back refreshed. And with plenty of fish!"

Mary Fran wasn't too thrilled over Garrett's decision to go fishing and leave her, but she couldn't go because of Billy. "Be sure you bring home enough fish so that we can have a fish fry for everyone," she said.

The trip to Marco Island took all day by the time they had a few refreshment stops. They took a small boat with them and rented a cabin on the inlet.

In the past, when the three went fishing it was always a camping trip to some lake in the area because of no transportation. Circumstances had now changed because of Garrett's good fortune with Mr. Langford. They were not now limited, because the pick-up provided all the transportation they needed. A trip to Corpus Christi might be too far, but Marco was definitely not.

Garrett did feel bad about leaving Mary Fran. They had been together through some tough times, and now some good times were occurring and he left her at home. Maybe he could do something for her after the fishing trip? Perhaps a weekend in an Orlando hotel might be just the thing?

Garrett did feel good, though, about getting away with Brett and Alan. They had always been friends, and Brett being his first cousin only made the tie much closer. In their past escapades Brett had always been the cook. Garrett cleaned up the pots and pans. Alan had no specific job because he wasn't good at anything of a domestic nature. He was best at hunting and fishing.

The three fished all night the first night and by daylight had more snook than they could handle. It was noon by the time the fish were cleaned and iced. Some of the snook were fine ones, weighing almost twenty pounds. A twenty-pound snook is one of the fighting sporting fish, so the three were worn out at daylight, but happy over their catch. They had two more nights to go.

After sleeping a few hours, the three decided they needed a night on the town worse than they needed more fish. Before the night was over, they had covered most of the lower west coast of Florida. Sarasota was the best nightspot, and this was where they spent most of their time. Staying up most of the night, they were not able to fish any the next day.

Deciding they needed a good meal, they picked the best restaurant they could locate. Sitting there having a drink when dinner was over, Brett said, "Well, boys, I might as well tell you some news that you're bound to hear from someone else if I don't tell you now."

"What is it?" Alan inquired. "I thought I was the only one with some news, unless Garrett was going to tell us Mary Fran is pregnant again!"

"Lord, I hope not. One kid is enough for right now," Garrett replied.

"Cassey and I have decided to get married," Brett said very bluntly and with little emotion.

"Well, are you happy about it?" Garrett inquired.

"Oh, yes, I think I'm happy. My problem is that it came before I thought I was ready for it. I wanted to wait, but Cassey didn't want to because things are so tough at home for her," Brett said.

"Congratulations are in order, and here is a toast to the both of you and your good health, and our hope is the future will be very kind to you and the family you develop," Garrett said.

"Thanks to both of you," Brett said. "You are my very best friends, and you should know well in advance of everyone else."

"Ol' Brett is getting married, Garrett. I sure didn't ever think I would hear this news," Alan said.

"It is just a little strange," Garrett said. "Do you think they are just possibly in heat and think they are in love?"

"Naw, it's love. See how all the color has gone from his cheeks? I've been noticing something was wrong with him the whole trip, just didn't know what it was. He's not the same fellow. He used to be fun. Now he is just about the deadest person I know, don't you think, Garrett?" Alan asked.

"You might be right. This love business is a mighty serious ailment," Garrett said.

"You fellas lay off, how 'bout it?" Brett asked. "If I'd known you birds were going to react this way, I would never have told you. Maybe it would have been better if a fertilizer salesman, or someone else, had told you. I thought you would appreciate getting it straight from me."

"We were just kidding, Brett, you know that," Alan responded.

"You're right, Brett. We would rather hear it from you, and, yes, we were just kidding. Now what's your news, Alan?" Garrett inquired.

"I can't top Brett's news, so maybe I should keep my mouth shut," Alan said.

"Come on, Alan, what is it?" Brett questioned with a threat in his voice.

"Well, I've got me a job, believe it or not," Alan said, with a beam in his eye.

"A job!" Brett exclaimed. "Who wants a job? Then you can't come on these trips with Garrett and me."

"That's right, Alan. You've really screwed up," Garrett agreed.

"Maybe I have, but I had no choice," Alan said. "I had to go to work."

"You also know we are kidding, Alan. I think it is wonderful you've found a job after completing your business course. You are ready to find something to do," Garrett said.

"Doing what, Alan?" Brett asked.

"I've got me a job as assistant to Richard Jennings, the state legislator. I'll be working for him as some sort of a gofer out of the Orlando office. I will be stationed in the courthouse."

"That's wonderful, Alan. I think this requires another toast. This one should come from you, Brett," Garrett announced.

With glass held high, Brett said, "Here is to the most deserving boy in Orange County. One who deserves a break, one who has worked hard to achieve an education and reach this place in life." They toasted again, and again, to all their good fortune.

During the evening Alan said, "You know, I'm proud of this job for one reason more than any other. You fellas know I never knew my dad, and my mother has worked like a dog all my life to put me through school—even taking in washing and ironing in our house. She's never had a dime she could spend on herself. She's never been anywhere. She's never done anything but try to raise me, and now maybe she can have just a little free time and a few pennies to call her own. If I can work it out, I'm going to see to it that she has some easy days."

"I'm sure you will, Alan, and, yes, she certainly does deserve some easy days, and I know you will provide them for her," Garrett said.

The three young men spent the next day fishing just a little and left for Homosassa Springs to fish for trout before going home. At Homosassa they had tremendous luck, and they were able to carry home almost a fifty-five-gallon drum of fish.

They arrived home late afternoon with their drum almost running over with fish, which were well iced. Mary Fran and Sally Haney had invited all the farmhands to the main house for a fish fry that night. Garrett bought enough beer for everyone, and they fried the fish outside in a large iron pot. Sally made a pot of grits and hushpuppies, and everyone couldn't have enjoyed them more.

The snook were eaten and the trout set aside to be either dried or smoked the next day. These fish would be divided among Alan's and Brett's families.

35

In an unusual gesture, Mr. Langford came to the office quite unexpectedly one morning. He was not accustomed to moving very far from his rocker on the side porch. This occasion not only took Garrett by surprise, but Mr. Langford was clearly not at ease in a situation where Henry Bates could hear their conversation. After a few minutes of pleasantries, which amounted to nothing, Mr. Langford said, "Garrett, let's take the pick-up and ride out to where the men are clearing land." Realizing Mr. Langford had something on his mind, particularly so after the one-thousand-dollar incident, Garrett said, "That's a good idea."

Leaving the main house yards, Mr. Langford, though not troubled, appeared concerned with something he wanted to discuss with Garrett. "Garrett, you know we couldn't have accomplished anything had it not been for the Depression and all these folks who were flat and needed help somehow coming to us. They are here because we had just enough resources to keep them from starving to death. What we've accomplished is in large measure due to them. Sure, you and Beau could have eventually arrived at the same place, but it would have taken us forever."

"Yes, sir, I'm well aware of that."

"This is really a great crew, and they work well together. Because of their loyalty and hard work, we ought to think about cranking into our company some sort of bonus arrangement. I mean, where else could one find this many people who would work for virtually food and shelter? Oh, it's true we have taken care of them when the money started to come in, but think of those months they worked for no cash at all. This type loyalty is unheard of, even in a depression time."

"What do you have in mind?"

"I don't exactly know. I was toying with idea of discussing

with you the idea of taking a small percentage of company profits at Christmastime and distributing it among the management help on the basis of their contribution to the success of the company. Maybe have some sort of Christmas party and give the money to them in time so they can buy their family something for Christmas, say the week before Christmas. I don't think we need to make too big of a deal out of it, just something to let them know we appreciate them and then prove it. Had it not been for these folks, you and Beau would still be in the swamp behind the barn sawing logs. Think about it. We've been going for a while now, and we can't even see the logging crew from the barn anymore," he concluded.

"Well," Garrett said, "now that we have Henry to keep up with our records, this won't be such a difficult job. It would not only allow us to show the folks how we feel about them, but perhaps they might feel more a part of the success of the organization and work even harder to do a better job next year."

"This direction to Henry should come from you, Garrett. And more, maybe we should do one other thing for those employees who hold straw boss positions. I've thought about giving each of them a lot for a home on the north end on the highway, then saw whatever lumber they need to build a house. Give the lumber and lot to them and allow each to assist the other in building their home during hours other than working hours. This should give them a sense of belonging and a home they can call their own. If they become disgruntled with us, or decide to sell it for any reason to someone outside the company family, it won't make any difference to the rest of our holdings. And more, I think you should, sometime in the future, consider sawing lumber for a fine home for you and Mary Fran, but let's make this after I'm gone. Our home is good enough for anyone, but I'm thinking of Mary Fran and her wishes in a new home. I believe she would like a home that was hers alone, not something someone else had worn out twenty years before she ever saw it. Pick out a place both of you like and build your home and enjoy it. After all, when you get my age and have the opportunity to observe all the things in life you've failed to do and enjoy until you are too old to do them, then a lot has been wasted. Promise me you won't do that, Garrett. Take care of Mary Fran and enjoy yourselves as much as possible while you are young."

"Well, I don't know what to say, Mr. Langford. I'm all wrapped up in trying to pay bills and the progress of the business moving and have never really looked down the road like you are doing this morning. But I can say this: What you are saying makes sense and sounds good to me; however, your home is fine enough for anybody," Garrett replied.

"I know that, Garrett, and you know that, but you might be missing the point. I believe Mary Fran is building air castles in her head trying to determine what her dream house is going to look like. It's wrong to leave her captive in my wife's dream home for too long. Give her the reign and let her decide what she wants, and then grit your teeth and do it for her," he concluded.

Later in the afternoon Garrett quietly slipped away for a visit with his dad. He had made a practice in all things that were of substance to discuss them with him. Garrett did it because he valued his father's opinion, and his answers were usually right. Additionally, when he described the situation to his dad, the right answers began to come within his own mind as he verbalized the problems or opportunities. And yet, this was a peculiar situation because he had always pictured himself working with his dad, followed by looking after his dad in his old age. Now the situation was completely different from what his thoughts had been over the years. But more, he was always proud to have the opportunity to come to his dad for a confidential discussion of his current problems.

When Garrett arrived, his dad wasn't around the house, but he was at the barn with a bunch of calves he was weaning.

He had about fifty of the most beautiful calves imaginable in his holding pen. The mother cows were already driven to the farthest pasture, completely out of hearing distance of the calves.

"What are you doing with the calves held up, Dad?" Garrett asked. "Going to take them to the market?"

"Naw, just weaning them, son. I've got their mammies in the back pasture and plan to keep the calves here on hay and dry feed for a day or two before turning them out, and then monitor them closely for a few days," he said. "I was just going to the house to have a cup of coffee. Why don't we both go?"

"Sounds good to me," Garrett said. When they arrived at the house, it was as Garrett expected—in a state of upheaval with nothing in its right place and every dish in the kitchen dirty. In fact, two cups had to be washed before they could have coffee. In a roughshod gesture, Mr. Gregson cleared the kitchen table so they could sit down.

"Dad, I don't know how you ever sleep, drinking this strong coffee. I get the shakes every time we have a cup of it," Garrett said.

"If coffee is worth drinking, it is worth making strong enough to taste," Mr. Gregson replied.

"Dad, Mr. Langford hit me with an idea I wanted to talk to you about," Garrett began.

"I'll be glad to listen, son."

"He thinks that since we were so fortunate in getting the original Alabama folks to help us beginning at virtually no salary, just food and shelter, that we should remember their gesture by setting aside a percentage of our profits, maybe 10 percent, each year and give it to them individually based on their contribution to the company. This should also include any other of the future straw bosses. We should give it to them at Christmastime in the form of a bonus in addition to their regular salary. How does that idea grab you?" Garrett asked.

"You know, son, dealing with John you know up front you are not dealing with an idiot. He has been right most of the time about his business dealings. I don't exactly know how he got his start, but I can tell you from observation, he hasn't made many mistakes. If you stop to think about what he has proposed, it isn't all that drastic. You can't leave them at their present salaries for the rest of their lives. You also remember those people could barely cover their bodies with clothes when they arrived. They had very little food and no shelter. When you think about running low on food with no prospects for more or shelter from the rain and cold, then you are much more humble than if you had some change in your pocket. The gesture you made by allowing them to live in the old Coble house and providing them with food was just like a fairy tale to them. You took care of them and they really couldn't ask for more. Now that you are feeding them, sheltering them, and also providing a salary, they have the best of both worlds. And remember this, they haven't let you down. If it hadn't been for these folks, it would have been a long haul for Beau and you. But now, pause and observe them, they are happy and content. The other side of it is that 10 percent to John is like me taking folks to town and buying them a hamburger. The bottom line is the Alabama folks are making money for you, why not divide a portion of it with them? I expect if you do, they will work even harder next year," Mr. Gregson concluded.

"Well, I don't disagree with the proposal. I just wanted to talk it over with you and get your opinion."

Mr. Gregson said, "Another thing: I think anytime you make the effort to be sure your people are well provided for, it will come back to you fourfold or more. You can't lose."

"Dad, Mr. Langford also wants to get up on the highway just out of town on the north side of the last section and deed each of the department heads, which would be the original folks, a lot and let them cut enough timber to build their house. They are to provide the labor, and we will give them the land

and lumber. He thinks this will add some stability to the group and give them a greater sense of belonging," Garrett said.

"Not a bad idea as long as you don't let it be taken for granted that everyone who works for you thinks they will automatically be given a house. I like the idea as long as it doesn't present a hardship on you trying to provide it."

Garrett continued, "The clincher came when he suggested that somewhere down the road I cut myself sufficient lumber to build Mary Fran a home that is hers. He thinks she is putting on a show of satisfaction now because we have had the good fortune since becoming associated with him. He feels she will want a home that is hers and hers alone. She will always feel she is living in someone else's home living in the Langford house," Garrett said.

"He's right! Mary Fran needs something someday she can call her own. She needs some solid roots someplace where she can raise her children. But you must realize this took some gumption on John's part, because he is just like the Alabama folks now that he has the two of you to look after him. He has the best of both worlds. He has someone to look after him and someone to run his business. Who could ask for more?"

"Well, Dad, maybe the strangest part isn't out yet. From our very first day, Mr. Langford hasn't been in the way at all. When he makes a suggestion, which is rare, like he did about the Alabama folks' money and houses, he always does it in a very low-key fashion, and I feel if I disagree he won't look back, and it will be okay."

"Well, just what has he got in mind for you when he's gone?" Gregson asked.

"We've never talked about it. I don't know. I look for him to leave me something and issue orders to sell the rest maybe, and give the proceeds to some charity. He is awfully charity minded. He is a soft touch to someone who is in need. He will give you his last dime if you need it. To adequately answer your question, we've never talked about it. I figure one day he will want to talk and we will. Until then, as long as we are being looked after in the manner we are, I'm not going to worry about it," Garrett concluded.

"Are you making money with the business?"

"On paper we are. Our problem is that we are expanding at a rate faster than we are taking in money to finance the growth, so we are always in a cash bind. It keeps Henry always in turmoil trying to figure how we can make the next payroll. But we are making good progress. Our land-clearing operation is going good. Our citrus plantings are proceeding ahead of schedule. We are clearing lots of pasture. And the vegetable operation is going well. We are making progress, but little cash," Garrett said.

"Then go home and don't worry about it. You could be much less fortunate. Take care of your folks and your business and your family, and everything else will take care of itself, if you work hard and smart enough. If you don't, it will let you know in a very forceful way," Gregson said.

All the way home Garrett thought about his conversations with his dad and Mr. Langford. He knew both were right in their ideas about what should be done for the Alabama folks. In his own mind, he was also aware that their hard labor was the key to the mushrooming success the company was enjoying. For no reason other than his inexperience, he was still wallowing in indecision. However indecisive, he also knew he did not need to speak to other employers regarding how they would handle this, because Mr. Langford and his dad were always on target with their thinking. Besides, few other employers were making money.

Garrett did have a soft spot in his heart for those who worked for him. There was no more loyal a person than Beau. He could always be counted on, because he was really more like family than a hired hand.

Bill and Cindy Mathews were like family also. About the same age as he and Mary Fran, and their kids were coming along together. Each couple provided the other companionship and good times together. Cindy and Mary Fran were close friends, and Garrett always thought that this was good for Mary Fran to have such a friend, because of her past.

The Alabama folks were remarkable, considering the circumstances under which they arrived. Their resourcefulness and ability to handle extremely hard work for unbelievably long hours, never griping or grumbling about conditions, was a great asset. Even though they had to fix and refix their tools, their attitude remained tops. Yet, as broke as they all were, none ever asked for time off or to borrow money.

The Alabama folks all had known hard times prior to coming to Florida. Looking at their hands, one could readily determine that their lives had not been easy. Covered with calluses and skin-deep brown from the effects of the sun was proof positive of rough days in the past.

Because of this, Garrett always had a soft spot in his heart for the women. A woman with split nails, doing man's work with dirty hands, was too much. It reflected too many days of hard, backbreaking days in the fields.

The good thing was they were on the job every day without fail and remained there until the sun was down. Sundays found them all in church and doing their part in the settlement with those who were sick and needed help instead of just relaxing. They were honorable and good people, always interested in the welfare of others.

As a result of their past, their Alabama roots, they possessed a tremendous amount of pride in themselves while attending church or in town shopping. They were always clean and dressed in clean clothes. Maybe their clothes were old and tattered, but clean. The men shaved weekly unless they unexpectedly went to town during the week. They seldom had a haircut other than from their wives.

With all these thoughts going through Garrett's head, he couldn't disagree with Mr. Langford or his dad. He knew where his success was coming from. He also knew that if he didn't take a dominant role in being sure the workers and straw bosses were taken care of, they would play a diminished role in his financial well-being in the future. His problem was knowing where the money would come from. He knew if he followed through, it would place the business in a bind after Christmas.

The new home for Mary Fran did have a great attraction to him. In fact, he already knew where he would like to build the home. There was a hardwood hammock not far from Bath Pond that he had had his eyes on for a long time—a beautiful spot that was not only secluded, but with black heavy land and very beautiful.

He wanted to tell Mary Fran about a new home when he could get the most personal mileage from it. How could he do it? When would be the right time to spring the news on her?

Garrett was also thinking about his goals for the future and how he was going to finance them all. The citrus nursery was growing well. In fact, he was growing more trees than he could ever clear land to set and care for. He was thinking 4,500 acres of citrus total. Yet for right now, he was content to plant about 100 acres per year until he had resources to do more. He was thinking the vegetable operation would help him increase the citrus plantings. His goal was to increase vegetables at the rate of 100 acres per year, hoping to get a minimum of two crops off the land yearly. Ranch land would eventually measure 10,500 acres, but included here would be a number of larger lakes. Maybe improving 50 acres of pasture each year would be a reasonable goal. Beau and Bill had the perimeter fence almost complete and had begun cross-fencing, which meant funds for additional stock had to be generated. New lands were planted each year in the summer after watermelons were harvested.

A vegetable packing shed was currently being constructed. The women wanted to operate the shed. He had agreed to this, provided they stay out of the fields, and they would be paid the competitive price that other packing sheds paid.

Garrett was thoroughly excited, arriving home as he carefully considered the possibilities, yet he knew the sawmill was still presently generating the funds to operate the entire place. John Haney was its key to success.

After Garrett's mind was made up that they could in fact do something in the way of a bonus for the Alabama folks, Bill, and Beau, he could hardly contain himself for the rest of the fall until Christmastime. He wanted to have a nice party, one that the employees could enjoy and that he could finance. Perhaps he'd kill a steer or two and a few shoats and have a barbecue with all the trimmings, or a fish fry or a large batch of chicken and rice. At any rate, at this moment he had Henry confidentially working on the bonus arrangement, and he was firm with the decision.

Of course, at the onset, Henry, being his usual conservative self, didn't know how they would raise the cash for the bonuses. He never had sufficient monies for the payroll, let alone a bonus in addition to the payroll. In his estimation, it just couldn't be done with all the expansion they were now undertaking.

In desperation, Garrett said to Henry, "Well, Henry, I'll tell you what. You figure out what the bonus arrangement would cost us, and if we don't have the money for the employees, we will find it somewhere, even if we have to borrow it. We'll do it. Just don't get all upset over it."

"That's what I'm afraid of. We'll do it, and it will take me until next July to find enough money each week for the payroll."

The bonus was Garrett, Mary Fran, Mr. Langford, and Henry's secret. Over the next few weeks until Christmas they all shared lots of excitement in anticipation of how the employees would react to such an arrangement. In fact, it was so exciting they had a problem at times not revealing their secret.

Early one morning as Garrett was coming onto the side porch, he found Mr. Langford already sitting in his favorite rocker, cigarette in hand. He said, "Garrett, I've been thinking about our bonus deal lots lately. Maybe we've approached it wrong from the very beginning?"

"What do you mean, Mr. Langford?"

"Wrong in the sense that if we had our heads screwed on, we would have realized at the beginning we couldn't give everyone a bonus and have it large enough to mean anything to them," Langford said.

"I know what you mean. I've been wrestling with the same question. I think we should give everyone ten dollars as a Christmas present. In addition, give the bonuses to our management people. After all, our management people are our Alabama folks who have helped us from the beginning, including Bill and Beau. This way everyone will get a nice Christmas gift, and Bill, Beau, John Haney, Jim Lawrence, and Jim Morgan will get the bonus in a very low-key manner. I don't think we should make a big thing about it in front of the rest of the folks," Garrett said.

"I like your idea," Langford said, "but what about Henry? You left him out altogether, and he plays a major role in our business. It's true he can't cut timber, but his job is just as important."

"I agree, but I wanted to have some fun with Henry. You know he will have to be in on all the calculations for the others. Let's just not say anything about his getting a bonus. Don't even mention it. He is already stewing about where he is going to dig up the money for the rest. Let's let him find the money, even if we have to borrow it somewhere along the line before Christmas, I'll tell John Haney that when a cash lumber sale comes along, not to turn it in to Henry, but to give it to me and we will use this money for Henry's bonus. After Christmas we will rectify the books as they should be, to keep it honest."

"That's good. Let's wait on Henry's until the rest has been distributed. He will be certain to have a sinking spell somewhere after they are so happy and he has nothing. Let's play this one by ear, and I agree we can have some real fun with

Henry. By the way, you know he is getting kind of sweet on one of the Haney girls, and this will help him buy her something for Christmas," Langford concluded happily.

36

Garrett noticed Mary Fran was running out of steam lately. She was listless and worn out all the time, and he felt a change was in order for her. He made arrangements with Sally to keep Billy for the weekend, and he surprised her with a weekend away from the house and the rest of the group.

During the entire time they had been married, they had never taken any time off together. They had never really spent any money at all that wasn't a necessity.

Now, they were really on their first weekend together with a little money in their pockets. They planned to Christmas shop and headed to town.

They checked into the best hotel in Orlando. Arriving mid-morning on Saturday, they decided to spend one night and leave after lunch on Sunday. After lunch on Saturday, they used the rest of the day Christmas shopping. Following a fine dinner in the hotel, they went out on the town like they had never done before. On Sunday they didn't awaken until late, and after lunch in the dining room they headed home.

"I could get used to this kind of living. I've really enjoyed the weekend. We ought to make a practice of doing this about once every two months. We could bring friends or we could come alone. We need an outlet away from the house and a change from the same people all the time," Garrett said.

"I couldn't agree more. I hope we can do this occasionally. It will do us good, I know I feel much better about going home now that I've had a little rest and change. The only thing I feel bad about is you letting me spend so much money on myself," she said.

"Big deal, you bought a few things you've never had, but needed," he replied.

The next few days until Christmas went fast. There was so much planning to do for the employees' party. Everyone was talking about it now that it was going to happen. They all decided it should be a barbecue, and each would bring the covered dish Sally instructed them to bring.

This barbecue wasn't like all the rest of the functions the employees had enjoyed together. Instead of one or two doing all the work, it was decided everyone would pitch in for the day and really do it right.

One group was digging the pit by sunup. Another had gone into town to get the beef and pork that had been butchered a few days earlier and hung there in coolers to age a bit. Another decided a little chicken would taste good, and they were killing a few fryers. And where there is anyone close to the soil who is barbecuing there will be a goat or two, and a goat was presently being slaughtered for the feast.

When Garrett heard of all the meat that was to be cooked, it appeared to him as though they could feed the entire settlement with it all. Sally had issued instructions to every employee what their dish should be: things like canned cucumber pickles, fresh cabbage slaw, home baked beans, a few green vegetables, and some sweets. Of course the only thing that was purchased was tea, ice, sliced bread (which was a luxury for the employees), and sufficient beer and some liquor for those who might partake.

"Garrett, I believe this day off and everyone cooking together will do something for our employees' morale. They are having fun now, and after they get their fill, they will be a much closer group. I believe it will do something for our ability to get out our work in the future, and we should plan these outings at intervals in the future," Mr. Langford said.

"I think you're right. Everyone seems to be having a good time and working harder than they normally do," he replied.

The meal had been planned for mid-afternoon. It would last as long as the food and enthusiasm did.

All through the day, excitement increased. The women kept coming to the pits to witness the progress the men were making with the meat. Of course, they were also offering instructions as to how they could be doing it better, to which the men paid absolutely no attention.

Shortly after lunchtime, the women came with tablecloths, straight chairs, and silverware and began setting up for the big meal. All sorts of substitutes were used for tables, such as boxes and boards. The tables were placed on the side porch of the main house so that those getting chilly could get inside if they needed to. Some tables were out on the lawn.

As the afternoon progressed, excitement picked up with the consumption of some of the beer and even a little liquor. Even the women got to hanging around the pits nibbling and nipping a bit. Nibbling on the barbecue while it is cooking is one of the best-tasting morsels one could ever expect to experience.

Mary Fran was busy with finding more table covers. She was rummaging through Mrs. Langford's trunks when Garrett walked in. "Garrett, I can't use these cloths of Mrs. Langford's. They're linen and fine materials. There will be no telling what is spilled on them before the night is over, and I just don't want to use them."

"Why not use a few sheets?"

"Every sheet we have is already out there. The lawn and porches now look as though we're having a ghost convention," she said.

"Do the best you can and don't worry about it."

Around three o'clock the food had arrived from the employees' house. The table was stacked high with sliced bread from the store. There were half a dozen washtubs filled with iced beer and soft drinks. There were crew barrels filled with tea, the meat was just about ready, and the people were standing around just waiting. Everyone was there and everyone was having a good time, expecting a real blast of a party.

Around four o'clock the meat was ready. Asking for the employees' attention, Garrett invited Mr. Langford to offer the invocation.

As he stepped to the center of the group, everyone removed their hats as he said, "Lord, this has been a good year for us. We don't have a great deal to show for it except a year of hard work. But the hard work is good for us, remembering there are countless thousands around our country who haven't had work in a very long time and who don't have enough on the table at this Christmastime. We pray for these folks with hope that their needs will be met. We thank you for the good health of our families and the place you have provided for us in this world. And now, gracious Lord, pardon our sins and bless this food to the nourishment of our bodies and our bodies to your service. Amen." The entire group said "Amen" in unison.

"Get yourselves a plate and move up to the tables," Garrett said. As he was speaking, Beau walked by and Garrett took hold of his arm and said, "Beau, how about getting Bill, John Haney, Jim Lawrence, and Jim Morgan and come to my office for a minute before you eat." Beau was off to round up the men.

"Mr. Langford, Beau and the rest of the men are coming to the office before they eat. I plan to give them their bonus and tell them about their lot on the highway. Why don't you come too?" Garrett asked.

"No thanks, Garrett. They work for you, and I know you can handle it just the way we decided."

Henry saw Garrett enter the office and the rest of the men following him and knew immediately what was taking place. He worried that the company couldn't afford such a luxurious bonus arrangement, and at this point he did not know anything at all about the lot as an additional gift. He also knew he had been overlooked, and it was souring his stomach. Yet he was trying to be big about it since he wasn't doing manual labor for the company.

Henry thought, *Here it is Christmas, and I have been robbing every cash source I could find for a month trying to come up with the money for a bonus.* He didn't know what he would do for the next few weeks about the payroll until they could take in some more money from lumber sales. But then the vegetable sales were good, and they could help out. If push came to shove, they could sell some cattle. With this thought, he and Jean Haney went toward the food.

Inside the office with the doors closed and only the appropriate people present, Garrett said, "The purpose of this conversation is to let each of you know that we appreciate your loyalty and hard work. The opportunity each of us has had here fell into place in large measure by your unfortunate circumstances elsewhere. Your eventual arrival here has been the greatest asset I've ever witnessed. We wanted to do something for you and couldn't think of a more appropriate time than Christmas. We hope you will accept our offering in the same spirit in which it is offered. Because you fellows are our management team, we decided to take a percentage of our net profits and divide it equally. We think you deserve this recognition, and we hope you can put $232 to good use. The amount of this management bonus shall remain confidential between only those who are present in this room. The rest of the employees will receive a smaller token of our appreciation."

With this announcement the men's faces went blank and the silence was shattering. They were squirming in the chair, none knowing what to say because this generosity was something they'd never experienced and they'd never needed it more. This amount at this time in their lives was in the same category of "big money" to these fellows.

Finally, and with a voice choked with emotion, Bill said, "Garrett, I can't speak for the rest of the fellows, but I can say truthfully I've never had a more unexpected gift, yet a gift that means so much to me. I'm just thankful Cindy and I have had sufficient food. You know things are rough in the area of food and shelter, and just belonging to a place has meant everything to us. We will never forget your generosity."

When Bill finished, the room went to a deafening quiet again. When the silence had lasted too long, John Haney, who looked as rough and grizzled as they come, tried to manage to speak and couldn't. When he realized he couldn't speak, he stood up and shook hands with Garrett and did manage to squeak out a "Thank you," giving him the biggest hug imaginable.

Jim Lawrence and Jim Morgan also offered their thanks with emotional voices.

Beau was different. Beau only received a token salary anyway because Garrett always saw to his needs. Beau, however, was just as speechless, and because he was, he was smart enough not to try to say anything. But looking into his eyes, Garrett knew his innermost feelings.

"Now there is another thing," Garrett continued. "Because all of you mean a great deal to us and have stuck to us when we really needed someone to stick, we want to do something else for you. At your convenience, take your wives up to the hard road just outside the settlement in the oak thickets and pick out a lot for yourself. Pick the one that you like, and we will deed it to you. When you are ready to begin construction, each man will be given the lumber for his house. The rest is up to you. Maybe you fellows together could help each other build your homes. Work it anyway you want to, but the land is yours and the lumber is yours and maybe the bonus will help you get started," Garrett concluded. "And, that is all the gifts for this Christmas. I will ask you this: We have extended these gifts to you because you are our management team. Obviously we can't do this for every employee as a gift from the company. Your wives should know, but please let's keep this to ourselves."

When the bombshell dropped regarding the lot, the men had already stood to leave. Now none could leave. No one knew what to say, and all sat down again because of weakness in their legs. Being given a homesite and some of the materials to build was a total shock.

The men expected nothing as a Christmas gift, for they were truly thankful for their jobs. Their job was gift enough. No one could have ever been more generous with them than Garrett over the short time they had been together. Who would have ever expected a nice bonus and a piece of land and lumber to build a house? In the desperation of the moment for these men—men who were physically tough beyond description—they did what anyone would have done under similar circumstances. They blew their noses and wiped a few tears and again shook Garrett's hand and hugged him.

"Now do me a favor," Garrett said. "What about going out there and showing the rest how to eat, drink, and have a good time with your families and friends? Just get out of here."

Everyone left but Beau. He stood there and looked at Garrett for a few minutes and finally said, "You know I don't need this money. I have saved most of my salary. Henry takes care of it for me, you know. As for the land, me being black, I can't build a house on the hard road outside the settlement. The Ku Klux will have me before the sun goes down. I'm happy right where I am, and if you need the $232 back you can certainly have it. You know that."

"Beau, I knew you probably wouldn't want to build a house in the settlement. You know you can continue to have the house you now have or build another. As far as the money is concerned it is yours. You earned it! You are a deserving human being to me. Whether you are black, red, or white doesn't matter to me. What does matter is that we appreciate all the hard work you've done, and we wanted to show you our appreciation. And," Garrett hesitated, "you know you are more family than employee." Garrett hugged Beau and Beau responded. Both men's eyes filled with tears of family and success never dreamed possible.

"I appreciate you and everything you have done for me. You know you can always count on me," Beau said.

"I know that. Now go eat some barbecue," Garrett said.

When Garrett was alone, the strangest feeling came over him after having given the bonus, land, and lumber to the men. He was sure he got a greater good out of giving the gifts than they had from receiving them. He was just as happy for them as they were to receive. He learned a good lesson, and that lesson was that giving is better than receiving, which was a good lesson at Christmas.

Pondering what had happened and how the men reacted, his eyes filled with tears. As they were running down his cheek and dripping off his chin, Mary Fran came into the office. When she saw him, she couldn't believe what she was witnessing. Everyone else was outside having the best time imaginable, and here was Garrett, the absolute toughest of them all, inside crying.

When Garrett realized she was in the room, he took his rough hand and wiped away his tears. On seeing her, he embraced her and couldn't hold it any longer. For a few minutes, he held her in his arms and sobbed.

"Garrett, straighten up and tell me what is wrong. I can't stand this. What is it?" she demanded.

Regaining his composure he told her the whole story, and both had another good cry before joining the rest of the folks.

Because of Henry's special physical problem Garrett couldn't get him away from the crowd quite as easily as someone who could readily walk. He had to wait before confronting Henry with his bonus. Garrett knew Henry knew what he was doing when he asked the men to come to the office. Of course, Henry knew he wasn't asked to come and thereby decided he was getting nothing. So the longer he stewed in his juices, the more upset he would become about it all. Garrett knew this and wanted to wait on him long enough to have some fun off him, but not too long to hurt his feelings.

Henry had eaten a sandwich Sally had made him from pork and was talking to Jean Haney by the pit. When Garrett walked by, he did not look at him at all, just passed in a hurry.

Garrett killed some time talking with the others, and when Jean went to get more food for Henry, Garrett took this as his opportunity. Henry was sitting on an orange box behind the pit and out of the way of the other traffic.

Walking over and sitting down beside Henry, Garrett said, "Henry, you've done a good job here. In fact, I don't know quite what we would have done without you. Everyone depends on you and you've never let us down. I wish there was some way we could adequately say 'thank you'."

Henry, being the pessimist, thought that his bonus was going to be lots of nice words and no money. Henry did not know about the lumber and the land.

Henry turned to Garrett and said, "Well, Garrett, you know I needed a job when you hired me, and no one except someone of your temperament would have put up with a cripple. I thank you for this and hope I can measure up in the future."

"Well, I know you will, Henry, but I did want to do something for you at this time of year when everyone is so happy." As Garrett was saying this, he handed Henry an envelope with four hundred dollars in it. As he handed it to Henry, Jean walked back up and Garrett stood up, saying, "Here, Jean, sit here. I was just leaving." As he did, Henry quickly slipped the envelope into his pocket with a noticeable expression of relief on his face.

While Jean spread their plates, Henry felt like he was sitting in a bed of ants wondering what was in it for him. While he couldn't say anything to Jean, he had to find out.

Garrett saw him headed back toward his office before he ate the food Jean had brought and had to chuckle. He didn't notice Henry anymore until about fifteen minutes later when Henry grabbed him from the rear saying, "Now I know where my shortages went. You were siphoning them off from John. You can't be trusted, Garrett." And with this comment, he stuck out his hand, and Garrett could see and feel profound appreciation written over Henry's face. He didn't have to say anything. He knew.

Henry said, "You know you shouldn't have given me this much when the rest got less."

Garrett said, "They don't know what you got. That is between you and me. Besides you weren't hired for your muscle. You were hired for your mind."

"Thanks, Garrett," and Henry hobbled back to Jean and his food.

"What was that all about?" Mary Fran asked.

"Don't ask, I might cry again," Garrett responded.

The eating went on until well after dark. As the evening progressed, someone slid Mr. Langford's upright Philco battery radio onto the side porch and tuned in the Grand Ole Opry, and the dancing began, ending only when the Opry signed off at midnight. The food wasn't totally consumed but what remained was divided between everyone, and there was barbecue in each house through Christmas.

As the midnight hour came, Garrett huddled the folks around him on the porch and said, "Folks, it is about time we called it a night. I don't know when I've had so much fun. I believe everyone danced with everyone, and it will be a night we will always remember. Tomorrow is Christmas Eve. Take it off, take Christmas day off, and we will see everyone the day after Christmas. Why don't we close with a prayer with everyone joining hands?

"Lord, you've been good to us. We thank you for this occasion and we thank you for the meaning of the season. Go with each family here tonight. Keep us safe within your arms until we meet again. Amen."

When Garrett had finished with the prayer, Jim Lawrence began singing "Joy to the World" and followed this with every Christmas carol the group knew. The last, of course, was "Silent Night."

"Merry Christmas, everyone," Garrett yelled. The same response came back to him.

37

The years since their wedding day of April 1933 had been good to Mary Fran and Garrett. Having the good fortune of becoming associated with the Langfords was the best stroke of luck of their young lives. In fact, while they both had worked very hard, it was difficult for them to equate the miserable time most folks were having just trying to exist in the Depression-riddled South. Existing is tough for anyone; however, having the opportunity to observe the Alabama folks gave some insight into their good fortune.

After Billy's birth in 1935, Jay was born in 1937 and Mary Jane in 1939. Their family was growing, and there was activity around the Gregson household.

Garrett's dad now lived in one of the smaller tenant houses close to the main house so that he could not only eat at their table, but also close enough to receive care for his needs. His health was fairly good; however, age was catching up with him. He now needed just a little assistance from time to time, and Garrett and Beau were always close by for him.

Bill and Cindy's daughter Sara Elizabeth was born in 1939, and their family was then complete. Jimmy Mathews and Billy Gregson were inseparable friends.

The Alabama folks picked the lots on the highway, and their houses were for all practical purposes finished. While they were rather rough in places, they did represent a monumental accomplishment for the year 1940.

Henry and Jean married and lived in quarters provided by Garrett in the rear of the office building between the main house and the sawmill.

The business progressed well. The citrus nursery not only provided all the trees Garrett could set each year, but also enough for selling to those who needed trees in the industry as well. The grove plantings were growing at a rapid pace, and fruit was beginning to show up for harvesting. The vegetable operation was becoming a larger part of the operation each year, and the vegetable packinghouse was providing sufficient work for all the Alabama women plus others in the settlement. John Haney was still operating the sawmill to capacity and had its daily schedule down to a fine-tuned operation. Beau and Bill had the pasture completely rim-fenced and were working hard cross-fencing and improving the pastures. The herd had been established long enough now that the bull calves were being sold each year and Beau was still training the four dogs he felt he must have. The dogs doubled as watchdogs around the main house at nights. New generations of Buford, Booger, Gator, and Precious continued to be members of the operation.

PART TWO

The Productive Years

38

The afternoon of Sunday, December 7, 1941, was a clear, brisk Florida winter day. This breezy clear day was not unusual but uncomfortable for those attending Mr. Langford's funeral. He had died the preceding Friday, and everyone in the settlement, including all company employees with their families, was present.

Even though Mr. Langford was an elderly man, his death was a primary source of uneasiness for Garrett because of the peculiar arrangement the two of them had, which was nothing more than a verbal agreement and a handshake. Because they were well suited for each other, there was never an argument. Garrett was the boss and Mr. Langford the senior advisor. Garrett always thought of Mr. Langford more as a member of their family because of their mutual attraction. They had only known each other since Garrett and Mary Fran's wedding in 1933, but the confidence they established in each other was far more stable than their relatively short acquaintance would indicate.

Leaving the cemetery, one of the younger Alabama folks, who was about twenty years old, came up to Garrett all out of breath with the news that Pearl Harbor had been bombed by the Japanese. No one really understood the magnitude of the bombing, nor was anyone really sure where Pearl Harbor was.

"How do you know such a thing?" Garrett inquired.

"We just heard it on the car radio as we were leaving the cemetery, and we thought you would like to know about it," the young man said.

"Yes, I certainly am interested and thanks for your thinking to come back to tell me," Garrett said.

"Sounds like we've been crapped on, son," Mr. Gregson said.

"Sure does," Garrett replied. "I thought Roosevelt said just the other day that we were not vulnerable to any attack, and no American boy would fight on foreign soil?"

"You can't put a lot of value in what a politician says, plus the fact they bombed us," Garrett's dad said.

Alan was walking with them to the car. He said, "Watch it now. You know I'm interested in politics, Mr. Gregson."

"Well, you know what I mean, Alan, all but you. Besides if it were you who told me something I couldn't depend on, you know what would happen to you, don't you?"

"I'm afraid I do. Something like kicking my butt until my nose bleeds," replied Alan.

"You've got it!"

Driving home, Garrett was in a state of shock regarding Mr. Langford's death and now Pearl Harbor. No one said much. Everyone sat thinking about the funeral and the consequences of the bombing and what it could mean personally. Garrett wondered how it would affect his operation, knowing full well it would in some way.

"This bombing business scares me, Garrett," Mary Fran said.

"Me, too. But I don't think it is anything we can't handle. How tough could the Japanese be to whip?"

"I don't know how tough they will be to whip, but you've got to hand it to them. They must have plenty of guts running up to a country like the United States, dropping bombs, and attacking us, as small as they are," Mr. Gregson said.

All during the rest of the day the war news continued to worsen as casualty reports were available. Each report was just a little worse, and the news from Washington was such that it was continually muddled. The reports were contradictory and confusing. Even so, everyone listened because of concern. It was the state of uncertainty, shock, and siege of the mind that disturbed everyone. Mothers could already see their sons and husbands marching off to war.

Since Mr. Langford's death on Friday, the kids had been filled with one question after the other. "What was going to happen to Mr. Langford now?" "Where is he?" "Where was he going?" "What about this business of one's spirit rising? How does it do that?" And all the other questions kids are apt to ask.

Billy, being six years old, Jay four, and M. J. only two, the questions came in a steady stream. The questioning became heavier during the dinner hour and into the evening until their bedtime. The kids felt as if Mr. Langford was family. They didn't know the difference since he was in their house prior to their births.

When the kids were asleep, Mary Fran came back into the living room with Garrett. "Well, Garrett, now that Mr. Langford is dead, what now? What will happen to us? What provisions will we make?"

"I wish I could answer that question, but I can't. I know Mr. Langford must have had a will. I think I will go up to Buford Casey's office tomorrow, if I can make it."

39

It was business as usual the next morning. Being Monday, everything that could go wrong did. Coupled with the bad news coming from Japan and Pearl Harbor, most working for Garrett were completely confused. The fluster was from the fact that most were finally beginning to get back on their feet after the Depression, and now this. Nothing went smoothly.

As is the case throughout the South when a loved one dies, there was a great deal of genuine concern over the death of Mr. Langford. They really did have deep and sympathetic feelings for him. It was true that he spent most of his time on the side porch rolling Prince Albert cigarettes, but everyone knew his past success made their jobs possible. His generosity meant the world to them because of a steady supply of groceries at a time when they were mighty scarce. The employees also knew of Mr. Langford's regard for Garrett. His success, coupled with their association, was the big reason for their jobs and good fortune.

Garrett was having problems with the operation because his employees were vitally concerned about the status of the war with Japan. Roosevelt, after consulting with Congress, did declare that a state of war existed. Garrett completely forgot about reassuring his help that their jobs were secure.

Late in the afternoon, somewhere around 6 p.m., a sleek-looking 1941 Ford coupe came to a stop in front of the office. It was Buford Casey, the attorney. Immediately upon seeing Buford, Garrett knew that before long the Langford mystery would be solved.

"Hi, Buford," Garrett said as Buford entered the small office where he and Henry were sitting.

"Hey, Garrett. Can we find a private place somewhere for a few minutes? I need to talk to you," Buford said.

"Sure, come into my office," Garrett said, stepping aside to let Buford pass.

"I'm just leaving, Garrett. I'll lock the front door on the way out," Henry said.

"Fine. See you tomorrow, Henry."

"I had thoughts of paying you a visit today, Buford, but so many problems occurred around here, plus the Pearl Harbor thing, that I just haven't been able to leave. By the way, what is the latest war news?" Garrett asked.

"Can't say as I know any more than you, Garrett. All I know is that Roosevelt declared war, and I guess a good-sized bunch of American boys will have to go to whup them Japs."

"I just hope we can get it over with in a hurry. I haven't been following the situation very closely, but I sure feel we don't need to be involved in an extended fight with them," Garrett replied.

"I don't think we have the necessary tools to wage much of a battle now. I think we might have to gear up and then fight. This will not only take time, but there is an upbeat side, I think. It will provide many jobs, and our factories can run again at full capacity. I think economically it could have a positive effect on us. It could also cause lots of our men to die, fighting a battle that shouldn't have been fought in the first place," Buford concluded.

"Any way you cut it, Buford, it is spooky, but you didn't come here to discuss a war. What's on your mind?"

Buford was a short, pot-gutted person with no neck whose collar was always opened and his tie loosely tied around his neck. Because he was balding, he always wore a hat, even inside if he could get by with it. He pushed it back on his head and grunted loudly as he bent forward to retrieve a large folder of papers from his briefcase.

"Garrett, Mr. Langford came to see me a few months, maybe a year ago, and asked me to bring his will up to date. Now that he is gone, you need to know the contents of that will."

"Well, I've wondered what was going to happen."

"In a nutshell, you will remember loaning Mr. Langford one thousand dollars some time back. He took that money to the funeral home and paid his burial expenses. You remember that, Garrett?"

"Why, yes, I remember giving him one thousand dollars, but what does it have to do with his will?"

"Plenty," Buford responded. "For one thing that one thousand dollars bought you the entire Langford estate. You bought it and paid for it with that single one thousand dollars. He said to me that besides this, you had earned the estate. What do you think of that?"

"You've got to be kidding, Buford. We're looking at more than fifteen thousand acres and all his other assets? You must be wrong," Garrett concluded.

"You might think I am, but I'm far from wrong. I drafted the will, and I know what is inside it. You and Mary Fran are the new owners. It is all legal and proper, and you will not be contested because he has no blood heirs. You are the sole owners. It is yours to do with as you please," Buford said.

Astounded, Garrett settled back in his chair and was totally unable to speak. How could such a thing happen to him? What did Mr. Langford have in mind? He had a thousand other questions he couldn't answer.

Buford said, "Garrett, the will is very simple. Nothing complicated. And it says exactly what I've told you. I have a copy to leave for your study, and the original will go to the judge. I also have a letter from Mr. Langford that my secretary wrote for him when he made this last will. He asked me to deliver the letter when I read you the will. Why don't you study the papers and come by my office in a few days, and we will get the wheels turning to close his estate?"

"Okay, Buford. Thanks for coming out." Because he was so overcome, Garrett simply sat behind his desk and let Buford find his way to his car.

Not knowing what to do next and because he was so excited, he sat dumbfounded until he saw Sally Haney coming in front of the office on her way to the chicken house to gather the eggs. "Sally, could you do me a favor?"

"Sure, Garrett, what is it?" she asked.

"Can you arrange to stay over at our house tonight and care for the kids? I need to be away for the evening, and I wanted to take Mary Fran with me."

"Not a problem," she replied. "You take her and leave the kids with me. They'll be fine."

Mary Fran was out in the backyard when Garrett found her. "Honey, how about you going inside and put on your best dress and go into Orlando with me for the evening? We will be back late. I have asked Sally if she will stay with the kids."

"Anything wrong, Garrett?" she asked.

"Oh, nothing like that. Some things I wanted to talk over with you, and we need to be away from here for a few hours. Now hurry, and I'll be ready when you are. We'll eat supper in town."

"Okay. In forty-five minutes, maybe less."

"Make it less, if you can."

Garrett quickly called the Orange Court Hotel in Orlando to make dinner reservations. He also reserved a hotel room.

While Garrett waited for Mary Fran, he did have the opportunity to scan Mr. Langford's will, and it did say exactly what Buford said it did. It was short, as wills go, very direct and to the point, written—except for a few legal terms—in language a grammar-school child could understand. There were no questions left unanswered in Garrett's mind.

Mr. Langford had left his entire estate to Garrett and Mary Fran. Payment was the one thousand dollars he had borrowed earlier and which also prepaid his funeral expenses.

"I wish I knew what all the fuss is about," Mary Fran quarreled as she stepped into the truck. "It sure is nice to get to go somewhere, but it isn't like it should be when one has to dress in such a hurry. Now, why the hurry-up trip to Orlando?"

"Why don't you just get hold of yourself and read Mr. Langford's will while I drive? Buford brought it out just a bit ago, and I wanted to get away for a few hours to think through what has happened."

"Don't tell me we've got to move out?" Mary Fran replied.

"That's just about it," Garrett said.

With a solemn face Mary Fran opened the papers and began to read. As she did, and not knowing fully all the terms used in the document, she was at first puzzled over its contents. Then when she had scanned its contents for the first time she paused and pondered exactly what she had read. When the contents begin to sink in, she went limp. Her face was blank and white as she turned to Garrett with the question, "Does this say what I think it says?"

"That depends on what you think it says."

"Does it say Mr. Langford's entire estate is left to us?"

"You've got it!"

"Garrett, I simply can't believe it. What did he have in mind? Why did he do it for us?" It was one question after the other as they came to her mind, and she continued to ask them of Garrett.

"I can't answer your questions. I can say that he had no blood relatives according to Buford, and it can't be contested. Furthermore, he left us a letter that hasn't been opened yet. I thought we would wait until we get to the hotel before opening it, where we can have some privacy and read it together," Garrett said.

The Orange Court's lobby was filled with guests and those there for dinner like Garrett and Mary Fran. When they entered, Mary Fran said, "I think if we needed privacy we should have gone to the Bath Pond. It would have been lots more fun. Just look at all these folks."

"Don't worry. I have a room set aside for our use. Let's go up and read the letter and then come down to supper."

Finding their room, they quickly sat on the edge of the bed, carefully opened and read the letter.

It read:

Dear Garrett and Mary Fran:

I wanted to say a word to you apart and aside from my will, which accompanies this letter. Therefore, I have chosen this private bit of correspondence that should be kept between the three of us.

Garrett, I know you would have had strong second thoughts about accepting my estate without having paid for it. Well, you have paid for it. Consider all the hours of hard work you put into trying to get the sawmill started, the trees in the nursery, the trees in the ground, and all the land clearing that has been going on. The pasture improvement that has taken place, the truck farming and the vegetable packing house and the other things you have done that have been successful and, in part, on my behalf.

In addition to this, you and Mary Fran are to be commended for the good care you've extended me since moving into the main house. Because I knew you would have second thoughts about not paying something for the place is why I asked you to come up with the $1,000 loan I used to prepay my funeral expenses. So there, you've paid money and sweat for the place! You will find more than enough to repay yourself in my personal checking account at the bank, which is now yours and transferred to your name. This has already been taken care of by Buford Casey.

Above all else, remember there are no strings attached to the will. The assets are yours. I've watched you very closely and fully believe nothing will be squandered. But there is another element of business you need to always have filed right behind your eyeballs. Sometimes it is more difficult to keep an asset than to acquire one. Keeping what we have developed will be much more difficult than taking the risk to acquire it.

You now have the beginnings of a great life together, a life that can be independent from the necessity of leaning on others if you will but make the most of it. You now have the assets for financial leverage. Use every element of the business to its fullest advantage. By assuming this role in your life there is another duty you now have. You should use your good fortune to provide as many benefits for other people as is humanly possible. This will come in the form of jobs and altruism.

Based on the way the both of you have worked and the way you started out with me, I am confident you will someday emerge a very wealthy couple. Wealthy, because you already know wealth isn't just money.

Because of your past, and especially yours, Mary Fran, the two of you know how to recognize others when they suffer. Because you know this, you should always remember to be of assistance to everyone who needs help if it is in your power to extend it. I like this trait in you and ask you to continue to develop and enlarge it. Take great risks in this regard. Whatever you do for others will come back to you manyfold. You know this and can count on this as a truism.

You "kids" are my family and my only family. Logically you are the ones to inherit my estate. No one could've expected any finer care than I have received since Mrs. Langford's death. Because she thought so much of the both of you, we had talked on several occasions of leaving you our place. It is what both of us want. We wanted to do it because of our love for you.

You should remember the secret to a successful life is to give back more than you receive. Win by giving, not receiving. Few realize this important lesson.

The two of you were gifts to my wife and me. You made our dreams come true. You are good people, and goodness has power. Use this power in every positive

> way you can for the rest of your lives and you will be the real winners, not those whom you have actually helped along the way. The life asset of winning will be yours. It will be a very good feeling that no one but you will possess, and it will be good. This feeling, for you, will be almost as good as the feeling I've had executing this will.
>
> Thank you for all you did for Mrs. Langford and me. Through this bequest, I hope I have demonstrated our love tangibly. Take our assets and do with them as you like, but don't wait until you are too old to have some fun together.
>
> My very best wishes as you pursue your lives remembering that as you love each other there are those who've gone before that love you, too.

The letter was signed John Langford and dated.

When they were finished reading the letter, neither could say anything for a few minutes. Both sat on the edge of the bed thinking about what they had read, stunned and with tears streaming down both cheeks.

When they had recovered sufficiently to talk, Garrett said, "I don't believe anyone has ever had a nicer thing done for them than this. I simply can't believe it. It's as if we are dreaming and we will wake up and it will all be over."

"I know it, Garrett. It is unreal, and we will soon be back where we were at noon today."

Garrett thought that few times in one's life would such a thrill occur. He could remember other times in his life when he was excited, but only one when this level of excitement was achieved, and that was the night of his wedding when he and Mary Fran finally had gotten to their house for the first time and the honeymoon began. He remembered Brett's words that the honeymoon was when the business of being "alright" would begin.

At the present moment, words could not express their emotion and feelings of the grand slam that had happened in their lives. Instinctively, the "alright" business of their honeymoon past began all over again. When the "honeymoon" was over, they skipped supper and went back home.

40

The next morning the war news had worsened. Even more devastating were the feelings of uncertainty that had invaded everyone who worked for Garrett. The employees were building up within their own minds what would happen to them and their families. Garrett had the same thoughts. He now had the place operating on a fairly solid basis, but was personally faced with having to enlist in the army to help fight a war.

Garrett entered the office at 7 a.m., and Henry was already filled with questions from the farmhands. What would happen to their families if they had to go? Who would take care of their families? How could they get out of going? All were legitimate questions from concerned people.

"Garrett, our folks are going crazy trying to figure out what will happen to them and their families. Just about everyone working here except the older Alabama folks are eligible for the draft, including you. I wish we had some answers for them. The problem is, our folks are listening to the radio and hearing of folks lined up blocks down the street trying to enlist. I don't believe a one of our fellows will try to shirk what they believe is their patriotic duty. I think they just need some assurance their families will be taken care of while they are gone," Henry said.

"How can I assure them their family will be taken care of if I'm with them, Henry?"

"I don't know, and I don't believe they ever thought it was your personal responsibility. I think they are looking for answers to questions that have no easy answers," Henry said.

During the next few weeks Garrett tried his best to make every provision for the farm to run without him. He filled in Henry and Mary Fran with all the details he felt they should be familiar with. In addition, he told his workers that anyone entering the armed forces for the duration, whether drafted or enlisted, could leave their family in their house if they agreed to come back to work after the war concluded. This seemed to alleviate much of the anxiety the men and families had.

Garrett expected to receive a notice to report to Camp Blanding for a physical examination preparatory to entering the armed forces for duty. The notice came. It was a sad day and a shocking experience to receive such a thing.

For Garrett it was an embarrassing experience since he was subjected to a mass physical examination. The truth was that he had never had even one physical examination in his entire life, and here was one full day without any clothes. Of course, no one else had clothes either.

He had no trouble with any of the mental and written tests he was subjected to. He thought he was passing the physical examination with flying colors until the doctor whose job it was to examine his heart and blood pressure decided he wanted Garrett to go into Jacksonville to be examined by another army doctor without telling him why.

An MP took Garrett and several other men into a military hospital. He wasted little time getting them there since their buses had to wait on them at Camp Blanding before leaving for their new assignments.

Garrett handed the doctor the envelope from the doctor at Camp Blanding. After studying its contents the doctor said, "Remove your shirt."

The doctor listened closely to his heart and then took his blood pressure. He asked an MP to take him out onto the lawn and have him run for three to five minutes and bring him back.

After the run, the doctor did the exact same exam and said, "Mr. Gregson, you have a heart murmur that will prevent you from being drafted for military service. In addition to this, you have what I consider extremely high blood pressure. I suggest you go to your family doctor when you get home and tell him what we have found and ask him to prescribe treatment. Do you have any questions?"

"No, sir. I will be sure to get him to examine me as soon as I get home," Garrett replied.

The military doctor asked, "Hasn't your doctor ever told you this before?"

"No, sir, I've never been examined before by a doctor. I've never needed it, I guess, but I'm sure glad you told me what you have so that I can have it looked after."

Leaving the hospital, an MP took Garrett and others to the Greyhound Bus station and provided them with a pass home. Garrett couldn't decide whether he was happy or sad at having been rejected for military service. He did want to do his part, yet he really didn't want to leave Mary Fran, his family, and his business. This physical problem was of some concern, but it would allow him the opportunity to really concentrate on his newfound fortune and continue the development of the place.

41

Before the draft was finished with the men in Garrett's operation, it had taken most of his younger men. Beau was gone in a flash. Close behind Beau went Bill Mathews, then Brett Moore and Alan Wright. John Haney, Jim Lawrence, and Jim Morgan did not have to go because of age, but each of their boys did. Those who did not want to be drafted into the army joined the navy or marines in advance. Garrett lost forty-two men to the draft. All he had left were their wives, many of whom worked on the farm, and the older men.

Haney used women to snake logs to the sawmill, and he was back using them in the saw operation itself. The farm and grove operation was run almost totally by older men and women. For all practical purposes, the pasture improvement and fencing operations had ceased since Bill and Beau were no longer there. Garrett did find some older cattlemen who acted as caretakers to watch over the animals, but it was a job he considered his. This, added to his regular responsibilities, kept him on the move.

Because of the loss of men, Garrett decided he must become more mechanized. Instead of using oxen to snake logs to the mill, he bought small tractors that could be used in the groves and pastures. Instead of clearing land by hand, he purchased a bulldozer. The large tractor could clear considerably more land in a day than all the field laborers together normally did. Mechanization took the place of men, and not much momentum was actually lost. The women continued to take care of the company garden and work inside the vegetable packing houses.

42

As the war in Europe and the Pacific heated up, the demand for farm products and beef also increased, becoming so great that Garrett was overcome with orders he could not fill. He was devastated not to be able to do more.

The problem for him most of the time wasn't providing the farm product, but the labor shortage. Supplying beef also remained a major concern. To meet this need, he found a ranch in southwestern Florida whose labor was almost completely taken by the draft. It was fully stocked.

In desperation to keep up with the demand for beef, he agreed to purchase the ranch with minimal money up front and a long-term mortgage with low interest rates. This presented another problem. His time was now spent on the road running from one operation to the other. The new operation was located in the Moore Haven area. During the early 1940s, there was no easy way to get from central Florida to this area.

Because the vegetable demand had risen far in excess of available supply, he directed the bulldozer to clear black land for truck farming instead of more citrus at the moment. He substantially increased this acreage, and with the addition of several tractors, he had little problem with working the new land. His problem now was enlarging the packing facility and locating parts for his machinery. His problems never ended.

One problem was constant. He couldn't buy new tractors because the former plants from which he ordered them had been converted to defense production. Used tractors were the normal purchase. Because of this, spare parts became the needle in the haystack. Here is where the Alabama folks shined. They had never operated with new equipment. All they knew was keeping junk equipment wired together and taking parts from an unused tractor and placing it on another for a day or the duration. For this reason, Garrett began to buy used tractors for spare parts. He had a very valuable junk pile.

The timber operation was having a great deal of trouble keeping up with demand. This was primarily because of the fact that most of the men who had been drafted worked in this operation. Because of this, Garrett sent Jim Morgan to Alabama to recruit more labor. In a few days he was back with almost twenty men well past middle age. Arrangements were made to house the single men, with the promise that their families could come as soon as housing could be secured.

With the changes made in the operation, Garrett was making new strides in keeping up as best he could with the demands of the market. He was now utilizing every acre of land he could to the best advantage with the available labor. He was developing an extremely profitable operation from almost all the ventures in which he was involved. Of course, the real brains behind the profits belonged to Henry, who constantly watched the income and expenses.

Garrett, of course, had never witnessed a time when the entire country was pulling together in an attempt to feed the folks at home while taking care of the boys overseas. Everyone had a part in a cohesive group vitally interested in doing everything possible to not only win the war but also to take care of its own. Allegiance to the country was at an all-time high. Folks were buying war bonds and stamps. Gas was rationed, but no one really minded because they knew the reason for the policy. Sugar and other items were also rationed, and everyone lived with this inconvenience. Although many grocery items were scarce, people survived.

While the Gregson operation was moving upward financially at a fast pace, the farm workers didn't suffer quite as much as those who did not have the capabilities to grow much of their food. Salt, sugar, coffee, and flour were really about all they needed in addition to automotive supplies.

With the war raging on two fronts, Garrett gradually took hold of the business while most of his original male employees were now serving in the armed forces. He had never attempted until now to run a business without the support and guidance of Mr. Langford. If it were not for Henry, the banker, and Buford Casey, he would have long since been sucked down the drain. Their expertise kept him afloat. With the war entering its third year, the personal stress from the workload was without let-up, and there was no end in sight!

43

One regret Garrett faced was turning into a real problem: his relationship with Brett and Cassey. When they were married, Cassey immediately thought their economic status was, or should be, equal to Garrett and Mary Fran's. This was not the case by far. Brett being Garrett's first cousin and lookalike, they were very good friends also. They grew up together hunting and fishing and doing all those things boys do. Of course, Alan was always included.

Upon Brett and Cassey's wedding, there was bad chemistry immediately between Cassey and Mary Fran. Because of this, there wasn't the closeness Garrett and Brett had hoped for between their wives. Not that either had done anything to insult or irritate the other. It just happened this way. Cassey was the only person Mary Fran ever knew in which this type of situation occurred. Not a big thing, but there was always Cassey's constant grinding jealousy.

After Brett and Cassey's marriage, Brett asked Garrett for a job. Garrett refused for two reasons. One was that the Depression was winding down, and he really didn't have a job to offer, unless he made one specifically for Brett. With the scarcity of money, he chose not to do this. Garrett also felt strongly that it wasn't good business to hire kinfolks. If Brett hadn't been kin, he probably would have made room somehow because of their closeness.

But because of the closeness and affinity for Brett, Garrett offered to set him up in business. Brett wanted to be partners, but Garrett refused because he did not have time to deal with anything he didn't fully control. Brett, therefore, was frightened to go into business and decided to pass up the offer.

By passing up this opportunity, Brett could find no work, and the two of them were reduced to living with their parents.

Fueled by Cassey's attitude, there was always resentment because Garrett had given so many of the Alabama people employment, and he should certainly be able to find a spot for Brett. To make matters worse, Brett and Cassey had nothing in the way of resources. They were destitute with no prospects for a job.

Garrett's reluctance also came from the fact that the management people in his operation had earned their position. Everyone elevated themselves through the ranks by nothing less than the sweat of their brow. He felt that Brett, with Cassey's constant bickering, wouldn't make it doing the grunt work that was required to work his way up the ladder.

Some months later, Brett softened a bit. He accepted Garrett's offer to set him up in business. Garrett wanted Brett to open a feed, seed, and fertilizer business so that he could do a sizeable portion of The Gregson's Company business with him. Brett, influenced by Cassey, didn't like the idea and decided on a grocery store.

To get started, Garrett advanced Brett the money from his small personal savings. In fact, he advanced him all the money he had at the time. The loan was to be used to stock the store, and when sales were made Brett was to repay Garrett at no interest. Garrett spoke to the owner and secured the building using his personal credit.

To begin with, sales were good. Everything looked rosy. Brett was turning over the stock in a hurry. However, when Garrett inquired, he learned Brett was doing it all on credit. None of the customers had any money to pay Brett. Therefore, Brett had no money to restock for future sales. And now, Garrett had no more money to loan either.

In desperation, Brett went to the bank to borrow money to restock. The only way the bank would agree was if Garrett cosigned the note. The bank's attitude hurt Brett's feelings. Cassey was furious. Because of their failure, she decided it was Garrett and Mary Fran's fault.

Garrett went against his best judgment and the advice of those around him. He cosigned the note for Brett to buy new stock. This action, Garrett figured, was going the last mile.

When Brett was restocked for the second time, sales decreased because of no credit extended to his customers. But Brett had now found a way to stay in business. Cash sales were the only answer during this difficult time. It was a long and difficult process for Brett to regain their initial financial position. But now, it was less the money he owed Garrett.

Brett and his wife had begun to have personal problems as the success of their business became evident. They wanted children, yet they were unable to have any. This was a constant source of pain. Cassey could never forget the fact that they were beholden to Garrett, even though he did everything possible to help them become successful. After all, Garrett had the most money in the venture and had guaranteed the rest of it at the bank. Brett knew he had to succeed, and Garrett had to see to it that he did.

To make matters worse, Cassey's friends were not the same friends Garrett and Mary Fran enjoyed. Her friends were always telling her how Garrett and Mary Fran lived and how they were taking advantage of Brett and her. It was the sad old story of how the rich get richer and the poor, poorer. Tragically, Cassey believed it.

Brett had talked to Garrett on several occasions about his problems with Cassey. They thought she needed to find a personal interest and pursue it. She disliked the grocery store and would find every reason to keep from working there. She faked sickness along with every possible excuse not to come in. Brett was sure she was drinking more than she should. Some nights there would be no supper prepared, and she would be in no shape to cook it.

When the building next door became available, Brett and Cassey decided to put in a department store and sell clothing and housewares. Because Cassey was determined to be someone she wasn't, she bought clothing for resale that wasn't right for the area. Her clothing purchases were too stylish and high priced for the folks in the settlement. Her customers were not as fashion conscious as she was. These folks were grubbing out a living from the soil. Because of the miserable success in the department store, the grocery enterprise had to struggle to keep the doors open.

Almost a year passed with no success, and Cassey lost her interest in the department store. Her drinking grew completely out of control. Because of this, she didn't keep the store open at regular hours.

What little Cassey did sell she sold on credit, and the credit business was wrecking Brett for the second time. The financial crisis for Brett worsened, and the relationship between Cassey, Mary Fran, and Garrett deteriorated further. She became public with remarks about her failure. She felt she had been taken advantage of by Garrett. She was talking to everyone who would listen.

Garrett and Mary Fran, of course, resented her remarks; however, they decided not to respond publicly. Even though it was their money and credit that put Brett and Cassey into business, this was their thanks.

Brett finally decided the department store must be closed to stop the losses. Debts had piled up, and he was very close to being bankrupt.

On top of all his personal and business problems, Brett was among the very first in the settlement to be drafted. Cassey was now at home to fend for herself, and she was not capable. Because of her excessive use of alcohol, she was placed in a rest home for a few months and eventually sent to a mental hospital.

When Brett left for military service, Garrett assumed the total debt of the store. Because he couldn't afford to absorb the losses, he put a manager in to run the store to keep it from wrecking him financially. With Brett's approval, the manager was to run the store until he returned to take over again.

With the new manager and additional residents at the settlement, the store slowly turned a profit. Garrett was also able to sell some of his beef through the store. With this in mind, he built a small butcher pen and slaughtered cattle on a regular basis for the store.

Because he was doing well by selling beef through the store, he decided to expand his slaughter operation and peddle meat to other stores in the area. This operation quickly turned into a fantastic success.

The beef operation, using the slaughter concept, was the beginning of Garrett's vertical integration in marketing. The calves were not only born on his property to his cows, but they also grew to slaughter weight on his land. He butchered them in his slaughterhouse and peddled them to stores without any middleman. Garrett liked this concept and decided to extend this type of marketing to all his other operations.

Cassey never recovered. In fact, she became so confused, she could not recognize anyone and didn't know who or where she was. When she died, Garrett buried her beside her parents.

Sadly, Brett was killed in Austria near the end of the war. He was also buried beside Cassey.

Being of a sensitive nature, Mary Fran never quite fully recovered from the rumors Cassey started about their relationship, even though when Cassey was admitted to the mental hospital, it was Mary Fran who saw that her personal needs were met. Mary Fran made sure that Cassey was adequately taken care of right up to her death, and she did it as if Cassey had never uttered any bad remarks about her or Garrett.

Garrett had always been thick-skinned and was more prone to let others' remarks about him slip off his back. Of course, they concerned him, but he felt when he was doing the best he could, then that was all he could do and no more could be accomplished. Therefore, after so long a time, whatever

Cassey had to say about him didn't matter. When Brett was killed, it was a sad day for him. After all, the two of them had almost been reared as brothers. Since his parents had passed away, Garrett was actually the only one left to mourn Brett's death. All Garrett could remember was their lives together and Brett's unhappiness in marriage and his miserable business performance. He would have been capable of much more under different circumstances, Garrett thought.

44

The war in Europe and Asia eventually came to an end. Truman's decision to drop the atomic bomb on Japan quickly brought the Japanese to their knees.

Within a few months after Truman's decision, all Garrett's men who had been drafted and were still alive were sent home. It was both a happy and a sad time for everyone in Garrett's employ. Forty-two men were drafted, but only thirty-seven were to come home. Of course, the grief was shared with the affected families regarding the husbands and fathers and sons who didn't make it. It was particularly painful during the initial grieving, but painful also when the others returned and there was celebration for them.

Because the wartime years had been good for Garrett, as a gesture of kindness he rented a house on Marco Island and as each serviceman came home, Garrett arranged for him and his family to be reunited during a few days there. It was totally a goodwill gesture of appreciation on his part. Even though the servicemen did have mustering-out pay, Garrett picked up the entire bill for the few days that each spent on Marco. He also placed each employee on the payroll while they enjoyed the sun.

45

Resuming normalcy, Garrett began again fulfilling the plans for development that he and Mr. Langford had initially visualized by planting citrus, including rejuvenating his citrus nursery. He fenced new lands and cleared new pastures.

In an effort to vertically integrate his citrus operation, he revamped the vegetable packinghouse into a fresh citrus packing facility. When this step was finalized, he decided to stop growing vegetables at the home location. Vegetables would now be grown in South Florida.

Bill Mathews was among the first to come home. He had been wounded in the Pacific and was hospitalized for the last few months of the war. When the war was over the doctors felt his recovery sufficient that he could be assigned to a veterans hospital near home. His homecoming was a happy occasion. The hospital allowed him to accompany Cindy to Marco Island, compliments of Garrett and Mary Fran.

Happiest of all was Beau. For the entire war, he had gone from one job to the other. He was a cook in about every base in the European theatre. He was always working in tents and makeshift operations. When the war was over, coming home to the peace and quiet was like being reborn.

On Beau's first night back, he and Garrett talked most of the night about his wartime experiences. Beau had horrible racial and battlefield experiences, and Garrett felt exhausted after the all-night session.

"Why don't you take a turn at Marco?" Garrett asked.

"I don't want to go anywhere, and besides, I don't have anyone to go with me."

"What would you like to do?" Garrett asked.

"If I really had my druthers, I'd go hunting and fishing with you for a few days. Nothing fancy, just get away and relax like we used to."

"No reason why we couldn't do that. I'm sure Henry can take care of things until we get back."

After telling Mary Fran, Garrett and Beau went to the Gulf fishing, then further south for a few days. It was a quiet and restful time.

46

Beau's early years had been spent with his grandmother Essay James. He took her last name. They lived in the room behind the kitchen in Garrett's father's home. Essay's job was to run the house and primarily care for Garrett after his mother died soon after his birth.

Beau's entire world was Mr. Gregson's backyard and following around the place with him. He was younger than Garrett by a few years, yet they grew up together and shared the same house, table, and family.

Even though Beau's world was limited at the time because he was considered black, he was not limited at the Gregson home. He and Garrett were constant partners, whether they were hunting, fishing, or doing their assigned chores.

Beau had two other friends, Alan and Brett. He was always included in every outing with them if it had to do with hunting, swimming, or fishing.

Because of Essay's reluctance, Beau was never allowed to venture far from her unless it was with his three friends or Mr. Gregson. She did not want him hurt because of his color. Yet he did not have the appearance of a black person since his father was white, yet unknown, and since Essay and his mother were very light-skinned, indicating they might be of some white ancestry also. When the boys were swimming, Beau appeared as one of them in color. His hair was not as other black people's, but straight like the white boys with whom he grew up. Because of Essay's hope for him, she constantly corrected his grammar, and more specifically his accent. He spoke as good, or better, English than most people in the settlement, with absolutely no Southern black accent of the day.

When Essay moved in to look after Mary Fran, Beau had a few sad months alone with Mr. Gregson because his world now was severely limited. Yet, when Mr. Gregson suggested that he help Garrett and live there also, Beau only had Garrett when Mary Fran didn't. He was limited again.

Losing his grandmother, he actually lost all connection with the black world because everyone considered him white and one of them. Yet, with all this he was always cautious about how far he ventured out.

Beau's was a world of work, with a few excursions away with Garrett, Alan, and Brett. Sawgrass Simpson was his first introduction to any kind of organized religious activity. He liked and looked forward to the preacher's Wednesday visits.

During World War II, Beau was introduced to a world away from the Gregsons. For the most part it was an acceptable experience, yet he was truly glad to come home.

His world changed significantly when he had the opportunity to meet girls, always white, while in service. He was introduced to a world he never knew existed, and he liked it. He took advantage of this opportunity and wanted to continue a social life after arriving home, yet he was well aware that his activities would have to be limited—that is, until he, Garrett, and Alan were on a fishing trip in Marco that changed his life forever.

Not wanting to haul their small boat to Marco every time they fished, they decided to rent a larger boat from a local guide. The guide sometimes fished with them for fun when he didn't have paying customers.

On one occasion during their first afternoon fishing, they caught more fish than usual. Alan said, "We need to get someone to cook these fish for us for tonight's supper. If we stay until Monday like we have planned, they won't last to get them home."

Garrett spoke up, "Yeah, I'd like that too, but who would cook them since we didn't bring a frying pan?"

Barney, the guide, said, "Maybe my daughter, Trish, would cook them. I can ask her."

"That's a good idea, Barney," Garrett said. "What do you think, Beau?"

"Sounds good," he said.

No one had ever noticed anyone else living with Barney. Yet when Barney went into his house to ask Trish if she would cook the fish, she came back with him and took the fish around behind the house to clean them prior to cooking. Beau instinctively went with her to help out.

Barney's deceased wife was part Seminole Indian. Trish's complexion was exactly the same as Beau's. She was truly a beautiful and shapely woman who took pride in her dress and appearance. Because of this, it wasn't difficult for Beau to want to help with the fish. For some reason he was drawn to her from the moment of his first glance.

Beau noticed Trish had a very slight limp, like someone who needed one shoe built up to be level with the other. It was only very slight and he didn't inquire. He later learned through Barney that she was in a tragic automobile accident and almost didn't recover. One leg was broken in several places. Her pelvis was fractured, and she had lower internal injuries that required extensive surgery to correct. She couldn't have children because of the accident.

Knowing he was on shaky ground, Beau tried to become acquainted with her over the messy job of cleaning fish. She was pleasant enough and wanted to talk, but she was more interested in learning about Beau than telling him about herself.

As they were finishing the fish and before taking them into the house, Beau asked her, "Could I come back sometime and maybe we could go fishing together?" This question was all he could come up with in the quick moment he had.

"Sure," she said. "I'd like that." This was all that was said.

A couple of weeks passed, and Beau asked Garrett for Barney's telephone number. Garrett immediately thought Beau wanted to call Trish, and he gave Beau the number.

After the office was closed, Beau went to Garrett's phone and called Trish. She was delighted to have him call, and they made a fishing date for the coming weekend.

At the time Beau had not bought any sort of transportation because everyone was in line for a new car to be produced after the war was over. So he borrowed Garrett's pick-up and left on Friday afternoon after work.

Beau arrived at about midnight at the little shack Barney always rented to them. A note waited on the pillow for Beau to come to the house if he was hungry, and he was.

Trish was sitting on the front porch and invited him in. Barney was out with his friends for the night, and Trish had a meal already prepared in the kitchen.

Their conversation went well, and they enjoyed each other's company—so much so that they sat up the rest of the night. Not being able to fish early, they slept in and met about lunch on the dock. Trish had a lunch she had prepared, and they went out in the boat to the mangroves. They found a small spit of dry land and took their lunch there.

They continued to enjoy each other and didn't fish at all that afternoon. They decided later in the afternoon to go out someplace for supper. Beau was a little shaky about it since he had not told her of his background but chanced it anyway. Nor had she told him of her Indian blood.

They went to a place in Ft. Myers where they were not known, and everything went well. It was a good meal, with great conversation.

When Beau walked out on the dock the next morning, Trish was already there with a lunch and the boat ready to launch. In no time, they were back at the very same dry spit and picnicking again.

During the night, Beau decided he could not continue to keep his background from Trish. He liked her very much, and he realized that telling her about him might mean he would not be welcomed anymore. He was extremely anxious and downright fearful of telling her. The longer he considered his options, the more he knew he should not tell her. Then he thought, on several occasions, *I can't let our relationship continue on an untruthful basis. If I don't tell her, she might break it off when it would hurt most.* So, after lunch was finished they lay down side by side under a mangrove.

"Trish, there is something I need to tell you," Beau nervously began. "Something I hope won't make any difference, but yet I feel obligated to say."

"What, Beau?" she asked.

"My grandmother was part white and my father was white, yet there is black blood in my background. You can see I have no features of a black person, yet I felt compelled to tell you before our friendship continued." He sat up and looked the other way.

Trish saw what was happening and was aware that up to this point he had not even tried to hold her hand, nor kiss her, and now she was putting it all together. He was afraid of what she might think if he did.

She sat up, got to her knees, crawled around to his front side, sat down in his lap facing him, put his face in her hands, and saw his eyes begin to glisten. Witnessing this, her tears started to flow. She looked into his eyes for a long moment and kissed him squarely on his lips. She then embraced him, he responded, and both had a happy cry.

Gaining control, Beau asked, "Why are you crying? I have something to cry about. You don't."

"Beau, I'm in the same shape as you. My mother's parents were Seminole. She married Barney. Barney is Creole. That's why we have similar skin. My mother was killed in the same accident that almost killed me. For the first time in my life I've found a person I like, and I'm not ashamed of my ancestors nor the person I like." She planted another kiss, and he responded.

Beau was not completely innocent in the ways of the world. During the war he had had plenty of encounters in other countries with women who could never trace him.

Beau and Trish spent until dark relishing their good fortune. They smooched away the day. Of course, this caused Beau to have to drive most of the night back home with no fish. No fish was difficult to explain. Everyone who suspected something wanted an explanation regarding why there were no fish.

Beau told Garrett on Monday what had happened, every detail. Garrett was happy that Beau had found someone with whom he could be friends. Beau walked around on air for the entire week.

Beau called Trish from the office Thursday night for the purpose of just talking. Trish invited him to come down since Barney was guiding a group to the Keys for a week's excursion beginning Friday. Beau accepted, provided he could borrow the truck.

"Beau, you are going to wear that old truck out between here and Marco. You may have to move," Garrett kidded.

Trish was waiting for Beau at the front door, and they decided to spend the night in the main house together. It was a weekend both remembered fondly.

Beau and Trish were married in Garrett and Mary Fran's living room. Rev. Boggs performed the ceremony. They took a weeklong wedding trip to Miami in Beau's new car, and they lived behind the big house in the same little house Essay and Beau had always lived in.

Beau and Trish were very well accepted by Garrett's workforce. In fact, the employees threw a fine wedding reception with food and drink far beyond what the newlyweds ever thought would occur for them.

They lived happily together. For the first time in his life, Beau didn't eat at the table with Garrett and his family. He now had his own. Trish pitched in and worked the garden and in the packinghouses just like the rest of the women.

When they vacationed, they always returned to some place that had been a happy experience for them, or they researched new, distant places. They had no children because Trish couldn't, and both agreed her misfortune was the best thing that could have happened for them. They belonged with Garrett and Mary Fran, living out their lives in comfort and what later turned out to be luxury.

47

Being eleven years old, Billy was now old enough to be assigned some farm chores. One of the jobs he liked best was taking care of the cow ponies. Billy's first love was horses, and he was becoming a good horseman. He took great pains to see that they were cared for adequately.

The dogs were another of his responsibilities. He took care of them and played with them every spare moment. The dogs were second nature and a wonderful part of his life. Sometimes the dogs would not mind the cowboys because of Billy's constant playing with them. They were beginning to play instead of driving and catching cattle.

Since the first day of the cattle operation, there were always four dogs. Buford and Booger were the catch dogs. They both had some bulldog mixed up in their ancestry.

Gator and Precious were drive dogs. Their job was to bunch the cattle and move them in the direction the cowboys wanted them to go.

Buford, Booger, and Gator all had very good dispositions and were easily handled. Not so with Precious. She was a female and the meanest dog on the place. She was very unpredictable and vicious. Only a few of the men could handle her. Billy could handle her because he fed her. Whoever was in the kitchen at the moment could handle her because the back door is where she ate. Few others were able to handle her, even with a cow whip.

The saga of the dogs was a strange story. When one died or was killed, the replacement dog always had the same name of the one being replaced. There had been many dogs on the place, all with the same four names.

Other than tending to the cow horses and dogs, Billy liked to work with the cattle themselves. Herding them and tending to their needs—like treating them for screwworms and giving them internal worm medicines—were the things he liked best. Billy didn't like grove work at all and only very few of the jobs in the packinghouse. However, he always did the job he was asked to do.

He definitely did not like being a part of slaughtering the cows. He always fell in love with the cattle and did not want to be a part of killing them. He was too kindhearted.

Billy wasn't a mean boy, but he was filled to overflowing with mischief. He liked to have fun, and he vanished many times when he was supposed to be doing chores. Chances were that he had talked some of the other boys into going to the Bath Pond for a swim since he wasn't allowed to swim alone. Sometimes he would take a leisurely horseback ride and become oblivious to time.

Billy's favorite cow pony was Peanut. Peanut was a smaller bay gelding with plenty of cow savvy. All the cowboys liked to ride Peanut when they were driving cattle—that is, if Billy wasn't along with them. Billy had begged his dad to let Peanut be his very own. He wanted a horse that no one else rode, the way his dad had his own horse. Peanut fit the bill perfectly and was the perfect horse for Billy.

Garrett had thought long and hard about giving Peanut to Billy and had decided, in his own mind, that he would do just that on the next occasion that called for a present for Billy. However, at this point in time, Peanut still belonged to the cowboy who could get to him first when a horse was needed. Everyone liked Peanut because he was an exceptional cow horse and also had a great disposition.

Garrett didn't mind Billy riding Peanut whenever he had a chance, yet he always warned him that cow horses are trained to stop and turn very quickly. Even an experienced rider sometimes had problems staying in the saddle.

Billy felt that with Garrett and Beau fishing, he could treat himself to a ride on Peanut. Billy usually rode through the pastures and into the swamps and thickets, imagining all sorts of cowboys and renegades. He always had a good time doing this, and he always encouraged the dogs to go with him. Somewhere along the way the dogs would seek a mud hole or a lake or ditch or something with water in it to cool off, and they usually remained in the first water hole until Billy came back.

On this particular afternoon Billy and Peanut had been out as deep as Peanut's neck in a small lake. Both had taken a swim. They wandered around the pastures south of the farm buildings. No one was nearby other than cattle while they galloped around having a good time.

There was an oak thicket with cow trails all through it. The trails were just wide enough for a horse and rider. All the saplings were about six inches in diameter and fifteen feet tall. Sometimes the horse would get too close, and a severely skinned knee would be the result for the rider.

On this particular afternoon, Billy and Peanut both knew better, but they decided to gallop through the thicket. They successfully traveled one trail all the way through and decided to try another one. The two were at full gallop and then came to a sharp turn in the trail. Peanut had no trouble making the turn and Billy was doing his best to hang on. What Billy didn't know as they made the turn was that before them was a sapling pushed into another by a bull or cow, and it was across the trail.

Billy saw the tree but was going too fast to stop. He then decided to reach up and grab the sapling with both hands and let it push him off the back of Peanut. All this was happening so fast that he did not have adequate time to assess the situation accurately. He had to make up his mind fast and act.

Peanut went under the sapling while Billy reached up to grab for it. His problem was that he missed the sapling, and it hit him squarely across the forehead, savagely knocking him off Peanut.

Late in the afternoon, when the fencing crew came to the barn at quitting time, they found Peanut standing at the gate of the barn with his bridle on. One of the men took him to his pen and fed him, thinking Billy had forgotten to do so.

The crew foreman thought he should report the situation to someone and located Henry at the office. "Mr. Henry, as we came to the barn at quitting time, we found Peanut standing at the gate with his bridle on. I don't know if he got away from someone who was riding him or what happened. We put him up and fed him. I thought someone ought to know."

"That's fine," said Henry. "I'll take care of the matter."

Henry was busy trying to balance a bank statement and thought little of Peanut being found at the barn gate. Soon he had forgotten all about the incident.

One of the things Billy could always be counted on every evening was to be on time for dinner. When he didn't show up, Mary Fran began to worry.

"Jay, do you know where Billy is?" she asked.

"No'm, I don't. I been off with the Haney kids all afternoon, and I haven't seen him. I wish he would come on to supper so we could eat though. I'm hungry."

Mary Fran went to the barn to see if Billy was with the horses. Henry was just finishing up his day at the office. Mary Fran said to Henry, "Henry, have you seen Billy? He hasn't come home for supper, and this just isn't like him. He is usually here early and nibbling."

"No, I sure haven't," replied Henry.

"Well, maybe he is at the barn with the horses. I'll just walk there and see," Mary Fran said.

Henry made his way toward his quarters when Peanut's mysterious behavior came to mind. With this thought, he went straight to the barn. Negotiating the sand wasn't easy with his crutches, but he managed to make it and heard Mary Fran calling Billy.

As he approached her she heard his labored breathing and saw his limited mobility and said, "Henry, what are you doing here?"

"I don't know if this has anything to do with Billy, but the fencing crew came to the office just a bit ago with the news they'd found Peanut standing at the barn gate when they knocked off. They put him up and fed him and thought they ought to tell someone. Peanut could have gotten away from him, and Billy is on his way in."

"I'll bet Peanut is part of the mystery behind Billy's disappearance," Mary Fran said. "You go home, Henry, and I'll call Bill and ask him to help me look."

The more she thought of what had happened, the more she knew Peanut had something to do with Billy's absence. Thinking about it, she became frightened. The more she thought of it, too, the more her mind ran away with her, playing tricks on her and impairing her reasoning capabilities. She knew she needed help.

When she telephoned Bill Mathews, Cindy answered. "Cindy, has Bill gotten home yet?"

"No, not yet, Mary Fran, but I expect him any minute now. Can he call you when he comes in?" Cindy asked.

"Yes, the minute he walks in the door."

The minutes dragged into endless moments of panic waiting for Bill to call. She kept telling herself that Billy was okay and that she would have the problem in hand soon. She further panicked when she realized that if Billy was in fact hurt, Garrett was fishing. How could she locate Garrett? *Where was he? Would he call in tonight?*

Bill mustered every available employee and their wives for the search. Some rode horses while others drove trucks and tractors. All of them were calling Billy's name, moving and searching.

Bill was aware he had about one and one-half hours of daylight left when the search started and so much acreage to cover. If Billy had ventured very far, daylight might run out. Regardless of the time element, Bill knew everyone would be on the job until Billy was found.

John Haney was visibly shaken about Billy's absence. His wife was one of Billy's closest friends because of her relationship within the Gregson home. Many times Sally would bring Billy home with her for one reason or another, and because he was such a likeable boy the entire Haney family loved him.

John was the first to come upon the oak thicket atop a slight sandhill. The thicket was about two acres, and he was really undecided whether to waste time going into such a place because he knew Billy would probably avoid it.

Just as he started to walk away he heard a dog bark and remembered Bill's instructions: "Not to let a stone go unturned." John turned around and walked in.

Walking through the thicket, John noticed a trail crossing the one on which he was walking. This trail was so thick, he couldn't understand how anyone would want to enter, given the briars and limbs in the path of the trail. Exiting the other side after walking the first trail, he felt it useless to go back in and walked away.

He heard the dog again. However, because he ran the sawmill he wasn't familiar with the sound of the cow dog bark. But then if Billy was on the other trail and was hurt, he would never forgive himself if he didn't investigate it.

John crossed the halfway mark where the second trail crossed the first. Making his way through the balance of the trail, John thought how it was getting dark and everyone would need some sort of light to finish the search if Billy wasn't found soon.

He was about out of the thicket when the trail made a sudden left-hand turn. Making the turn, John immediately saw Billy lying there with blood all over his face. John then had another problem that he originally felt was much more serious. All four dogs had taken up positions on either side of him. The worst part was that Precious was between him and Billy.

John couldn't, because of the coming darkness, visualize what had happened. He also knew he had to get past Precious to get to Billy. John began to talk to Billy. Billy didn't answer. He just made a low moaning sound.

Not knowing what else to do, John approached Billy and said, "Come on with me, Precious. Let's see if we can't help Billy." Precious moved aside as John approached and let him kneel beside Billy.

Billy only moaned, never spoke. John knew better than to try and move him, but he could tell Billy probably wasn't very comfortable, given the way his body was positioned on the ground. Nevertheless, John decided not to touch him but to go for help. He turned to the dogs and yelled "stay," pointing his finger at them.

Exiting the thicket he saw several ranch hands on horseback. He instructed one of them to ride to the office and ask Henry to get an ambulance and for him to wait until the ambulance arrived and bring it to the thicket. He instructed another to locate Bill and Mary Fran and bring them to the thicket. He asked the other to tie his horse and come into the thicket with him.

As they approached Billy's body, they heard him moaning with a little greater force. The dogs backed up and John thought Billy opened his eyes momentarily.

"Billy, can you hear me?" John asked.

Nothing came from Billy but a moan. His moaning was in the same rhythm as his breathing.

John took a sweat rag from his pocket and tried to remove the coagulated blood from Billy's face and eyes. He didn't want Mary Fran to see all this, yet he knew better than to wipe his forehead where the wound itself was located.

John spoke to one of the ranch hands. "Take this rag and find the cleanest water available. Wet it and bring it right back to me. Make it snappy." When the man turned to run, the dogs almost caught him since he startled them. John's quick reaction stopped them.

Returning, the hand said, "Here is the best available, Mr. Haney," and handed him the wet rag.

Time stood still for John, who now realized that Billy was in serious trouble if help didn't come soon. He dreaded the thought of facing Mary Fran, whom he was sure would make the trip to the thicket once she was aware of what had happened.

Seeing Billy, Mary Fran was devastated. She initially had to be convinced Billy was alive. She spent her time until the ambulance arrived trying to figure out what had happened. When Bill Mathews arrived, his first job was to remove the dogs to someone who could handle them. Since he and Beau normally worked them, they minded him well. He simply had another cowhand take them just a little bit away from where Billy lay, and they gave him no fuss. This action at least stopped the ferocious growling every time another person walked up.

Bill studied the trees and Billy, even finding slivers of the oak bark embedded in Billy's forehead. Figuring out what had happened was fairly simple, given that Peanut's hoofprints were all over the trail.

When the ambulance attendants attempted to remove Billy's body, Bill had to restrain the dogs. Billy was moaning even louder when they moved him. The dogs did not like this and lunged toward the attendants.

When the dogs calmed down, the attendants began their task of removing the boy. Billy was strapped to the stretcher, which would restrict any movement, thus protecting any broken bones he might have.

"Bill, I'm going with Billy in the ambulance. You go to the office and help Henry locate Garrett. John, please ask Sally to look after Jay and M. J. until I can get back," Mary Fran instructed. It was amazing how calm and collected she was at such a scene. The normally easygoing woman, who always yielded in conversation and conviction to Garrett, was in full charge and no one doubted her authority.

Bill said, "Mary Fran, as soon as I can get to Henry and find Garrett, Cindy and I will come to the hospital. In the meantime, call if you should need anything else."

With these words, the ambulance driver took it very easy exiting the pasture. In fact, because of the apparent seriousness of the accident, the ambulance attendants decided not to rush at all for fear of doing more harm to their ride.

48

Arriving at the hospital, the emergency room staff took over and ushered Mary Fran to a small waiting room just to the side of where the doctors were hovered over Billy.

Because of the slow pace of the ambulance, given Billy's apparent condition, Bill and Cindy were just moments behind Mary Fran and were ushered into the waiting room with her. The person assigned to sit with Mary Fran until family or friends arrived quietly left.

"Mary Fran, Henry is working the phone trying to locate Garrett and Beau. In addition, the highway patrol has been alerted to watch for them and send them in," Bill said.

"Has there been any word on Billy, Mary Fran?" Cindy asked.

"None," she replied.

Sordid things were running through Mary Fran's mind as the moments turned into ages in the waiting room. *Was Billy's accident God's way of punishing us for something? Maybe I haven't been the kind of mother I should have been? Maybe I should have kept stronger reins on Billy, and all the kids? Maybe I can make some sort of deal with God if he would just heal him?* She decided her mind was playing tricks on her. *I should get control of my mind and emotions,* she thought.

Wiping tears away and literally shaking with fear, Bill sat down on one side of Mary Fran. Cindy sat on the other, trying their best to console her. Not being able to talk to her, they just sat close, and Cindy held her hand in silence.

Garrett and Beau were driving out from their guide's house. The road out was a lime rock fill along a mangrove swamp.

"I'll bet that last snook weighed at least twenty pounds," Beau said to Garrett as they entered the highway from the Marco coast.

"Beau, you've been around so many liars in the army you have taken up the habit. You know dang well that snook couldn't have possibly weighed more than twelve at the most, probably closer to eight."

"Eight, my butt," Beau retorted.

Just as Beau said this, a siren blasted from behind. Garrett said, "What the heck is wrong now?"

"The law is probably going to get you for trying to convince me my fish weighed less than twenty pounds," Beau replied.

Bringing the truck to a stop off the road, Garrett immediately stepped out and approached the patrolman. "What's the trouble?" Garrett inquired.

"Could I see your driver's license' please?" the trooper asked.

Garrett fumbled with his wallet, finally locating his driver's license. He handed it to the trooper.

Studying the license carefully the trooper said, "Mr. Gregson, I hate to be the bearer of bad news, but I have been instructed to ask you to telephone your office. There has been some sort of accident on your farm and you are needed there immediately."

"Do you know what has happened?" Garrett asked.

"No, sir, I'm very sorry. I don't."

"Thanks, Officer. I'll stop at the next phone and call in."

Garrett called Henry, who said, "Garrett, it is Billy. He had some sort of accident riding Peanut and has been taken to the hospital. Bill and Cindy are there with Mary Fran, and we haven't had any word other than that."

"You call the hospital and tell Bill I'll be there as soon as I can get there. I'm leaving Marco now, and it is probably five hours home," Garrett instructed.

"Yes, sir. You can count on it," Henry replied.

Driving home, Garrett started to stop several times and phone the hospital to try and find out the extent of Billy's injuries. His next decision was that he couldn't waste the time and kept driving. The uncertainty and extent of his injuries were tough for Garrett to take and keep driving. The trip home was tough.

It was past 2 a.m. when Garrett and Beau arrived at the hospital. The security guard directed them to the room where Mary Fran, Cindy, and Bill were waiting. The smell of the hospital initiated fear inside Garrett, and he was soon to experience a moment that was dreadful.

When Garrett entered the room, the three of them were huddled in one corner with their backs to him. As he was walking in front of them and looking into Mary Fran's face, he instinctively knew Billy's condition was not good.

"What happened?" Garrett asked.

Mary Fran started to speak and broke into tears as she stood up and moved toward Garrett. He simply held her until her sobbing ceased. When she was in control of herself, Bill said, "Billy was riding Peanut and was evidently galloping through an oak thicket past the south cow pens. He rounded a curve on a cow trail and collided with an oak sapling that was pushed across the trail. He saw it too late and the sapling struck his forehead, knocking him off the rear of the horse. This was a brutal lick to his forehead. It was a couple of hours before we found him after Peanut came to the barn. It was another hour before the ambulance arrived, which we had to pull part of the way with a tractor because of the wet areas. Because of Billy's condition, the ambulance couldn't move fast, and it was dark before we arrived at the hospital with Billy."

"What's his condition?" Garrett inquired.

Bill continued, "The doctors still don't know his condition. He took a heavy lick to the forehead. The doctors think it's very serious. They are worried about brain injuries."

"Garrett, what are we going to do?" Mary Fran asked.

"We have no choice but to wait and see what the doctors think about his condition, and they will direct us what to do."

"But what if he dies?" Mary Fran asked.

"Mary Fran, you know we will do everything we can to keep him alive. Why don't we see what we have to worry about and the battles we have to fight before we begin worrying about something we know nothing about?" Garrett replied.

At around 3:30 a.m. the doctor came to the waiting room as he was leaving to go home for the rest of the night. "It looks like Billy's condition has finally stabilized," the doctor said. "He's a long way from out of the woods, but for now he's resting and his vital signs are within acceptable ranges."

"Do you know the extent of his injuries?" Garrett asked.

"No, sir, I'm sorry to say. I can tell you his injuries are confined to his head. There are no broken bones or injuries of any kind except to his head. Now, the nature of the injuries are still unknown," the doctor concluded.

"Is he conscious?" Garrett asked.

"No. He is in a semiconscious state when we try to awaken him. We had a problem stabilizing his heart rate and blood pressure. It was all over the board. I can also tell you his temperature is rising at a very slow rate. I can't tell you how far it will go, but it is on the rise presently."

"What's the next step?" Garrett inquired.

"I'll be back around 9 a.m. if not called before. We will further evaluate his case and determine the next move."

Garrett asked, "Can we see him?"

"Sure," the doctor said. "Follow me."

Entering the complex next to the emergency room, they passed a number of very sick patients in various stages of consciousness. Billy's bed was enclosed by curtains and was next to the last in the long line of patients. When they arrived there was a nurse by his side who looked very gentle and who was holding his hand and talking to him even though he was asleep. She gradually backed away when she saw them.

Garrett could only see his face since the rest of his body was covered. There was swelling around the injured area. Billy was in no apparent distress and appeared to be resting easy.

The group of people gathered around his bed and silently looked at him for a moment. When it was apparent there wasn't going to be any sort of response from him, they followed the doctor back to the waiting room.

The doctor said, "Let me make a suggestion. Why don't you folks go home and get a nap or a bath, and meet me here at 9 o'clock? If you can get a few hours sleep, it would be good for you."

With a very frightened look, Mary Fran said, "Oh, no. I don't think I could leave."

"Mary Fran, we've done all we can. There is nothing you can do for Billy now. Let's go get a bath and be here when the doctor arrives." Garrett stood up and so did Mary Fran, and they silently left the hospital.

After leaving the hospital and when they were in Garrett's truck, Mary Fran said, "Garrett, I couldn't stand it if anything happens to Billy. I feel responsible for him since you were not at home. He's just got to pull out of this."

"He will. You put those kinds of thoughts out of your head. Give him a little recovery time. It will amaze you how a strong kid like Billy can snap back," Garrett said.

Not much more was spoken as they made their way home, except for Mary Fran browbeating herself for not watching him closer while Garrett was away from home.

"Put that kind of talk behind you, Mary Fran. Bill's accident is not your fault. Had I been home, I would have let him ride Peanut, you know that. His accident is not your fault, like it isn't anyone's fault," Garrett said. Mary Fran sat silently and cried. Sally and John Haney were both asleep in the kitchen with their heads down on the kitchen table. Both were anxious for news of Billy.

"It's 4:30, Mary Fran. Let's sleep until 7:30. Sally will look after M. J. and Jay. Let's sleep until then and go back to the hospital," Garrett said.

"Okay, I'll try."

Trying to sleep was no use for Mary Fran. Every time she closed her eyes, she saw Billy as they were loading him into the ambulance. Sleep was impossible, so she got up and went into the kitchen. John and Sally had gone home for a few hours, and Mary Fran made herself a pot of coffee.

When the clock went off at 7:30, Mary Fran was already dressed and ready to go.

"Did you sleep any?" Garrett asked.

"No, I'm afraid not. I just couldn't. Hurry now, Garrett, and let's go."

They were at the hospital by 8:30. The nurse on duty told them Billy was still asleep, just like they left him.

The doctor arrived promptly a 9 o'clock and went directly to Billy's chart and then to his bedside. After a few minutes he returned to the waiting room.

"Folks, I'm sorry to report his condition has worsened overnight." With this news, Mary Fran went into deep fits of weeping. Garrett put his arm around her and retrained his attention on the doctor as she cried.

"I want to call in a doctor who specializes in brain injuries. We need some help that no one here is able to provide. With your permission, there is one such doctor I would like very much to call."

"You call anyone who can help us," Garrett replied. "Where is this person?"

The doctor said, "Unfortunately, Jacksonville."

"Get him here as soon as you can," Garrett said.

Garrett and Mary Fran sat around the hospital waiting room for the rest of the day and far into the night. It would be the next day before the specialist could get to Billy's bedside. Other than the continual rising of his temperature, Billy's condition wasn't changing much. The nurses were not able to get any response from him now. He just lay there. At first he would eat ice and take liquids. Now nothing.

They sat and talked. They tried to diagnose the outcome,

knowing nothing of the seriousness of his condition except that it was bad. They kept trying to predict the outcome, and each time they had to conclude they knew nothing of what they were talking about.

Folks from the farm and the settlement dropped in from time to time to offer encouragement and support. Feeling the concern of those who mattered in their lives was a comfort to Garrett and Mary Fran.

The pillar was Garrett's dad. He seemed to realize when he was needed most, and there he was.

Mary Fran would not leave Billy, and Garrett couldn't leave her alone at the hospital. Even though she couldn't sit with Billy, she couldn't leave. She felt better if she was at least close by. The hours dragged.

As the day changed to night, the small waiting room filled up with folks, not all of whom were talkative, just silently waiting for some word from the doctor. Realizing there were too many people there, they began to drift out after offering their reassurances to Garrett and Mary Fran.

It was about nine in the evening when the doctor came out and said to Garrett, "There is absolutely nothing you can do here. I know you want to be close by, but you should know I've asked the nurses watching after Billy to call you as soon as they notice any change, either good or bad. I'll promise you that if I am called during the night, I personally will alert you of the change. Now, please go home and try to rest. The specialist should be here by noon tomorrow. Can you do this for me?"

"What do you think, Mary Fran?"

"Well, I'll go, but I certainly don't want to," she replied.

"I know you don't want to, but what is the use of tearing yourself down by remaining here when it is so utterly useless? Billy needs you to keep your strength up. The way to do this is to get some rest," the doctor said.

Reluctantly, Mary Fran decided to leave after visiting Billy's room once more. It was tough. She wanted to help so much, yet she felt totally useless because she could do nothing. If he were conscious, there might be some way she could help. Unconscious, all she could do was sit and wait.

On the way home Mary Fran asked Garrett, "What are we going to do if the specialist wants to move Billy to Jacksonville?"

"If he says it is our best hope, we are going to order the ambulance and move. That is all we can do."

There was a long period of silence. Then she asked, "Will we move to Jacksonville to be with Billy?"

"I don't think 'move' is the right word. We will certainly go to Jacksonville for the duration and stay close by. Don't worry about something like this, Mary Fran."

"Well, if we go to Jacksonville, you certainly won't leave me up there, will you?" she asked.

"Only if it is absolutely necessary, and we find that you can get by alone there," he said.

"You know, I've never even been to Jacksonville. It must be a big town, and it is certainly unfamiliar to me," she said.

Henry met Garrett for a few minutes at the office when they arrived. There were some routine business matters they needed to discuss. He was with Henry less than an hour. When he left, Garrett was confident he could be gone for as long as necessary and his business would be in good hands with Henry. Besides, if it wasn't, he certainly couldn't worry about it now. His family was the most important thing on his mind.

Both Mary Fran and Garrett were sitting at the kitchen table at 5 a.m. when Sally arrived to cook breakfast. They were drinking coffee and looked as though they hadn't slept for days. The night had been horrible. Garrett dropped right off to sleep, only to awaken a couple of hours later finding Mary Fran wasn't in the bed. He found her looking out of the living room window with tears streaming down her face. He couldn't help but think of the times he saw Mrs. Langford at this same window. After some discussion, they decided to try the bed again. Mary Fran mercifully slept for a couple of hours, but Garrett was never able to go back to sleep after he was once awakened. Both were up by 4 a.m., bathing and getting ready for another day at the hospital.

The morning was endless. They both were hopeful of finding Billy improved when they arrived, but their hopes were dampened when they saw him. He was just lying there. It had been three days now, and nothing was happening.

The doctor did his best to help their feelings when he made his rounds. He took great pains in explanation and all the time he could spare to reassure them.

Garrett asked, "When do you think we can expect the specialist to arrive?"

"I can't rightly say. I thought after our telephone conversation he might have taken last night's train or one early this morning. If he left this morning, he should be here not later than 1 p.m. The truth is, I don't know."

Waiting was Garrett's worst character trait. He could not wait on anyone. His worst anger always came when another person had told him he could meet Garrett at a certain time, and then was late. Garrett's day was always planned so that he could keep all his appointments and keep them on time. Now he was being put to the test. Waiting, endless waiting.

Just when the world was collapsing around them, and they couldn't stand another minute of waiting, Garrett's dad walked in. Somehow his strong presence made it all seem better. Now there was some new strength, new muscle to help bear the burden.

Mr. Gregson walked over to Mary Fran, put his arms around her, and said, "You know everyone is praying for Billy. They are sincere prayers from sincere people. Believe that."

"I know, Dad," Mary Fran said with tears streaming off her chin. "Everyone has been so nice and considerate. Everyone has tried to make things easier for us, but I guess there just isn't anything anyone but the good Lord can do now. Of course, we are waiting on the brain specialist from Jacksonville, and we hope he is going to be able to offer some good words."

Garrett's dad turned to him and hugged him just as he always had. His arms felt good to Garrett. He was a strong man with a strong faith. "Son, has there been any change at all in Billy's condition?"

"No, sir. Not that I can tell. If anything, I believe he is even less responsive now than last night."

The doctor came in as they were talking. "The specialist is with Billy now. I hope he will be able to talk to you shortly."

"Has he said anything to you, Doc?" Garrett asked.

"No, he just got here," replied the doctor.

"Keep your chin up," the doctor said as he started to leave.

The specialist was an older man. His hair was white, and somehow the white hair added stability to the situation. Dr. Watson was a tall, stately man of perhaps sixty years of age. He was very confident and sure of himself. Because of this, Billy's family felt good that he had arrived.

"Mr. and Mrs. Gregson, my name is Tom Watson. I've examined your son briefly. I've looked over his chart and reviewed his tests, and I have some things I would like to discuss with you. Would you like to go somewhere private, or is this room okay?"

"This room is fine. This is my dad," Garrett replied.

"Fine," the doctor continued. He took a seat and suggested they all sit. "The medical attention your son has received thus far has been top-flight, though limited in what this hospital can provide. I think Billy has a very severe head injury to the frontal portion of his brain and perhaps some other areas as well. He is not responsive, as you know. He has a temperature, and I can tell you his brain is swelling. There is pressure beginning to form and it certainly will become worse if it can't be alleviated. I wish this hospital had more sophisticated equipment so that we could run more tests, but unfortunately Jacksonville is the closest place with the equipment we need."

"Are you saying you don't have enough information to adequately diagnose Billy's condition?" Garrett asked.

"At this point I don't, and his injuries are so serious I don't want to act on impulse. I can't afford not to be accurate now," the doctor said.

"What do you suggest?" Garrett inquired.

"The best of both worlds would be that we charter an air ambulance and send him to Jacksonville where I can take much better care of him," Dr. Watson said.

"You've got it. Can the hospital order an air ambulance?" Garrett asked.

The nurse standing with Dr. Watson said, "Yes, I can take care of this for you in short order."

Another nurse came for Dr. Watson, "Dr. Watson, can you come?"

Both nurses followed the doctor out of the room.

Mr. Gregson said, "You two get hold of yourselves now. The doctor here can handle this. You've got to believe in him and believe that he can get Billy back on his feet."

It was only a few minutes until Dr. Watson was back. "I'm afraid Billy had a convulsion. It is over now, and I think he is okay for the moment. The air ambulance can leave mid-afternoon. Would you folks like to drive or go with Billy in the ambulance?"

Garrett turned to Mary Fran, asking, "Would you like to go with Billy?"

"I've never flown, but I don't want to leave him," she said. "Do you think it is okay for me to go?"

"Sure, it's okay," Dr. Watson said. "In fact, I will be in the plane myself."

"That's the best news I've had in a long time," Garrett said. "I will drive and arrive sometime tonight."

"That's good," Dr. Watson said. "I'll see you at the emergency entrance as soon as we can get an ambulance to take Billy to the airport." He promptly left the room.

"Mary Fran, you go to the phone and call Sally. Tell her what you will need for me to bring for you in Jacksonville. Also tell her what to pack for me. Tell her to tell Henry to cut out some time for me to talk to him at the office before I leave," Garrett said.

Within a matter of minutes the nurses had Billy ready to travel and loaded into the ambulance for the airport. The doctor got into the ambulance with Billy and Mary Fran. Garrett followed with Mr. Gregson. It was a half-hour drive to the airport, and the little entourage slowly made its way there.

The plane was a small two-motored cargo plane that was occasionally used as an ambulance. It was clean, and the crew was standing by ready to go. It didn't take long for it to get off the ground, and Billy was on the way to get the best help they could provide, which he desperately needed.

Mr. Gregson said to Garrett, "Son, what do you need me to do for you while you are away?"

"Nothing, Dad. Henry can hold it down with the help of the managers. Of course, Beau will be there to help with the kids and help Sally if she needs anything. Why don't you go over to the house and stay there until we know the extent of Billy's injuries? It'll make you feel better, and I can get in touch with you there," Garrett said.

"That's a good idea, and I can get some of Sally's good cooking."

It was late afternoon before Garrett loaded the pick-up with the suitcases and left for Jacksonville. Leaving this late would certainly put him arriving around midnight. It was a long, lonely trip for Garrett. Long in the sense that he didn't know what was happening in Jacksonville. Long also in the sense that he didn't know how Mary Fran was faring in a strange place after her first plane ride. She was also facing the same uncertainties he was. It was a desperate trip, and he knew Mary Fran was counting the seconds until he arrived.

It was 12:45 a.m. when Garrett arrived at the hospital. Mary Fran was sitting in a waiting room that was filled with perhaps thirty others who had the same sad duty, waiting to know the conditions of their loved ones.

When she saw him, she immediately stood up and came to him, saying, "Garrett, I still don't know anything. Dr. Watson came out around ten o'clock and said he was going home. He had finished all the tests for tonight and would know the results early in the morning. Then he left."

Garrett sensed Mary Fran was upset that Dr. Watson had gone home and said, "Well, I'm glad he has the tests behind him. This is a good time for Dr. Watson to sleep while the results are being tabulated. Let's go find a place to stay for the night."

"We aren't going to stay here?" Mary Fran asked.

"No, we'll call them and let them know where we are," he said.

Garrett asked the security guard where accommodations were close by. "Right down the street. It is a hotel that caters to families with hospitalized relatives." He then gave them directions.

Utter exhaustion allowed both to sleep until 7 a.m., which was unheard of for them.

They arrived at the hospital around 8:30 a.m. and made their way to the waiting room. They asked the receptionist about Billy's condition.

"He had a restful night, and we expect Dr. Watson to be in around mid-morning," the nurse replied. She continued, "Have you folks had breakfast?"

"Not yet," Garrett replied.

"Why don't you go to the employees' cafeteria and show them this family pass? They will let you eat there. If Dr. Watson needs you before you can get back, I'll phone down there and get you up here on the double," she said.

Garrett and Mary Fran left for the employees' cafeteria. Mary Fran remarked, "Wasn't that a nice lady?"

Garrett's response was, "Sure was, but everyone has been very nice to us, I think."

Time was dragging again for Garrett and Mary Fran. It seemed as though mid-morning would never come. When it did, the time from then until Dr. Watson's appearance passed even slower.

It was 11:45 a.m. when a nurse came to the waiting room and asked them to follow her. She led them to a private room down the hall and said, "Dr. Watson will be with you shortly."

"Billy isn't going to get well, Garrett. I just know it," Mary Fran said with panic in her voice.

"Don't talk that way. You have to believe, and expect, the best."

Dr. Watson walked into the room at that moment. "Good morning, folks. I hope you got a good night's sleep."

"Well, better than we've been getting. I guess we were both so tired, we couldn't stay awake any longer," Garrett replied.

"Tell us about Billy," Mary Fran asked.

"You know we ran tests last night, which I'm sorry to say haven't told us much more than we already knew. His responsiveness hasn't improved, and we are having a problem feeding him other than through the veins. The thing that disturbs me is that there is a great deal of pressure in his head that must be relieved. We will do this surgically, but not at the moment. This decision will be made later in the day. If necessary, we can schedule it immediately. There is one more test I need to hear about prior to making this decision," Dr. Watson concluded.

"How serious is the surgery?" Garrett asked.

"Anytime you put a patient under anesthesia it is serious. However as surgery goes, and this is considered major surgery, it should be labeled serious. Billy's age and health are the best things he has going for him now."

"If surgery is necessary, you will do it immediately?" Mary Fran questioned.

"That's right," Dr. Watson replied. "However, whether surgery is necessary or not, I have asked a couple of colleagues to come by and evaluate Billy's condition today. I need their input, and they are top professionals in their field."

"Are we looking at a decision by late afternoon?" Garrett asked.

"Yes, unless his condition worsens during the day, which I don't expect."

"We are confident he is in good hands under your care," Garrett said.

"Why don't you folks come with me to visit with Billy for a few minutes and then take some time away from the hospital either to rest or go to lunch and come back mid-afternoon?" Dr. Watson said.

When they entered the room, Garrett felt like he was in another world. This sanitary world seemed to embrace a kid much more fragile than the Billy he remembered. Here was a little boy who was sick, pale, and void of energy and perhaps even life. *This couldn't be Billy,* he thought. The sad truth was, it was Billy. The stark reality of it all hit Garrett with a jolt, a jolt that for a moment he didn't know whether or not he would be able to handle.

Mary Fran walked slowly up to the bed and took Billy's hand and rubbed it. It was completely lifeless.

The two stayed for a few minutes, and a nurse came in to check on him. At this point they left.

It was 6 o'clock when Dr. Watson sent for Garrett and Mary Fran. They were brought to the small private consultation room they had occupied earlier.

"I thought the two of you should know we've done about all the testing and examining we can do without a decision. We've collected all the data we know how to collect, and it is now time for action. Billy's condition is unchanged, and I can't honestly tell you that I think his condition will ever improve," Dr. Watson laid it out bluntly.

His remarks hit Garrett and Mary Fran like a bolt of lightning. Up to now, Dr. Watson had never given them anything but hope, and now he was saying Billy might never get better.

Dr. Watson continued, "I think we should only do sufficient surgery to alleviate the pressure to his brain. Exploratory surgery at the same time would be in order to determine if there are other factors we know nothing about to this point. I think all this should be done in the morning."

Garrett asked, "Has there been any new or different information offered by the other specialists you called in?"

'Unfortunately not," Dr. Watson said. "How do you feel about surgery at this point?"

"We've both known that surgery was a possibility, and I personally have not wanted to have to face such a decision. However, our trust is in you and your knowledge and abilities. Our reliance is in you, Dr. Watson," Garrett said.

"How do you feel, Mary Fran?" Dr. Watson asked.

"I don't know," she said. "I just want Billy well, and if surgery is the way to do it and there is no other way, then let's get on with it as soon as possible."

"Okay. I'll schedule the operating room for first thing in the morning," Dr. Watson said. He continued, "Both of you know there are risks involved with surgery. However, in this case, I really don't believe there is an alternative. Enough time has passed since Billy's accident that he should be making improvement on his own if he is going to. We'll do our best. Now you folks can go in and visit him, and I suggest try to get a good night's sleep, and I'll see you in the morning after surgery."

After a short visit with Billy, they both left. It was a time when they needed support, and they had only each other. It was an uncertain feeling and a time when one wonders if someone else could do better.

When they arrived at their room, the phone was ringing. It was Henry, who had Mr. Gregson on the line.

"Son, what can you tell me about Billy?" he asked.

Garrett went through the entire story. He told him of the surgery scheduled for the next morning.

"What do you and Mary Fran think of all this?" he asked.

"We're both afraid of it. We feel uncertain and uneasy about it all. We don't know what else to do, but we do feel we have the best we can get in a doctor," said Garrett.

"Well, son, I believe you have the best doctor and hospital you can get in the state. Believe that you've done your best, and I'm sure everything will work out. Keep us posted, Garrett," Mr. Gregson said.

"Sure, Dad. I'll call you tomorrow when we have something to report," Garrett said as he hung up.

Both felt much better after some reassurance from Mr. Gregson. They made the effort to go out to supper and returned by way of the hospital for another visit with Billy prior to going back to their room for the night.

49

Entering their room, Mary Fran turned to Garrett and embraced him. She started to sob. Her sobbing was without ceasing until she ran out of breath, at which time she had to pause.

Garrett tightened his embrace, and she felt as if she had gone limp. He held her for a brief moment and said, "Hon, you know we've faced tough times in the past. We will continue to practice what we say we believe, and we will be strong."

He loosened his embrace and they both kneeled at the bedside with arms wrapped around each other. Garrett said, "Lord, you know our problem. We've talked to you several times every day since Billy's accident. Our strength comes from you. We not only ask you to allow Billy some relief from his tragic accident, but provide Mary Fran and me with the strength and backbone to face tomorrow, fully aware your hand is guiding Dr. Watson's hand as he operates on Billy.

"We know you will not place upon our shoulders more than we can bear. We ask for strength and your presence with us as we face tomorrow. Walk with us every step that we might make the right decisions. Amen."

They stretched out on the bed, fully clothed, arm in arm, and mercifully slept the night through.

They were at the hospital by 6 the next morning. They were allowed a brief visit with Billy and then ushered out. The doctor did speak to them briefly with assuring words. He placed his hands upon both their shoulders and offered a brief prayer for Billy's recovery.

Surgery began at 7 a.m. and lasted until after the noon hour. The morning dragged as no other morning ever had.

When Dr. Watson came out, he sat down with them in the conference room. "Billy came through surgery and is in good shape. He will be in the recovery room for some time, and probably won't come out to his regular bed until tomorrow afternoon, if not later. We were able to relocate some crushed bones and hopefully reduce the pressure. We, unfortunately, didn't accomplish much more than this. I believe he will be more responsive after a short recovery from surgery. Only time will tell. I expect him to be much improved over his earlier condition; however, you must prepare yourself for the possibility that he might not be. A brain operation is a tricky and difficult surgery to perform. There isn't much a surgeon can do to rectify severe injury to the brain. We do our best, and Mother Nature does the rest. Mother Nature is usually better at healing than surgeons. I do hope for the best, and I want you two to expect it as well."

"Can we see him now?" Mary Fran asked.

"Sure," the doctor said.

"Remember when we go in, he had his head shaved and has a massive bandage. Don't let it throw you," Dr. Watson said.

He stood up and motioned them to follow him to the recovery room.

50

Two weeks passed, and there was little response from Billy. He would open his eyes when asked or was shaken, but this was about all. He wouldn't talk; however, he did make some sounds of a deep gurgling nature. Worst of all, he was having the seizures more often now.

Dr. Watson said to them, "I can't say I know how you feel because I've never experienced this sort of tragedy with any of my kids. Unfortunately, we've done all we can do for Billy. I wish it had turned out to be more, but I am afraid this is it. I wish I knew where to send you to get more help, but there is nowhere to suggest. Insofar as I know, no one can be of any more assistance."

"Are you telling us this is what we have to expect for the rest of his life?" Garrett asked.

"I'm afraid so. I'm so sorry," Dr. Watson replied.

"You mean he isn't going to get any better?" Mary Fran asked.

"I don't think so. All you can do now is pray for a miracle."

Mary Fran lost all composure. Her mournful sobs were sounding throughout the care unit. Garrett put his arm around her, and Dr. Watson motioned for all of them to enter the private conference room. When Mary Fran regained control, Garrett asked, "How long can he live in this condition?"

"Barring other complications which can occur, like pneumonia, he could live for years or he could die shortly," he answered.

"Will we be able to keep him at home?" Mary Fran inquired.

"You can, but I certainly don't suggest it if there are alternatives you can utilize."

"What type facility are you referring to?" Garrett asked.

"Some type of nursing facility with twenty-four-hour care is best," Dr. Watson said.

"What if we provided twenty-four-hour care at home? Will he need specialized medical equipment?" Mary Fran asked.

"You can try this, but I don't recommend it for your sake. I know you have other kids, and this would not be in their best interest. The main reason being you—Garrett and yourself—will never be finished for the day. You can never relax, and this isn't good. Your home's use is intended for relaxation, and you can't with this type situation. His needs will be simple, like administering medication on time and someone to be close by twenty-four hours each day."

"When does this decision have to be made?" Garrett asked.

"Whenever you are ready to make it. He will be perfectly fine here until that time comes."

Garrett and Mary Fran decided to go home for a visit with M. J. and Jay for a few days and make the decision and follow through. It was difficult to think about Billy not ever being responsive and full of life as he once was. He was the perfect child, full of life, yet submissive to parental control. It was a blow to have been told what to expect for the rest of his life.

Garrett knew instinctively Mary Fran was opting to keep Billy at home, yet he knew in his own mind that Dr. Watson was right. Quitting time would never come if Billy were at home.

It was late afternoon before the couple could leave for home. When they returned to their room, Mary Fran completely collapsed in tears, and they flowed all the way home. Garrett felt that if she couldn't handle Billy's condition and get hold of herself, she might suffer some sort of personal sickness.

This was a tough decision and of a degree of seriousness they had never before faced. In fact, few had.

It was well after midnight when they arrived home. Because of the newness of the decision in front of them and because it was one of a frightful nature, they didn't talk a great deal about it as they drove. Most of the time they were sitting silently, considering the options that faced them with Billy. Occasionally, after a long pause, one would ask the other a question relating to Billy, and they briefly discussed his recovery prospects.

The big question was never brought up, yet they both knew what they had to decide.

Arriving home, the few hours in their bed were spent sleeping more soundly than they had known for some time. Garrett was particularly worn because he and Beau didn't do lots of sleeping while they were fishing. The only sleep they had in Jacksonville was when they were completely exhausted and sleep came before they collapsed.

Garrett was in his office by daylight, reviewing the current status of his business. Henry was there when he had arrived and it took them all morning to discuss the problems and decision they had to consider. Even with the load of business worries, Garrett could not keep his mind off Billy and his problems. The phone rang constantly with friends around the community inquiring about Billy.

Mid-morning Mr. Gregson came in and closed the door to Garrett's office. "I've heard around the farm the news isn't what we had hoped for with Billy."

"That's right, Dad," Garrett began, and for the first time he lost his composure. Of course, he and his dad had faced this sort of moment before, but this time it was Garrett's son and totally different. Mr. Gregson moved over beside Garrett and put his arm around him and held him tight as he himself shed tears. After a few minutes, Garrett said, "Billy's life isn't going to have much quality to it from here on out." Tears began streaming down his cheeks and he was unable to speak. In a fit of desperation he put his face in his hands and sobbed.

Observing Garrett, Mr. Gregson wasn't able to control himself either, and the two sat crying. They wept until they had it under control a few minutes later. Henry heard what was going on and left the office, locking the front door behind him.

"I can only imagine how tough it is, son. It's tough anytime something happens to one of your family members. You must remember not to give up, because God is still in charge. He has something in mind for you and Mary Fran. Time will tell you what it is. Maybe the doctors don't give you much hope, but there is still one Power higher than all the doctors, and I believe He has the power to heal Billy. Whether He will or not is not for us to decide. Never forget that, and always pull and pray for his complete recovery."

Garrett responded, "I know, Dad, and we haven't given up. We'll make it somehow."

"I know you will, and you remember everyone here is praying for his recovery and praying that Mary Fran and you will find sufficient strength to see it through, whatever the conclusion. You've got lots of friends and lots of support."

51

When Mr. Gregson left, Mary Fran was coming across the office lawn. "Garrett, everybody is trying to be helpful and everyone is inquiring about Billy. The phone hasn't stopped all morning, and the house has been full of people with the best intentions, but it is all about to drive me insane," she said.

"I know, the same thing has happened to me. Tell you what, you call Sally from here and tell her to deliver us a couple of sandwiches and a thermos of coffee and we'll take a horseback ride," Garrett said.

"Sounds good to me," and Mary Fran picked up the phone.

"Come to the barn when you get them, and I'll have the horses saddled," he said.

Mary Fran was there before Garrett had the horses saddled. As they rode out from the stable, Peanut was in the corral and looked as though he had lost his last friend. He was standing with his head down and hardly noticed them as they passed. Their eyes moistened passing by the little cow pony.

Garrett had no idea where they would ride, but he did know they wouldn't be back anytime soon. They rode out through the new ground where pasture was being planted. They skirted the orange grove and the laborers. They rode through a portion of the vegetable farms and talked about everything but Billy.

Eventually they came to the oak thicket where Billy was injured. Both left their horses outside the thicket and walked to the spot where he was injured.

When they came to the curve in the cow trail, they both stopped and looked quietly for a moment, and when their eyes eventually met it was more than they could take. They each held the other and sobbed uncontrollably. It was several minutes before either had any composure at all, and it was the first time this had happened. Until this time Garrett had been able to remain in control, but not now. They both wept unashamedly until they wept no more.

They moved over to a fallen tree and sat on it looking at the spot where Billy was hurt. "Garrett, I can't get Billy out of my mind. I can't close my eyes without seeing him with that bandage lying in that bed."

"I'm having the same trouble. It never leaves me."

She continued, "I'm glad others are trying to show their support and concern, but I've told the same story so many times it is like a broken record. I feel like I'm operating on nervous energy, and I'm weak in the stomach and can't eat. I can't sleep, and I can't bear the pain of Billy's condition."

"It is the same with me."

She said, "You sure don't look like it most of the time."

"Maybe not. Pain is invisible, yet the pain is still in there," he said.

With saying this, Garrett moved closer to Mary Fran and put his arm around her, bowed his head, and said, "Lord, we don't know what to do. Our son who is precious to us is severely injured, and you know we've already come to you on countless occasions over the last few days asking for help. We've secured what has been reported to us to be the best medical attention we could provide him. The doctors have done their best, and we believe their talents came from you, yet we've got some decisions to make and we don't know what to do. Speak to and lead us, as we come to the best decision on Billy's behalf that we can make. He is totally in your hands. Amen."

"Okay, Mary Fran, it comes down to you and me, with God's help. What do you think?" Garrett asked.

"First, I cannot leave him in a place where I cannot visit every day," she said.

He replied, "Okay, what options do we have?"

She said, "The first option I want to consider is bringing him home. I believe the familiar surroundings would be helpful for him. If we can do this, it would be best for our family."

"You don't think there might come a time when he will need more medically than what we can provide?"

"This is not the time to discuss that, and we will talk then about moving him."

"How can you get any rest if he is home?"

"How could I get any rest running back and forth every day to see about him? I wouldn't have any time with the other kids."

"How much additional help will you need?"

"I don't know, and I can't think about that now. We'll have to wait and see what it takes," she said.

"Okay. We'll bring him home. You call Dr. Watson in the morning and tell him our decision, and ask him what sort of equipment we will need to care for him, and we will bring him home as soon as we can get it all together."

Garrett privately thought Dr. Watson could talk her out of bringing Billy home. He was beginning to see the wisdom in providing for him elsewhere.

It was almost sundown when they left the oak thicket. It was dark when they passed Bath Pond, and both decided a swim would be good for them. They also took up some more "honeymoon business" while they were at Bath Pond, which had a way of making things "alright," even if just for a little while.

52

Dr. Watson was not thrilled about their decision to bring Billy home instead of placing him in a nursing home. But when he saw they were determined, he agreed and listed the equipment, facilities, and assistance they would need.

Mary Fran was busy for a couple of days painting the room and redecorating it. She picked a room close to the kitchen so that Sally could help look after Billy, and if any extra help was hired, they could use the back wing or the kitchen wing as their part of the house. The rest of the family normally lived in the front wing, and that is also where their bedrooms were located.

It took the ambulance most of the day to come from Jacksonville to the house. It was a slow trip that seemed never to end. Mary Fran rode in the ambulance with Billy. Garrett followed along behind. There was a nurse who accompanied them, and she told Mary Fran that it would be good therapy if whoever was watching after Billy talked to him. Talk to him just as if he were responding to the conversation. Don't ask him questions, just talk to him. She said further that this would also help the caregiver.

Billy's room was fixed to look after him, including a hospital bed she bought and had set up. She had more light fixtures installed and a sink nearby.

It was set so that she and Sally could watch after him during the day with additional help during weekends. In addition, there were those who would come in for the night every night so that he could be adequately cared for.

Billy actually didn't know he'd been in an ambulance, had surgery, and was now in his bed at home. The truth was he didn't realize he'd been to Jacksonville.

Sally fussed around trying to get him to eat. He did eat sparingly at around 9 o'clock just prior to her going home.

The night sitter had come, and Mary Fran was giving her instructions as to how she wanted her to care for him. In an instant Billy straightened out stiff in the bed, opened his eyes wide, and was straining every muscle in his body with his mouth clamped shut. He bit his tongue and it was bleeding. His face began to turn blue. After a few minutes, maybe two or three, he went limp. All during this time, Mary Fran and the sitter were frantically trying to do something that was effective for him, yet nothing seemed to work.

When it was over, Mary Fran sat down in the chair unable to stand any longer. "Is he dead?" she asked.

The sitter reassured her with the words, "No, ma'am, he isn't dead. He's had a convulsion. He is now over it, and he has passed out. I'm sure he'll come around in a few minutes and be okay."

"I don't know if I'll ever be okay again," Mary Fran said. "That came close to scaring me to death."

"I've been sitting with patients for a long time. A convulsion is a scary thing to watch, but the truth is there isn't much you can do for one. In fact, nothing except keeping them from biting their tongue. When it's over, it's over," she said.

Mary Fran weakly left the room when she thought Billy was okay. Garrett was in the living room with M. J. and Jay. When she entered, he could tell immediately something was wrong and asked the kids to go to bed since it was time.

"What's wrong?" he asked.

"Billy just had a convulsion, and it scared me out of my mind. I don't know if I can take this if it happens often," she said.

"Dr. Watson told you to expect this, you remember?"

"Yes, I know, but I didn't know they would be this scary."

"Is he okay now?"

"I think so," she said.

Both went to Billy's room and found him resting easily.

They sat down with the sitter and stayed for a couple of hours. Though he was in terrible shape, it was good to have him home.

Convulsions were frequent for the next few days. In desperation Garrett called Dr. Watson, and he prescribed additional medicine that seemed to slow them down, but not totally.

A couple of months passed. Garrett could see that Billy's being home was clearly getting the best of Mary Fran. She couldn't sleep or eat, and had no time for herself or anyone else. M. J. and Jay were not completely forgotten because she had Sally working full-time looking after them, but she sat with Billy all the time. She had a full schedule; it was Billy, nothing else.

53

Garrett spoke to Dr. Watson often. His opinion was that Billy's condition was never going to improve. He would be completely bedridden for the rest of his life. He would not be able to converse with anyone and would never be able to even partially care for himself. Dr. Watson suggested he be placed in a home where Mary Fran had only visiting privileges.

Garrett agreed with Dr. Watson. He didn't believe Mary Fran could stand up under the pressure she had now assumed. The problem was that the immediate area didn't have what was needed in the way of a nursing home. Those who needed such stayed in the hospital as long as they could and were subsequently sent home to be taken care of as best they could be.

Garrett went to all the surrounding larger towns and was unable to find any opening available in the existing homes. Coming home one day, he suddenly came upon the idea of building one, a building large enough that could take care of Billy and other patients too. Maybe if he put up the construction money, the other patients would generate sufficient profit to pay for Billy's upkeep.

Then there was the question of who would run the home. He discussed this with Henry. It turned out this would be no problem at all. Some of the Alabama girls were looking for jobs. Further, Jim Morgan's oldest daughter Aline had almost completed nurse's training. Henry talked to her, and she was interested in running such an operation.

Garrett asked John Haney to deliver the necessary building supplies to a small piece of property on the north end bordering the highway close to where the Alabama folks had built their homes. The design of the home was to be simple. There would be a reception area with one long wing of rooms. There was a kitchen and along the backside a long sunroom where all the patients could come to be with others when they weren't in their rooms. Initially, there were twelve rooms to the facility. Construction began at once and progressed rapidly.

During this construction period, Mary Fran never left Billy's side. She agreed with building the home because she could tell being with him was getting her down. While she was interested in the construction of the home, she didn't feel compelled to watch every moment.

Aline Morgan finished her training prior to the completion of the home. Because of this, Garrett suggested she come to the house and look after Billy until the home was finished. She accepted, which gave her the opportunity to help plan the final decorations and furniture purchase. She also bought the supplies and hired the necessary staff to adequately operate the facility.

The day finally came when Billy was ready to be moved to the new facility. The staff was in place and ready to begin. Area doctors had heard about it and recommended several patients who were admitted during the first days.

The place was well suited for Billy. He never left his room because he could not tolerate sitting up. He couldn't communicate with anyone, and there was a real question as to how much he actually comprehended. Within the first few months, the home filled to capacity. In fact, Aline had to hire more help to operate the facility.

When Billy left home, Mary Fran could again get some rest. She scheduled herself a visit with Billy on Tuesdays and Thursdays and anytime in between she wanted to. With it all, she could never get him off her mind. She mourned his condition and suffered every day his loss in life. However, this time did give her the opportunity to become reacquainted with M. J. and Jay, and they were gradually getting back on a regimen of doing things together.

54

Billy's accident occurred in 1946. After he returned home, his condition seemed to remain the same through the remainder of the 1940s. The nursing home had gone through some significant changes to get to the point where it could sustain itself. Actually, instead of a nursing home, it had evolved into a home for children with special physical needs. All the patients now were children in much the same condition as Billy. Most had the same outlook.

The medical facility seemed to function more professionally with all the patients sharing somewhat the same condition. Mixing older and younger people together somehow did not facilitate the same level of service that the more specialized approach did. Because Mary Fran was always on top of the administration of the facility, she was sure Billy was afforded the best care possible. The same care was extended to all patients.

When Garrett and Mary Fran had the opportunity to observe how many folks had the same need, they constructed another facility to house older patients. Many of the patients were bedridden with all the types of illnesses one normally expected to see in a nursing home.

In addition to these two structures, a third was eventually built. It was unique in that it housed only those folks who were able to go home during the day. The third home was a place that an older person could come for the night. Late in the afternoon a bus picked up each resident, transporting them to Garrett's new facility (their night residence), where everyone had dinner together. Their room was furnished with their own furniture if they wished. They played cards or had some type of group activity. After breakfast, they were bused back to their homes, and all could do whatever they wanted to during the day. Using this method, the residents were with other people at night and had two good meals provided. This residence was filled to capacity very shortly.

Aline Morgan was able to oversee each of the facilities. Because of her increased responsibilities and success with each of the three ventures, she needed more assistance from others than had originally been contemplated. Local physicians approved of the way she was running the facilities, and the regulatory agencies gave her high ratings.

The real credit went to Henry because of his financial expertise in handling funds. Garrett could not afford either of the facilities at the time, yet they were built. Somehow Henry was able to see them to fruition by using the cash flow from all the farming operations.

Garrett had another requirement. Henry was to determine the financial capabilities of each of the patients and residents. If they were either unable to pay or needed a little assistance but really needed the service, they were never turned away, even if Garrett absorbed the entire loss.

55

During the late 1940s some changes were taking place in Garrett's business. His idea of vertically integrating his beef operation was providing a market few other producers had. In fact, the cattle business was not as lucrative as it had been during the war. Garrett was still selling his meat through his store and peddling to others. He needed more markets to fill, but he wasn't willing to take the prices buyers offered.

Henry's idea was to attempt to sell already-butchered beef directly to the larger packers in the North and Midwest. Garrett's operation would buy the trucks to deliver the beef and develop some sort of back haul. This way they would be receiving more for the beef than they could get locally, and with the trucking operation they would develop another profit source.

Henry had been working on this project without approval from Garrett for months because he could see its potential. When Garrett returned from Jacksonville with Billy, the program was almost ready for them to begin serious discussions about where the money would come from to complete the deal. When they felt they were on fairly solid ground, Garrett decided to visit the packers to make the final arrangements. Henry could not accompany him, though needed, because of his physical condition. Henry set up all the arrangements for Garrett to fly. Driving would have taken too long, given the distance he had to cover.

It was an exciting opportunity for Garrett. The contacts Henry made for him rolled out the red carpet, and before Garrett could comprehend what was happening he had made the arrangements to sell two semi-loads of butchered beef every week.

He bought one tractor-trailer truck and delivered the two loads weekly. When one driver returned home exhausted, he put another on the same truck and turned it around. In time, they were able to develop back hauls, bringing the truck home profitably. Of course, with Henry's expertise, the trucking company charged the beef unit for hauling its beef to market. This way he could monitor whether or not the trucking company was profitable.

The apparent success of the beef operation was really giving Beau and Bill a workout. Keeping the stream of beef coming was tough. They made mistakes, but they did get the operation working smoothly.

56

The vegetable packinghouse and farm were on their way to less profitability, primarily because the vegetable markets had been taken over by muck farmers in the southern part of the state. Their volumes per acre and quick production, plus not being as prone to cold weather, allowed their crops to come to fruition sooner than the farms in Central Florida. Therefore, the early market prices were going South Florida, not Central.

Because of this situation, most farmers in Central Florida were putting their farms into citrus. Citrus was the coming agricultural pursuit. It was shipped as a fresh fruit product. At the end of World War II the market became glutted with single-strength canned juice that wasn't fit for human consumption. Not until frozen concentrated orange juice appeared, which proved to be the "Cinderella child of the Florida citrus industry," did greater returns became apparent.

Instead of phasing out his vegetable operation, Garrett decided to grow corn and other products he could use to finish his cattle for slaughter. It was a good arrangement since he was already set up to handle the farming operation. He simply revamped his vegetable packinghouse to an orange packing facility and used the same labor to operate it. His groves were now producing enough fruit to supply a fresh fruit house.

And so, in 1950 Garrett found himself hauling his own beef to northern markets already slaughtered. His trucking company was growing at a respectable pace to service the beef program. John Haney was going wild sawing timber for sale from their sawmill, and he only had a short time before he would have to begin buying saw logs. Beau and Bill were still fencing more lands but the end was in sight. Because of all this, Jim Lawrence's land-clearing operation was coming to an end unless more land was purchased. The citrus nursery, under Jim Morgan's leadership, was slowing because of their citrus land running out. If they didn't buy more, he would have to begin to sell trees to other growers, which he was already doing.

57

Alan Wright's job with the politician rubbed off on him. Since returning from service, he had served as county commissioner and had begun contemplating running for state representative. With Brett gone, Alan was the closest friend Garrett had. At every junction they talked to each other before making momentous decisions. They knew each other like a book. They hunted and fished whenever they were able to, and they shared their successes. Yes, they also cried with each other in the sad times. They were family.

After Alan was discharged, he married a girl he met in Baltimore while in service. Her name was Mildred Smith. Mildred moved to Florida with Alan and became very good friends with Garrett and Mary Fran. Being from another part of the country, her customs were different, and they all had laughs at each other occasionally.

Alan and Mildred never had children. She was sadly killed in an automobile accident in 1950. When she was buried, Alan and Garrett went fishing for two weeks while Alan recuperated from his loss. His political career became his primary life's work. Garrett was always on the front row, supporting him with his energy and finances.

58

For some time Garrett had been experimenting with cross-breeding his cattle in an attempt to develop a cross more able to stand the temperatures and insects found in Florida. His preference in cattle was the Brahman cross with other breeds. The Brahman can tolerate warm temperatures yet seemingly was not any more suited than other breeds to withstand the ravages of insects. During his studies on the subject he was told of a rancher in Texas who had worked on the same things. The rancher had been cross-breeding and had what he thought was an improvement. After discussions via telephone and the mails, Garrett decided to visit the rancher and see his animals.

"I really don't want to go to Texas, Garrett," Mary Fran said. "I want to stay close so that I can check to be sure Billy has everything he needs."

Garrett had been unsuccessful in getting Mary Fran to venture far from Billy. Even though he had hatched up little outings, she still wasn't very interested in doing anything but looking after family and being close to Billy. He was doing okay, except from time to time he did experience frightening convulsions.

"Why don't you ask Alan to go with you? He needs some time away from politics, and it would do the two of you good to be alone together," Mary Fran said.

Alan wasn't difficult to convince. In fact, he jumped at the chance to get away for a few days.

They decided to drive Garrett's new car. He had an Oldsmobile 88, the hottest car of the year. Since Mary Fran had been visiting every day at the nursing home, Garrett bought the car for her instead of her using a farm truck. The car was such a pleasure to drive, Garrett now decided he needed one himself.

Garrett and Alan took a couple of days in New Orleans, thoroughly enjoying the town. It was a new and different experience for both, but two nights was enough for Bourbon Street. In fact, they determined that if they didn't leave the sights and sounds of the city, they might die there!

Payne Gilbert's ranch was in South Central Texas in a little town called Reid's Station. Payne was a tough Texan who looked as though the sun had parched his skin for years. His every breath was talking about his ranch. Garrett thought that compared to his, Paine's ranch was mighty poor. Where he averaged one cow per acre per year, Paine needed close to five acres to handle one cow for a year. Garrett did like his cows and decided to buy a bull and a couple of cows. They spent one night and most of two days before deciding to head east.

Instead of sending one of the drivers to pick up the cattle, Bill Mathews decided to come himself. He brought his son Jimmy, who was the same age as Billy, and Jay, who was a couple of years younger. It took five days to make the trip. The boys told everyone when they returned that they had been almost around the world.

One day during the following week, Bill came into the office and said, "Garrett, I like those cattle you bought in Texas, but that bull is probably the meanest animal I've ever been around. He's sneaky and mean, and I'm afraid he's going to hurt someone."

"You still have him in the pens at the barn?" Garrett asked.

'Yes, and I think he should stay there until he calms down. Maybe it is just because he is in a new place that keeps him upset. Feed and water seem to do little to take the edge off," Bill said.

Garrett's dad had fallen in love with the cattle. He spent a good bit of time just looking at the new cows and bull. He was, however, cautious of the bull and gave him a wide berth.

After about a week the bull seemed to be getting accustomed to the ordinary hustle and bustle of the ranch. He was beginning to tolerate all the activity.

The center of the lot had a watering trough with the water pipe up inside of a cross tie so that the cattle wouldn't constantly rub against it. One day the float in the trough got hung up and the water was overflowing and running everywhere around the center of the pen. Mr. Gregson happened along and decided to cut the water off until someone could fix it. The cattle were under the barn and so was the bull.

Just as Mr. Gregson entered the lot, the bull snorted and blew heavily before quieting down. When the bull calmed, Mr. Gregson continued. Before he could get to the water trough, the bull made a lunge for him and, of course, he tried to avoid him by running to the lot fence. Unfortunately, the bull was faster and hit him squarely in the back, knocking him into the board fence. He fell back from the blow to the fence, and the bull hit him again in the same place. This had the effect of slamming him into the cross tie on which the boards were nailed. The second blow knocked the old man unconscious.

No one saw the accident and no one really knows how long Mr. Gregson lay in the lot with the bull over him. Every time he would stir, the bull would hit him again until the stirring stopped.

John Haney was coming from the sawmill to the office and saw the bull standing over Mr. Gregson. He opened the lot gate and drove his pick-up inside and ran the bull into the pasture with the cattle. John knew when he saw what had happened that Mr. Gregson was beyond any sort of help. Because John knew he was dead, he went into the barn and brought enough burlap feed bags out to cover him and went to the office as quickly as possible.

Without stopping in the reception area, he walked directly into Garrett's office and closed the door. "Garrett, I've got some bad news for you," he said.

"What's that, John?" As he spoke he was slowly looking up from some papers and standing up.

Not knowing how else to break the news he said, "Garrett, the Texas bull has killed your dad."

Garrett slumped back into his chair and sat for a brief moment trying to get a handle on the moment. "Are you sure?"

"Yes, I'm sure," he said confidently. "I saw Mr. Gregson on the ground in the lot with the bull standing over him, and I opened the gate and ran the bull into the pasture."

"You're sure he's dead?" Garrett asked, reaching for his hat.

"There is no question, Garrett. Please don't go out there. I have some mill hands watching him so that the kids won't see the mess. Stay here, Garrett, while I get Henry to call the authorities."

John left Garrett and asked Henry to call the sheriff and undertaker and also Mary Fran. He promptly turned and went back into the office with Garrett. Garrett was at this point devastated. His grief was real, and tears were flowing down his cheeks.

Completely incompetent to know what to do or say, John stood there for a moment, walked around the desk, hugged Garrett, and said, "Maybe you want to be alone for a few minutes. I'll close the door on the way out. Henry called Mary Fran." John Haney left the room, closing the door behind him. Inside the room Garrett was simply overcome with his private grief.

It wasn't long before the sheriff and undertaker arrived. The sheriff brought the justice of the peace with him for official purposes. The body was promptly removed. Garrett went home with Mary Fran when the body left. Everyone on the farm made their way to the house, offering their condolences within minutes and beginning a vigil that would last for a few days.

An hour before sundown, Garrett left the house. He did this quietly without any word to anyone. He made his way to his pick-up and quietly left his office parking space. No one was around when he went through the lot gate toward the south pasture to locate the bull. He found the bull grazing with a few cows about two miles south of the barn. The bull was content and paid little attention to him. Not for long, however.

Garrett stopped a short distance from the herd and retrieved his 30-30 from behind his seat. He checked it to be sure it was loaded and quietly made his way toward the herd on foot.

The bull carefully watched as Garrett slowly made his way to the angle he wanted. The cattle began to slowly move away while continuing to graze. The bull stared at Garrett and didn't move. In an effort to move Garrett back to the truck, the bull snorted and shook his head violently. When Garrett didn't scare, the bull made the same movements but even more ferociously.

Garrett wasn't going to scare easily. The bull decided to rush him. This was his fatal mistake.

The bull was about forty yards from Garrett when he started toward him. The closer he came, the faster he ran. When he was within twenty yards of Garrett, he was running full blast. This is when Garrett shot him. The shot dropped the bull in his tracks. Only his momentum allowed any forward motion.

The moment Garrett knew he was down, he cut his throat. He then walked away.

The shot rang out across the flat woods. Those who knew Garrett were aware of what had just happened.

Beau was standing on the side porch when Garrett returned. "Beau, take the bulldozer and drag the bull to the butcher pen. Tell them to grind him up in hamburger tonight and see that he is on the truck going to Chicago tomorrow morning. This way maybe the bull will be in the Chicago sewer by this time next week."

Garrett slept little that night. He was obsessed with thinking about the past and the role his dad had played in it, what his dad had meant to him. He had always needed his dad, and his dad was always there to support him. Because of this, he always sought to please his dad in everything he did. He wanted his dad to be proud of him. He wanted to do right. Besides his dad, Essay and Beau were the only close family he had ever had until he married Mary Fran.

At first light the next morning Garrett was standing in the lot of his home place. His dad had built it and it was grown up now. Dog fennels head high. All of the buildings and fences were falling down. This place represented his beginning. He had lived here with his family. Somehow coming back to this place provided strength for Garrett. He felt close to his dad here, and it felt good.

Garrett thought he would restore his home and preserve it so that he could come here often to sort out the tough decisions that would surely come. The years ahead brought many.

The funeral was attended by almost everyone in the settlement. The church was full of folks who considered themselves simple. Not a big shot there, unless one considered State Senator Alan Wright a big shot. Garrett certainly didn't.

When the funeral was over, most of the folks brought food to Garrett and Mary Fran's. The settlement gathered to offer all they had, which was their companionship and sympathy, to the grieving family. Their generosity was heart-warming, but there was also a giant empty spot inside Garrett that just couldn't be filled. Perhaps time would help.

Mr. Gregson's body was buried next to his wife's in the old cemetery. The double tombstone was already there. Garrett just had to have someone etch the date of his dad's death on it.

59

Since his dad's death Garrett could only cope with the loss by losing himself in his workaday world. The day never ended for Garrett. He seemed to be continually operating on nervous energy, never resting unless he was asleep, which seldom lasted more than a few hours at most. He never took any free time for himself and never went for a few days away with Mary Fran. They had promised this to themselves. But he became a workaholic as a means of dealing with all the heartache he experienced in the past and with Billy's continuing illness.

Mary Fran wasn't any better off. She spent all her time at the convalescent center, always looking for ways to improve Billy's care, and indeed that of all the patients there.

The home now had more rooms and was always full, with applications for others. It was in a constant building program.

While the home didn't make any money to speak of, it paid off in the satisfaction of knowing that a constructive good was accomplished for people who needed it. Billy certainly received the best care possible.

When a person who needed the center didn't have the money to pay the bill, the door was always open if a bed was available. Ability to pay was not a prerequisite for admission to the convalescent center.

The year 1952 wasn't a banner year for agriculture, particularly Garrett's operation. His vegetable operation had been phased out, so the land was used for either pasture or citrus. The vegetable house was transformed to accommodate citrus, but fresh citrus continued to decline in price. This situation was particularly frustrating because the annual employee bonus was tied to profits. Garrett could only justify running the fresh fruit house to generate cash flow.

Citrus was taking on a different complexion, and Garrett knew that eventually the big money would come from here.

Without the advent of frozen concentrated orange juice in the mid-1940s, the citrus operation would have disappeared completely. Garrett never liked the canned single-strength orange juice because of its terrible taste. The canned grapefruit juice could be swallowed if sufficient vodka was mixed with it, but this was the only way.

Because of his investment in citrus and the acres his groves were accumulating with the steady planting that had been proceeding for years, Garrett decided to build himself a small concentrate plant large enough to handle just his fruit. His thought was to develop a market for his juice. His trucks could haul it since they were already refrigerated.

The most lucrative operation profitwise was his transportation system utilizing the vertical marketing program started with his cattle. He was raising the cattle, butchering them, and using his trucks to deliver them to the markets he had developed. The transportation markup was much better than the cattle business, yet one fed on the other.

The long-range idea was to develop the concentrate market vertically as well. Garrett's operation could then not only be diversified but, in a sense, self-sustaining.

Frozen concentrated orange juice is a unique process. The idea is to remove the water from fresh citrus juices, can and freeze it, then ship it to the grocer. The consumer buys the juice at the grocer's, takes it home, adds the necessary water, and has something very close to the fresh product itself.

Several larger grower cooperative associations and private companies were investing in processing plants. It seemed the logical answer to a serious marketing problem for citrus.

Garrett could visualize concentrate's potential. He was one of the few who could. Henry was against it mainly because of the amount of money required to construct a plant and staff it with management that they did not have. Labor had never really been a problem for Garrett. When he needed more, he hauled in some new families from the south. This was a different deal, however. The needed management required some knowledge. Management had to have expertise in manning such an operation. The greatest problem for Henry and Garrett was the uncertainty of it all.

Local bankers were reluctant to loan monies for such a venture because of the amount needed and the uncertainty of its success. Because of this obstacle, Garrett began using out-of-town bankers for all his larger business-related expansions. His cash flow was sufficient to develop most any type of expansion he had previously undertaken, but a concentrate plant was a little too much. He needed help.

One of his big daily responsibilities was keeping Henry from having a nervous breakdown because of the amount of money required. Henry's reactions were primarily because of his conscientiousness and because they started with nothing. Because of their continuing expansion programs, which were by design, they kept all of their available cash tied up. The money never accumulated. Now Henry couldn't see the end with the monumental amount they had to borrow.

Apparently Garrett didn't let it bother him. Mary Fran had ultimate faith in his ability, and it bothered her not at all.

Because of the tremendous amount of transportation involved, Garrett decided to build his concentrate plant on the highway away from the rest of the farm buildings and residences. Because of its proximity to the existing slaughtering operation, his trucking company could work both of them with little effort. Also, both operations might be able to use the same cold rooms to some extent.

The plant was constructed of concrete block. Garrett made sure he left sufficient room for future expansion for both the citrus and slaughter operations.

Located in the center of both and closer to the highway, Garrett decided to build a main office that would house the necessary personnel to handle the paperwork for all the operations. Within the office complex was a very nice conference room, and Henry was set up in executive offices.

Garrett decided he would keep his office where it was in the little building under the oak thicket near his home—for no reason other than he liked it that way. He was a maverick and loner when it came to business matters. His private telephone lines could be hooked to the main switchboard in the office, and it would be as if he were in the main office.

Being the workaholic he was, he had phones inside his home hooked to the switchboard. The phone hookup was to become a real problem later for his family, only because the phones would ring all night. A cutoff was soon attached for his private lines.

With the capacity of his plant more than he produced to begin with, Garrett needed to buy about one-third of the raw tonnage necessary to operate the plant at optimum efficiency. Purchasing this tonnage from other growers was Garrett's responsibility. He chose to purchase the fruit already harvested and delivered to his plant so that his picking crews would harvest only his fruit.

Instead of buying on-tree outright from growers, the option was offered for growers to share in total revenues on a patronage basis. Because the growers were carefully screened before offering this deal, it turned out to be good for everyone. The expenses of the operation were subtracted from the total returns plus an agreed-upon markup for Garrett's investment in the plant. This allowed the plant to run at optimum efficiency.

Because of the magnitude of his business, Garrett was totally consumed with his responsibilities. Mary Fran was fully involved with the center caring for Billy. Given this arrangement, they only came together as a family at the dinner table at night. With the phone constantly ringing, there was not a great deal of in-depth family conversation. The kids were teenagers, and this situation should have been different.

60

At fifteen, Jay was quite different from the "anxious to please" boy that Billy would have been expected to be at that age, had it not been for his accident. Prior to his accident Billy was always the boy who openly displayed a willingness to mind his parents and always do the right thing. Jay wasn't a bad boy but one filled with mischief. A willingness to mind his parents wasn't necessarily his primary character trait. Jay lived on the edge of doing what was in his own mind, usually in the gray area of what was right.

The greatest difference in the two boys was that Billy was more serious minded than Jay. Jay liked to have fun. He also liked girls. Girls would always play a large role in his life, and he went out of his way to take advantage of them. He also liked all those things in which he shouldn't indulge, like tobacco—both smoking and chewing. Alcohol was also one of his weaknesses. He really didn't abuse alcohol because he knew he would get caught and that the consequences would be more than he was willing to pay. But he did take advantage of it every chance he had. Of course, Garrett and Mary Fran never condoned any of his off-color behavior. They didn't allow him to smoke or drink in their presence, nor did he try to, but they were privately suspicious.

Many times Jay and M. J. had to fend for themselves while their parents were away. Sally always saw to their meals, however, and Bill took care of their transportation needs. During these times also, Sally spent the night at the main house with them.

Jay was a brilliant kid, but one of his problems was not applying himself at school. He was always full of himself, and studying wasn't his greatest interest. Some subjects, however, held so much interest for him that in spite of himself he did study and receive acceptable grades, many times A's in sciences. He loved sports and was quite a good athlete.

His choice of friends was always what kept him in plenty of trouble, the kind of trouble that was usually hard to explain sensibly—like the time he and his friends passed by Garrett's watermelon patch to the Smith patch where the kids knew there was always a guard posted, a guard they knew had instructions to use rock salt to shoot any intruders.

On this particular still summer evening with a bright moon, the boys decided the time was right to raid the Smith patch. Not that they couldn't get a melon out of Garrett's patch to eat, but to see if the possibility existed that they could get away with it at the Smith patch. It was a Saturday night, and the idea suited the boys well.

Jay said, "You fellas already know the patch is located on a hill and the guard sits on top of the hill. What we should do is attract his attention in one direction, and those of us who will get the melons will come in from the opposite direction." It being early evening, the decision was made to attract his attention from the moonlit side of the hill, the east side, then attack from the west side, the dark side. This planning sounded good, and everyone divided into two groups. Jay happened to be on the team that was destined to steal the melons.

At the prescribed time, a distraction was raised in a scope of woods that joined the field on the east. Jay's group started up the hill in the same manner as a soldier would crawl along on his belly. They crawled under the barbed-wire fence and made their way up the hill to the particular melons they had selected. They started rolling the melons down the hill in front of them while still on their bellies. The guard heard them and yelled to stop. Instead of stopping, they elected to pick up their melons and run. The guard let them get to the fence and roll their melons under the wire, and as they started over the fence the guard shot Jay squarely in the rear end. Two others were also shot. The salt had sufficient power to penetrate their pants and skin and lodged firmly underneath.

The reason for shooting someone with rock salt in the first place is that when the salt begins to melt, it starts to sting. There is no way to put out the stinging.

Within fifteen minutes, Jay's rear end felt like it was on fire. The pain took a while to subside.

Oddly enough, at fifteen, Jay didn't have the capacity to learn from experience. This group of boys continued to try different tactics to rob the Smith patch without detection. Sometimes they succeeded, but most times it resulted in another night spent in misery.

One day Jay was loading packed fresh fruit onto a long-distance truck at the packinghouse. This wasn't a favorite job, nor was any, but Garrett insisted he do something. Garrett was trying to give him a job in every division of the family business so that he could finally figure where he was best suited—that is, if he wanted to become a part of it.

The long-distance truck drivers were laughing about things they did when they were in high school. One of their favorite tricks was taking about fifteen deep breaths, then to stick their thumb into their mouths and blow hard without any air escaping. This chain of actions reportedly caused them to pass out for a few seconds, and it would scare the teacher out of her wits. On hearing this, Jay couldn't stand it. He walked over to the driver and asked for further explanation.

"It's simple," one driver said. "All you do is take the deep breaths and blow on your thumb, not letting any air escape. You pass out, it's that simple."

"I'm going to try it," Jay said.

"Okay," said the driver. "Why not over here where this box material is located so that you won't fall on the floor and hurt yourself?"

Positioned properly, Jay followed their instructions. Those watching said it took about thirty seconds for him to regain consciousness. He felt okay and elated because he knew a teacher at school he couldn't wait to try this on. Several of his schoolmates who worked at the packinghouse also saw what happened.

The next day, entering Miss Smithers's classroom, Jay knew this was the day. She was already upset with the preceding class and not in a good humor. Jay's friends could read what he was about to do. Several of the boys had agreed to get her agitated with them, and at the height of it Jay would pull his unconscious act.

She had just about had all she could take and was outlining what was getting ready to happen to those who were agitating her. Jay had not been a part of her problems of the day, and then he fell out cold on the floor right under her feet.

Witnessing what had happened, she immediately knelt down trying to revive Jay. The floors had been oiled to keep down the dust, and her white skirt was ruined. She patted Jay's hands and cheeks, and tears were streaming down her face. In desperation she yelled at a student to get the principal.

"Jay, honey," she pleaded, "wake up now." She begged and patted every way she could.

When a situation like this presents itself, a few seconds seems like an eternity. Everything was going wrong for Miss Smithers, it seemed. She couldn't make enough money teaching to be independent. Her car needed repairs she couldn't make. Her room at the boarding house wasn't the way she wanted to live. She was having problems with her boyfriend. He was interested in hunting and fishing, and she wanted someone interested in the arts. And now, with all her problems, Jay Gregson had to die on her!

Just as the principal entered the door, Jay woke up. He began to try to sit up, but Miss Smithers wouldn't let him. All she could think of was getting him out of her classroom until he was okay.

After making Jay lie a few minutes on the floor, the principal accompanied him to her office where she promptly made him lie down on the daybed. Jay hadn't counted on this scenario. He thought that when he came to, Miss Smithers would let him continue as before in his seat, or better yet, send him home. The bad part of this was that Jay couldn't get rid of the principal. She had a wet washcloth and positioned herself over him, intent on continually rubbing his brow with the washcloth. After thirty minutes of this, Jay convinced her he was fine. It was time for lunch and the principal had to be in the halls anyway. When she went into the halls, Jay escaped.

During the lunch period Jay's buddies congregated around him, and they hatched a plan that took real genius. They decided they would all do the same thing sometime during the afternoon and recruited all the trusted souls who would agree.

Beginning the first period after lunch, classmates begin to fall out all over the school. When the epidemic of the "mysterious illness" hit its peak, the principal called an end to school for the day. Since it was Friday, everyone would have time to recuperate over the weekend, she thought.

After school Jay's buddies thought him a hero. The other kids attempted to stay clear of those "contagious" so as not to catch the same ailment.

Several weeks passed before school officials caught on to what was happening. When reckoning day arrived, those who participated were summarily lined up in the football coach's office and given the beating of their lives. Then the coach and principal took each boy home, and their parents inflicted whatever serious punishment they doled out individually.

The problem with Jay was he just wanted to have some fun. Fun at any cost was the way he thought. However, he did shy away from that in which he was certain to get caught because he was extremely aware of not wanting to hurt his parents, since they had about all they could handle with Billy.

Jay never really felt he was getting second-rate attention from his parents because of Billy's problems. Garrett had included him in every hunting and fishing outing he planned, and they really had fun together. Jay hunted and fished with every person working for his dad.

Mary Fran was always aware that M. J. needed her, and she tried to always be there for her. There were times, however, when Billy needed her, and he took first place. For whatever the reason, there were times when Sally substituted for Mary Fran, which seemed okay with M. J.

With all Jay's fun-loving times, he was never really addicted to anything. He could take cigarettes or leave them. He never really seemed to have a problem leaving the chewing tobacco at home when he and Garrett were fishing. Alcohol was not a problem. He was unusual in this way.

On one occasion Jay was driving a farm pick-up to a party after a high school football game. No one was with him because he was headed to his girlfriend's house to pick her up. He had a drink from a bottle that a farmhand had procured for him. While driving down into the settlement, a car backed out of the driveway directly in front of Jay without seeing him. Jay stopped, but the car didn't and backed into him.

The driver of the other car was very apologetic and had only done minuscule damage to the farm truck, but he insisted on calling the police to investigate the accident for insurance purposes. The older fellow had already admitted his guilt.

While the fellow had gone into the house to use his phone, Jay hid his liquor in the bushes so the law couldn't find it and use it against him. He hid it very carefully inside an azalea bed.

When the police arrived and the investigation was almost complete, the officer asked Jay, "Have you had a drink?"

Jay replied, "No, sir."

The officer replied, "You sure smell like it. What is it I smell then?"

"Oh, I don't know. Could be Listerine. I'm on my way to pick up my girlfriend, and we are going to the school dance."

An old lady, who was rocking on her front porch and witnessed the whole thing, said, "He's lying, officer. The young man hid his liquor in the bushes behind him."

The officer walked over to the bed and retrieved the bottle, "Is this yours?"

Jay answered, "No, sir. I've never seen it before."

The lady and Jay got into an argument, and the officer sent her home. He then told Jay to get into his car.

The officer looked at Jay and said, "Is this yours?"

Jay replied, "Yes, sir."

After releasing the man who backed into Jay, the officer said to Jay, "You can't leave. I think I need to take you to see the sheriff for your drinking offense."

Jay knew that couldn't happen because his dad was a supporter of the sheriff and the sheriff would go straight to Garrett. Jay said to the officer, "You know, it is not like I'm drunk. I admitted I had a drink, but one drink doesn't make you drunk. Besides if you take me to see the sheriff, he is going to take me home to see my dad and then I will really be in a mess. Can't you just overlook this little incident?"

After some begging, and the officer realizing Garrett was the sheriff's prime financial supporter, the two came to terms and the officer decided to let Jay go. However, he did take his liquor away from him.

Because of Jay's personality, everyone who knew him loved him. Everyone who worked in all his dad's satellite operations loved him, as well as everyone at school and in the settlement. He was basically a good-time kid whom everyone immediately liked, and Jay liked almost everyone himself.

61

One of the younger Alabama boys decided he didn't want to be a farmer all his life and took a barber's course. He felt that if he was working for himself, the inside life would be lots more fun for him. Prior to leaving the farm, he and Jay were friends and liked to slip a drink together only to see if they could get away with it. Because "Alabama" was older, he was Jay's "keys" to the liquor store. All the storeowners knew Jay and had some connection with Garrett, so without Alabama Jay had to drive a long distance to get something to drink. The two had always been friends.

It was a January day. This was a month in which the cheap Yankees visited the area to fish. They all had cabin fever from being hemmed up inside with the snow piled up outside. These people were called the "twenty-dollar Yankees." That is, they brought a twenty-dollar bill and wore a pair of long underwear and didn't change either one while they were in Central Florida. They pulled a little wobbly two-wheel trailer to sleep in, and it was fully stocked with food when they arrived. They bought nothing while they were in the area and hauled home lots of freshwater bass and speckled perch.

On this day, Jay was in town and decided to go by the barbershop and visit with Alabama for a while. When he arrived, Alabama and his partner, Charlie, didn't have any customers. Both were sitting in their chairs talking.

"Hi, how's it going?" Jay inquired.

"Fine, Buddy, how 'bout yourself?"

After a few minutes of pleasantries Alabama said, "Jay, I've got a bottle of vodka. How about a drink?"

"You drink here in the shop?" Jay asked.

"Oh, sometimes, but we never drink anything but vodka, so our customers can't smell it," he replied.

Never to be one who refused to drink with a buddy, Jay said, "Sure, why not?"

Time passed with no customers, and they continued to drink. Just as the last drop was being divided, a couple of Yankees started across the street headed into the barbershop.

Alabama said to Jay, "You'd better get into the chair. Here comes a couple of Yankees." Jay got into the barber chair.

Feeling absolutely no pain, Alabama asked Jay when one Yankee was in Charlie's chair and the other seated to wait, "Now, Mr. Gregson, how would you like your hair cut today?"

To which Jay replied, "Only a light trim, please, Mr. Alabama."

Alabama picked up his electric shears and starting in the middle of Jay's collar on the back, removed a streak to the scalp all the way to his forehead. Then he proceeded to shear his entire head. All the while Alabama was shearing, they were talking about all sorts of things.

The fellow waiting for the next available barber chair couldn't believe what he had heard and was now witnessing. His expression was one of extreme astonishment.

When his head was sheared, with bundles of hair all over Jay and the floor, Alabama backed up and studied his head. He then took out his straight razor and lathered Jay's head with about two inches of soap foam. He very methodically sharpened his razor with about twenty-five licks on the strap.

When his razor passed his test, he started at collar level and slowly shaved Jay's head everywhere hair had been growing with the exception of his eyebrows. When this job was complete, he backed off and took another look.

Not satisfied, he reached under the counter and brought out a box of strong detergent and shook it all over his head, then placed a hot towel on it for a few minutes. The towel melted the soap powder, and Alabama gave Jay's head a good scrubbing. After the scrubbing came a good rinsing, and then Alabama dried it off.

Still not satisfied with his customer's appearance, Alabama then put a thick layer of some sort of salve on his head with another hot towel. After a few minutes passed, he took the towel off, wiped off the salve and summarily took a box of talc powder and shook it vigorously over Jay's head.

With the job complete, Alabama backed up, smiled profusely, turned Jay's chair around to the mirror and said, "There, isn't that nice?"

To which Jay answered, "Perfect, just what I wanted."

After Jay's reply, Alabama removed the cover and he stepped down. When he was safely down and had his balance, Alabama pointed his finger at the remaining Yankee who was sitting there in a trance watching the haircut unfold before his eyes, and said, "You're next!"

The Yankee quickly stood up from his chair and headed toward the door. He said, "I just remembered, I've got to tell my wife something." He promptly left.

Jay followed him out with his hairless head shining in the bright Florida sunshine—all smiles and drunk as a hoot owl.

62

Garrett and Mary Fran had little time to sit and think of that Sunday afternoon long ago and the little church in the settlement when they were married. Little did they think of on that day with so little else but love and the will to pursue all their tomorrows. Of course, they really didn't have any dreams other than trying to survive.

The sequence of events within their lives couldn't have presented themselves at more opportune times. Everything just seemed to fall into place.

They never really forgot how all the neighbors came to their rescue with a garden, pigs, chickens, and of course his dad's gift of cattle. From that herd there had been countless offspring. At the birth of each of their children they gave them ten heifers and kept track of them. Of course, the kids didn't know it, but Garrett and Mary Fran did, and they knew which were theirs and how many they had.

Their success multiplied manyfold when they met and established themselves with Mr. and Mrs. Langford. No one could have been more fortunate than to have had such wonderful mentors.

By fulfilling the Langfords' lifelong dream in the role of their surrogate son and daughter, Garrett and Mary Fran were able to take the assets the Langfords provided, and with a great deal of grueling work, somehow over the years make it pay off.

Everything fit into place as they grew. The sawmill initially provided the operating cash to keep eating and going. The Alabama folks falling in with Bill and Beau seemingly couldn't have happened even in a storybook setting. Of course, if everyone were not on the edge of starvation, they wouldn't have endured the difficult days with which they were faced.

The operation went from the sawmill, to cattle, to vegetables, to citrus, to packinghouses, a transportation system, and now a juice plant that was manufacturing frozen concentrated orange juice. Looking back, the story appeared like a fairy tale. Remembering what it was like looking forward in the early days was a completely different story.

The real problem from the beginning was where the next dollar was coming from to buy the needed supplies for the rest of today and then to begin tomorrow. It was extremely tight all the time financially.

Were it not for Henry's financial expertise, the overall operation would not have come together for Garrett. Not only Henry, even the idea coming from Mr. Langford to give the employees a portion of the profits was sent from heaven. This percentage now, among the management cadre, amounted to more than their salaries in some cases. This type of compensation was unheard of in that day and time.

For the last few years Garrett had been trying to face up to the gigantic task of marketing. He was attempting to improve and polish his concept of vertical integration—that is, marketing from the ground up though company channels. Every step had to be a profit center.

The only profit center that was not a part of the farm itself was the trucking company, yet the trucking company was the asset that made the rest of the marketing concept work.

For years now, the daily drain on Mary Fran with her activities and Garrett always bouncing his head off some difficult problem was taking its toll. The blood pressure problem that was discovered at his army physical had been growing worse. Mary Fran was thin as a rail and operating on nervous energy. There had to be relief somewhere for them both.

During one low-energy point, Garrett said to Mary Fran, "We've never really taken any time for ourselves away from here. About the only breaks we've ever allowed were Bath Pond breaks. These are nice but only last about an hour. I think we need to think about taking a vacation, just the two of us."

"You mean leave M. J. and Jay here?" she inquired.

"Sure, I mean, do something we'd like to do that would allow us some rest."

"I really don't know. Leaving them is not something I'd want to do."

"If we take them, we will then do something we don't want to do. There has to be a compromise here some place."

During the next few days Mary Fran responded to an emergency at the convalescent center. A doctor was called to a patient, and Mary Fran was in with Billy. The doctor happened to stop by his room and sat down.

"Mary Fran, how much time each day do you spend here?" he asked.

"Whatever is necessary, I guess."

"I've never been here that you were not here."

"It does take a lot of time. But look at the good it does," she justified.

"I'm sure it does, but you can't withstand this strain. You need some time away."

She replied, "You've been talking to Garrett, haven't you?"

"No, I haven't seen Garrett in several weeks. But you do need to begin to think about other things and allocate a little time for yourself."

On the way home she thought that maybe they were entirely right, but the real clincher was that she didn't know what she wanted to do. She'd never really done anything but go to the coast with Garrett or to town shopping.

Sitting on the side porch after supper that night, she told Garrett what the doctor had said. "Maybe we should think about doing something. But I want the kids to have something to do themselves. I can't just leave them here."

During the course of the next few weeks the plans jelled. Garrett and Mary Fran decided to go on a slow drive through the Shenandoah Valley in Virginia and take a few days in Washington, D.C. Maybe drive up into the New England states. The more they considered a vacation, the more their imagination began to work and all sorts of ideas came to the forefront.

M. J. wanted to attend a music camp. She had made all her plans and was excited about it. She would be home before her parents, but Sally always looked after her.

Jay wanted to attend a rugged survival camp. He thought he could conquer the world. After inquiring about the camp, Garrett figured it would tax his strength, both physical and emotional, to their limits. It was perfect!

The kids left a day or two prior to Garrett and Mary Fran. On the appointed day they left in a new car, and Garrett really had trouble realizing it was a vacation and not just another business trip. They left from the convalescent center after telling Billy good-bye.

The first night they had dinner in St. Simons Island, Georgia—a wonderful seafood dinner, and they talked of spending the rest of their time there.

The second night they had another delicious seafood dinner in Charleston, South Carolina. The next morning they felt a little tired, and because it was a vacation, they decided to stay over another day and look the city over.

A few days later they were in Roanoke, Virginia, enjoying the Shenandoah Valley. After seeing the Smoky Mountains of North Carolina, they didn't think any sight could overwhelm them ever again. However, the Shenandoah was equally as beautiful.

Garrett's habit was to talk to Henry every morning. Henry purposely, on Mary Fran's private instructions, did not tell Garrett anything he did not have to. Things Henry could handle without Garrett's concurrence were out of bounds.

They decided they couldn't visit all the sights in Washington, D.C., in one day, so they decided to spend about three days there. On the second morning, the phone rang in their hotel room prior to first light. It was Henry.

"Garrett, Billy had a severe convulsion around three o'clock this morning and didn't come around. I'm sorry to have to tell you, but he died," Henry barely got out.

Garrett couldn't say anything. He just sat on the side of the bed as if he was listening for Henry's next words.

"Garrett, are you there?" Henry asked.

"Yes, Henry, just speechless," and his voice broke and his emotions were more than he could handle. When he was in control enough to talk, he said, "I'll have to call you back." He hung up the phone.

Mary Fran was already up and had come around to Garrett's side of the bed. Garrett looked at her with tears streaming down both cheeks and couldn't speak. He was beyond any conversation for the moment.

"Is it Billy or one of the other kids?" she asked.

"Billy," he managed to squeak out.

"Is he dead?"

Not being able to answer, he nodded his head affirmatively. He stood up with her and took her into his arms, sobbing uncontrollably.

When he regained control, his first notice was that Mary Fran had not shed a tear. Her face was one at peace with herself. Of course, she wasn't smiling, but she appeared truly filled with peace and tranquility.

She pushed Garrett away and down to a sitting position on the side of the bed. She pulled up a straight chair in front of him and said, "Garrett, if we believe what we say we do, we must ask ourselves the question: Is Billy's death a bad thing? Yes, we will miss him because he was our firstborn, and we loved him as much as any parents ever could. Billy died years ago, that day riding Peanut in the oak thicket. We've kept him alive and nurtured his every need. We've kept others who needed the same assistance. The truth is, if we believe what we say we do, Billy is in heaven. He now has his wings. He is in the place the Lord has prepared for him. How can we be sad? We will see him someday, and he will show us around heaven. Don't weep for Billy; he is in God's hands. He's home!"

Garrett began to control his emotions. He thought how very strong Mary Fran was, how strong her faith was—and here he was sitting on the side of the bed weeping.

He said, "You're right, Mary Fran. Billy's home, and you are an inspiration for me, and I thank you for sharing your outlook."

"Our problem now is contacting the kids, getting home, and planning Billy's funeral," she said.

During the next hour, they contacted both kids. Both would be on their way home shortly. They contacted Henry, who executed the funeral arrangements.

Garrett stored the car. They caught a taxi to the airport, and the Delta agent had tickets for them for which Henry had already arranged. They were home by mid-afternoon.

During the next few days, Mary Fran was an inspiration for everyone with whom she was acquainted. The kids needed her desperately. Jay found he wasn't as tough as he thought with this kind of circumstance. He needed his mother and father.

M. J. handled the death better than Jay because she was actually so much like Mary Fran in thought and deed. She spent all the time she possibly could with Mary Fran while growing up and picked up most of her good qualities. Though different personalities, they were very close and personal with each other.

When Garrett weakened, he always thought of the conversation with Mary Fran in Washington and recovered quickly, yet he definitely had his weak moments. Mary Fran had weak moments, moments of indecision, but never wavered with her thoughts and beliefs about Billy's death. She wasn't happy it occurred, but she felt a release that was welcomed.

Mary Fran was also totally confident she and Garrett did everything humanly possible to provide the best care for Billy, including building a facility that was professionally staffed with all sorts of trained attendants to take care of him and others. She did not once look back and say or think, *I could have done more.*

When the funeral was concluded and Billy was buried in the Gregson cemetery plot, the family went home. They hosted a buffet dinner for those who would come, and it appeared that everyone in several counties had taken them up on their offer, about which they were very proud. Being around others at a time like this is healthy emotionally, and it helped Garrett and Mary Fran.

Sitting on the side porch drinking coffee at daylight the next morning, Garrett and Mary Fran were waiting on breakfast and talking. They talked about the day before and the effort others had made to comfort them. Some folks became tangled and mixed words spoken under pressure that normally would embarrass the speaker. Some were unable to say anything. Some were very eloquent in what they said, and it was very meaningful.

Garrett asked, "What do you plan to do with the center now that Billy no longer needs it?"

"We will keep it, enlarge it, and change its name to The Billy Gregson Convalescent Center. We will do as much good as we possibly can for as many as we can, regardless of their ability to pay, for as long as we can," she said. "How 'bout that?"

"Sounds good to me," he said.

PART THREE

The Payoff

63

Garrett enjoyed other people socially, yet when a decision was required, he needed solitude with no interruptions to arrive at the answers that best suited him. He did have the ability to make a sound decision, but he was basically a loner when decisions were required.

On one such morning, he had his favorite horse saddled before first light with a thermos of coffee slipped into his saddlebags. He rode south.

While he liked all kinds of agriculture, his favorite was cattle. He enjoyed riding among them, watching them graze. When the turmoil of life needed a calming influence, he either drove his pick-up or rode a horse into a herd of cattle and watched them graze. Slowly he meandered within this gentle herd and lost himself in total enjoyment of the moment.

His decision-making capabilities always followed the same pattern. Being in solitude, he would revert in his mind to the beginning, mostly with Mr. Langford. His dad taught him the basics of becoming a cattleman, but Mr. Langford taught him the basics of the business world. Prior to Mr. Langford's death, Garrett felt he had a graduate degree centered squarely on the profit motive while providing the assets and will to allow others to prosper also.

Garrett's decision-making capabilities required different parameters from others who managed larger corporations and answered to a board of directors and then the stockholders. He was with Mary Fran the sole owner. The two of them were the boss, board of directors, and stockholders. Fortunately, their business in recent years was financially sound. Banks did not play the role they once had in his thinking. The truth is, he now owned a small bank.

Leaving the herd he rode into a grove located adjacent to the pasture. He enjoyed the grove but one needed to cover more ground than a horse could if the grove needed to be inspected properly in a short period of time. Because of this, he rode only into a small section and then retreated to the pasture.

After about two hours, he came upon a hardwood hammock and stopped, allowing his horse to graze. He took the coffee and found a place to rest comfortably. *The solitude of this hammock is habit-forming,* he thought.

Sipping the coffee he thought of all the problems facing his cattle interests. The market was flat, and if he were not vertically integrated in the marketplace, he could not survive. He thought of all his friends who were losing money because they weren't diversified into other businesses.

The citrus industry was beginning to develop a multitude of marketing problems because South America was shipping concentrate to Canada. Canada then shipped into the U.S. market, and Florida growers were competing with juice that cost much less to produce than local juice.

Even with his superior marketing program, his profits were dwindling and he wondered about the future. His multiple problems were serious. Even his trucking company now faced new and difficult regulations from state to state.

He sat in the hammock for a couple of hours considering an offer he'd had from a national food company. At first, he would not consider selling because of Jay and the allegiance he felt toward the Langfords and his employees. He also knew Mr. Langford didn't achieve his success in life by being a dummy. Times change, and so do the fortunes of those who manage with the times.

Certain problems he, along with every citrus grower, had experienced. One of them was disease. Another was adverse weather. Because of both of these problems, Garrett actually had to buy juice from other plants to accommodate his customers and keep them in his camp. After freezes the groves had always come back, yet he thought that one day the granddaddy of the freezes would occur and it would be the end.

Cattle prices continued to worsen. Foreign markets were difficult to work with. Health officials were heralding the downside of eating red meat.

Labor was becoming increasingly difficult to solicit and train. Everyone wanted the check at the end of the week, but they didn't want to earn it.

His greater problem was that his managing ability was spread too thin because of the enormity of the operation. Yet, even though he had interviewed a number of prospects to help him, he found no one who was suitable.

More than this, he was getting tired and wanted to spend more time with Mary Fran. With all these considerations, he still didn't want to take the easy way out. Yet, if he made his mind up to sell to a qualified buyer, what would he do with the money?

He pondered all these problems throughout the day, arriving home without having made any decision. The more he thought about all the problems facing him, the more confused he became.

When he arrived back at his office, there was a note from Henry asking him to call. This was unusual because Henry usually handled everything under his management with Garrett's input.

"Chalmer Products has been hard on me today. They want to know what we are going to do with their offer. I told them the time for acceptance wasn't up, and I'd talk to you when I had the opportunity. This didn't suit them because they didn't want to be left hanging without some idea of what you were thinking," Henry said. "Have you given it any more thought?"

"Yes, I've been out all day trying to think it through, only to become more confused. Have you any new thoughts?"

"Not really. Thank goodness this is your decision," Henry said.

"I know it's my decision, and to sell or not sell is not the problem. The problem is my allegiance to the family, the employees, and in particular Mr. Langford. I'm especially concerned about Jay," Garrett continued.

Henry said, "Why don't you let it soak a few days? We actually have another ten days before a decision is required."

"Okay." Garrett hung up and looked over his mail for the day.

Mary Fran came in, "I was beginning to worry about you. You missed lunch and have been gone all day."

"I ate some oranges for lunch. Tasted good," he said. "I've also tried to get my mind made up about what we should do about selling to Chalmer."

"Do you know what you want to do?"

"That's the problem. I don't. The more I think about it, the more confused I become. I want to do what is in Jay's and M. J.'s best interest, while also remaining loyal to Mr. Langford and the employees who are counting on us. These are big things."

About this time Garrett's secretary left for the day. Mary Fran stood up and locked the front door to the little office.

She came back, sat down, and said, "Now, Garrett, I want you to listen to me."

He said, "The floor's yours for as long as you wish."

"M. J. has finished college, is happily married, and her husband is financially capable of taking good care of her and their family. Jay has finally gotten a handle on himself and is growing into quite a good manager. You took an asset the Langfords had bought for another purpose and made something out of it they couldn't. I don't think you owe them anything but doing what is in the best interest of your family. The thing here is whatever is right for us and honorable."

She continued, "Your problems have arisen because you were at the mercy of the weather with the groves. Disease and market have been the problem with the cattle. To me, if you want to keep them, that's fine. If not, sell them. That's okay. The question is: Could you live a happier, longer life without all the worries you now have? Stop and think about the problems you have every day on your shoulders, and you know you won't delegate responsibility except to a very few. Stop and consider the problems centered around the fresh fruit packinghouse, the concentrate plant, the butcher pen, producing the beef and the citrus, and on top of all this the trucking company. Ponder how much machinery alone you have to keep going. All these things are your problems, and you still have the responsibility of generating the finances."

"Yes, I know," he said. "But remember, I've had lots of fun and satisfaction getting us to where we are today. It hasn't been drudgery when you look back on it. The uncertain future is the problem."

"If you sold, what would you do with the money?" she asked.

"I don't know. We already have everything we need. It would have to be invested in some way. I guess Henry could work it out if we did sell," he concluded.

Mary Fran caught her second wind and said, "Well, we started with fifteen dollars and twelve cents and about one change of clothes each. A rented house, some chickens, pigs, cattle, and a garden that others helped us get. Look at where we are today. It's true, we couldn't have done all this if it hadn't been for the Langfords. But you need to remember this: Look at the number of years we took care of him. Not that we minded. We enjoyed him, and he certainly made it worth our while. What you need to stop right now and remember is that he left the property to us with no strings attached."

"I know."

"Remember, Garrett, in his letter Mr. Langford said we ought to provide as many benefits for others throughout our lives as was possible. He said take the place and do with it as we would. If The Gregson Family Foundation owns the convalescent center and every other asset we own, think what we could then do for others. He also said don't wait until we are too old, like they did, to have some fun together. Do you remember, Garrett?"

"Yes, I remember."

They walked toward the house for dinner. There were only the two of them now. Occasionally, Beau and Trish ate with them, which made four.

64

Early the next morning Garrett called Jay down to his office while his secretary was up at Henry's offices in the executive building to retrieve the mail. "Jay, you know Chalmer Products has submitted a contract to buy us out?"

"Yes, sir, I do," Jay replied.

"What do you think of this?"

"Dad, this is up to you and Mom. You made the place what it is. I made a mess of my life when I could have been much more help."

"No, you didn't make a mess of things. You were a kid and you did kid things we expected. You served your country honorably. You were severely wounded, and thank God you survived."

"Yes, sir, I am lucky to be alive."

"Our problem is we don't want to shoot you out of the saddle with your dreams in place, and we also want to provide for M. J."

"Whatever you decide, I know our best interests are at heart. We know this, and you've always given us far more than was necessary. Now is the time in your lives when you need to think of yourselves and live a little easier."

After their conversation was finished, Garrett paid an unexpected visit to Henry. He never went to the executive office building. He usually telephoned. In fact, some of the employees there didn't know what he looked like in person.

"Henry, how much longer do you plan to work? Tell me the truth."

"I've truthfully never given that any thought. The answer is I don't know. I've always known that if you hadn't given me the chance, I would probably still be a cripple with nothing to do," Henry replied.

"You've more than carried your weight around here. You know that. The real question is your ideas as to what we should do with the Chalmer people's offer."

"Based on the value of what we own, it is short considerably," Henry said. "That is, even if you wanted to sell. Besides that, their offer only covers the headquarters property with the plants. What about South Florida? That would be of no value to us without our plants here."

"You be thinking what the deal should amount to if we decided to sell, and we will talk later. Remember, I do not want to be in on the negotiations. You bring the deal to me, and after we discuss it I can either reject or accept it. I won't be put on the spot for an answer by high-pressure buyers."

"Yes, sir," Henry concluded.

Garrett went home and asked the maid to fix a picnic lunch for him and Mary Fran. He told Mary Fran to meet him at the barn with the lunch, and they would take a horseback ride together. They rode to Bath Pond. Bath Pond was off limits to every employee without express permission from Garrett personally. There had been erected a dock with a screen room on the end for their enjoyment.

They rode through the pastures and a couple of blocks of grove on the way to Bath Pond, arriving in time for lunch. They took a swim and had lunch. Afterwards they settled back and discussed the deal with Chalmer.

Their decision was to sell if the money was right. Pay the taxes, putting the residue into The Gregson Family Foundation to be used in various ways to help others. The board of directors consisted of Garrett, Mary Fran, Jay, M. J., and Henry. The funds granted each year would be 75 percent of the returns from the invested corpus. Henry would begin as the investment head. Each of the directors would become an employee of the foundation and receive a salary. Jay would become Henry's assistant, finish his last year in college, and get an MBA. Eventually, Jay would head the foundation.

Early the next morning, Garrett called Henry to his office. "Here's the deal, Henry." Garrett outlined the decision he and Mary Fran arrived at the preceding day.

"Sounds good to me," Henry said.

"Here is what I want," Garrett continued. "I want my house and one hundred acres cut out of the deal, and they must take the South Florida property to get this place. I want Bath Pond with fifty acres and a sixty-foot roadway to the highway deeded to The Gregson Family Foundation. When the smoke settles, I want $750 million in the Foundation and the guarantee that every person now in our employ will at least have a job with Chalmer except you and Jay. I want Beau retired at full salary with a cost-of-living increase annually until he dies and the right to live in the house he now lives in for the rest of his life. How far am I away from your thoughts on the money?"

"We are $50 million apart. I wanted to net $800 million for the foundation," Henry replied.

"Go for it," Garrett said. "I want a clean contract, no contingencies, and cash at closing. Any deposit required when we execute the contract is nonrefundable."

"Yes, sir," said Henry.

Garrett felt good about finally having arrived at a decision. It was the beginning of the fresh fruit season, and the packinghouse was attempting to open with a soft market, not the usual opening with the demand exceeding supply. Garrett alone had to wrestle with these early problems. He was considerably over his head with all sorts of fresh fruit decisions at the moment.

65

Mary Fran was on her way over to Garrett's office as he got to the front door. Watching her approach, he was sure that his family success was in large measure because of her effort. She made all the family decisions without bothering him with them. She took care of the kids, seeing to all their needs, and still found time to assist friends, employees, and most important, the grandchildren. All this gave him time to do those things he had to do relating to the business.

"Garrett," she began, "we need to talk a little. Let's drive down to the south block."

They got into his car and off they went. As they began to move she said, "I want the name of the convalescent center to always remain The Billy Gregson Convalescent Center. It has grown now to the point where it accommodates almost one hundred people in serious need, regardless of their ability to pay. Strangely it is paying its way, except that you built and maintain the buildings."

She continued, "The Gregson Family Foundation was established and totally funded by 10 percent of the profits the family made annually, which picked up any deficits of the Convalescent Center but also funded all the other projects we have going. I think the foundation and the Center are two of our greatest achievements. They should remain two separate entities, with the understanding that the foundation will always pick up any deficit the Center incurs."

"I agree," Garrett replied. He had pulled to the top of a high sandhill, and they were looking over a block of Valencia oranges. "It is tough for me to think about selling this."

"I know it is, but the decision has been made, hasn't it?"

"Yes."

Mary Fran said, "I haven't finished yet with what I wanted to say."

"Okay."

"M. J. has finished college and is married to someone who can more than adequately provide for her and their family. We have much to be thankful for with their little boy and girl. Now Jay has flushed from his system the necessity to have a good time all the time. I think this is because of his close call in Korea. He sees now that there is more to life than a good time. One of my worst days was when we went into that military hospital in Frankfurt and saw him in the shape he was. I never thought he'd come home. But he did, and now he is doing a good job according to his bosses, and I hope he will continue to make good progress. He is married, and we have another grandson.

"Think about the Alabama folks," she continued. "The original groups are old now and retired in the homes we allowed them to build from the sawmill, and they live at the edge of the settlement. They've been replaced largely with members of their family and friends, who have never worked anywhere but for us. Today the old-timers have a fully funded retirement program you've seen to, and they spend part of their time every day under Henry's nose drinking coffee in the break room.

"Just think," she said, "Sally's retired and in good health and enjoying her retirement. We had to replace her with two people for just the two of us. One for the kitchen and one for the house."

"Is all of this history lesson going somewhere?" he asked.

"The point is we couldn't even crawl until Beau came. Then Bill and all the Alabama folks were sent to us by a Higher Power, I believe. They arrived and couldn't leave. The only way out for them was to walk. You took them all in. They did a great job for us their entire lives. The point is you've taken care of them their entire lives and even now funded, from your pocket, their retirement and they contributed nothing. Everything all the original employees have you gave them. I believe you can take great comfort in knowing these things.

Nothing really was given to you. You earned every penny with the Langford property, property he could do nothing with but sell. But you took it and the last days he had were happy watching you develop it. That's good! Good because you did all these things. I want you to be proud of what has happened here."

66

Garrett was walking from the barn area when Henry drove up to the little office under the oaks. Instead of letting Henry hobble out, Garrett got into the car on the other side.

"You coming to see me?" Garrett inquired.

"Yes," Henry said. "I'm afraid I didn't get the news I wanted from Chalmer."

Garrett chuckled, "They wanted to pay us more than we asked, I'll bet?"

"No, sir. They thought we were too high."

"Tell them to forget it then," Garrett replied. "However, you might put it in a more diplomatic manner."

"We are a good piece apart, and I don't believe we are close enough to worry with them."

"We don't have to sell, Henry. Don't let them spook you." Garrett stepped out of the car and walked inside his office.

That night Garrett and Mary Fran were discussing the sale after the house help had left for the day. Neither of them felt upset since they had agreed that if the sale were meant to be, it would happen. If not, they weren't going to worry about it.

It was 9 p.m. and the telephone rang. It was the Chalmer people. The person handling the negotiations said to Garrett, "Henry said if we couldn't meet the price then you weren't interested in selling?"

"If that's what Henry said, that's it," Garrett replied.

"I can't believe you are walking away from this amount of money."

"I don't know why not. You approached us. That's our price. If you can meet it, fine. If not, we don't have much to talk about." Garrett thanked the man for calling and hung up.

Henry called early the next morning stating that the contract had another few days in its time for acceptance. "I've also received an indication that others might come with another contract. Word must be getting around about the Chalmer deal."

"We don't want folks to think we are in for a fire sale, Henry," Garrett said. "If Chalmer backs out, maybe we ought to back off."

"Yes, sir, if that's what you decide, we will do it," Henry replied.

"Just let it soak until the expiration of our time for acceptance. Then we will decide what to do."

67

The day after the Chalmer contract expired, Henry had heard nothing more from them. Later the same day an eastern attorney showed up in his office. He said he represented some eastern interests and wanted to talk about buying the business. Henry called Garrett.

"I have an attorney in the office who has come from the Eastern Shore district and wants to talk about buying us out. What should I tell him?"

"Find out what his deal is and let me know. Don't bring him here until we talk his offer over."

Henry called back in an hour. "He wants to come see you."

"You bring me his deal first if it is our asking price. If not, send him on his way," Garrett said.

In about thirty minutes Henry drove up to Garrett's office. Garrett went to his car.

"Garrett, based on the offer we can net in the foundation $761 million after taxes. However, I'll need to check this out further before we hang our hats on this figure. Tell me what you want me to do," Henry asked.

"We are apart $39 million based on your asking price, right?"

"Yes, sir," Henry replied.

"Get him to split the difference, and tell him we will deal. Otherwise, no deal."

Henry called in about an hour and said the fellow left and said they didn't have a deal. Garrett put Henry's mind at ease with the words that they all still had a job and no harm was done.

The next week the Eastern Shore representative of the produce group called Henry by telephone and said the group was able to increase its offer by $9 million to $770 million, and that's all they could scrape up. If Garrett couldn't accept this figure, they would have to back off. Garrett asked Henry for an hour to think.

Garrett called Henry back in a few minutes and said, "If they put up substantial money up front, so that we will know it is sold, I'd say go for it."

"How much?" Henry asked.

"At least 10 percent, nonrefundable," Garrett replied.

Henry called back later that day stating he had verbal acceptance and that he was waiting on the contract. Further, they stated that when the contract was fully executed, 10 percent would be transferred to the bank.

A special messenger hand delivered the contract to Henry the next day. Henry brought it to Garrett as soon as he had gone over it and after he had taken it to the attorneys to secure their approval of its validity.

The contract had thirty-six hours as a time for acceptance, and Garrett told Henry to tell the messenger it would be thirty-six hours before he could expect it to be executed. Garrett wanted to be sure it was for their exact agreement and that the employees kept their jobs, that the house and one hundred acres were excluded, and that Bath Pond was left in place with a sixty-foot parcel of land to the highway included.

Henry said, "Garrett, I think everything is as it should be. It is a simple contract as you requested. The lawyers have agreed to its validity, and I think you will find it acceptable. I'll come back when you tell me."

"Come back after lunch tomorrow," Garrett said.

Garrett and Mary Fran talked it all over again that night and decided it was acceptable as written. They signed it that night.

Henry was there about 2 p.m. the next day. Garrett said, "Henry, here is what I want you to do. Use our present funds to alter the foundation to do what we need it to do. Then when the dust settles and the deal is complete and closed, I want

$5 million placed in such a manner that Mary Fran and I have use of it for the rest of our lives. At the survivor's death, the remainder goes into the foundation. Set up $2.5 million each for Jay and M. J. without too many limitations, but still enough so that it will last the rest of their lives. Then write yourself a check for $1 million without any strings. Set it up any way you want it to be set up. Place the remainder in the foundation, including the remaining funds in our family corporation, and close the corporation after being sure all the retirement accounts are in place for the employees, and Beau is adequately provided for as we discussed."

When Garrett was finished, Henry couldn't speak. In fact, he didn't really hear what Garrett said after instructing him to write a check for $1 million to himself. He was white and speechless and began to mutter, "Garrett, I can't do such a thing. It wouldn't be right considering the rest of the employees. What would they think? Particularly those who came before me? What would I say to them about what I got? It just isn't right."

Garrett said, "Anything is right that Mary Fran and I say is right, and we want it this way. Without your help all through our association, we wouldn't be where we are today. Your expertise is what has made the company. Now you take the money, and you and your wife do some of the things you've wanted to all these years. Believe me, you've earned it. If anyone ever finds out about this, it will come from the two of you. It will be our secret unless you spill it."

Henry left the office in a state of shock. He got hold of himself between the two offices and began the conclusion of the deal.

Garrett told Mary Fran that night after the kitchen help left of Henry's reluctance to accept the money. "Well, Garrett, you and I can keep the secret. We'll see if Henry and Jean can."

"We don't have a problem with Henry now and never will. He will be totally loyal until he draws his last breath. I want him to fashion Jay in such a manner that Jay can step into Henry's shoes before he kicks out. He needs to monitor Jay for a few years," Garrett said.

"You are right. Jay doesn't realize the job we have in mind for him. I just hope he can fill Henry's shoes," Mary Fran replied.

They talked for several minutes and then Mary Fran asked, "Garrett, only our family and Henry know about the sale. How do you plan to tell our employees?"

"I don't know. I've been thinking about that, and the more I think about it, the more I don't know how to do it. Why don't you think about that, because I've really got lots of fresh fruit problems on my mind? It will be nice not to have the phone ringing all the time with all sorts of problems," he said.

When the deposit money was safely transferred to their bank and the original contract was properly executed with their attorney's approval, Mary Fran said to Garrett, "Why don't we have a real blowout of a Thanksgiving party for everyone who works for us? Really do it up right for the last time?"

"Why Thanksgiving?" Garrett asked.

"According to the contract, Eastern will take over April the first and Thanksgiving will be the last time we could, unless we do it Christmas. We could keep the secret until Thanksgiving, but it will surely leak out before Christmas."

Garrett thought for a minute and said, "Let's sleep on it. We don't have to make this decision now."

68

Mary Fran came down to Garrett's office early the next morning and asked him, "What do you think about the Thanksgiving party idea this morning?"

"It is a good idea. You carry the ball," he said.

"Get ready to spend some money then, because we are going to do this up right," she said.

The printer delivered to Mary Fran printed invitations to a Thanksgiving Ball, coat and tie required. Garrett looked at the invitations and said, "You have lost your mind, Mary Fran. Most of these folks don't own a tie."

"If they don't, they can buy one. This is going to be a party they will remember. Besides, everyone needs a tie for their burial."

The day before Thanksgiving a semi-truck entered the main gate. Inside the trailer was a tent that was about the same size as a football field. Henry thought Mary Fran was going to have a three-ring circus.

The tent had flaps in case of wind or rain, but the weather had been predicted to be nice. Mary Fran was counting on that.

There was a second tent placed beside the larger tent. The larger tent had tables and chairs and a dance floor with a stage for a band. The tables had white cloths on them. Electricity was available, and the appropriate lighting was developed with candles on the tables. The adjoining tent had a magnificent buffet. It was not only the traditional Thanksgiving meal, but it included professional attendants with portable barbecue pits, a station with raw oysters and boiled shrimp and hors d'oeuvres of all kinds, everything imaginable. Most of the folks who worked for them had never seen such a set-up, and they walked around bug-eyed for the first few minutes until someone told them they could begin to eat. Beverage stations were set up in several locations with every kind of drink.

One thing that startled and amazed the employees was that Mary Fran had place cards at each person's place setting. Most had never seen such a thing. Located by the place card was a solid gold–framed picture of some scene on the property. Most of the pictures had the person seated in that place in the scene. There were flowers on each table, and some lucky person would be able to take them home when the festivities were over.

When their guests arrived for Thanksgiving dinner with all the trimmings at 5 o'clock, the flaps to the big tent had not been raised. Everyone was enjoying music from a small ensemble stationed outside. Some listened to the music, and some began to eat. At 6 o'clock, the flaps were raised, and a twenty-piece band started to play. This was the first anyone saw of the dance floor that had been installed. Guests could enter the larger tent only in certain locations, and waiters assisted everyone with finding their tables. Regal treatment for royal guests!

The buffet had not been opened. At 6:30, Garrett went on stage using the band's microphones and said, "This Thanksgiving celebration has been developed for everyone's enjoyment. We want you to enjoy the food and have a good time because we've lots to be thankful for. The dinner buffet will be open shortly, but I think it only proper that we pause and ask that everyone join with the singers and the band and sing the Doxology, after which you are free to eat. The party will last all night if you decide to stay and dance. The band has been hired for all night, and they will be here until you leave." The band started to play the Doxology, and everyone began to sing, "Praise God, from whom all blessings flow; praise him, all creatures here below; praise him above, ye heavenly host; praise Father, Son, and Holy Ghost. Amen."

"Have fun everyone. The evening is young," said Garrett, and then he left the stage.

The band begin to play dance numbers that attracted a goodly number. Those who were not dancing were in the buffet line.

The buffet had the traditional items. It also had a round of beef being carved, a country ham, and all sorts of country-style dishes. The vegetables were fresh, and the food was outstanding. Looking at the dessert table, most attending could hardly wait, because it was so beautifully filled with all sorts of desserts most of these folks had never seen.

The eating and partying went on full blast until 9:30 when Garrett again went on stage. The band stopped and turned the microphone over to him. He turned to the band members and said, "Why don't you folks take about a thirty-minute break for food and rest?"

He gave them time to get off stage and turned back to the group. "Those of you who are not sitting, please find a chair." He gave them a chance to sit down and approached the microphone again.

"Tonight is special. Special in the sense that we work together and most of us have been here long enough to be considered family. This truly is a Thanksgiving celebration, because we've all a great deal to be thankful for.

"This coming April 1, Eastern Produce will take over all the Gregson farming enterprises." The room became totally silent. Garrett smiled and said, "No, this is not an April Fools Day joke.

"The purpose of wanting to tell you now and tell you myself is so that you will not hear this from someone else. You've nothing to be concerned about, because one of the elements of the sale is that everyone who currently works here will continue. Your retirement and health benefits will continue just as they are. Based on the people I've met from Eastern, you will be impressed with them. They are farmers just as we are and have always lived close to the soil.

"Mary Fran and I thought long and hard about this difficult decision. We felt it was in our best interest, given our ages and yours, to align you with someone who will be here for the long pull. If you will give the new owners a chance, I believe, based on what I know about them now, you will be satisfied.

"Most of the old-timers in our outfit have already retired and are here with us this evening. To them I say: Without you, tonight would have never happened. Where else would you find others who would virtually work for nothing just to find some way to eat? For those of you who don't know, that is exactly what we did for a long period of time. I would like to ask all the original employees to stand where you are so the younger folks will know who you are."

Bill, Cindy, Beau, and all the original Alabama folks stood. It was apparent, by observation, the older folks were completely worn out. They needed rest and were enjoying their well-earned retirement. The rest of the group gave the old-timers a standing ovation. It was an emotional time, since nothing like this had ever happened to this group of folks.

"In case you are wondering, your bonuses will be paid just as they always have been at Christmas time. This has always been something we've looked forward to doing because, in a sense, you really earned this extra money. We have been glad to do this.

"Mary Fran and I feel particularly close to each of you because of the role you've played here and within our lives. We don't cherish the idea of leaving, but we know it is in the best interest of our family and also yours. We thank you from the bottom of our hearts for all you've done, and we look forward to continuing our acquaintance and friendship as we go into retirement ourselves. Our door is always open to you.

"One last thing, you would make an old man happy tonight if you will eat all this food and wear this band completely out. We used to be able to party all night, and I think we still can."

Garrett stepped off the stage to another standing ovation from the crowd. When he did the band struck up a number he had asked for, and he and Mary Fran danced. It was midway though this dance that the dance floor filled to capacity. Those who were stunned by the announcement were lined up at the beverage stations.

Garrett and Mary Fran walked onto their side porch just as the sun was peeping over the horizon. The band members were loading their equipment, and cars were headed out the main gate. Ironically, the older folks were the ones who left last and had stayed with the band until it was over.

69

Garrett and Mary Fran spent the entire weekend reminiscing. They talked about the good times of the past and the bad they had to endure. They tried to remember all the people who had been a part of their lives. They were able to know that on April 1, a few months away, they would no longer be in the same business. Knowing that all they had built would be someone else's was not a happy thought at times, yet certain assurance they had done the right thing. They, of course, were considering this to be almost the end of their lives. Sometimes they thought they were getting ready to die instead of live.

Bright and early Monday morning Garrett's phone rang nonstop. This was an unusual fresh fruit season in that it was warmer than usual. There was also much fog early in the mornings and not good for fresh fruit's carrying qualities. The fruit was more prone to break down en route to the customer. Every call this particular day was bad news, it seemed.

Strangely the entire month would be the same. It was a miserable month in that nothing went right. The closer Christmas came, the more problems there were to solve, just no let-up.

Mary Fran wanted to take a trip to get away while the transition was in progress. Henry needed to change gears from the family business to the family foundation, and he needed time alone, but more than this he also needed rest. His rest would come when Garrett was not around to disturb him. She had suggested this to Garrett, and he had agreed, but a destination had not been agreed upon. These were all things the two of them discussed in the midst of all the operational problems Garrett was trying to work through.

70

This maze of problems had Garrett completely preoccupied when he was ushered to the head table at the surprise appreciation dinner where Alan Wright, governor of the state of Florida, had referred to their wedding of more than fifty years ago.

While Garrett had, in his own mind, relived almost his entire life during the course of a few minutes, he was aware of Alan talking about their childhood together and all the fun things they did. He realized the folks in the audience were employees and their families, business associates and friends from every station in life. He didn't realize he actually knew this many people.

Some of their friends had laudatory things to say about the accomplishments they had achieved with the hospice and convalescence center. Some of the employees had some touching remarks regarding their association over the years, particularly the Alabama group and Bill Lawrence.

At this point in the ceremony, Alan stepped up to the microphone and said, "The next person I would like to introduce is the best hunter and fisherman I've ever known. He catches the most and largest fish. He is a crack shot whether it is deer, quail, or dove. He is so good with a gun I wouldn't let him shoot around a corner at me. Ladies and gentlemen, Beau James." Garrett and Mary Fran were amazed that Beau, knowing him as they did, would want to offer some personal remarks and be a part of such an evening.

Beau came to the lectern, paused for a few seconds, looked around at the great crowd and said, "I am an illegitimate black person. I don't know who my father was. Nor do I believe my mother knew who he was. My mother left me as a baby with my grandmother. Her name was Essay James, and I took her last name.

"Garrett's mother died when he was a very young child. His father hired my grandmother to come cook and keep house and raise Garrett. Our room was the room behind the kitchen in the Gregson home place.

"I've always considered Garrett's father as my father, too. He disciplined me and helped my grandmother raise me. I grew up eating at the Gregson's table with the Gregsons.

"Garrett and I did our chores, got into trouble together, were disciplined together, hunted and fished with the governor here and the late Brett Moore. I was always accepted by who I was, not what color I was. In fact, given my light skin and Caucasian facial features, few ever realized I possessed black blood.

"When Garrett married Mary Fran and moved out, a part of my life moved also. But then, I received a reprieve. Garrett needed me to come help him and Mr. Gregson let me go. My grandmother came when Mary Fran was ill, and our family was complete again. Only Mr. Gregson was left behind.

"We had some tough years. There were some years when we scuffled to exist. But then Garrett and I, in a sense, gained another father in the form of Mr. Langford. No one could have ever asked to be associated with a finer person.

"Then Bill and Cindy came along and things were just a bit easier. The Alabama folks came, and little did I realize the day we all stood out on the side lawn in the rain with those folks, we would end up at a place like this tonight.

"Progress began for us when there existed no money, only sweat and muscle. Sweat and muscle and pure determination on Garrett and Mary Fran's part made Gregson Family Farms.

"I am so happy my mother left me with my grandmother. I am happy Mr. Gregson was my father. And ladies and gentlemen, I can't begin to express to you how very grateful I am to have the privilege of introducing to you my brother Garrett and his wife, my sister-in-law, Mary Fran."

With this introduction, the audience went wild, standing, whistling, and yelling. While the commotion was going on,

Beau approached Garrett, whose face was filled with tears. Garrett stood up and hugged Beau and both sobbed. It was such a touching scene that Mary Fran couldn't sit still. She moved into the hugging match. Right behind her was Jay and M. J. The crowd continued to roar.

When the commotion in the dining room was subsiding, Beau took his seat after escorting Garrett to the lectern. Garrett's emotions were running away with him, and he was aware he had to get hold of himself. *Only by keeping it light will I be able to get out of this,* he thought.

Garrett paused longer than he had intended, but finally said, "When I left home this evening I had at least two dozen things left yet to do today and, of course, bellyached all the way here tonight to Mary Fran, who had not the foggiest idea what the plans were either. To arrive and find all our friends waiting with the governor heading the posse is just a little heady. But to be completely upstaged by Beau is past anything I could ever hope to put into words. Let's give him a hand."

The crowd roared again with a standing ovation. Beau responded by standing to acknowledge their applause.

Garrett continued, "Beau had the opportunity to consider what he wanted to say. Had I known outside the door I'd have to face you folks behind this microphone, I would have left Mary Fran holding the bag." The crowd applauded again.

"Actually, I really don't know of anyone I'd rather spend this evening with than those of you who are gathered here. This is the greatest honor Mary Fran and I have ever had bestowed upon us." The crowd responded again.

"Everything Beau told you about tough times was true. However, looking back they were not nearly as rough now as they seemed then. We always managed to eat, but never even once in the early days did we have any money we could afford to spend on anything but the bare necessities. After Henry became associated, spare money became a thing of the past. I don't know what he did with it, but we never had any. That is, according to him." The crowd got a kick out of this.

"I can tell you, however, that without Henry we would not be here this evening. Whatever success we have enjoyed to this point has in large measure been Henry's responsibility. Let's give him a hand. Stand up, Henry," Garrett concluded. Henry made the difficult effort to stand, and not only did the crowd applaud but gave him a standing ovation for an extended period. Garrett let it go for as long as it would, to Henry's very great embarrassment.

"It is true that we've finally gotten to the point to where we eat regularly, but this didn't just happen. Had Bill and Cindy Mathews's car not collapsed, we would have never met them. To this point, Beau and I not only ran a sawmill, we looked after the cattle and all the odd jobs. Now our workforce had increased by 33 percent with the addition of one man. Stand up, Bill and Cindy. Thanks for all you did." The crowd responded.

"Then there came that special day. What do you think happened? John Haney, Jim Lawrence, and Jim Morgan along with their families came into our yard in an old truck that wouldn't go any further. There were more people in that old truck than a Greyhound Bus could haul. They thought they were poor, but they really looked like solid gold to us. If they had known how badly we needed them that day, they would have settled for nothing less than top management positions." The crowd applauded. "Now, all the originals in that truck please stand." A good number stood. "Now, all the offspring of that group stand with them," and fully 40 percent of those present stood. The crowd roared again.

Garrett turned to Mary Fran and asked her to come to the lectern and stand with him. She reluctantly did so.

"The truth is, whatever success we've enjoyed has been through the people we've been associated with over the years. We had nothing but grit and determination and two older men who counseled us. Those of you here are the reason we were successful.

"We are no different than anyone else. There are lots of things we wish could be reversed but never can be. We lost

Beau's grandmother in a nasty way. My dad was killed by what I considered a prize animal. Our older son left us at far too early an age. We've all lost family and friends who were very closely associated in World War II, Korea, and Vietnam. We can't reverse any of this, nor can you reverse the heartaches in your lives. The thing that got us all through the rough times were each other, and we can never repay our debt to each of you for standing by us when we were hurting." The crowd was silent with the exception of a few noses blowing and faces grimaced.

"The business successes we've enjoyed are soon forgotten, but the association with friends such as yourselves will never be forgotten. Mary Fran and I have been reminiscing since our Thanksgiving gala, and we've talked about people, not about things. You people are our memories. If we live long enough to get old, we have a memory filled to overflowing with remembrances of each of you. For this we are thankful."

Garrett looked down at Mary Fran and paused and as if on cue she stepped forward to the microphone. "I went from foster home to foster home as you know until I finally found a home with Garrett." The crowd loved it and exploded.

She continued, "We've had a wonderful life together. And Garrett's right, you people are our memories. It isn't property or money but you folks, and I thank you for being a part of our lives. It hasn't been a one-way street. We didn't help you nor did you help us. It has been a give-and-take life that we've shared with you. For this, we are grateful."

With this, she backed away. Garrett paused and stepped forward again. "It is true. Our hope is to lead a life with a little lower profile. It is time we stepped aside and let the younger folk take the lead. We don't plan on going anywhere but home for the time being. Then we plan to go to our heavenly home for all our tomorrows and we will be there sharing it with you. Please accept our grateful appreciation for your kindness and generosity, not only here this evening, but throughout our lives. It is an evening we shall remember every day for the remainder of our lives. Thank you." The crowd again stood and applauded until the governor stepped up again.

"It has been a wonderful evening, Garrett. We thank you and Mary Fran for sharing your lives with us. Before we call it quits this evening, I wanted to say something. Everyone already knows we've been associated as friends all our lives. I know, and everyone here is aware of the Gregson family's altruism. You've given far more of your time and resources than could ever be expected of any couple. Therefore, because of this, your good hearts have rubbed off on the group assembled here this evening. We know the two of you are interested in adding a unit to the center, whose specialty is in caring for the brain damaged. Because of what you've meant to those assembled and to the community, we have raised the money to build this unit amounting to twenty additional rooms plus physical therapy and treatment facilities. It will be a part of the standing center and carry absolutely no additional name of donors. We feel what we are, in large measure, has come from you, and we are just giving a portion of it back. We hope you can accept this gift in the same spirit it is offered."

The governor walked over and hugged both Garrett and Mary Fran, both of whom were in tears. The governor's protective officers stood close by and allowed all who wanted to do so to come by and greet Garrett and Mary Fran. Not one person left the room without first coming to them with some expression of appreciation.

When the last person filed by, everyone was standing, and in the clearest voice imaginable Jim Lawrence started to sing, and everyone immediately joined in, "Blest be the tie that binds our hearts in Christian love." The group sang all its verses and stood reverently until Garrett, Mary Fran, and their entire family had exited the building.

71

The farm changed hands on April 1. The foundation was up and running and was funded sufficiently to do a great deal of good. Jay was successful in eventually getting his MBA and was further schooled under Henry's tutelage. Henry was thinking of retiring and going home to Jean.

For Garrett and Mary Fran, they were satisfied with their children's lives. Both were happily married with kids, and both were leading productive lives.

As for themselves, they traveled until they wanted to travel no more. Mary Fran never lost interest in those facilities they had funded over the years, and she kept in close touch with each operation and participated where it was possible. In fact, she died in the Convalescent Center she developed after sixty-one years of marriage to Garrett.

Garrett sometimes saddled a cow pony and rode over to Bath Pond, but mostly whiled away the days sitting on the side porch at home with the current successors of Buford, Booger, Precious, and Gator at his feet. He was there when the sun rose every morning, listening to the birds sing while gathering food for the day. He died there at sunup on his eightieth birthday, with Beau beside him.

About the Author

A native Floridian, Lowell Teal was born into a citrus and cattle family. After graduation from the University of Florida, his executive career began with an international agricultural marketing organization representing citrus growers and other producers nationwide. Fifteen years later he established a management-marketing-public relations consulting firm. The company is known today as Austin Teal Corporation, a real estate sales organization, from which he is retired. He is the author of *A Happy Heart Is a Good Medicine* and *Company Stewardship*. Both present a how-to-think educational process for the person within the workaday world balancing job demands with family responsibilities. He is married, the father of two and grandfather of two.

For more information about Lowell Teal, go to his website at www.LowellTeal.com.

For more information about his book *Bath Pond,* go to the book website at www.BathPond.com.